SWIM THE MOON

PAUL BRANDON

SWIM THE MOON

Edited by Jack Dann

Book design by Jane Adele Regina

A Tor Book
Published by Tom Doherty Associates, LLC
175 Fifth Avenue
New York, NY 10010

www.tor.com

Tor® is a registered trademark of Tom Doherty Associates, LLC.

Library of Congress Cataloging-in-Publication Data
Brandon, Paul.
    Swim the moon / Paul Brandon.—1st ed.
        p. cm.
    "A Tom Doherty Associates book."
    ISBN 0-312-87794-3
    1. Fathers—Death—Fiction. 2. Women singers—Fiction.
3. Scotland—Fiction. 4. Fiddlers—Fiction. I. Title.

PR6102.R36 S9 2001
823'.92—dc21

                                                2001027823

First Edition: September 2001

Printed in the United States of America

0 9 8 7 6 5 4 3 2 1

For Julie . . .

contents

author's note

The first healthy dose of thanks has got to go to my editor and pal, Jack Dann. Without his bottomless well of optimism and pure enthusiasm, this book quite literally would not be in your hands now. I also have to thank Charles de Lint and MaryAnn Harris for all the kind words of encouragement and for poking a first-timer in the right direction. Tom Doherty, the late Jenna Felice, and all the folks at Tor; Merrilee Heifetz, Ginger Clark, Caren Bohrman; Janeen Webb; my families on two continents (particularly Karen and Mark for their unfailing faith in me); and Helen, Mannie, and Rachel for all the tunes.

Music is such an intrinsic part of my writing process that to fail to mention some of the inspirational sources for this story would be an injustice. In addition to the usual classical stalwarts, I owe a special debt to the vast talents of Martin Hayes and Dennis Cahill, Kevin Burke, Silly Wizard, Loreena McKennitt, Lúnasa, Kevin Crawford, Luka Bloom, the Waterboys, Sharon Shannon, Kavisha Mazzella, the Bothy Band, and Solas, to name but a few.

This is a work of fiction. Though Sandwood Bay and some of the other locations in the story are real places, my depictions of them are not. I have no doubt taken great liberties with geography and possibly history, so all mistakes are utterly of my own making. Any resemblance to actual people or happenings is purely coincidental.

—PAUL BRANDON
Brisbane, Autumn 2001

"Wouldst thou"—so the helmsman answered—
"Learn the Secret of the Sea?
Only those who brave its dangers
Comprehend its mystery!"

—Longfellow,
"The Secret of the Sea"

prologue

SCOTLAND, 1876

The prow of the curragh rose and fell as the man deftly angled the small boat toward the shore. The waves were heavy and swollen with the promise of a late autumn storm and the clouds that gathered out to the west were dark and sullen. The oars wheeled, dipping into the gray waters of the Minch with a practiced precision born of a life on the sea. The fisherman threw a glance over his shoulder, using the solitary pillar of rock to mark his position. Above him, expertly riding the squalling breeze, gulls tumbled, their cries loud and raucous as they battled each other for scraps from the meager catch. His heavy woolen coat and trousers were soaked through with the salt spray, and his clean-shaven face was flushed and raw from the wind. The only flashes of color were two gold hoops that hung from both his ears, an odd counterpoint to the palette of grays and browns that surrounded him and his tiny vessel.

Behind him, the steady waves rolled up the shore, the sound like distant thunder, and with a quick flick of the oars, he caught one, riding it in steadily till the boat thumped into the soft sand. Unmindful of the wet, he jumped over the side and took hold of the thick rope, fighting the sea for a moment as he sought to drag the curragh clear.

Once up the beach and safely secured from the sea's searching fingers, he reached inside and hefted out the slippery mass of his nets, absently checking through them for holes as he laid them out on the sand to dry.

With the nets pinned down and the small sack of fish slung over his shoulder, he made his way up toward his home.

Sitting back low against the dunes, the bothy still looked as new as when he'd built it himself, barely a half-dozen years ago. Fresh turfs covered the roof, browning and dry from the brittle wind yet still sound enough to keep out even the coldest chill. Smoke plumed out from the thin chimney, spiraling around the roof before being pulled away by the freshening wind. The grasses surrounding the house bent and swayed, and further away, he could hear the branches of the cluster of trees in the spinney knocking together.

Dumping the fish at the door, he doffed his cap and stepped inside. Familiar aromas met him, burning driftwood, food, and earth, and as he closed the door, he called out, "Sheelagh? Where are yeh, lass?" His broad accent marked him as an Irishman, though the Scottish landscape had chipped a few rough edges into his speech.

No one answered, and with a slight frown, he walked through the kitchen and into the darkness of the bedroom. Muttering to himself, he crossed the room and flung open the course fabric of the curtains, letting in a stream of washed light. The room was empty, and the bedclothes were strewn over the pallet. Calling again, he returned to the door and looked out over the beach. The storm clouds were closer now, and the horizon was nothing more than an indistinct smudge of gray.

With the wind pulling at his dark ringlets, the man stepped out onto the grass and walked along the beach, shouting out her name. His eyes scanned the foam-flecked sea, the sand, and the dull green of the grass beyond, but saw nothing. Breaking into a run, he felt the first twists of concern in his stomach.

He found her amid the rocks at the north end of the beach.

Curled into a fetal position, she was naked and covered in a sheen of sea spray. One arm reached away, toward the ocean, the hand submerged in a trapped pool. Long sloe-black hair blew wildly about her, framing a face that was at once beautiful yet haunted. Her cheekbones were high, almost regal, and the line of her jaw strong, aquiline. Her body would have once been described as perfect, flawless, and her legs impossibly long and slender.

Once.

Now she was pathetically thin, wasted; pale skin stretched tight over protruding bone.

For a moment, he though she was dead, but her head lifted weakly and she looked up at him with liquid brown eyes. The breakers shattered against the rocks, sending cascading shivers of brine over them both. Her pupils were wide, almost dilated, and as he stood over her, she uttered one word, her voice weak and sibilant:

"Please . . . ?"

Her eyes bored into his soul, searching, pleading. For a moment he stood still, his arms hanging loosely by his sides, fighting the overwhelming, conflicting feelings of love, pity, and cold determination. Shrugging off his coat, he crouched down and covered her, then, gently, for she weighed almost nothing, he lifted her. Her gaze still held his, and for a moment, he thought he could see himself in there, trapped, imprisoned.

Bottomless eyes silently voiced the plea one last time, her thin skeletal hand coming up to tenderly touch the side of his face.

Please . . .

He held his breath, held her; then, with the barest shake of his head, turned and started back for the bothy. She lowered her face into his shoulder and wept.

His resolve hardened. It was like the land around them, harsh yet at the same time severely beautiful, and as he slowly walked back toward his home, he blinked away the tears that gathered in his eyes.

part one

THE CALLING

In dreams begins responsibility.
　　　　—William Butler Yeats, *Old Play, Epigraph, Responsibilities*

I saw the new moon late yestreen
Wi' the auld moon in her arm;
And if we gang to sea, master,
I fear we'll come to harm.

　　　　　　　　　　　　　　　　　—*Anonymous*

1

Sorrow washed over me completely, like a flood-fueled winter tide.

There's been so much loss in my family that I think the death of my father had come as no true surprise. I had been mournful at first, conveniently far away, but once I'd arrived here, one sadness had been replaced by another. I was beyond tears, and although his absence left a hollow place inside of me, I knew I would not cry.

I would grieve later, on my own, like I had before.

Shrugging the unaccustomed weight of my black coat slightly, I slipped through the impressive crowd to where the front doors stood open. The church hall was old, and smelled strongly of smoke, old ladies' perfume, and varnish, but once on the threshold, my senses broke through the cacophony of noise and aroma. I could hear the distant thunder of the waves breaking on the fractured cliffs and the squabbling gulls fighting over the scraps thrown to them by the net menders. I was aware of the salty tang of the sea breeze, tainted only slightly by the smell from the fishing boats, and of the damp, heady fragrance of the purple heather that collared the hill behind the church.

I took a deep breath, and a hundred scenes flashed through my mind like someone flicking the pages of a journal, the faces and scenes blurring into a collage of memory, sorrow, and dream. My father acted through some of them, but most were of another, even dearer person that I'd also lost to the water. The images were fierce in their poignancy, complex and overwhelming. I'd shut them away, guarded and secure for six years, but here, in this small Scottish village just about as far north as I could possibly get from the place I had grudgingly called home, they had found a key, and were returning triumphant. I lowered my head a little, trying to submerge them in a lake of the mundane, the commonplace, but it was no use. They had been awoken, and I thought that perhaps this time it would not be so easy to run.

Sniffing slightly from the cold air, and absently trying to warm the ache from my chilled hands, I once again ran over my last few days, trying to pick out moments from within the chaos my father's death had created.

Most of the twenty-seven-hour flight passed as a gray, timeless haze interrupted only by meals, the snoring of the man next to me, and the complaints of children too long bored. I spent much of the journey just gazing through the thick square of window at the clouds so far below; the rolling sea of white occasionally punctuated by the sharp gray peak of an unknown mountain or the shining blue of a distant sea. I pointedly ignored the in-flight movie—my mind being too prepossessed by other thoughts.

At last I departed the controlled climate of the aircraft into the waning light of a Glaswegian summer evening. It was supposed to be a lucky time of year to cross the world. I had left Brisbane on a cool winter morning, so the change of temperature was not as sudden as it might have been. In fact, I think Glasgow was the warmer of the two, but then that might have just been my imagination. I stopped for a moment at the top of the mobile stairs and stood, eyes closed, just breathing the air and remembering. I didn't know Glasgow that well, but it was the thought of returning to the Isles after so long. The years had passed as suddenly as the flash from a camera, but it felt like it had been in another life that I had lived here last.

It seemed to me almost as if I had been another man, living a different time that was now forever denied me.

I opened up my eyes, returning resentfully to the granite reality of the funeral. For a moment, the images I had released were so overwhelming that I didn't realize my sister was leaning against the jamb next to me. Short, rounded, and fair-haired, she appeared the complete antithesis to my rangy, dark form, but although we looked at the world through different pairs, we shared the same eyes.

Those that knew recognized us as kin, and once, we had been inseparable, but now we were more like cousins that are reunited only for weddings, or funerals. She too lived in Brisbane, but still, we hardly ever spoke; only the occasional Christmas or birthday, or the odd time when she would turn up wherever I happened to be playing. Florence was the strong one.

"What is it about the men in this family and water?" she asked heavily. Her large blue eyes were ringed from crying and tiredness, and I noticed the clump of tissues she clutched in her small hand. I shook my head and shrugged, not really knowing what to say. She saw my reaction and pressed on. "I mean, I could understand them drowning if they were all fishermen or something, but they weren't—Dad was an architect, for Christ's sake."

Habitually, I removed my glasses and rubbed them clean, my fingers tracing the round metal of the rims through the cloth as I absently listened to her. After a moment, she looked up at me critically, brushing a few strands of gray-coursed, dark curling hair away from my face. I might be nearing forty, but she'll always be my older sister.

"How are *you* doing?" she asked softly, her gentle eyes searching my downcast face. I just shrugged, pushing my glasses back on.

I mumbled some reply, my voice thick, then in a clearer tone, said, "I know I should be here for Dad, but . . . I see her everywhere, Florence. I can't help it. I don't think I should have come back."

She took my arm and steered me down the slick steps and out into the graveyard. The tombstones reared around us like old, decaying teeth, and the bell tolled mournfully. To one side of the church, almost as big and certainly as ancient, a massive, red-berried yew tree stood, wide and spreading, its dark green foliage a stark contrast to the pale stone of the building.

"Perhaps you shouldn't have come," she agreed quietly.

I shrugged again, the gesture barely perceptible under the thick woolen coat. The wind chased the leaves around us, sculpturing them against the headstones like snow. The clouds were rolling in from the sea, and from the leaden, almost metallic feeling in the air, I knew there was rain coming.

I drew a slow breath and looked around. Below us, houses dotted over the gentle slope of the hill like milling sheep, the village of Kinlochbervie lay silent, most of the villagers being inside the church. Beyond the harbor the water stretched away like a rumpled gray blanket, and even from this distance I could see the white flecks of foam as the wind brushed against the tips of the waves, coaxing them higher up the rough beach. To the south, glittering a vivid sapphire blue on the clearest of days, sat Loch Inchard. A few indistinct triangles of white cloth floated across it, and I smiled slightly as memories of a hundred sailing trips with Dad scuttled through my mind, then felt bitter tears gathering as I remembered the last.

Forcibly, my view traveled back over the untidy straggle of the village, and I followed the single road out across the low, cliff-faced glen that sheltered the tiny bay. It carried along another four or so miles, toward the remote outpost of Blairmore that was nothing more than a collection of three or four buildings, then on as a naked track toward Sandwood Bay, and the tiny bothy.

Our ancestral home.

Local tales tell of how Padraig Brennan, a young Irish fisherman from a small village in County Donegal, set out early one morning, intent on hauling in a record catch. He rowed for most of the day and half of the night, then cast his nets when he reached still waters. The story continues on about how, when he pulled in the fish, the boat was so full that the water was lapping about his ankles. He struck out in what he thought was the direction home, but instead landed in the most beautiful bay he had ever seen. Liking the feel of the place, and having enough fish to last him a lifetime, he built himself a crofter's cottage—a bothy—and fell in love with a local lass of breathtaking beauty. Apparently he never realized he was in Scotland. The story was affectionately known as the Brennan Voyage, in obvious reference to the incredible journey made hundreds of years ago by the legendary St. Brendan, the unofficial Irish discoverer of America.

The tale was often told in the pubs and inns around these parts, and it changed with each telling. I don't know what really happened, all those years past, but somehow, an Irish fisherman *did* build a cottage, and Brennans have been here since.

Until now.

I'd lived there for a time, sharing the peace and wonder with my beloved wife, Elisabeth, but then she'd been lost in a boating accident, and my world had died around me. I'd been forced away, driven, if you like.

There were just too many ghosts.

And now the pain was there once more, as raw and aching as the last time I'd walked this graveyard, those six years past.

Within two months of her funeral, I'd packed and moved as far south as was possible, following the trail of my mother and only sister, who had both emigrated, separately, to Australia.

But I had returned, and a wound that I realize now had never really been healed was open again, and once more raw and bleeding.

Treading through the wet-bladed moor grass with my sister, the sorrow nearly choked me. It seemed a lifetime since I'd looked upon Kinlochbervie, but nothing had changed, not even me.

I suppose in a place like this, nothing ever does.

Her gravestone was here—somewhere underneath the spreading canopy of the old tree, but I'd only ever visited it once. To see it was to admit she was really gone.

The people were beginning to file out of the church, a black-clad line of somber-faced Scots, hard and resistant outside, shelling warm and passionate interiors that glowed like the coals under an old fire. It was this land that cultivated my love of folk music—taught by a stone-faced man who only came to life when his bow ignited fire along his fiddle strings. As they passed us, each offered their condolences; a prayer, a word, sometimes only a nod. How different we must've seemed—the pair of quasi Australians complete with tans and fledgling accents—but we were embraced all the same, like children come home.

With the funeral over, and the body laid within the damp earth, the wake was to take place in the Compass, the local inn: a low-ceilinged, smoke-walled place that was older than the country where I now made my home. For a time, when life was perfect, it had been my second favorite place in the world after the bothy, and the memories of the late night lock-ins were some of my most treasured. The music flowed as easily as the rich, dark beer, and despite the heavy hearts, I knew that once they all got inside, the merriment would ring forth again as they celebrated Dad's life. Although his death had been an accident, Dad had lived to a ripe old age, and those who knew him would mourn his loss, but not grieve.

It was the time I dreaded most.

As if reading my mind, Florence's hand slipped down my arm to grip mine, and she said, "Come on, let's go. I'm looking forward to this about as much as you are, but it's what Dad would've wanted."

"That's what I'm afraid of," I replied as we started off down the hill.

ii

The two small rooms that made up the drinking area of
the Compass were full in regard to all five senses: the noise
reminded me of the chatter of the seabirds, with only the
occasional word ringing out clearly from amid the gabble.
The weighty, opaque smell of tobacco, beer, and the sea
clung everywhere, hanging like a miasma, visible as tene-
brous, upswept currents above the orange-shaded lights
and palatable, lying thick on my tongue as I breathed in;
people pressed around us, and hands patted my shoulder
or gripped my arm briefly as Florence and I battled our
way through to one of the quieter tables against the far
wall. Unconsciously I ducked beneath the low rafters: vast,
pitch-painted spars that had been stolen from some
beached ship centuries ago.

No sooner had we sat down than drinks were placed
before us with a quiet word. I raised the dimpled pint glass
to my lips, sipping slowly. The familiar, fruity bitter trickled down past my throat, evoking yet more memories, and
I cast my eyes over the humming crowd as I drank. Music
blossomed out from one corner; a trinity of flute, fiddle,
and a melodeon, and the jaunty hornpipe struck a peculiar
counterpoint with my own feelings.

Recognizable faces slipped in and out of view: worn,
wrinkled countenances, most weathered to the color of old
leather by a life working the ocean. Glasses were raised to
purpled lips, and throats above starched and unused collars
worked easily in their regular actions. The whole scene
took on a surreal image to me, like an old photograph
discovered behind a drawer. The subdued light cast a sepia
tone over everything, and as I sat unobtrusively observing,
I felt like I was watching an old movie.

I put down the glass and spoke with Florence; at first just general conversation, but eventually, it turned to Dad and the funeral. We shared old thoughts, images really, of the time when we had all been happy here, before the marriage had turned sour.

Our childhood.

But I was still reticent and a little withdrawn. We both danced around the subjects for a time—I think that Florence was wary of going into too much detail; I was so close to Elisabeth here, closer than I had been for a long time, and it was more difficult than I had ever imagined. With the exception of Dad's weekend visits, I had been the last to really live in the bothy. Florence knew of the pain, and tried to avoid it, but here . . . questions and concerns were thick about her, like midges near a stream.

I asked suddenly, "Have you been up there?"

Florence shook her head, not having to ask where 'there' was, and caught my eyes with hers. "You?"

I grunted a negative, picking up the glass and taking a sip. Hiding behind the commonplace once more.

"Do you think you will?" she asked, and I shrugged. I think a small part of me wanted to see the bothy again, but had no desire to pour fuel on the fire. Someone shouted my sister's name, and Florence was drawn away by another woman, and taking her drink with her, she left me alone.

But not for long.

I sat with my head bowed, absently listening to the music while my fingers shredded a damp beer mat. A shadow fell across the table, and I looked up to see a face I most definitely did remember. Ruddy and burned by the wind, the man's features were dominated by a huge bulb of a nose that was crisscrossed with red and purple veins like the markings on a road map. Dark dead eyes looked out from under salt-white brows, and a thinning thatch of colorless hair sat, approximately combed, on his head. He was dressed in a heavy, moth-eaten tweed jacket, and without any preamble whatsoever, he sat down opposite me.

He was called MacKay—I don't know if anyone actually knew his first name—and he was as old as the hills hunched around the village. He lived down near the old harbor, in a ramshackle house that always looked about to collapse, but had stood firm for more years than anyone could remember. I had strong memories of being frightened of him as a child; God help any miscreant who would venture too far down the beach—MacKay's choloric shouting would strip the skin from a youngster's back as he ran in terror. But as I had grown, I had come to know him, although only slightly. I'd heard that as a boy, he had nearly drowned out near Cape Wrath, and since that episode, folk claimed, he had never been the same again.

Touched by the sea.

Or those within, they'd say.

He had an uncanny knack for knowing just where the best fishing was to be found from season to season, and despite their mistrust and, perhaps, fear of him, the locals heeded his predictions as a London city broker might the *Financial Times*.

He was at his worse when drunk, which, if I remember rightly, was fairly often, and then he would reek with stories of merrows, selkies, and mermaids with a disturbing feel of rightness that left his reluctant audience unwilling to travel the cold paths to home.

MacKay shifted heavily in the chair and regarded me with his shark eyes. He looked the same as I remembered, as if he hadn't aged any in six years. His left hand was sheathed in a filthy woolen fisherman's mitten, and held a tumbler half-filled with what looked like whisky, straight, while the other gripped the edge of the table like a vice. His nails were yellow and fractured like the veins of quartz in the mountains, and the skin of his hand as brown as an old nut except for his fingers, which looked chaffed and raw. For a long moment, he said nothing, and the creeping feeling I had always experienced increased tenfold. There was a moment's tension, like the space between the notes of a tune, then he nodded and said, "I'm nae sorry about your father."

It took a second for it to sink in, then, startled, with my cheeks flushing, I replied, "What?"

His voice was heavily accented, like the sea raking back across the shingle, and as he pinned me to the wall with his stare as easily as a butterfly in a child's collection, he continued, " 'Twas what he wanted. He died a *happy* man. I'm nae sorry."

"But it was an accident," I managed to reply.

His wide-set shoulders raised a little—a gesture?—and he sipped at the drink, merely coating his lips. "P'raps."

There was the stink of both mystery and menace about him, and I found myself fearing once more. Like the deck of a ship in a storm, my mind rolled with a hundred questions, but before I could give voice to any of them, he waved a meaty hand, dismissing my curiosity.

"We'll talk o' it another time. Soon," he said, with an undertow of finality.

No, I wanted to say, *tell me now,* but all I could do was nod numbly, afraid.

"When are yeh coming back?" he asked, lowering the whisky.

I blinked as if struck. "I'm not."

He smiled then; a slight turning up of his chapped and

split top lip, revealing stumps of teeth long since gone to rot. He raised the glass to his mouth one last time, finishing off the potent drink with a single, noiseless swallow that made me shudder. He looked at the tumbler regretfully, then discarded it onto the table.

Leaning forward, he inched his face closer to mine. His breath was fetid and ripe with the alcohol, but his eyes were as clear as a starless winter night. The noise around us dropped, as if the pub were suddenly a theater and the lights had dimmed, and in a sibilant voice, he whispered, "It's nae yet over. The son must finish what the great-grandfather began, lest none o' them find peace. You'll be back. Despite what yeh may think now. Yeh won't know why, but yeh *will* be back."

The silence that followed that statement was palpable and eerie. I heard myself breathing, heard the working of my throat as it strove to contain the saliva that was building in my mouth, heard the slight scuffing sound my boots made on the stone floor as I moved them uneasily.

MacKay rocked back and stood in one smooth motion, his eyes never leaving mine. He remained still for a moment, overbearing, powerful, and knowing, then, with a bare, almost mocking wink, he stepped away and was instantly swallowed by the crowd.

I sat there for an indeterminate time, my long fingers clenching and relaxing around the slick sides of the glass while my restless mind battled with what he had said. I felt coldly sick, and I knew I was sweating profusely despite being chilled by his words. I wanted to question him further, to take his heavy shoulders and wring some answers out of him, but I couldn't. Other people spoke to me, and I nodded and gestured like a marionette. It was the oddest sensation; I felt like my mind were a jammed clockwork mechanism, and he had somehow reached into me and shaken it free, releasing the cogs and gears so that they ticked over under their own will. I had no energy, and despite what he said, no desire to return to Sandwood Bay.

It all ended eventually, and Florence and I parted company with the villagers, promising to visit again before we went back to Australia.

We had just under a week left.

We were due at Inverness in a couple of days to discuss the will with the solicitors. Despite his frugal last years, Dad had been wealthy; and as well as the small bothy, there was another, much larger residence further to the south near Edinburgh, and a substantial sum distributed about the local banks.

We had both declined offers to stay at Kinlochbervie, and instead had rooms at a guest house in the village of Ullapool (at my request), a drive of a little over half an hour away. I tried to concentrate on the task at hand, but I found it difficult to focus. The bright beams of the headlights cut a bright swath through the black, and occasionally, glowing signposts would rise up out from the darkness like the dead from the grave. Rabbits ran across the road, their eyes wild and terrified, and several times I was forced to swerve hard as they doubled back into my path suddenly.

My mind was the sea, my thoughts bobbing like flotsam upon it, sinking, only to rise again moments later in a different place. I turned on the stereo, sifting through the stations and static until I found Atlantic 152. I wound down the window slightly, admitting a steady rush of cold air, but the music and breeze didn't help.

The cogs were still turning.

2

It had stopped raining.

The clouds were clearing as we drove west out of Inverness and on through Dingwall, and although the sky was still moody, there was an air of change gusting through the mountains around Strath Conon. Florence was driving, but I could see from the way she was chewing her bottom lip that she was as distracted as I. My hands tightened around the rolls of mock vellum as I mulled over what had happened.

The solicitors had been curt and precise, delivering Dad's will with a practiced air of solemn sincerity. Florence had inherited the expansive Edinburgh manor house, and I, his savings (I already technically owned the bothy). On paper, the values worked out just about even, a fair half each (Mother had been struck off long ago), but I knew Dad's ulterior motives.

He wanted us back.

With the sheer, rugged visage of Sgurr a'Mhuilinn to our right, we traveled along the clear path of the A832, speeding past the blurring green-gray fields. Posts and fence markers flashed by, as repetitious and seemingly never-ending as the railway line that was occasionally visible alongside the road. Until we reached the turnoff to the A835, we neither spoke nor saw any other cars.

It was Florence who finally broke the silence, and as usual, she was direct. "What are you going to do?"

I shook my head. "What *is* there to do?"

She flicked a look at me, holding my eyes for a second, and replied, "Move back?"

"I don't think so," I said, the words of MacKay echoing through my mind. "I'm quite happy where I am." I fingered the cloth of my coat, feeling uncomfortable. "What about yourself?" I asked her after a moment. "You and Dan are set for life with that house."

"You're not exactly poor."

I shrugged and made a sound. Money had never really been that much of a concern for me. I only ever needed enough to get by, and if anything, I was more alarmed by my sudden wealth than pleased.

"I'll have to talk to Dan first, of course," she continued, eyes on the road, "but I can't see us relocating to Scotland—there's Dan's and my jobs first of all, and then there's Mum to think of."

Mother.

She lived on her own and didn't want all that much to do with us, but still . . .

"You're almost in a perfect position, you know." Her voice brought me out of my reverie.

"What do you mean?" I asked, squinting slightly as the sun came out from behind a huge white cloud and struck the car with brilliant gold light. I handed Florence her sunglasses.

"Well, you don't have too many ties in Brisbane—no mortgage, debts, those sorts of things, only Bronwyn, me, and Mum. You've not got a proper job. . . ."

I objected to that.

"All right, you've not got a job that holds you down to one particular place. But think about it; you're a musician, where better to make music than Scotland?"

"Ireland?" I offered, with a smile.

"Shut up, Richard, you know what I mean. It's not like you don't have the money now—Dad left you a packet."

"It's got nothing to do with money or ties—I don't *want* to come back, really!" I told her. It was true.

"I'm not saying you *should,* only that you ought to *think* about it."

"I don't even want to do that. I can't wait to leave. God, Flo, everywhere I look I see memories, and they're all painful."

"They can't *all* be. It's been over a half-dozen years since the accident. You've been fine in Brisbane, happy."

"Exactly. I'm happy because I'm away from *here.* The minute I got off the plane I felt like I'd stepped back in time. *Everything's* the same. It may well have been six years but . . . Jesus." I shook my head and pulled at my seat belt as if it were suddenly too tight.

"Why didn't you bring Bronwyn?" Florence asked after a moment.

I sighed, rubbing at my face a little before answering, "She wanted to come, but I . . . I thought that it would be best if . . ."

"You wanted one last time with the memories?"

I looked over at my sister, startled. She could be oddly perceptive at times. "That's about it," I admitted. "But I had no idea they'd be so vivid. I didn't really return here for Dad, it was more than that; I really just wanted to be close to Elisabeth one last time. I guess I thought I could come over here, have a look around, remember how good things were, then go back, finally cut free."

"I don't think it works like that."

I chuckled mirthlessly. "No, it doesn't."

"What did she say?"

"Who?"

"Bronwyn."

"I think she was a little upset."

Florence looked over at me again briefly. "Did you tell her why you wanted to go alone?"

I shook my head slightly. I reached down and unwound the window a little. The cool afternoon air whipped at my face. "I just said it was a family-only funeral."

"Richard!"

I held up my hands. "I know. I should have told her."

"Then why didn't you?"

I swallowed and searched for a reply. "At first I was going to," I said, "but then, the more I thought about it, the more it seemed best if I didn't."

"She's your partner, Richard. She would have understood. You shouldn't have lied," she scolded, her voice sounding exasperated.

"I *didn't* lie, exactly. I just didn't want her thinking . . ." I threw up my hands. Feeling helpless, all I could do was shrug again. For a moment, Florence looked like she was going to say something else, but her mouth closed and silence descended upon us once more. For a time I just sat there, gazing at the gray tarmac of the road as it vanished under the car. Then I looked over at her face, at her profile lit by the sun. She understood better than most, but still she didn't really know how deep the hurt went.

I doubted even I did.

"Perhaps it *was* for the best," she murmured. "As long as things really *are* over now."

I looked at her, but said nothing.

We reached Loch Broom, and for a moment, both of us were distracted by the stupendous view off to our left. We passed the old skeletons of ancient crofters' cottages, now nothing more than pairs of triangular chimneys that looked all too much like gravestones as they poked out from within tangled clumps of briar, flower, and fern. Florence slowed down here, for the road was wrought with twists and sharp-angled bends, and she didn't speak to me while she concentrated. I was glad of the respite, for my sister's words had struck a chord within me, and I was afraid that if I began to look deep enough, I would find a spark of me that wanted to return.

We passed two massive, blue-black ravens sitting on a twisted stump of rock. Their glassy, fathomless eyes followed the car as they regarded me dispassionately; then, as one, they took wing, effortlessly lifting into the clearing sky.

Ullapool was visible now, a strange sight that used to amuse me, for the growing town was built upon a finger of land that protruded into the shining loch, and on a clear day with the sun reflecting off the water, Ullapool appeared to be floating. But today, it too just served to rekindle the past.

The guest house was a three-story, rambling affair that looked to have done its best business a decade earlier. There was a relaxed, almost tired feel to the building, an outlook that was certainly not mirrored by its almost annoyingly effervescent landlady. Most of the rooms were taken up by holidaying families from the north of England,

and sun-browned children clattered and chased down the carpeted halls, seemingly at all hours.

With the car parked and unpacked, we made our way wearily through the corridors and up to my room. Despite the well-placed bunches of fresh flowers, the house still had that typical smell to it, one common of all guest houses, and although not exactly unpleasant, it still served to remind me just how far from . . . home we were.

With bags off-loaded, Florence sat down heavily in the easy chair, contemplatively regarding me while I filled the tiny kettle with water. When the tea was made and my thoughts mustered, we sat and talked into the evening, but neither of us broached the subject of the future.

ii

In the four days between the meeting in Inverness and the flight home, I got in a great deal of hill walking and visited a couple of old haunts from my days as a musician here, renewing acquaintances with people who were not so much friends as friendly.

We spent the Wednesday night in Kinlochbervie, sharing stories of our Australian histories with folks who really had no conception of what we were speaking of, having spent their entire lives in and around the remote district of Sutherland.

It was after dinner, and with a growing sense of unease, that I excused myself from their company. I told them I wanted to visit a few more friends, and after a moment's protest, they let me go. Florence looked at me oddly as I put on my coat and slipped out of the door, and as I winked at her, I saw her smile thinly.

Out of the house and on the black tar river of the road, I felt an immediate relief. A nauseous twisting had begun in my stomach, and I had felt sick, but here, in the night, breathing the cold air, I began to feel better. I buttoned up my coat, trying to seal in the last of the warm air before the sea breeze stole it away. I looked around slowly, wondering where to go. I had no wish to visit anyone, but felt the need to just walk for a while. Around me, the old street lamps cast circles of light onto the glistening road, and the row of cottages were all lit with squares of warmth in each window. Thin trails of gray smoke seeped out of the chimneys, borne away slowly westward by the salty breeze. I stepped away from the gate and began following the slight incline down toward the sea. The night was cloudy and very dark; there was no trace of the moon, not even a chalky smudge. As I walked, I heard the distant murmur of voices from within the houses, and the occasional crackle of laughter. Wood smoke and burning peat colored the air, a comforting smell that always haunted me. It was a smell that the Australian night, suffused with the dusky aroma of the eucalyptus trees, came close to emulating, but never quite close enough.

My footsteps tapped rhythmically as I turned a corner, coming within sight of the Atlantic. So complete was the dark that the sea appeared only as a blackness even deeper than the sky. I left the narrow road and crossed the causeway that led to the new pier, then walked along the wall of the old harbor, careful of my footing on the old worn stones. The waves broke steadily against the cliffs to the north, and what was a roar there was no more than a dull rushing here. Below me, the still waters of the harbor licked gently at the wall. I sat down on the damp stone, hanging

my legs down and watched the night, the sea, while absently rubbing my wrists against the biting cold.

Occasionally, I saw a brief flash of light, like a watch-
man's beacon, and thought that perhaps it was a trawler,
out for the night's catch. There was a lighthouse further to
the north, on the fractured pinnacle of Cape Wrath, though
its warning was blocked here by the cliffs and hills that
towered to my right.

I'm not sure how long I sat there, but by the time I got
up, my legs were stiff, as if the stone had sucked the
warmth from my marrow. The wind had picked up a little,
breaking apart the clouds so that patches of star-spotted
sky were visible. I turned and made my way back up toward the town.

As I passed the inn, I stopped to listen. The usually
rowdy chatter was subdued and somber—even for a mid-
week evening. After a moment's silent thought, I pushed
open the heavy door and stepped in out of the cold. The
main room was almost deserted, and I crossed on quiet
feet to the bar. The woman nodded to me in greeting, her
smile as warm as the thick fire that bloomed under the
hearth.

I paid her and picked up my drink. As I turned, I noticed
the small knot of people gathered in the corner, sitting in
a circle around one of the tables. There were perhaps a
dozen bodies there, mainly old men with the look of the
sea about them, but there were women also, equally hard
and hardy. I recognized a couple of faces, but no one
looked up at me as I sat down in the shadows of the corner
opposite. They were looking at one man who was sitting
on a stool, his back to me. Broad shoulders were encased
in a thick, dirty tweed jacket, and a red, blotchy neck,

fringed with white, closely cut hair met with a head that was large and capped with a hat of the same material as the old coat. I could not see the face, but in one of the hands that rested on the table was a glass half-filled with whisky.

I cowered within the darkness of the corner, hardly daring to breathe lest he hear me. I was afraid, an irrational, childlike fear that was disarming and embarrassing. No one was talking, and I got the sense that they were waiting for MacKay. His heavy hand raised the tumbler to his mouth, out of my sight, and when it returned to the table, the glass was empty. The noise of it hitting the rough wood sounded loud, and I likened it to a herald's staff hitting the floor.

Then he started to speak. Even though he was facing away from me, I could hear every word, every inflection that he put into his speech, and I sat there, not drinking, not moving, as beguiled as the rest.

"There are many tales as t' their origins," he began, his voice rich and low, "many sources, many stories. The *Lebor Gabala*, the Irish Book of Invasions, tells how Balor of the Baleful Eye, giant king o' the despised Fomorians, ha' revealed t' him a prophecy tha' his own grandson would be his downfall. So, fearing the revelation, Balor ha' his only daughter, the beautiful Eithne, imprisoned in a distant island cave. Now, it came t' pass that Cain MacCainte, a hero o' the mythical Tuatha de Danann, discovered her whereabouts and, disguised as a woman, gained entry. He seduced Eithne and all o' her twelve guardian-women, and in time, all bore children, with Eithne bearing triplets."

MacKay paused, picking up the refilled glass and drinking before continuing. "In his rage, Balor had all the children drowned in the black waters o' the sea, where they became selkies: neither living nor dead. One escaped, a single boy, Lugh, the father o' Cuchulain, but tha' is a story for 'nother time.

"So the Irish, God forgive them, believe the daughters o' Eithne and her women t' be the selkies. The first children are said t' be immortal while they dwelt in t' seas, but as a consequence, all the males we' also infertile. So 'tis that they steal mortal men. The original descendants still dwell within t' Irish Sea, while their halfling children live o' the coast all over the Isles, though they have favor among the west. 'Tis these that can shed their skins and walk the land among us, and as yeh all know, to find the skin is t' trap the ghost."

He stopped again for a moment, and I finally took a swig of my beer. When he continued, his voice was lower still, and I had to strain to hear his compelling words.

"South o' here, round the islands of Mull, Skye, and Iona, folks believe them t' be fallen angels, like the daonie sidhe; those tha' stood by when Lucifer made his stand against the Almighty, neither good enough for Heaven, nae wicked enough for Hell.

"I knew a man," he said, turning his head slightly so that the side of it caught the light of the fire. "A little ways from here. He was selkie-born." He held up his right hand and splayed his fingers. "He ha' webs here, like a fish, and there was something in his eyes, always a kind of longin'. He was married t' a woman, a plain, fisherman's daughter that I never knew. He lived wi' her for six or seven years, and they had many children, but one day, some years back, when she was in town, he found his skin, tucked away behind a loose turf in the roof, and he, and the children, disappeared.

"She still wanders t' beaches, calling out their names, but

nothin' answers her, save the occasional bark o' a seal, and o' course, the laughter o' the sea."

The glass was once more drained, and MacKay said, reflectively, "They are an exacting people, as are the daonie sidhe and like t' Good Folk, the selkies always retrieve their debts, one way o' another."

As he said this, he slowly turned around to look at me. His half-hooded eyes glimmered in the shallow light, and for a moment, we both shared something. The rest of the inn, the other people, ceased to exist. There was only me and MacKay's stare. My blood ran through my veins as cold as the Celtic Sea, and the tiny hairs along the back of my spine stood stiff. The fire crackled and popped, sending a whorl of sparks up the chimney.

I rose from the chair, aware that everyone was watching me. I stumbled to the door and hurried through, slamming it excessively. For a long time I stood there, my back against the hard wood as I breathed deeply. The old man had touched something, something deep within me that even I hadn't known was there. It was as if the story had been for me alone. Had he known? All that time, had he known I was seated over there? I was positive he hadn't seen me enter, but still . . .

After a few more minutes, I made my way back toward the house. As luck would have it, just as I turned to open the gate, the front door swung wide and Florence emerged, saying her farewells to the people. I hovered by the car, saying a few perfunctory words when they saw me, anxiously waiting for my sister to open the door.

As we drove home, she inquired as to my health, saying I was as white as a sheet. I made my excuses, blaming it on something I had eaten. She accepted that, but I doubt she believed it.

iii

Our last couple of days in Scotland passed quickly.

We made arrangements with the solicitors to contact them via letter or fax as to our intentions for the future. The money was easy enough, and in fact had already been transferred to my meager account in Brisbane (minus the substantial inheritance tax and the fees, of course), no doubt whetting the expectations of my bank manager to no end. What was a considerable sum in pounds sterling would become a veritable fortune in Australian dollars.

In the end, Florence was sorry to go, as she realized it would be quite unlikely that she would return to live, even with the house here she had inherited.

I was only too glad.

Despite her reasonings and my expectations, there were two things that failed to happen.

I didn't see MacKay again.

And I didn't visit the bothy.

3

Saying farewell to Florence for the time being, I caught a cab from the airport to my rented house in Auchenflower.

I sat in the front seat trying to rub the tiredness from my eyes as the car hurtled down Kingsford Smith Drive, running parallel to the glistening, silverlit Brisbane River. It was about two in the morning, and the city was deserted.

The return trip had been awful. Despite the silence of the overnight flight, I'd not been able to sleep for more than a minute or two. Every time I began to nod off, something would happen that made me lurch back upright, be it a dropped plate, turbulence, or even just my own mind. I'd spent most of the time in a kind of half-doze that only served to deepen my tiredness. By the time we had cleared customs and said our good-byes, I was just about ready to drop.

Turning right off Milton Road, the cab traveled down under the drooping branches of the jacarandas, the dipped beams of its headlights arcing the way before us, and came to a stop outside of my dark cottage. I paid the woman clumsily, then stepped out onto the street. I locked my hands together above my head and stretched, feeling the knots in my muscles protesting. The light from the street lamp filtered down through the trees, flickering on the close-cut grass around me. The night was cool, but the smells from the gardens were rich, comforting.

Lugging my case up the wooden stairs, I stopped outside my door, fumbling for my keys. Once inside, I didn't even bother to turn on the light. The red eye of the answering machine winked at me, but I ignored it. The room was almost totally dark, with only a slight slab of gray light entering through the uncurtained window in the kitchen to low-light the furniture. Dropping my case by the door, I made my way through to the bedroom, only pausing briefly to get a drink of water. I removed my clothes hastily and fell onto the mattress, longing for sleep.

When I awoke late the next day, I felt little better. Although I thought I'd slept soundly enough, I was still bone-numbingly tired. I lay in bed, staring at the ceiling and listening to the distant noise of the traffic as I tried to sort through my feelings. There was a random, almost frantic quality to the images, almost as if I had not really woken properly. I closed my eyes, trying to concentrate on something in particular, but it was no use. It became hard to separate the recent from the distant. They merged as one.

Out in the living room I heard the phone ring, but I let it go. The answering machine kicked in, and I didn't hear the voice or the message. My breathing steadied, and once more I slept.

ii

Three sharp knocks echoed through the room.

I marked my place, then closed the book and got up from the easy chair. Before I reached the door, I heard the sound of a key, and I stepped back as it swung quickly open. Standing there, in perfect silhouette against the bright afternoon sun, was Bronwyn.

Two things went through my mind as I saw her: I felt terrible for not ringing her since I'd got back, and I didn't want her here right now. She stood still, not speaking while we regarded one another across the threshold. Her hazel eyes were angry, and her lips were drawn tightly together. I was about to speak when she started forward, raising her hand suddenly.

"Don't even try to think up some goddamn excuse, Richard." She dropped her small bag down on one of the chairs and turned to face me, one hand gripping the edge of the table. I shut the door, the bottom of my stomach dropping away at the expectation of the argument.

"Do you *know* how many times I've left messages on your fucking machine? *Why* haven't you rung me? Three days you've been back—I didn't even know *that* till I spoke to Florence—and not so much as a short call to say you're all right."

I stammered some sort of reply. She was *really* angry; her language was proof enough for that. Bronwyn only swore when she was close to losing control, which wasn't very often. On reflection, it was usually with me. The truth was, I didn't know why I hadn't contacted her. I knew I'd received a number of messages, but I hadn't answered any of them. To be honest, I hadn't replayed the machine at all.

"I'm sorry," I said lamely, instantly regretting it. Sorry was the last thing Bronwyn wanted to hear. She wanted a row, a way of blowing off the steam. I played fiddle to relax, Bronwyn had fights. They'd been sort of fun at first, but I'm really nonconfrontational at heart, and they hurt.

Her eyes blazed, and to try and stave off the impending rebuke, I stepped quickly past her, saying, "Let me get us some tea."

I went into the adjoining kitchen and quickly set the kettle to boil, all the while feeling Bronwyn's eyes upon me. When there was nothing more to delay myself with, I turned to face her. She still stood by the table, tall and angry. Her long blond hair wafted slightly in the gentle breeze from the open doors to the verandah, and she looked quite formidable in her black suit. She was staring at me intently, though the wrath seemed to be fading slightly.

Bronwyn and I had met about a year ago at a café, on the banks of the Brisbane River, out near Hawthorne. I'd been playing one of my extremely rare classical concerts with a quintet, and she had approached me during the last of the breaks asking about lessons for her younger sister. We'd got talking, and although I didn't teach, for some reason I agreed.

I found out later she didn't have a sister.

She was a copywriter for a small advertising agency just outside of the city, and was exceptionally good at her job. She had pursued me voraciously and relentlessly, it had seemed, though I didn't think I was running all that fast. Our relationship was passionate, yet still withdrawn, even after a year. I knew the distance came from me, but there was nothing I could do about it, and I think we argued about as many times as we made love.

The house was still quiet, and only the pure voice and music of Loreena McKennitt filled the silence between us.

"You look like shit, Richard," she said finally.

I was forced to agree. I still don't think I was over the jet lag. She crossed the room and I turned and opened my hands. With one last sigh of resignation, she stepped into my arms. My fingers met around the small of her back and I pulled her close. For quite a time we just stood there, holding each other.

"God, it feels like you've been gone years," she murmured.

"It's only been a week."

She lifted her face from my chest and looked at me. "Nearer two," she corrected.

I shrugged and made a face. "Sorry," I said again. "I was shattered."

"You still look it," she replied, her lips finding mine. The rising shriek of the kettle forced us apart, and reluctantly, with one final kiss, Bronwyn moved away. With a weary sigh, she moved to the couch and sat down. I poured the boiling water into the pot, put it onto the tray next to the mugs, and carried the whole affair into the lounge, placing it on the table next to the sofa. I sat down beside Bronwyn, looking at her for a moment. She was so very beautiful, too beautiful for someone like me.

During the weeks before I'd gone overseas, she'd been making overtures to me about moving in. I'd managed to avoid most of her questions, begging the funeral as an excuse, but now, I knew, the topic would come up again at some point. I hated myself for not being able to commit fully to her. It wasn't that I had other women—far from it. I'd only had a smattering of relationships since I'd been here, and all of those had been within the last three or so years and had not lasted longer than a couple of months. I don't know what it was about me. God knows, I was attracted to Bronwyn, I'd not felt such fire with someone since . . . well, I guess I've just answered my question.

I once thought that if I looked hard enough, I'd find another person like Bethy, that life would be able to go on as if nothing had happened. But there was no one like her. There was no one like Bronwyn either.

"It brought back all the memories, didn't it?" she asked softly, her eyes dark and searching. I nodded, taking a deep breath and wrinkling my brow.

"Too many," I said.

Her arm went around my waist, and she pulled me close, resting my head against her shoulder. Her perfume was strong, some French concoction that I could barely pronounce the name of, but I could still smell the somehow reassuring residue of shampoo in her thick hair. It was a little while before I pulled away, remembering the tea. The tension had eased, and though she had forgiven me, I knew Bronwyn would bear some resentment for a little time yet. It had only been three days, but for her, it had verged on an affront.

With the tea long gone, and the blaze of the sun giving way grudgingly to the cooler shade of the afternoon, I looked at my watch and asked, "Don't you have to be back at work?"

She shook her head, stirring her golden hair into restless life. "Not today. I figured I'd need the whole afternoon to kill you."

I smiled, though part of me knew that had probably been her original intention. The large room was split by a brilliant slash of sunlight, and within the column, tiny particles of dust whorled and glittered. Outside, its call raucous and mocking, a kookaburra laughed from its perch somewhere within the mango tree that shaded the garden. The insects were chattering away, and the smell of flowers was on the breeze.

"So what do you want to do for the rest of the afternoon?" I inquired.

"I'm not sure," she replied, pulling me close again. "Let's just see what happens."

When he awoke, the bed next to him was empty, though the rumpled sheets and slight depression were still warm with the heat of a body.

Stretching out his arms, he yawned and raised himself up a little. Above his head, the clear, milky light of the full moon poured through the window, bathing the small room in an ambience that was both churchlike and serene. For long moments he just lay there, watching the play of the silver on his skin, waiting for her return. The wind was quiet tonight, for once not playing its tricks with the chimney, and far away, only audible if he concentrated, the sea murmured restlessly against the shore.

Shaking the last of the sleep from his mind, he swung down from the bed, planting his feet on the cold stone of the floor. Running long fingers through his hair, he put on his glasses and stood up. Softly, his voice questioning, he called her name, but received no reply. His feet padded on the stone and his pajamas whispered as he walked from the room. Pools of light spilled onto the floor from the windows, melting into a lake where they joined the wedge that ebbed in from the open door.

His curiosity was aflame, and a small dervish of worry had begun to twist deep within. Looking around once more, he crossed to the open door and, resting his hand on the fresh paint of the jamb, called her name again.

The wind answered him, a single, sudden squall that carried on it the tang of salt and the slightly bitter smell of seaweed. Outside, the small bar of land between the loch and the ocean was illuminated dramatically, and the small river connecting the two was a shining cord between the mother and her child. The sands shone, and high out over the water, a moon filled full to bursting hung precariously in the sky.

He left the house, his step quickening as the worry spun faster, grew larger. He shouted her name, loud enough that it echoed off the cliffs that fringed the tiny bay.

Something splashed in the water, large, heavy, and he broke into a trot. The night air was cool as it brushed across his chest, and his curling hair tapped at his forehead as his loping run quickly ate up the short distance to the sea.

Before him, the water spread away, an infinite mirror, impossibly smooth and eternal, older than life. From the distant horizon to the shore, the water was lit with a thin, tapering corridor of pearled light, surrounded on both sides by the night-haunted ocean. Within the passage, like a monolithic shape, a single rowing boat floated. It was impossibly black, no more than a recognizable silhouette, its shadow extended and still as it reached away from the moon toward him.

It was empty.

Ripples expanded outward, from a point near the prow, as if something had been dropped. The miniature waves made their way toward the shore, dying out long before they got there.

Panic built within him, consuming like a fire in a forest long denied rain. He met the water but carried on running, churning up great glittering sprays as he tried to reach the solitary boat. He screamed her name again, torn with anguish and realization as he waded through the clinging sea. Coldness sucked at his flesh, sudden and spiteful, and as he leaped forward to try and swim, he took down a lungful of water. He surfaced, coughing and frantic, trying to beat his way to the boat, but the sea would not let him.

On the shore, the two seaward windows of the cottage looked out impassively, the glass reflecting the glare of the moon like pupils of a cat. The wind gusted again, moaning through the open door then back out, down the beach and toward the two shapes in the stillness of the sea. The man's silhouette stood waist-deep in the water, clawed hands raised either side of his body, water falling slowly through his fingers as he wept. The wind picked up his tortured cry, the almost animal wail of the demanded question that ripped from his throat along with the keening sounds of his loss. Cradling them both, the wind carried on out into the darkness, following the silver channel for a time, before it grew bored and once again skirted back inland.

I awoke suddenly, my eyes wide and my nostrils flaring as I fought for breath.

The visions faded quickly, though some of the images lingered pointedly. With one arm straight behind me for support, I ran a hand down my face. I shuddered violently, as if I were about to cry, and slowly let out the breath I had been holding. The curtains blew wildly around the square of the window, and the light that washed into the room was pallid and weak. It was midwinter, but the night felt uncannily humid, and even with the fan ticking overhead, I was intolerably hot. I swung out of bed, and without bothering to put on any clothes, walked on crooked legs to the bathroom. After I had relieved myself, I bent down over the sink and splashed some cold water over my face, then looked in the mirror. I barely recognized the face that peered back at me. The bags under my eyes were getting bigger, and my skin looked loose and unhealthy. I flicked off the light and quietly returned to the bedroom.

I sat on the edge of the bed, and for a long moment just stayed still, looking down at Bronwyn. She was lying facedown on the bed, her limbs spread out almost wildly as she slept on, unknowing of my nightmare. Like me, she was naked, and the dim light cast her lightly tanned features with a milky tint. Her skin was flawless save for one spot just below her right shoulder blade where she had a birthmark shaped like a crescent. It wasn't so much a flaw as an enhancement. The events of the night came to mind, and though they still stirred me, I looked at them in a different light. Our sex had been almost merciless at first, then had slowly slipped into a languorous half-reaffirmation of our relationship, and we had both finally fallen asleep at some point in the very early hours.

Quite suddenly, I felt incredibly guilty.

The emotion came upon me quickly, punching through my mind-fogged barrier of sleep with alarming ease. It was the same feeling that I'd had when she'd first opened the door; I didn't want her here. My stomach was churning, the sensation all too close to unwillingly being on a ride at a fair and knowing you can't get off just yet.

It wasn't just that I wanted my solitude; well, in a way it was, but there was more to it than that. Things I couldn't put into words. I . . . loved her, of that much I was certain, but was that enough?

I screwed my eyes shut as a vivid afterimage streaked across my retinas. It was of a face, another face, and as I sat on the bed watching Bronwyn sleep, my right hand absently began to twist the cold silver Claddagh ring I still wore on my finger.

Bronwyn didn't stir, and for that I was glad. I think she had sensed something was wrong—I'd been withdrawn and distant both during the lovemaking and after, and although she had questioned me gently, she had not pushed, which was unusual for her.

A time was coming when we'd both have to sit down and talk about the future. I dreaded the coming of that day, but a growing part of me could not wait for it to arrive.

4

The dreams became a nightly occurrence.

They started out as nothing more than tenuous images that fled cloudlike when I awoke, but as time passed, they grew, becoming stronger, more poignant, more compelling. They were never quite frightening enough to be called nightmares, although on many occasions I would lurch upright in bed, sitting there for long moments just listening to my ragged breathing, the sigh of the wind outside the window, and the echoes of the ghost I had brought back with me.

I remember one of the dreams intensely; I had been swimming. Swimming through water so black and glossed that it might have been oil, yet it was smoothly cold and comforting, like cool silk slipped on over a warm body. I swam slowly, my strokes broad and effortless. I didn't need to breathe, and though it felt like I were, my chest wasn't moving. There was no sense of direction, no up or down, just forward. I curled into a ball, suspended and motionless, delighting in the lack of control. I could taste the salt of the water on my lips, and its smell was in my nose, strong and urgent, almost demanding. I opened my eyes wide and looked around, rolling weightlessly. The glimmering sheet of the surface was above me, stretching away into infinity, as flawless as glass. Straightening out and lengthening my strokes, I made for it. There was no perception of rising slowly to the surface, nor any indication of what lay beyond. With my fingers pointing before me, I broke through the silver barrier suddenly, and with little resistance.

I was flying.

It was as if gravity had been reversed, and I was tumbling from the water into the air. Voices, both male and female, spoke, soft and whispered, and though the words were familiar, I could not quite understand. I knew from the tones that they were questions. They seemed to become agitated, perhaps from the lack of a response from me, and the wonderful freedom of flight turned swiftly into the terror of falling.

I awoke shouting, my arms tangled in the thin sheet and my body sheened with perspiration. A moment passed, and my sense of reality returned gradually. I clicked on the bedside light and sat back against the pillows, raking my fingers roughly through my damp hair. I glanced up at the clock on the wall, and groaned as I discovered it was ten after five. There would be no way I'd get back to sleep now. The light through the curtains was already beginning to brighten, and the dawn chorus was enthusiastic and animated. Mercifully, tonight I had been alone. Bronwyn had become worried at my sudden wakings, the shouting and mumblings, and though she had been nothing but supportive, I was glad to be alone.

I took a few deep breaths and a swig of warm water

from the glass next to the bed and tried to settle myself. The images stayed with me, haunting, as they had before. Most of the dreams I had been having in the three weeks since my return had followed the same basic theme; swimming and falling, exultation followed by terror.

Sometimes I saw a face, her eyes always following me. She never spoke, not like the others, but just watched.

Waiting.

Even just after the accident, when the memories and images had been at their most devastating, I never dreamed of Bethy. I suppose it was a blessing really, because dreams can be so real. At first I dreaded falling asleep in case I slipped into a world where she still lived, where things were as they had been. I would have stayed there. The waking would have killed me.

But I never did dream of her. Until now.

Time can do a great many things. I've spoken to a few people in similar sorts of situations, during periods when I'd thought that talking was the best thing, and there seem to be two conflicting thoughts: the passing of time dulls the pain, or it amplifies it. Of course there are those who hide it away, leaving it to fester until it bursts forth and consumes them utterly. I don't think I ever tried to hide the pain, at least not like that. Until recently, I'd honestly thought myself over it.

I tried to make sense of the kaleidoscope quality of the dream, the tumbling pictures and sounds, but as always, it slipped through my mind, the moments falling like sand through fingers. That was another image that stuck with me, though I couldn't place it within any dream.

My heart gradually slowed and I slipped down the bed, once more resting my head on the clinging cotton of the pillows as I turned off the light. The faint glow of the morning sun was just coloring the thin gauze of my curtains, and I closed my eyes and listened to the excited birdsong until I grew restless and got out of bed. I showered and made a pot of coffee, then sat on the verandah watching the dawn.

ii

Life carried on.

Bronwyn's relationship with me resumed its normal path, though I was still distant. She didn't bring up the subject of moving in, and for that I was glad. I'd been feeling a space growing between us of late, an area of uncertainty I knew *I* was cultivating. To me, nothing had really been the same since I'd returned from Scotland. She sensed the discord, of course, but each time she questioned me, I shrugged off her concerns; making light of the situation or turning away her inquiries deftly. She took my assurances in good stead, but I could still see the doubt in her eyes, and the confusion in her heart.

There was one particular time when I came very close to telling her my doubts about our relationship. It was a Thursday evening, and with nothing better to do, we had driven over to New Farm Park for a walk. The night was cool, just the barest hint of a breeze sighed through the huge jacaranda and fig trees that lined the narrow path. The park was still and quiet, and only the occasional distant glow from a car's headlamps and the seemingly far-off sparkle of the city reminded us we weren't miles from nowhere.

Holding hands, we strolled past the shadowed shape of the closed tea shop and on toward the river. We barely spoke, each of us lost in our own private world of thoughts. Possums chattered to one another in the high boughs, and occasionally, I heard the rhythmic beating of wings as a flying fox took flight. We were almost alone; only one or two dedicated joggers pounded the grass this late at night, and they stuck to the illuminated sections further toward Sydney Street.

Reaching the river, Bronwyn sat down on one of the wooden benches, motioning for me to sit next to her.

"What's the matter?" she asked me, her steady voice sounding loud after the quiet. The river lapped gently against the breakwater in front of us.

I took off my glasses, rubbed them clean on my jumper, and looked her in the eyes. For a moment I was going to do it, I was actually going to tell her about the nightmares, my doubts, about Bethy, everything.

But then; "Nothing," I replied softly, slipping my glasses back on.

5

On a more mundane level, I continued to scratch a living playing in the pubs and bars, refusing to touch Dad's money until I really had to.

It was vaguely comforting to know that it was there, complete and intact despite a few fancied thoughts during the return flight.

Rubbing my wet hair briskly with the towel, I walked from the bedroom into the kitchen, trying to remember where I'd put down my coffee cup. It was a quarter to six on a rainy Friday night, and I had landed a fairly large gig with the residential Irish band, Tallafrae, at a pub called Gilhooley's in the heart of the city.

The regular fiddler had been called away on some emergency family matter, and through a telephone conversation barely an hour ago, I'd been asked to step in. The music was no problem, just the usual infectious jigs, reels, and songs, but I was weary from lack of sleep, and wasn't feeling too well. Still, if there was anything that would cheer me up, it was a few hours of decent music.

I eventually found the mug (above the wash basin in the bathroom, of all places) and, alternating between gulps of coffee and drying my hair, I managed to get dressed. I was due to arrive there at about seven, and although it was only a fifteen-minute drive, I hadn't checked my equipment, so I was rushing.

At five to, I pulled into Charlotte Street and was jammy enough to find a vacant meter right outside the back door. With my gear bag tucked under my arm and my fiddle case slung over my shoulder, I entered the smoky pub. The band were already set up, and shaking hands as I passed, I put down my case in the far corner of the stage, next to the wooden partition that separated it off from the bustling bar. I took out my fiddle, tuned it carefully, then hung it from the microphone stand. My only other pieces of gear were a small equalizing box and a delay pedal that both sat at my feet. I took the offered lead and plugged in, taking a moment to set my levels, then I was done.

Joey, the bouzouki player and a good friend, appeared from somewhere near the bar, carrying two pints of Guinness, one of which made its way into my eager hand. For a while we talked about my father, my trip overseas, and the night's set list, discussing possibilities. I was familiar with their music, and had played with Joey and most of the other members of the band many times before. I had free rein, which was just what I needed; I wanted a way of release, and I was even able to add a few of my own tunes to their set.

The sound check didn't take long; they were professional musicians—it was all second nature to them—and as we whiled away the time until half past eight, I began to experience the welcoming rush of expectation that I always get before playing. I was feeling much better, the tiredness was gone, banished by anticipation, and the sickly feeling in my stomach seemed to have subsided a little. The building crowd was a pleasant mixture of both young and old, and there were a few people that I recognized from other times.

The kickoff time arrived, and with the large bar full to bursting, we began with a lively set of jigs that gave me an opportunity to judge the audience and adjust my playing accordingly. They seemed receptive and eager, and as Sophie, the singer and flutist, launched into a very bawdy version of "The Raggle Taggle Gypsy," I felt myself relaxing and settling in.

By the beginning of the third quarter, the place was throbbing. The room was filled with smoke, and the ceiling fans and supposed air conditioners looked to be better at distribution than dispersal. My eyes were stinging, but I didn't care. My bow knifed across the strings, and my fingers fluttered as they found the notes of the reel on their own. The wooden flute would stream forth with a complex melody, and as it stopped, I would take over, my fiddle screaming out a reply as Sophie and I played off one another, riding atop Joey's percussive bouzouki. The bodhran stuttered out the rhythm, hypnotic and galloping, and couples jumped up and down before us in a rough approximation of Irish ceilidh dancing. The reel drew to its climax, but the anticipated ending didn't arrive. The rest of the band cut off exactly, leaving me to weave an intricate, spiraling melody on my own. There were whoops and shouts from the crowd as my playing rose to a frenzy, then dropped back down as the rest of the band once more picked up the threads of the tune, and we all finished it together. The applause seemed deafening, and I blushed as Joey pointed to me, grinning.

There was the briefest of pauses, then I struck up once more: a solo piece that was one of my favorites. It was a

slow tin-whistle air by Mary Bergin, a stunning Galway
musician, but it worked just as well on the fiddle, and as I
played I closed my eyes, letting the music flow across me,
swallowing me.

I can't honestly say what happened.

The tune took form, as it always did, and I released it
without really being aware of what I was doing. The pub
went quiet, or at least my hearing faded, attending only the
slow swell of the notes that continued. Pictures came unbidden into my mind's eye. I felt the cold soak of the salt
water that rose to my waist, felt the sea breeze against the
tears that ran unchecked down my cheeks. The music was
on the wind, in the wind, everywhere. The distant murmur
of the waves against the shore was my metronome, the beat
constant, coaxing, and gentle. I could feel myself moving,
rocking slightly on uncertain feet as the tide resisted me.
My clawed hands raked through the impenetrable water as
I screamed her name, my throat scoured raw by the terror
in the single word. The music stopped, the sound of the
tide hushed, both cut off suddenly by the manifestation of
my fear.

I dived under.

And was swimming.

I opened my eyes and saw Joey standing over me, the
worry obvious on his face. For a moment, everything
crashed round my head, reality mixed with fantasy, and I
had no idea where I was or what had happened. I could
remember nothing, only the music. I was sitting outside at
one of the tables that courted the potted fig trees along the
street. The wind that coursed up Albert Street from the
river was damp, cool, and refreshing, and from my right, I
could hear the muted cacophony from inside the pub;

voices fighting over taped music and laughter.

"Why am I out here?" I asked after a moment.

"You passed out," Joey replied, his voice soft and accented. "Clean as a whistle."

To those that didn't know the difference between Irish and Scots, we sounded a lot alike.

I swallowed thickly. My head was clearing, and despite what had happened, I felt fine. I still couldn't remember though.

"God, I'm sorry," I said, sitting up straighter and taking the offered tumbler of water.

After a couple of sips, Sophie crouched down in front of me and asked, "Are you all right?" I could see concern in her eyes. The other tables around us were scantly attended, and passersby slid along the pavement like featureless ghosts.

I nodded. "I've not been feeling too well this past week, you know, not eating, that sort of thing. I hope I didn't ruin the set."

Joey brushed a hand through the air and dismissed my concern. "Course not. We were just about finished anyway. Besides, I don't think any o' that lot noticed. They probably thought it was part of the act!"

I smiled and took a deep breath, then I had a sudden stab of fear. "My fiddle . . ."

"It's fine. Sophie here managed to grab you." The sense of relief I felt was tremendous; that fiddle was more precious to me than my own life. "Oh, here," he said, handing me my hat. It was one of those floppy peaked affairs beloved of folk musicians and train drivers.

I slipped it back on my head, then rubbed at my chin mechanically. I felt fine, except for the familiar churning in

my guts and a little splinter of a headache. I looked up at
Joey and asked haltingly, "Did I . . . did I *say* anything before I fell?"

Puzzlement crossed his face, and he shook his head.
"Not that I heard, why?"

Once more, relief flooded over me, relief tainted with
confusion. "I just remember shouting . . . something."

Sophie grinned mischievously. "You probably had a
flashback to one of your arguments with Bronwyn."

I groaned an agreement. Everyone knew about us. We
were famous for it. I waited another minute, finishing the
water. I stood up slowly, expecting my feet to be wobbly,
but they were surprisingly steady, and with Joey and Sophie
following behind, I went back inside.

Again, I made my apologies to the band, but no one
seemed particularly bothered by the incident; they all just
wanted to know if I was all right. Irish friendship. My gear
was already packed away, and my offers to help with the
rest were politely but firmly ignored. Usually after a Tallafrae gig there is a fair amount of drinking, joking, and
talk, while the last few stragglers weave their way to the
door. Still not recalling what had happened, I agreed to
stay for a time. It had been ages since I'd seen them, and
was quite keen to catch up. Ideas were offered for my situation, with Sophie's suggestion of low blood sugar seeming the most probable. Talk quickly turned to the regular,
and for a time, I forgot about what had occurred.

I remembered it that night.

I awoke suddenly, my throat harsh and dry. I knew I
had been shouting.

The scene, the landscape of the dream was there, painted
in my mind indelibly with heavy strokes. My cheeks were
wet and my knuckles white from gripping the sheet. From

that moment of grief came a single point of clarity.

A decision had been made.

ii

"Oh, hi Flo, it's me. If you're there, pick up, if not . . . well, it's a quarter before eleven on Thursday, and I . . . I was wondering if you could meet me a little later for a chat? There are some things I need to tell you . . . nothing serious, so don't worry.

"You know that coffee shop I'm so fond of? The little one down on Elizabeth Street, under the Hilton? Well, could you be there about fiveish? God, I feel like such an idiot talking to this thing. Sorry it's such short notice, and if you can't make it, ring me back. If not, see you later. Bye now."

iii

I stood up and pulled out a stool for her.

"I'm so glad you could come," I said as she lowered her small shoulder bag to the floor and sat down. Florence's face was a little flushed, as if she had been hurrying, and there was a sense of . . . of what? Anger? No, I don't think it was really that, just expectation and . . . concern, I think.

I sat back down, taking off my glasses and rubbing them clean. When I put them back on, I saw her regarding me seriously. Our eyes locked. She opened her mouth to speak, but was interrupted before she could do so by one of the waiters. In a pleasant manner, he took our orders and swiftly disappeared. The void between us reopened.

I took a breath and decided not to waste any more time. "I'm going back to Sandwood Bay," I told her softly.

One of Florence's eyebrows raised up, and she supported her chin on her hand. "Really?"

I nodded. I was uncomfortable. I had expected confusion, delight, or even raw outrage, but not cool, questioning indifference.

Her eyes never left mine. "When?"

"A little over two weeks."

A flicker. "Two weeks," she repeated. Her eyes blinked slowly, and she shook her head a little. "Why so soon?"

I shrugged.

"Because you realize that if you stop to think about it you'll change your mind?"

It was a point. "Perhaps," I admitted.

"Come on, Richard, you're the one who wanted us to meet, so talk to me." Further conversation was halted briefly while the flax-haired waiter deposited our drinks with a quick smile. Florence pulled the speckle-topped cappuccino toward her, thanking him absently. I stuck to tea; my third small pot.

"I mean," she continued after he had gone, "it's a bit of a turnaround. What was it you said in Scotland?" Her eyes scanned the ceiling as she fought to remember. "Oh yes: 'I can't wait to leave,' wasn't it? You were so adamant— almost insulted that I'd suggested it, if I recall."

"I know, but things have changed." I paused, looking at her. "You're mad at me, aren't you."

Her blue eyes softened a little, and she smiled: a tiny uplifting of the corner of her mouth. "Of course I'm not mad. I just want to make sure that you're not doing this on a whim."

"Flo, I don't think I've ever been more serious in my life."

I lifted the metal lid and stirred my tea while she battled through the froth on top of her coffee. I poured myself a cup and sipped at it, abstractedly watching the people who passed by. The afternoon was clear, warm, and bright—a typical Brisbane winter's day, and a freshening breeze was chasing the remains of the old leaves up the gutters. The coffee shop was almost deserted, being slightly off the shoppers' beaten track, and with us and one other woman being the only occupants of the small lower room, we had more than enough space.

I knew I would miss Australia; it had been my home for the last six years, and it had also been my refuge. It had taken me a while to settle in. The first two years had been almost impossible, and I don't really remember that much about them. The music was there, more healing than any balm, and of course my sister had never been too far away. I hardly ever saw anything of Mother, and, as I explained before, she didn't really want anything to do with us. I'd got over that hurt a long time ago, as had Florence. I don't know what Dad thought. He never really talked of her.

Dad had been the first Brennan to break from the tradition of fishing. When he had been old enough, he had traveled away from Sandwood Bay, enrolling with false documentation into Sterling University, where, for some unknown reason, he had studied to be a draftsman. He had always joked that it was the one subject they had let him into with his suspicious past. He poured his heart into the four years of study, excelling and finishing top in his class. Not bad for a poor son of a fisherman with no formal education. After enlisting at the latter part of the war, he had relocated to London, overseeing sections of the great rebuild before returning to Scotland. As well as London, his designs can be seen in every Scottish city, and quite a few towns. Despite the money, he still spent a great deal of his time at the bothy, paying for its upkeep when his parents passed on.

He met Mother while she was over in Edinburgh working for some department on behalf of the Australian Embassy and, although I doubt if they had truly fallen in love, they decided to get married. For a few years, I assume, they were happy, but Dad rarely spoke of it.

They had Florence, then me, but I suppose the quiet Scottish life wasn't for her, and she had walked out, leaving us with him. Dad cut back on work, designing from home while he raised us. He encouraged us both to study; Florence taking to teaching like a cat to cream, while I delved into music. We both left home when we were old enough, going first into university, then out into the world, as children do. I don't know if we ever thanked him.

With my tea half gone, and the rustle of the other woman's paper seeming loud in my ears, I said to my sister, "I've spoken to the solicitors in Inverness; everything's in order, I've booked the flight—Friday week, the real estate office takes back the house on the Thursday before, the gas and electricity . . ."

"You've been busy," Florence interrupted.

I smiled ruefully. "Actually, I arranged most of it this morning. I lose half my bond money on the house, but it doesn't matter."

She spoke up again. "What about Bronwyn?"

I took a gulp of tea and managed to meet her eyes. "I . . . I haven't told her yet," I said quietly. "We're meeting later on this evening."

Florence's voice was filled with consternation and no small measure of disgust. "Richard!"

I felt terrible. Almost sick with worry. Looking back, I should have confided in Bronwyn early on, when my doubts about us had begun surfacing within me, but I hadn't been able to. At first, I think I thought that once I slipped back into routine, the memories and nightmares would pass, but they hadn't. They'd got worse.

"Does she have *any* idea?"

"I'm not sure; I think so. She knows I've been having problems lately, but I don't think she realizes how serious they are."

She looked at me steadily. "Probably because you don't discuss things with her." There was a pause. Her eyes still held mine, then she asked, "What are you going to tell her?"

Now it was my turn to be quiet. When I did answer, my voice was hesitant, subdued. "I don't know. The truth, I suppose."

"Don't lie to her, Richard. You owe her that much."

I nodded slowly, looking down at my cup again. She saw my distant expression, and for a moment, didn't speak. The waiter returned on his rounds, asking if there was anything else we wanted. I came back from my memories with a jolt, and declined, as did Florence.

"Have you thought all this through, Richard?" she asked. It wasn't meant as a recrimination, only a genuine caring question. "What about living, and transport? And don't forget . . ."

I held up a hand. "Do you remember my old agent, Jack Radford? He's more than willing to put me up for a few days while I look for a suitable car, and there shouldn't be any difficulties when I get to Kinlochbervie. I *know* the bothy needs a little work; I'm willing to do it, and if there's any trouble, I can always impose on the MacDermots.

"Besides, like you said, money's not a problem, and once I'm set up properly, working'll be easy—I've still got all my old contacts, it's been six years, but I don't think I'll have any problems getting gigs or session work." I smiled a little. "Failing that, I can always busk at Glasgow station."

She put down her near-empty cup and looked at me evenly. There was a long pause, punctuated only by the sound of footsteps and the turning of the paper, then she said, "Why, Richard?" I caught all the different nuances held within that word.

I leaned forward slightly, raking my fingers through my hair as I exhaled slowly. My façade was crumbling. For a time, I didn't reply, then: "I need to put Bethy to rest, Flo. She's . . . she's still with me. I thought I had it under control but . . . it's consuming me again. It's been fine for the past few years but, going back, well . . ." I trailed off slightly. Florence's hand came across the table to take mine. "I can't get her out of my thoughts," I continued, the anguish coloring my voice. "I see her in the face of strangers, walking down the street; I'll look up during a show and glimpse her watching from the shadows; I wake up at night, feeling her warmth next to me . . ."

I swallowed thickly, fighting back the tears. The woman opposite us was watching me, and I smiled thinly, embarrassed at my condition. Her eyes held mine for a moment, and there was something there, perhaps sympathy and compassion, then she raised her coffee cup and the contact was broken. I shifted my gaze to Florence and, trying to lighten the mood, said, "I think I'm putting people off their drinks."

She smiled and gave my hand a reassuring squeeze. "Is there anything I can help you with?" she asked gently.

I sniffed and dug out a tissue from the pocket of my jeans. "Could you send on my mail? I'll have it redirected to your house."

"Of course."

I looked up at her. "Can I stay at your place the night before the flight?"

She nodded. "Anything else?"

"Not that I can think of, but there's bound to be other things. You'll probably have to drive me to the hospital after Bronwyn's finished with me." I tried to laugh, but couldn't.

"What about Mother?" she asked.

"I'm going to see her next week."

"She won't like it," Florence warned.

I shrugged. "She doesn't care, neither do I."

"That's true."

I finished my tea and we both decided to order again, taking the time to enjoy the rarity of each other's company despite my sick feelings of worry. Florence told me how she and Dan had decided to rent out the manor house on a long-term basis, thus supplementing their own incomes without the trouble of having to sell it. She talked of visiting for a time—perhaps for a couple of months, showing Dan the place of her birth, and was even more enthusiastic now that I would be over there. I liked Dan; in spite of the frugality of our meetings, we both got on well. He'd appreciate Scotland but, like Florence once said, he'd never truly love it, and certainly not understand it.

Few really do.

The sun was setting by the time we left, reflecting off the suffocating structures of glass and concrete, painting the roads and footpaths a vivid amber. Nature in the human world.

For the first time in years, I longed for the foam-capped sea and the curve of the glens.

6

I pulled into the dark driveway and turned off the engine. For a while I just sat there, my elbows resting in the gaps of the steering wheel while I held my face in my hands. My head was throbbing with the pressure of a building headache, or perhaps it was just the tension from the night.

I don't think I'd ever felt so small and terrible in my entire life. For what I'd just done I knew I was truly sorry, and yet truly to blame. For a long time I just stared at my deformed reflection in the windscreen, wondering if I really knew the person I saw there. After what had been happening just lately, I was beginning to doubt it.

I got out of the car and walked up to the front door. The street was quiet, but somewhere over the other side I could hear a child arguing with his mother, and a few doors down, someone was laughing. There was a peculiar fragrance on the air tonight, like the smell of the beach mixed with the heady aroma from the jasmine bushes at the end of the path. The breeze was deliciously cool on my hot, flushed face, and for a few minutes, I just stood on the verandah with my eyes closed.

When I finally ventured inside, I went straight to the

kitchen, pulling out a bottle of red before returning to the lounge. I turned on a single side light and sat down on the sofa, smothered by the shadows. My gaze traveled around the room slowly, lingering on bits and pieces that I knew belonged to her. Without looking, I uncorked the bottle and poured a large drink, absently running through what had happened tonight.

I stood up hesitantly as I saw her threading her way between the tables toward me.

My eyes followed her as she slowly filled my sight. The practiced precision, the economy of movement, that which had so often thrilled, now only daunted, intimidated. Her long hair, unbound for a change, poured down over her shoulder like molten light, catching the flickers from the candles and stirring restlessly as if alive. To my mind, it seemed to take her an improbable time to cross the small room. I watched her the whole way, doubting myself, my convictions and reasons. Before I had time to reflect, she was standing there, beautiful face filled with the look of warmth and love she was giving me. She leaned forward and kissed me on the lips, lingering for a moment.

"Sorry I'm late. The traffic through the city was hell."

I smiled as best I could and pulled away slightly. "That's okay, I've not been here too long. How are you?"

Bronwyn said, "Tired," then sat down opposite with a long, drawn-out groan.

Seeing her here, all the lines I had thought of, all the different possibilities with which to tell her, dissipated like mist in a storm.

I realized I had been staring and, clumsily, for my hands were shaking, I reached over and filled her glass with wine.

When I looked up, I saw her regarding me, her eyes quizzical, and a slight half-smile on her face.

"Have you ordered?" she asked, bringing the goblet to her lips.

I shook my head. "Just the bottle."

Her gaze left mine for a moment, and I took a sip of the straw-colored wine, having to work it down past my dry throat. We were pretty much alone. There were only three other people in the restaurant, and they were over the other side of the room. A world away from our tiny candlelit island.

"God, I love this view," she said absently, looking out through the large window. The lights of the Story Bridge glowed golden against the river, and beyond, the city sat silent, its twin wavering gently below it on the black, restless water. The effect was made all the more spectacular by the rippled belt of low cloud that hung over Brisbane, its belly brushed by the light of a million windows and street lamps.

Bronwyn looked back at me, her face half in shadow from the single, glass-ensconced candle that sat between us. I held her eyes for a long time, just looking into her. All the memories of our time together chose that moment to parade through my mind. I could remember everything about our relationship, from the terrible, raging arguments down to the smallest detail, like Bronwyn biting her nails when she was mulling over something important, or how she always put the milk in coffee before the hot water. I remembered the last time we made love, the last time we went to a movie, the last time she rang from work to say she loved me. Some of the thoughts surprised me, scared me, and I wondered silently if I had the strength to do this. It was just too much like the residue after the dreams: half-forgotten happenings, like scenes from a film remembered only distantly.

Despite the air-conditioning, I felt a thin bead of sweat run down the side of my face. As I brushed it away, I opened my mouth to speak.

"Bronwyn, I have to . . ."

"May I take your orders?" the waiter appeared from nowhere, shattering the tension within me with those five words. Bronwyn's eyes left my face as my sentence floundered, and as she told him what she wanted, I took another sip, relieved and frustrated.

I only ordered a starter—I had no appetite, and when he had gone, I turned to her again.

"What were you about to say?" she asked, resting her head on her hand.

I swallowed and took a breath. God, why did she have to be in such a good mood, so happy. I couldn't do it. I just couldn't. I smiled painfully and shook my head. "I forget. It doesn't matter. How was your day?"

My face felt as if it were beet red. I waited for her questions, the insistence that I tell her what had been on my mind, but she said nothing. She looked at me steadily, the tiny smile not leaving her mouth. Then she blinked, and the subject was changed.

We talked of little things, inconsequential matters that two people totally familiar with each other can speak about without fear of appearing boring.

I hardly listened.

The meals came and I began eating steadily. I didn't taste any of it, but the food provided me with a genuine reason not to converse. My eyes kept straying to her face, as if I were trying to lock away all the details one final time. Each time she caught me, I would hurriedly look elsewhere, as if I had been found guilty of some trespass. It occurred to me suddenly that this might well *be* the last time I saw her, and as we both finished up, my hands were shaking once again.

The waiter was over almost immediately to remove the spent plates, and as I filled up our glasses once again, Bronwyn said, "All right, Richard. What's on your mind?"

I looked up suddenly. Her eyes were almost sparkling in the gentle light. I don't think she had any idea. Carefully, I placed the bottle back down, swallowing to try and lubricate my dusty throat. There could be no more delays now. "I've got to go back to Scotland."

It came out quietly, quickly, but it came out.

Bronwyn said nothing. The light didn't leave her eyes, her chin didn't leave her hand. I looked at her fingers, her gold rings, then her face.

"Why?" her voice was curious, inquiring.

I shook my head. "I can't exactly put it into words. It's just something I've got to do . . . I've been wanting to tell you for a while but . . ."

"Yes," she said lightly.

I blinked. She was smiling now. I felt a weight plummet in my stomach. "What do you mean, 'yes'?"

"Have you been worrying about this? You should have known I'd want to come with you. Hell, you've talked about the cottage often enough, and since you inherited it, I'd been wondering how long it would be before . . ."

I felt physically sick. This was something I had not even imagined in the darkest rehearsals in my mind. I moved in my chair, sitting up slightly. "Bronwyn, no. I'm . . . I'm going alone."

She stopped talking and looked up at me. I actually watched the excitement slide from her face. The hurt that fell in its place was heartbreaking to behold. I so desperately wanted to take it back, to apologize and say everything was all right, but it was too late.

The silence that swallowed our small table was awful. I could feel the gulf between us widening with each passing second.

Finally, it was Bronwyn who spoke. "How long this time?"

"Excuse me?"

She picked up her glass. Her eyes were clouded, but her voice was still steady. "How long are you going for this time?"

I took a breath. There could be no turning back now. "I'm not coming back," I said softly.

I could see she didn't believe it. "What do you mean?" she said, her voice picking up. "What do you mean you're not coming back?"

"I'm going over to live. I'm going home. . . ."

She raised a hand before her face, cutting me off. "Wait a minute, wait a minute, just why have you *got* to go back?" There was a pause. "There's someone else, isn't there," she accused.

"Kind of," I admitted. "Though not in the way you think."

"Just what the fuck is that supposed to mean?"

I lowered my voice, looking around us. "Bronwyn, please . . ."

"*That's* why you've been acting so strange since you came back, why you didn't return my calls." She shook her head and looked at me contemptuously. "There I was, thinking you were all upset over your dad's funeral when in fact the whole time you'd been fucking some bitch. You're pathetic, Richard, spineless. She must be incredible if you're going twelve thousand miles for her."

"Will you stop!" I hissed. "I've not been seeing anyone. Jesus, you know I wouldn't do that."

"How do I *know* anything anymore? For some reason *I* thought we were happy!"

I lowered my face. "It's the nightmares," I said softly, feeling wretched. "I've got to go back and sort out what I left. I can't continue until I do." I didn't want to mention Bethy. I couldn't.

I looked over to her. She was silent, though I could see her chest rising and falling as she strove to contain her building anger, but when she spoke, her voice was soft. "If there's no one else, then why can't I come with you?"

"It's something I've got to do on my own."

"Richard, it's been over six years, for Christ's sake. Don't you think you might be overreacting just a *little*? It was obviously going to be painful, going back there, especially for a funeral, but . . ."

"I *know*," I replied, my voice almost a plea.

"Shouldn't you think about it first?"

"I have thought about it—too much. Besides, it's too late."

"What?"

"I've booked the flight. I leave in two weeks."

"You've booked the . . ." She stopped and shook her head, stirring her long hair. "And you didn't tell me? You son of bitch!" The momentary calm was shattered. Bronwyn's face colored and she went on, "I'm surprised you even had the courage to tell me now! Why didn't you just go and leave me a fucking note!"

I didn't reply. I knew it had gone beyond the stage where I could justify my actions even slightly.

Bronwyn stood suddenly, jogging the table, and her glass

tipped over. The white wine pooled on the tablecloth, then began trickling onto the floor. She looked down on me, tall, severe, furious. "You know, in a way I wish there had been another woman," she told me. "That I could live with, but . . . leaving me for a ghost?"

"Bronwyn . . . I'm . . ."

"No, Richard, don't you *dare* say you're sorry. Don't you *dare* lie now."

Her eyes held mine for a long moment. I could hear my heart thumping, my breath leaving my mouth. She looked like she was going to say more, but then, without another word, she turned and strode away quickly. I watched her leave. Part of my mind, the rational, everyday part, screamed at me to follow her, to apologize, to tell her I was wrong, to tell her I loved her . . . but I didn't, I couldn't. I stayed in my seat, my face low as she walked from view.

Reaching over, I righted the glass, then sat back, looking out over the river.

7

When I first arrived in Australia, I had traveled around in a state of almost constant numbness.

The wonderful and perfect life that I had known had been spilled away as suddenly as a kicked-over cup. As I began to live, to exist again, I started to appreciate the land I had fled to. I don't think I'll ever truly love Australia, purely because to me it will always be a place of uncertain solace.

There's a sort of young naiveté about Brisbane, a sense that nothing you do here matters because it is only a practice for the real world that exists elsewhere. During the earlier part of my life, I'd stayed in a few different cities; from metropolises like London, Dublin, and Glasgow to the more cosmopolitan Naples and Prague, and although each has its merits, memories and downfalls, there is a similar feel to all of them, a pulselike thrum signifying some sort of sentient life. Brisbane central is still just a large collection of buildings spread over the meanders of a river. A big country town. But then, by true definition, I am just a big country boy, and I'm acutely aware of my dislike for crowds and bustle, so my opinions are probably not that objective. I suppose there are many folk who could not survive each day without feeling and interacting with that heartbeat. I'm just not one of them.

Looking back over those hectic last two weeks, when life turned into nothing more than a dimly lit kaleidoscope displaying scenes of haste and fervor, I still find it hard to believe that I actually managed to get everything done in time.

Separating my things into what to keep and what to sell proved relatively easy, and a lot less painless than I had anticipated. All of my books and music (and I never realized how much I had) were to be sent on via ship, along with some of my clothes and a few odds and ends that I was loathe to throw away. The extensive sea voyage would take about three months, and the company had assured me they would be able to deliver the tea chests right the way up to Kinlochbervie. I'd left the final destination as the MacDermots—the family my sister and I had visited with— as the actual bothy had no real address. The rest of my belongings I either donated off or gave away to friends and neighbors. Florence kept some stuff at her insistence, against the day of my return, and I also gave her 'custody' of my little blue Datsun. Once I started, it was surprising how little time it took to clear the house of my material belongings.

I would have to pick up quite a lot of things when I arrived, and although I could have purchased them in Brisbane, it made more sense to wait and save luggage space and the effort of having to carry it all. Then there were the things I couldn't buy here; I had no proper winter clothes to speak of, and although it was still midsummer in Scotland, I knew full well that really meant nothing, especially as far north as Sandwood Bay. I hadn't forgotten the ferocity of the Sutherland winters—minus thirty degrees was a common temperature, and snow was practically guaranteed.

I spoke to Jack Radford a couple more times, mainly just to confirm that it was still convenient to stay with him awhile.

"Of course it's all right, you fool," he laughed, his bluff voice loud, cheerful, and unsoftened by twelve thousand miles of fiber optic. "Nothing's changed since last week. Just hurry your arse up here—I need the company! I'm already decanting three bottles of my best."

The final day drew closer.

I said good-bye to the small number of friends I had accumulated in my time here. Despite my solicitude, I went to see Bronwyn, but on both occasions she was out, and I was reduced to leaving a fragmented and pathetically apologetic message on her answering machine. She didn't ring back, and I returned from town one afternoon to find her things gone and the key on the table.

ii

As always, I was faintly apprehensive as I walked down the path toward the heavy front door.

Mother's house in Kenmore Hills says pretty much everything about her. From the outside it looks somewhat normal (for the area): overtly opulent, somewhat imposing, palatial perhaps; inside it was as cold and as impersonal as an old museum.

I only came here when I had to, which wasn't really very often. We barely stayed in touch—there was just no need, and mostly, I saw her ironically on days of celebration such as Christmas and the odd Easter. Flo's relationship with her was little better. She never really accepted our career decisions—as if a son of hers could settle for playing Paddy music for a living while her daughter was nothing more than a common school teacher. I don't know, maybe I'm just trying to rationalize our detachment the only way I can.

Perhaps she's nothing more than a bitter old woman—or me, a rejected son.

Taking a final steadying breath, and quietly hoping that there would be no one here and I would be spared this, I rang the bell. Somewhere off within I could hear a loud chiming and almost immediately, her irritating little dog began yapping.

Within moments, the door opened inward and I was face-to-face with Clive, her third husband.

Mother remarried not long after the divorce with Dad was finalized, but that, too, had been short-lived. After a period of traveling on behalf of the government, she had finally settled down in the western suburbs of her home-town, Brisbane, with an oddly quiet and rather likeable man called Clive Johnstone.

A barrister with absolutely no aspirations of the Scottish in him.

Clive was good company, and whenever I visited, I always found a great deal of sympathy in my heart for him. He was one of those loose-jowled old hounds that had a preternatural air of silent suppression about him. To me, it was almost as if Mother had taken him and beaten him down into this stoic, obedient butler.

I harbor a secret fantasy that perhaps one day I'll see his name in the paper as the main offender in a lewd high-court orgy affair or suchlike. I love to wonder about the outrage that would cause within the house.

With a welcoming smile, as if my appearance had somehow lifted the day out of the monotonous, he held out his hand and said, "Richard. Good to see you."

His skin was as dry as old parchment, and somehow the smell of old chambers, books, and smoke lingered about him, despite the fact that he was dressed in a loose set of white trousers and a sunset-yellow shirt.

"Clive," I responded. "You're looking as fit as ever."

He smiled, and for a moment, I could see the sharp intelligence in his eyes. "It's the garden, you know," he said, ushering me past him into the hall.

"I shut Rex in the drawing room," he said, indicating with a nod of his head to a closed door, behind which came a constant stream of high-pitched barking and scratching.

I smiled. Clive knew how much I hated mother's pathetic little Chihuahua, and it me. "Good idea."

I took off my sunglasses, put on my normal ones, and looked around. As always, the place was exactly as I remembered it. The barley-tinted wall-to-wall carpets looked as if they had just been laid, the furniture looked untouched and unused, and the place still smelled new. Off to one side of the hall there was a great glass-fronted cabinet that was filled with an expensive china tea service, and even the plates and cups were laid out according to size and with an exact precision that went far beyond the pedantic. The other side of the hall was the only part of the house that looked like it wasn't transplanted from a designer's head. Dozens of framed photos covered the wall for all to see: pictures of my mother shaking hands with Nelson Mandela, four different U.S. presidents, Mother Teresa . . . hell, even Elton John. She'd always paid more attention to people not in the immediate family.

I removed my light jacket and slung it over the bottom post of the banister. Clive raised an eyebrow but said nothing. He knew as well as I did that it was a planned move.

As we walked through the house, I asked, "How's things?"

He shrugged, was quiet a moment as if considering the question, then replied, "Same as always. You know what it's like, nothing ever changes. Joan is in the garden." I nodded and followed on. "You're not going to get her all angry again, are you?" he asked as we reached the patio doors. I looked out over the huge expanse of perfectly green lawn and saw Mother sitting at a table under a huge sun umbrella.

Smiling without humor, I said, "Probably."

Clive sighed. "At least let me find something to do in the house, preferably in the attic, before you set her off. She was snippy for two days after your last visit."

"I'll do my best, but I can't promise anything. In fact, if I were you, I'd find a reason to pop into town for an hour or so."

Clive raised an eyebrow. "That bad?"

I nodded. "Probably worse."

He sighed and patted my shoulder. "You go on down, Richard. I'll get us all some tea."

I thanked him and stepped out onto the lush grass, making my way slowly down toward her. I'd only got about halfway when I heard her say, "Well, what have we here? Have you run out of money again, Richard? Or maybe it's something else you're after this time? A second inheritance, perhaps?"

"Hello, Mother," I said as neutrally as I could.

Although Joan Hoffman-nee-Brennan-nee-Hargrove-nee-Johnstone was only in her mid-sixties, she looked much older. Her hair was bottle-blond and still long, but her skin was dried and withered from too much time in the hard Australian sun. She was wearing one of those ridiculous pairs of huge wrap-around sunglasses that made her somehow look like an astronaut.

But despite the amusement I might have gained from her appearance, there was nothing at all humorous about her expression. Her lips were closed in a thinly veiled line of contempt, and her whole demeanor was that of hostility.

Without waiting for the invitation, I pulled out one of the wooden chairs and sat down opposite her, slouching as best I could. The sun was almost directly in my eyes, but I refused to show any discomfort.

"So to what do I owe this honor?" She made a show of looking around. "It can't be Christmas already, surely?"

I smiled. "I just thought I'd pop round to see you."

She sat up slightly. "Oh, don't give me that bullshit, Richard. You never just 'pop' round. You want something. You always do. You're as bad as Florence."

"Oh, leave Florence alone."

"Yes, well, at least *she* makes the scant effort to come and see me, unlike you."

In spite of myself I could feel the anger building. "And just *why is that,* do you think?"

She opened her mouth to retort, but was thankfully cut off by Clive coming across the lawn with a tray loaded down with the makings for tea. He smiled, no doubt fully aware that we had been arguing, and also no doubt sure that he would now have to act as mediator.

"Here we go," he said quite cheerfully. "I made a fresh pot, and I dug out some cakes."

I accepted a cup and sat back, sipping at it while I gathered my thoughts. I was mulling over how best to break it to her that I was going home.

In the end, it was Clive who broke the uneasy silence. "Sorry to hear about your father, Richard. How was the funeral?"

I put down my tea and replied, "Ah, as good as can be expected, I suppose. Most of the village turned out. It . . . it was a good service."

"Lots of memories?"

I nodded. "Probably too many. I didn't realize quite how much I'd missed it."

Mother snorted. Clive threw her a reproachful look and went on. "If you'd rather not talk about it . . ."

"No no, it's fine . . . ," I assured him.

"Of course it's fine," she interjected, looking to Clive. "He's a rich man now he's got all of Peter's money."

"Joan, that's not fair."

She looked to me. "But true, nonetheless, eh, Richard?"

I didn't reply. There was nothing I could—or wanted—to say.

"Tell me," she said. "Did you and Florence get it all, or did he leave some to that other slut of his?"

I blinked and raised my head. "Excuse me?"

"Oh, spare me your surprise, please. Give me *some* credit, will you."

"I have no idea what you are talking about," I told her.

"I *know* you kept in contact."

"Of course we did, he was my *father* after all, and at least *he* had a passing interest in my life."

The barb went unheard. "So do you mean to tell me you knew nothing of . . . oh, what was her name, Clive? Something ridiculous . . ."

"Sulika," Clive offered, his eyes low, as if he wanted no part of this.

"That's right! What a delightfully eccentric name. But then, your father always was one to buck convention."

I was shaking my head. I sat up straight and pushed my glasses back up on my nose. "I still have *no* idea what it is you're getting at. Are you saying Dad remarried and didn't tell us?"

"Oh, nothing so noble as *marriage,* my dear Richard. Just a relationship, nothing more." She removed the stupid sunglasses, folding them up carefully before putting them on the table. She picked up her tea and sipped at it delicately. I could see the sick amusement in her eyes. She was enjoying this immensely.

But I refused to play her game, and after a minute or so of silence, she grew tired of waiting for me and continued, "I don't know how long he'd been seeing her. After all, I don't matter at all. I only found out after my old friend Maggie Cunningham rang and said she'd seen him out and about with her. She's only young, you know, perhaps twenty. Barely legal. I think it's disgusting."

"But I spoke to Dad all the time," I said. "He never told me . . ."

"Well, of *course* he wouldn't," she interrupted, with a smug smile. "He was probably ashamed. I mean, she was practically a *child* . . ."

Clive shook his head and sighed.

She put the tea down and regarded me a moment, with a pair of eyes that looked remarkably like a vulture's, before saying, "Come to think of it, I wouldn't be surprised to find out she had something to do with his death, you know. . . ."

"Joan," Clive warned in a surprisingly firm tone.

I was struck. I thought I'd known Dad well. We'd always had a good relationship, even after the accident, and I'd always thought there were no secrets between us.

Apparently I was wrong.

Unless, of course, the old witch was making this all up. "Is this your idea of a sick joke?" I asked her.

The sly smile returned and the bird eyes blinked. "Would I joke with you, my darling boy?"

"Stop being so obsequious. It suits you too well."

She leaned forward, closing the gap between us. "It's the truth, Richard. I don't know how long ago it started, but happen it did. I'm just surprised he left nothing to her—after all, there was plenty to go around, wasn't there, if, of course, one was . . . favored. She couldn't have meant that much to him really," she sighed. "Like everything else in his life . . ."

I refused to listen to any more of it. I stood up suddenly. I leaned down and placed my hands on the table and leaned across to her. "You are a poisonous old woman with the heart of a shark. I'm ashamed to call you my mother. Dad has been twice the parent from twelve thousand miles away than you have ever been. I came here today to try and bury the hatchet because I'm moving back to Sandwood, but I see that nothing in you will ever change. And quite frankly, I don't care."

I leaned back, and for a moment I saw her face fall before the mask was raised up again. Surprisingly, I felt no sense of victory, only shame, and deep disappointment.

"My only hope is that Flo has the sense to get away from you as well," I finished. "Clive." I nodded, then left.

I didn't look back.

8

Florence drove me out to the airport, that confined building of glass and metal that resembled more a modern shopping center than a place of departure to the world.

Checked in and waiting, we sat in one of the cafés, drinking coffee and talking about useless, small things.

Time dragged, I was anxious to be off, yet reluctant to leave, and I think Florence sensed my anticipation and was uncomfortable around me. I sipped at the cold coffee, not really noticing any difference, hot or cold, in the foul plastic taste. My hand luggage sat obediently at my feet; a single overnight bag for the stopover and my slightly larger fiddle case. I was not about to trust that to the cargo hold. The vast lounge smelled the same as all the others over the world: of carpet, burnt coffee, and food. It wasn't an altogether unpleasant aroma, as it hinted at travel and change. I felt good, eager, like I had finally taken off shoes that were too tight, or suddenly found a fifty-dollar note in an old pair of jeans.

A metallic voice fuzzed out from the speaker, and although I only caught a few splinters of speech, Florence stood up and said, "It's time."

I blinked, finishing the brown liquid quickly, and rose. Picking up my cases, I followed her down the departure lounge, following the bold numbers to gate three. Florence fussed around me like a wren, asking a dozen questions but not waiting for the answers. I handed my ticket to the woman behind the tall counter, who smiled mechanically, ripped off a portion, then handed it back. Through the vast panes of glass I could see the gleaming white plane, massive and hulking as it sat on the black tarmac. Three square lengths of passage reached out from the building, attached like umbilical cords. Stuffing the stub into my pocket, I turned to face my sister. She had become oddly quiet, and was looking at me seriously.

"Take care of yourself," she told me. I grinned and bent down to kiss her on the cheek.

"Of course I will," I replied.

"I'll try and explain things to Mother."

I shook my head. "Don't waste your time."

Flo nodded reluctantly and didn't say anything. A suited man pushed past us, his beard bristling as he hurried unnecessarily. To our right, a young couple were embracing, the man crying unashamedly as the girl picked up a backpack and stepped away from him. Families gathered, saying their last good-byes to grown children off to see the world before they changed it. There were no tears between us, and with a final, almost resigned wave, she walked off into the crowd.

I had one brief argument with a member of the cabin crew about my fiddle case; they wanted to stow it down below, and I was adamant that it would not leave my side. Eventually, I divulged its worth and, paling, the steward suddenly managed to find an overhead locker I could use.

After a twenty-minute delay, the plane began taxiing.

There was more waiting, a few perfunctory messages from the bored-sounding captain, then the engines shrieked and we surged forward. The green marshlands that supported the runway blurred, then dropped away alarmingly. The twilight view over the city was breathtaking. The golden ball of the sun was setting far to the west, and as we circled, its light arced onto the plane, momentarily blinding me.

When the brilliance cleared, all I could see was the ocean, blue, bottomless, and infinite.

I was going home.

9

I caught a taxi from the airport out to Jack Radford's house in the suburbs of Glasgow.

The trip took just under forty-five minutes, and I spent the time dozing in the seat next to the driver, listening absently to his heavily accented and likewise exaggerated stories of previous fares. Cab drivers may well be the one constant the world over.

I hadn't been able to sleep much on the flight, not because of dreams, but due to the more mundane reason that I'd been positioned two rows before a mother and her newborn baby, and the child had cried for most of the trip. Even the small headphones I slipped over my ears failed to drown out the wailing.

I was aching like hell. My back hurt and both of my wrists were throbbing. My eyes were sandy, and my mouth full of the aftertaste of the terrible half-cooked 'food' I had been served for dinner. I was just a walking whingebag. My Australian friends would have been disgusted.

All I wanted in the world was a cup of fresh coffee, a decent shower, and a warm bed.

With tires scrunching on the tiny, bleached gravel of the driveway, the cab stopped. I paid the small man and had just stepped out of the car when the drive was illuminated and the front door opened. Jack Radford strode out into the light, crossing to me with a great smile on his face and an outstretched hand. Two golden retrievers bounded past him, stopping either side of me, tails wagging furiously and tongues lolling. One was a large, old dog that I thought I recognized as Sock, but the other was no more than a pup. Jack whistled once and they reluctantly left me alone. Leaving the driver to unload the single large bag, I met my friend.

"Bugger me. Richard, you've got even taller," he declared by way of greeting.

I took his thick hand, grimacing slightly at the sudden squeeze and replied, "It's good to see you again, Jack."

He laughed. "You even sound like an Aussie now!"

There was a brief silence while we both evaluated one another. Short of the odd photo, it had been nearly seven years since I'd last seen him, and although he'd changed a little physically—a few more lines and pounds here and there—he was basically the same. Short, and looking a little more rounded, Jack Radford had the feel of a wrestler about him. There was a certain power, an undeniable feeling of strength that was at once disarming yet reassuring. His face was flat, and his features ruddy, even in the white halide light. He looked like that dignified British actor from the sixties—Leslie Phillips, I believe his name is—that man who always played the charming doctor with the voracious sexual appetite. Wispy blond hair blew atop his smiling face, and a pair of slightly squinted blue eyes evaluated me.

He still had the small, similarly colored moustache, and his lips were thin and pink. A cigarette was gripped between his fingers, and it made its way to his mouth frequently.

Jack Radford had once been kind of my agent, although only in the very loosest of terms. He worked as a manager, a booker, and an agent for bands, big bands with big appeal. We had first met at one of my solo gigs a little further north, Dundee, I think it was, and had become friends straightaway. I wasn't looking for representation, and he wasn't looking for individual performers, but we kept in contact all the same, often meeting when I came to Glasgow, or he took a trip up to the Highlands. He began tossing me a little work here and there, mainly studio stuff, a session musician for groups that didn't have a fiddler but wanted the sound on a song or an album. Those sorts of jobs paid very well, and I got to work with some great young bands. He'd also been the driving force behind the first of my four solo recordings. The actual albums had done reasonably well, and I owed most of their success to Jack.

Then, one summer, he offered me a position in a group about to embark on an extensive tour of Ireland. I'd been over there many times before and loved it, so I jumped at the chance. Bethy had accompanied me, and it had been one of the best times in my life. The band were fairly prolific, and after many of the shows, we would adjourn to the local pub—a building that had perhaps been a post office during the day—and have a session. It was during these impromptu gatherings that I'd met some of the most influential players in the world. Few fiddlers could claim to have played with and had advice from the likes of Seán Keane, Martin Hayes, and Kevin Burke. That tour had opened the doors for greater things. My name had got around, both in Great Britain and, more importantly, in Ireland.

Then fate had stuck in its knife.

The taxi driver asked, "Just here, sir?" and his voice brought me back to the present. I looked around to see him struggling with my bag, and as I nodded, he dropped it with a relieved-sounding grunt onto the gravel and returned to his cab. With a spray of stones, he turned the car around and pulled away. Jack picked up my bag, lifting it easily.

"Let's get inside. I'll pour us a pair of single malts and you can tell me what brings you back to Scotland after so long."

He led the way, carrying my heavy case as if it weighed nothing. I followed him into the warmth.

I told him about Dad, about the funeral and the inheritance, but I didn't mention the dreams.

Jack had known Bethy well, and often we met as two couples. That was before Bethy's death and Jack's divorce. Now we were just two men talking over old, changed times. He still worked as a promoter, and if anything, was even busier now than before. His home was expansive and beautiful; Jack collected porcelain antiques, and the walls of the lounge were covered with cabinets made from rich dark wood and glass that were filled with small shining oddments. The house smelled a little too much of polish and beeswax, as if it were not properly lived in, though not at all to the same degree as Mother's. Despite the opulence of the surroundings, Jack himself was wearing a battered old pair of jeans and a white turtleneck sweater.

"So, it's back to Sandwood, eh?" he said, handing me a gleaming tumbler. I smiled at him, then looked into my glass as I swirled the pale amber liquid slowly around.

I took a sip and smiled in appreciation. The whisky was wonderfully smoky and smooth, and after the long flight, it seemed an age since I had tasted something so perfect.

It was a chilly night, and the small, fake-coal, gas fire had been lit. We both reclined in deep, well-stuffed leather chairs. At first, I had been tired, but I had perked up, and as night fell about us, we continued talking.

"I think it's about time."

He lifted the drink to his lips, then asked, "What about the ghosts?"

I looked up suddenly, but when I saw the innocent expression on his face I relaxed. "I suppose they'll always be there, but I can't run forever."

"Damn right," he said, shifting up a little. "I've ghosts of my own, you know." He nodded sagely when he saw my look. "Aye. Cathy haunts me every month for money. You should hear her wail. Sends shivers up my spine."

In spite of myself, I grinned at him. The fine whisky warmed my insides, and although my body ached, I ignored the discomfort. I wanted the conversation.

"So what *did* happen with Cathy?" I asked him, foregoing tact for simple directness.

He shrugged and looked at the fire. "I suppose she had enough of it," he said somewhat softly.

"It wasn't really surprising," I told him. "She was *more* than tolerant."

"Aye, that's the truth," he conceded.

We'd all known about Jack's affairs, even Cathy, though she'd never openly spoken of them. She'd put up with it well enough, just so long as he eventually came home. He called it a peril of his position. What with all the new bands trying to get representation and the fans trying to get to the bands, Jack always had his hands full—literally. I couldn't understand it myself, and neither could Bethy, but it was one of those unspoken things that everyone knows about but doesn't discuss. I suppose it just became all too much for Cathy—and about time too. Jack was a friend, but that didn't mean I had to approve of his social habits, and it made it all the more difficult to voice concern.

He took another gulp, made a satisfied sound, then changed the subject by inquiring, "How long do you want to stay here?"

I made an indistinct gesture. "A few days?" I offered hesitantly, unsure how much leeway I would be granted.

He looked at me reproachfully. "Richard, you know you're welcome to stay as long as you like. I've this great big house and no one to share it with but the two dogs and the occasional . . . visitor, eh, Sock?"

At the sound of his name, the dog looked up sleepily from where he was curled by the fire. Seeing nothing amiss, he lowered his large head back down onto his paws and went back to sleep, periodically opening one eye to make sure all was still well. The new puppy, who I found out was called Sall, was snoozing opposite him, and gave off the odd whimper in her sleep.

"Thanks, Jack," I said gratefully. "But I'll only stay as long as it takes to find a car and pick up some things."

Radford shrugged. "Whatever. You know you're more than welcome."

I thanked him again, but he beat off my gratitude with a wave of his hand and stood up. He crossed to a drinks cabinet and pulled out the quarter-full decanter of fine scotch, refilling first my glass, then his own.

"So," he said, lowering himself into the chair. "What are you going to be doing up there?"

I told him my plans for restoring the bothy, and also my thoughts about getting back into the local scene. He punctuated my explanations with jokes about getting back to nature, but also asked some interesting questions and offered advice. I thought about telling him what Mother had revealed about Dad, but at the last I stopped myself. I needed more time to think on it. I still didn't know if it was true.

By the end, he had refilled both of our glasses again and lit yet another cigarette.

"I see you still smoke like there's no tomorrow."

He pursed his lips and blew out a stream, then said, "It's my only vice."

"Along with whisky and women," I pointed out.

Jack chuckled. "You *have* been away too long—you should know that as a Scotsman, whisky's no vice, it's a necessity. And as for the women . . ."

A pause. Sall raised her head and shook it violently, flapping her ears, then settled back down. There was hardly any noise in the house, and it was a welcome change after living close to a city.

"So what's happening in good ol' Scotland at the moment?" I asked him, feeling the need to break the sudden hush.

"What, workwise?"

I nodded.

"Don't worry about that. I'll be able to help you out when you decide to go public again. After all, it would be such a waste if your none too considerable talents were confined to farmhouses and tiny pubs in Sutherland and Caithness."

I smiled at his compliment, but felt myself blushing all the same. The seeping warmth of the drinks had spread from my stomach out into my limbs, and I felt myself beginning to doze slightly.

Jack saw my tiredness. "I think it's time you went to bed," he told me, putting down his glass and stepping across the deep pile of the carpet. "I'll show you to your room. It's got a bath en suite, so you can shower if you want. Sleep in as long as you like tomorrow. I've got to go to town in the morning for a few hours, but I should be back about oneish . . ."

Wearily, and with my feet dragging a little on the carpet, I followed him up the wide, gently winding stairs, listening to the familiar chatter of an old friend.

ii

I slept soundly through the next day, emerging blinking, slightly dazed, and very hungry in the late evening.

Jack cooked up a feast, and we spent the evening talking once more, with each of us filling in the other with tales of the past.

Two days later, and feeling sufficiently recovered from the exhausting flight and the change of time, I borrowed one of his cars and made my way into Glasgow. With the address written down on the back of one of his business cards in one hand, and the street directory in the other, I drove to the dealer that Jack had recommended. He was true to his word, and with one mention of my friend's name, the salesman became instantly helpful without becoming overly unctuous. By the end of the day I was a hideous number of pounds poorer, but I had bought a new Land Rover.

It may be considered loose of me to splash out so much money on what is basically just a car, but I know that in the northern glens of Scotland, like the Australian outback, a four-wheel drive is not really a luxury, it's a necessity. I'd been caught in enough snowstorms to appreciate their abilities, and I also remember well how many of the roads were little more than barren tracks—especially up around Sandwood Bay.

I'd spent a great deal of money this afternoon, but I didn't regret it. Well, I did, but I'd soon get over it.

The garage said they would prepare and deliver the car in three days—just enough time for me to buy some essentials.

Glasgow hadn't changed.

I wandered around the shops, unconcerned with time, unlike my fellow shoppers who pushed and bustled as if their lives depended on the last second. I bought a long, thick coat, some boots, and a number of other articles of clothing that I knew I'd need, as well as linen and towels, etc. Despite my dislike for disrupting the peace and solitude of the bay—and my own soul—I purchased a mobile phone. I knew I'd need it for work, and it might come in handy generally. When I'd last lived there, the bothy'd had no telephone line, indeed no power. The nearest phone was in Balchrick, and the postmaster there had had to relay messages to me by driving out. With the progress in technology, that would no longer be necessary. The man in the shop had checked and although I was at the edge of the far north cell, I'd be able to get reception.

I felt guilty, spending the money on something that I used to vehemently regard as frivolous, and after that, with my conscience tugging at me, I went back to Jack's.

···

iii

The garage delivered the car three days later, as promised, and after taking Jack for the perfunctory spin, I set about packing.

The day had dawned bright and clear. Not a cloud was visible, and although the sun shone warmly, a keen wind gusted down from the north, making my nose run and my eyes water slightly.

"Are you sure you won't stay for a few more days? We could hit the town and I could reintroduce you to the blissful wonders of a Belhaven bitter hangover."

"I don't think so, Jack." I sighed. "There's going to be a lot of work to do when I get there."

He passed me my bag and I hefted it into the back. "Well, as long as you're sure . . . ," he said regretfully. "To tell you the truth, I kind of like having the company."

I shut the boot carefully. "Nah, I really want to get up there—in case I lose my nerve." I smiled. "Thanks a lot though," I said, turning to face him. "For everything."

"It was the least I could do, Richard." He was silent a moment, regarding me, then: "Don't forget; give me a ring when you're on your feet again."

We shook hands and I was about to get into the car when he said, "Oh, I nearly forgot. I've got something for you. A present. Here." He handed me a neatly wrapped parcel that he'd been trying to conceal bchind his back for the last five minutes.

Bemused, I pulled off the paper and stared at the cover. I gave a slight chuckle, then read the title aloud: "*The Automobile Association Book of the Road.* Just what I need: a map!"

"Who knows," Jack said, with a grin and a shrug. "Some things might have changed up there."

iv

The drive from Glasgow to Kinlochbervie is just over two hundred miles, and I decided to break it in two by spending the night in a hotel near Fort William, roughly halfway.

By doing that, I could take my time, driving slowly through the beautiful countryside.

Absorbing Scotland back into my blood.

It took over an hour to clear the traffic surrounding the hub of Glasgow, but once free, I lowered all the windows, breathing deep of the pure Highland air. I stayed away from the motorways, picking my way instead along the thin ribbons of B-class roads that snaked north. There were particular places I wanted to visit, to renew my acquaintance with, and Jack's leather-bound A. A. road atlas became invaluable. Fumbling through my new CDs, I dug out the one I wanted and slotted it into the player. Fairly soon, the raucous music of a local band, aptly named Silly Wizard, was flooding from the speakers. I loosened my shoulders and changed my grip on the wheel, trying to take in the stunning scenery of the hidden road through Glen Orchy while still concentrating. It felt so right, so appropriate, driving through this sacred land listening to this perfect music. My Gaelic blood was boiling in my veins after having been subdued and cold for so long.

I was alive again.

———

Even though it was only a Thursday, I had a little trouble finding accommodation in Fort William, what with it being peak period, and instead stayed at a delightful guest house in the nearby village of Onich.

After a huge dinner and polite inquiries by other residents as to my destination, I retired to bed, satisfied and happy.

I dreamed again that night.

It was peculiar not only in its content, but also in the vividness with which I remembered it in the morning. It broke through my wafer shield of happiness like a boot stamping through the thin crust on a winter lake.

I was in a car, and it was night. I felt restrained, but as I looked down I saw that my body was cocooned within a sleeping bag. I was in the passenger's side, the seat fully reclined to support my supine shape. Although I didn't make the connection while I was dreaming, when I awoke I remembered a time when I had traveled around Scotland by myself, sleeping in the car as much as a tent. Although it was impossibly black, I instinctively knew where I was— just around the corner from Fort William, 'camped' on a grassy lowland on the shores of Loch Eil. Outside the car, the land was as silent as a tomb, the murmuring of the water was only vaguely suggested at the edge of my perceptions. The interior light of the car was on, and the small bulb threw forth a weak, wetly amber light.

Then it began to rain.

At first I just lay there, savoring the deliciously wild sense of freedom and safety as the hills around me were gently saturated. But the rain took on a more serious, determined note, beating like a hundred angry fists against the thin metal above me. I became alarmed, somehow remembering how close I had come to being bogged down when I had driven down there earlier. I couldn't free myself from the sleeping bag, and as I struggled upright, I looked through the fogged window. The water of the loch had risen, had climbed onto the flat grass, and was now sucking at the tires. Panicking, I tried to free my arms so that I might start the engine and move further inland, but no matter how hard I squirmed, I was held tight, watching, completely helpless, as the loch inextricably filled.

The dark water reached the windows, lapping like a tongue at the glass as it rose steadily.

Submerged. Outside: blackness, even more complete than night.

I lay there, arrested, confined, yet subdued.

Tiny beads of moisture chased down the insides of the clear panes.

Noises: the gentle hum of distant machinery, as if a ship were passing somewhere overhead.

I was strangely at peace. I knew I should be frantic, but the dream held me, caressed me, reassured me.

A shape swirled within the darkness outside. I wormed my way upright again, eyes squinting slightly as I looked out into the void.

Something slapped up against the glass, like the tail of a large fish. The sudden sound startled me, and I shouted out, my voice sounding dull, tinny.

It moved past the windscreen, the form masked but its size undeniable. I caught a suggestion of scales, of fins.

Darkness again.

Fingers tapped at the roof, soft but urgent, like children seeking attention. I turned first one way, then another, frustrated by my inability at motion.

The fear built within me.

A face appeared at the window, just inches from my

own. Broad, swollen lips sucked at me, a thick tongue prodded as if searching for entrance. Wide, upturned nostrils flared as they heaved in water like gills. The skin of the face was pale, pallid, fishlike, but not scaled, and the eyes that stared at me were a startling green, and so human. Red-gold hair, somehow illuminated by the fading light, fanned about her (how had I known its sex? There was no suggestion in the face), framing the features like a silk pennant ruffling in a warm breeze.

More faces appeared around me, the eyes questioning, the mouths searching. I caught glimpses of tails, impossibly thin and wide like dolphins, yet scaled.

I should have been terrified, but I felt oddly safe.

They were selkies.

I knew the legends, anyone living near the coasts of Ireland or Scotland did.

The creatures continued watching for a time, as fascinated with me as I was with them; then, as one, they scattered, like a shoal of tiny fish threatened by a predator. . . .

Fear.

I waited, my throat dry, my heart sounding loud as blood drummed in my ears.

I looked through the windscreen; my reflection stared back, distorted, wet, as scared as I. For long moments, nothing happened, then the car, the capsule, was lifted, toyed with, and tossed around like an petulant infant's plaything.

I screamed as I was thrown about. My face slammed against the glass, and for an instant, I thought the sudden impact might shatter it, letting the water come flooding in.

With my features pressed up against the window, I gazed out into the dark, unable to move.

It came for me, swimming through the blackness like an eel.

My mouth opened to scream.

Teeth . . .

V

I sat in the dining room, silently eating my breakfast while my mind mulled over the peculiar dream.

No matter how much I battled to remember, I just could not recall what I had seen coming for me at the end. It was nothing more than a dark thing of ebon suggestion, a phantasm. Something nagged at me, but I just could not grasp it.

My tea went cold while I lingered at the table, long after everyone else had left and the places had been cleared.

Eventually, I settled my bill and, packing my bags once more, I began the final leg of the journey.

My demeanor had changed since the dream, and I refused the inclination to stop and admire the scenery. The voices of Sandwood Bay were calling me, and although I had always heard them, they sang louder in my ears the nearer I came.

I did stop briefly at Dingwall, just to relieve the driving fatigue I was feeling and to refill the slightly parched fuel tank, then I was off, once again traveling the road Florence and I had used barely a month before.

No hesitation. No doubt.

I maneuvered the car across Laxford Bridge and continued on through Rhiconich toward Kinlochbervie. My heart was beginning to sound loud, like the deep rhythm of a

distant bodhran, and my hands were cold and slick upon
the wheel. The small village appeared before me, delicately
veiled amid the subdued gray of the sea cloud, but still
looking alive and hospitable.

I didn't stop. The post office, the pub, all flashed past as
a momentary smudge of color as I drove through the town,
following the narrowing road on toward Sheigra.

I branched off to the right just after the two homesteads
at Blairmore, following the treacherous two miles of winding, fragmented gray road that was really little more than
a shepherd's track.

Nothing much has changed, I thought to myself as the
small shape of Loch Aisir passed on my right. Just off to
my left, sitting on top of a low hill, were the ruins of another bothy, abandoned decades, perhaps centuries, ago. I
followed the path slowly down to where it forded the tiny
trickle of a brook that emptied into the dark waters of Loch
na Gainimh, then carried on until I reached a barely perceptible fork. Without even thinking about it, I veered off
to the left, skirting the fringe of the hill until I reached yet
another lake. As I came to the end of the marked route just
before the shores of the loch, I turned and drew the Rover
to a gradual halt before the ancient, rusting barbed-wire
fence that approximately marked the borders of our prop-
erty. The gate was closed, looking for all the world as if it
had never been opened in its lifetime.

This far away from "civilization," the land was fre-
quented only by sheep, deer, and a scant amount of well-
informed travelers who have heard of the beauty of the
little cove from word of mouth. Today though, as was
usual, the little turnaround space was deserted, and no cars
sat on the soft verges awaiting their owners' return from
the remaining two-and-a-quarter-mile trek along the path

to the sea. I stopped, my palms pressed flat against the wheel as I looked at the rude path that continued on, struggling its way up the slight hill, then running down toward the delight of Sandwood Bay.

Toward home.

10

I had my first real stab of doubt.

Steering the Land Rover between the two narrow posts, I stopped to close the protesting gate, then continued slowly along the narrow ribbon of overgrown lane that wound down the croft to the sea, and the cottage. The track looked like two parallel footpaths with tall grass growing between, and as I followed it, two wheels in either rut, I could hear the feathered tips of the rushes stroking gently against the underneath of the car. It was just all so familiar: the twisted, wind-blasted trees, the moss-smeared rocks, the purple sprays of heather, the rich, velvet grass.

I passed the two hilltop lochs, and as I crested the slight rise I stopped suddenly. Away to the right, the glittering expanse of Sandwood Loch lay, silent and seemingly bottomless. A thin stream led off from its westernmost edge to cut through the dunes, tall marram grass, and the clear sands to issue out into the sea between the two clusters of sea-rough stone locally called the mermaid rocks, because of the legend of a mermaid seen there combing her hair on calm nights. Just off to the south past the sands, a tremendous solitary finger of rock, Am Buachaille, the herdsman, prodded into the air, daunting and almost frightening. On the far side of the bay, the cliffs resumed their solemn parade, carrying on in a fractured, erratic line to the desolation of Cape Wrath, about five miles to the north.

Without knowing it, my eyes were on the bothy. It sat midway between the clear waters of the loch and the stippled sea, on a wide strip of rough, brilliant emerald grass known as *machair*. From this distance it looked almost miniature, a black-and-white, L-shaped toy placed on the green carpet. I could make out all of the detail, and what my eyes missed, my memory filled in. The land rippled, as if an invisible hand had brushed gently over the grass to imitate the sea. Despite the rolling of the waves, the wind, and the wheeling fulmars, there was an inimitable sense of silence and solitude, of patience.

Of waiting.

My breath faltered and my heart beat against my chest like a caged bird as I finally looked down upon my old home. I fumbled with the door of the car, swinging it open and stepping out from the warm interior into the blustery sea air. I hesitated, leaning against the fender as I dug my hands into my pockets. For some reason I wished for a cigarette, though I'd not smoked in nearly seventeen years. Then I started forward, chilled and numb feet moving of their own accord.

Immense white clouds floated silently like ancient sailing ships against a perfect backcloth of blue, and the sun that shafted out between them gilded the shimmering sea with a precious sheen of gold. The wind was fresh and biting, coming in off the Minch and circling the hills and mountains before sweeping back down the glen. My boots made little sound on the soft, spongy grass, though my coat rustled where the wind teased at it.

My mind was flooded with memories, snippets of the past, and before I had a chance to reconsider, I was down the hill and before the bleached timber door. I stopped again, just for a moment, taking in every last detail. The whitewash that covered the walls was peeling slightly, scoured slowly away by the harsh briny wind, and here and there, the large, dark stones were visible, like muscles under an old skin. The roof was turfed, and had weathered well. In the back of my mind I acknowledged that Dad must've kept the place fairly tidy.

There was a small, new-looking building just off to the right, and it had a functional air about it, perhaps some sort of toolshed, but I resisted the urge to investigate just yet.

I pulled the small, new key from my pocket and slowly twisted open the lock the insurance company had fitted. The shiny new disk around the keyhole looked out of place amid the old wood. I pressed my hand to the heavy door, feeling the rough grain against my skin as I opened it slowly, not knowing who was the more reluctant, the old hinges or myself. Damp air seeped out like a released breath, and I finally crossed the invisible barrier my imagination had erected.

It was larger than I remembered, swelled with the feeling of a place too long alone. Although it was here that he had drowned, the old man had not lived in the bothy in the true sense of the word, rather just used it to escape from the chaos that had become his life.

The main room was dark; shadowed but welcoming. The smell was still there, that homely mix of burnt wood, dry stone, and the sea, and I paused for a moment, just breathing in. Massive, pitch-painted rafters crossed the ceiling above me, supporting the framework of the roof. Odds and ends, bits of fishing nets, trophies, beach finds, were hung or nailed up like Christmas decorations. One wall was taken up by the massive range, in the area that had always been referred to as the kitchen. Black and gleaming, it looked archaic and forbidding, sitting under a triangular chimney. Off to one side, and partially hidden by a stone partition, was the old sink. There was no hot water, but the cold was fresh and clean, and the tap ran clear almost straightaway. On the other side of the central room there was an open fireplace, and within, the charred grate had been swept clean. A cord of ready wood was neatly stacked to one side, and a well-used poker and tongs hung from the mantel.

I looked along the thick beam and my heart skipped a beat as I recognized one of Bethy's carvings. It was of a small cat, and as I picked it up and caressed the stone with my hands, I thought my composure would finally shatter. Gently, I put it back. It would be painful there, in plain sight, but no more than the other pieces of her memory I kept with me.

There was a small amount of furniture left around; the old table, a few chairs, shelves, and an empty bookcase that looked lonely under the dirty window. It took me a moment to realize, but there was a bare bulb hanging from one of the spars, and my eyes followed the well-concealed cable down to a relatively new-looking switch. Instinctively I flicked it on, and nothing happened; then I realized that the little shed outside probably housed some sort of small generator that Dad must've purchased. Investigating further, I found a plug socket alongside where the table used to be placed, and another just across from the sink.

With my hands back within the cold comfort of my deep

pockets, and feeling a little reassured that I actually had power, I wandered from the dim room into the single bedroom. It too was empty, save for the old metal frame of a large bed, upended and resting against the wall, next to a worn and weary-looking mattress that someone'd had the foresight to wrap in a thick sheet of polyethylene.

The door to the bathroom stood open, and I wandered in. There was the definite, though familiar, smell of damp in here, damp, soap, and ammonia. The old enamel bath, stained beyond reclamation, rested behind the door, deep-sided and almost forbidding. I opened the window, letting in some fresh air, and as I cast my eyes over the little room, I saw the small cupboard over the sink was slightly ajar. With my reflection flashing before me, I looked inside at the clutter that sat on the small shelves. An old tin of scouring powder, two colorless cakes of soap, and a brown, moldy cloth took up the lower, and above them, silent and slowly rusting, sat my father's old single-blade razor. A long-empty bottle of Old Spice stood just behind it, its stopper missing, and next to that, upended, fraying, and cobwebbed, was the black-and-white badger's-hair brush. I smiled as I picked it up and ran the bristles, soft as silk from many years' use, across the palm of my hand. There were other things in there too: deep amber bottles of medicines, cough mixtures, and cold cures, their labels faded into nothing more than furred squares of paper; a bleached packet of Andrew's liver salts; and an old twisted tube of what I supposed was toothpaste—the last of it looked to have been wrung out years ago. Of the brush there was no sign.

But it was all his.

Again I thought about the woman he was supposed to

have shared the end of his life with. I assumed she'd stayed here with him—if indeed she ever existed and wasn't a fantasy of my mother's twisted mind.

If she had lived here, there was no longer any indication.

But then I suppose she would have come and taken her things away long ago.

As I slowly closed the mirrored door, a long-limbed spider scuttled out. For a moment, I watched as it crawled aimlessly across the wall, then, cupping it carefully in my hand, I put it out of the window.

"Time to find a new home," I told it as it disappeared over the ledge.

I left the bathroom and ambled back through the cottage. I did a mental stocktaking, trying to note what would need to be replaced or bought new. I walked slowly around my old home, submerging my mind with a hundred little details from the important to the paltry, just to keep the threatening memories at bay.

Eventually, I left the house and walked the short distance across the grass and onto the fine white sand of the beach. With one hand holding my wind-tossed hair back from my face, I gazed out across the rolling waters for what seemed an age. The tide was out, and down at the waterline, the waves broke against the shore, stirring the exposed shingle into hissing life as the waters retreated like an intaken breath, only to surge forward again. Above me, black-backed seagulls, the living souls of the dead fishermen, turned cartwheels on the strong breeze, their cries haunting and almost mocking as they dived and swooped. To my right, nestled within the lee of the rocks and drawn up safely away from the mark of the high tide, a single boat, a curragh, lay, upside-down as it rested on two ancient rotting railway sleepers. I crossed to it, slowly running my hand along the rough, barnacled keel. It was old, and had been in our family since the beginning. There was even talk it was the very boat Padraig had used to cross the sea, but I doubted that. Still, it was old, and under the barnacles, it was sealed with many layers of crusting tar.

Crouching down, my fingers traced the fading, inverted letters of its name: *The Seal Maiden.*

That had been my grandfather's idea and insistence, despite the objections of his believing wife. She had known it would bring the family nothing but ill omen, and she had been right. But still none of us had had the courage to change the name.

But nothing could really be changed.

I took a deep breath of the cool air and let my hand fall. I sat down, my back to the hard wood of the boat as I again looked out over the water. An empty sensation built within me, an unresolved feeling of expectation. I picked up a handful of sand and watched as the grains trickled through my fingers. I gave up trying to hold them back. I'd spent so much of the last years restrained and concealed, hidden away like an ashamed leper. In another place, with different people, it's so easy to be someone else, to conceal from yourself all that you are, or are meant to be.

The last of the sand drained from my hand, and the image plucked a note somewhere within my subconscious. I looked at the dust that remained, until that too was taken away by the wind. I flicked my gaze from my hand to the bothy, then to the sea. The emptiness bloated within me, expanding until it possessed me. I placed my palms over my eyes, finally surrendering as old memories overwhelmed me.

———

*T*he brisk breeze chased the last of the dry leaves up the gutter, carrying them with invisible fingers until they were piled against the old stone wall.

Around the historic courtyard, the great beech standards stood solemn, their once-green crowns, now the color of burnished copper. They shook majestically in the chill breeze, shivering their frail leaves down onto the students who sat seriously around the tables below.

With a slight look of disdain, the young man picked the dead leaf off his paper, frowning at the slight smudge of black ink it had caused. He raked back his hair and looked about. His nose was red and running from a recent cold, and his hands, carefully wrapped in pauper's gloves against the chill, shook slightly. He cast his gaze across the court-yard, brushing over the collected faces that all sat hunched over various books with only one purpose: to learn. A face caught his attention; a young woman with long hair the color of summer straw. She was sitting under the university clock tower, obviously sharing some joke with her friends.

He didn't realize he was staring until she saw him and challengingly returned his look. Blushing furiously, he blinked and went back to his books, losing himself once more within the lines of written music. But every so often, he would find himself looking up tentatively to make sure she was still there.

*O*h, will you please just go up there and ask her! If you don't, then I bloody well will!" A pint glass was raised to his mouth again and a hearty amount of beer consumed.

"You wouldn't!" The second, taller man said.

The glass lowered, revealing a pale, freckled face dominated by a huge grin and topped by a shock of ginger hair. His eyes depicted a look of pure ingenuity and hapless daring, challenging the speaker without using words.

"Okay, I suppose you would."

"Besides, what's the problem with that? I got you into Maggie Priestley's knickers, didn't I?"

"Don't be disgusting."

"Do I lie?"

He pushed back his glasses and snorted. "No, you just twist the truth close to breaking. And don't talk like that about Maggie."

"Prude."

There was a pause while they both drank. Around them, clouds of cigarette smoke floated lazily, fogging against the glass of the closed windows. Without the solace of the small noisy pub, the streets of Edinburgh were cloaked in a mantle of three-day-old snow, and cars and trucks crept carefully through the dirty slush.

"Well?" asked the bright-haired young man.

"What?"

"Are you going to ask her?"

"Not with you threatening me, I'm not."

"Fine," he said, banging his glass down against the bar with exaggerated drama. "Well, I am then. You spend too long cooped up with that screechy violin of yours."

"Screechy?"

"Yes. Like a cat being fucked by a rhino. It's time you grew some balls, Brennan." He started off toward the round table at the other end of the bar.

"No no no, wait!" the other said hurriedly, grabbing his arm. He looked at his friend and sighed, the mock anger flashing in his eyes before turning into a lopsided grin. Without speaking, he reached for his tumbler, finishing the scotch with a single swallow.

"That's my boy."

"Jackson, two words: Jane. Wilkinson."

The leering face took on a look of pain that was very nearly convincing. "You know about that?"

"Thirty seconds, wasn't it?"

His friend opened and closed his mouth like a fish.

Richard smiled mischievously and moved through the crowd, pushing past those who wouldn't move when he asked. Without thinking about it, he took off his glasses, buffing them quickly before hastily putting them in his pocket. He stopped for a moment, his brow creased with thought before digging them out and slipping them back on once more. He couldn't believe how slick his palms felt, nor the tumbling sensation that was overwhelming his stomach. His eyes smarted from the heavy miasma of smoke, and there was a noticeable tremble in his hands.

Halfway there, he stopped again, looking back at his friend for reassurance, but Jackson had his back to him, doubtless ordering more drinks. Swallowing, he looked back to the table, half-hoping, half-dreading that she might have seen him and left, but she was still there, surrounded by a half-dozen or so companions.

Oh God, what was he doing? Wouldn't it be better to wait until he bumped into her on her own?

She threw back her head and laughed loudly. The amateur and unoriginal poet within him likened it to a brook cascading down a valley.

He sighed, stretching out the moments while he watched her. He knew her name, Elisabeth Stockton, from asking around, and he had also discovered she studied Fine Art, specializing in wood and stone sculpture, and she occasionally had a stall at the Sunday markets. He'd wandered by, but never had the courage to stop.

She'd seen him.

He dry-swallowed again. There was no way he could go back now. She smiled, an illuminating, welcoming gesture that flooded his heart with warmth, and he felt his stomach knot again. Her face was so beautiful: rounded yet well-defined, her cheekbones high and distinguished, her eyes large and the color of spring. He was so nervous he felt physically sick.

For Christ's sake! I'm twenty-one, not twelve, he thought, trying to summon a response to her smile from his distraught features.

His legs began working again, and like a marionette, he made his way to the table. The talk ceased abruptly, and he became aware of the eyes of her friends boring into him, questioning, wondering.

A bead of sweat dribbled down from his forehead. He brushed it away, his mind trying to shift through the thousands of colliding thoughts to make a coherent sentence.

Eventually, he didn't need to say anything. It was his legs that let him down. He had just opened his mouth to speak, to ask her if he could buy her a drink, when he bumped against the table. He never remembered if he was pushed from behind, or if he merely stumbled, but he did remember the sound the full glasses of beer made as they toppled into the two laps; hers and the nearest of the friends.

*T*he matinee had been terrible.

Well, the performance itself had been superb, but Richard had spent the entire three hours being acutely aware of the woman next to him; anxiously waiting for first the break and then the end with a mixture of appre-hension, excitement, and sheer terror. He'd decided the the-ater would be the best place for their first date. Neutral ground; no music or galleries. He'd thought about nothing else for the last week. After marinating her best pair of jeans in MacKewan's Export, the last thing he thought he'd get that night was a phone number, let alone a date. But as he was to find out, Elisabeth Stockton had a remarkable sense of humor.

With conversation misting in the freezing air before them, they left the theater in high spirits, and for at least five minutes, Richard deliberated whether or not to hold her hand. In the end, it was her arm that slipped wordlessly through his as they made their way to the restaurant. The streets were cold and dark, filled with the menagerie of people hastily making their way home in the freezing win-ter evening.

Richard dug out his wallet and looked inside worriedly as the waiter removed the dessert bowls. He had blown most of the remains of his grant on this evening, but to his slight relief, Elisabeth insisted on at least paying for half of the meal. After a token resistance, he gave in.

Unmindful of the bitter cold, he walked her home via the botanical gardens, where they stopped for a while on one of the snow-dusted benches. With the floodlit sight of Edinburgh castle groping the sky behind them, they kissed for the first time.

A fter the third knock, the door swung open, and with a silly smile, Richard brandished the single rose. "Sur-prise!"

There was a slight pause as the woman stepped out into the light.

"Nice try," said Jacqueline, Elisabeth's flatmate. "But you're really not my type." She looked down at the red rose. "So, do you want Beth or are you just doorknocking on behalf of the labor party?"

Richard blushed to the roots of his hair and mumbled an apology.

"Go on through. She's in the kitchen," Jacqueline told him wearily, stepping aside to let him pass.

It was late summer, and the university bar was filled to bursting.

The back patio doors were wide open, and the bustle of people extended out onto the wide balcony. Just in front of the stage, a sea of jumping bodies heaved in time to the music blaring out in front of them. Playing a mixture of traditional folk and thumping rock, Romany Tales were just finishing the second set of their first-ever gig. All had gone well, and despite his initial bout of nerves, Richard had thoroughly enjoyed himself. He only wished Bethy would hurry up and appear—she was off trying to negotiate the sale of one of her important pieces. He knew she'd make every effort to see his first gig, but he also knew how important her work was to her.

The song finished to a cacophony of noise and cheers and as Neil, lead singer and guitarist, announced they'd be back after the break, Richard caught sight of Bethy pushing her way through the double doors at the other end of the hall. Waving vigorously, he jumped from the stage and made his way through the press of close-knit bodies. They

*met just about halfway, she as eager as he, and he knew
from the look of joy on her face she'd made the sale.*

*They both started their sentences at the same time, and
after a brief pause and a laugh, Richard said, "You first."*

*A wide smile warmed across her face, and she held up a
hand stuffed with ten-pound notes.*

*"A hundred and thirty pounds!" she cried, eyes sparking
with light. His mouth opened with surprise, and for a moment, they just stared at one another, then they hugged
fiercely and began jumping up and down, chanting, "A
hundred and thirty pounds!" The people around ignored
the odd pair; they'd seen a lot more peculiar things than a
happy couple within the campus.*

*They made love for the first time that night. Jacqueline
was out for the week so Bethy had the place to herself.
They'd waited so long to consummate their relationship,
not through any reservation about each other or unsurety,
but through the sheer sensibility of not wanting an addi-
tional worry through the weeks of the finals. In the months
of their being together, they had rapidly pulled down the
barriers of shyness and hesitation, so their first time was
unhurried, passionate, and exquisite.*

*T*hey both reached the letter box at the same time.
Three envelopes tumbled down onto the coconut
mat. Bethy reached forward and picked up the last one,
holding it before her seriously. Richard was at her side,
clutching a similar one.

"What if we both fail?" she asked suddenly.

Richard shrugged. "We can both jump off the castle."

"What if one of us fails and the other passes?"

He shrugged again. "I guess they get to watch instead."

She laughed and the tension was broken. They held the letters before them warily, as if they were somehow alive.

"Ready?" he asked. She nodded.

"Go!"

The tour was three weeks old, and for the first time, Richard and Bethy actually had a day off.

It had been a grueling time; spent mostly in the small coach traveling from town to town, gazing out of the windows at the beautiful Irish countryside that flashed past. But it was tremendous fun, and the band had decided they would much rather play dozens of small gigs than a number of large ones. So, with the rest of the group entrenched at a hotel in Bundoran, Richard and Bethy had stolen off for some time on their own.

Pulling the hire car onto the wide verge, she turned to Richard and smiled.

"Where are we?" he asked, getting out of the car and looking out over the lush green hills to the sea.

"Glencolumbkille," she replied, locking the driver's door. "I came here once with my parents, when I was ten, and I've always wanted to come back."

Richard made an exaggerated groaning sound and she punched him on the arm. "You can hardly comment—you call trudging around Falcarragh for two hours fun?"

"I was looking for relatives!"

"It was boring! Do you realize how many Brennans there are in County Donegal alone!"

"Point taken." He shuffled his feet and slipped his new cap over his hair. "Lead on, my dear."

They followed the winding path down onto the golden sands of the beach. Although late autumn, the day was mild and the wind crisp, and the waves that rolled in were small and gentle. Reaching the sands, they both stopped to remove their shoes and socks, then, hand in hand, they strolled slowly along the crescent of beach. At the other end, they were forced to leave behind their carried shoes and Richard rolled up his trousers in order to paddle across the wide stream that lapped across the sand.

"This reminds me of home," he said as they reached the rocks.

"You keep promising to take me there," replied Bethy, swiftly clambering up the nearest.

"One day."

From where they stood, a small finger of grass-topped rock protruded out into the sea, flanked on one side by the sickle-shaped bay and the other by a low cliff. Gulls wheeled above them, swooping down into the tide-filled gully between the headland and the outcrop.

The feeling of the cool grass between his toes was delicious, and as they reached the end of the little island, they sat down on the thick carpet of turf, gazing out to sea. She leaned back into the circle of his arms and he rested his head against her shoulder.

"This is so perfect," he murmured. Her head nodded with agreement.

They were both silent for a long time, listening instead to the sound of the sea and the rush of the wind through their hair.

It was Richard who finally broke the silence, and when he spoke, his voice was soft and serious. "Bethy?"

She turned slowly, brushing the errant strands of slightly curled hair from her face, and looked at him. Her green eyes shone, reflecting back the sunlight, and her mouth was shaped into her usual half-smile.

Richard swallowed, the feeling of nervous fear creeping over him once more.

"I . . . I was wondering . . ." He paused, looking out to sea for a moment before finding her face once more. As if knowing what he was about to ask, she laid her hand over his. "I was wondering if we could get married . . . if you'd marry me." It came out haltingly at first, then all in a rush, but it came out all the same.

The smile that illuminated her face sent a thrill of wonder through him, and as she reached forward to embrace him, she said, "So that's what's been bothering you all week."

His arms came around her and he held her close, marveling at her warmth. "Of course I'll marry you," she said into his ear. "You'd taken so long over it that I thought I was going to have to ask you!"

He held her so tight he thought she might snap, then he remembered something and pulled away. "I got these in Galway," he said, producing two silver Claddagh rings from his pocket. "I know they're supposed to go on the other finger and all that, but I don't think it'll matter."

She held out her hand and he slipped the ring on. It was a little loose, but that was just the cold. He looked at her face, his hand rising to brush the hair from her eyes. "I love you," he said softly, feeling as if his heart were about to burst from his chest and jig around them.

Her voice echoed his, and she pulled him down onto the grass. After a few moments, he said worriedly, "Hey, what if somebody comes?"

"Let them."

With the ceremony and reception finally over, the new "happy couple" stepped down toward the waiting car that would speed them away to the hotel, then on in the morning to the airport.

The driver, a wide grin on his moustached face, held open the door, but just as Bethy was about to enter, a voice called out, "Richard, Elisabeth!"

Richard turned to see his father approaching, a smile on his usually worn and serious face. The wind gently tousled his salt-and-pepper hair. "I've one last gift for you both. I wish I could say that it's from your mother and me but . . ." He spread his hands and shrugged slightly. Joan Brennan hadn't even been able to make it to her own son's wedding.

"Here," he said, handing them a thick envelope. Richard looked at his father questioningly while Bethy opened it. She unfolded the sheaf of paper and her eyes scanned the first page. They suddenly widened, and she crossed to embrace her father-in-law in a flurry of white silk.

"Oh, Peter," she cried. "Thank you!"

Richard took the gift from her, and after looking at it, said, astonished, "These are the deeds to the cottage!"

"I want you two to have it—with my blessing."

"Dad . . . ," said Richard hesitantly. "It's too much."

Peter Brennan waved away his son's concern. "Nonsense. I'm hardly there anymore, and I'd rather you both had and cared for it than the place fall into ruin like most of the others. It's a little remote, I know, but you've got that old Jeep, and with your two jobs being home-based . . ." He didn't finish. Richard stepped forward and embraced him heavily.

"Thank you, Dad."

*S*he opened the door and stepped into the inviting warmth of the room.

Under the stone mantle, a bright, cheery fire threw forth shadows that chased tails across the walls while the smell of simmering soup filled the air. The table was cleared of its usual collection of half-finished sculptures and reams of sheet music and was instead set for dinner. To one side, Richard stood facing away from her, unaware, as he uncorked a bottle of wine. She closed the door softly, put down her case, and padded across the flagstone floor. Her arms encircled his aproned waist as her face burrowed into his curly hair. He turned in her arms, his eyes sparkling in the flickering candlelight as she smiled and kissed him warmly.

*Y*ou're selling them quicker than you make them," Richard noted as he watched her delicately chipping away at a fist-sized lump of rock.

Earlier in the evening it had been just that, a rock; now it resembled a small bird. It was utterly fascinating to watch her work, to watch how she shaped the unshapeable.

"Isn't that the best position to be in?" Bethy replied, absently picking up a different-sized miniature chisel.

"Mind you don't cut yourself," Richard warned.

She stopped what she was doing and looked at him steadily.

"Never mind," he said, going back to his coffee.

*A*nd now, it's your turn. Happy tenth anniversary," Bethy said, dropping the present onto the bed.

"What did you do?" Richard asked, grinning as he pulled off the decorative paper to reveal a large cardboard box.

"*I put it in there so you wouldn't guess,*" *she told him.*

He opened the box, his gaze flicking questioningly to her beaming face as he pulled out the fiddle case. It was brand new and was made of contrasting pieces of light and dark wood, polished until they practically glowed. Richard let off the latches and carefully opened it up. His eyes widened as he saw the fiddle within. Reverently he took it out, running his hands over the deeply polished mahogany. It was a stunning instrument, obviously made with a great deal of time, care, and love. Putting it back in the case, he took Bethy in his arms, thanking her profusely.

"*It's handmade by that fellow over in Lettermullan, Connemara—you know, that little old man's workshop you spent so much time in last summer?*"

"*How could I possibly forget?*" *Richard murmured, gazing at it in wonderment.* "*It must have cost you an arm and a leg.*"

She waved the question away. "*Ahhh, phhhht. I've got spare limbs. Besides, you only live once. And I thought your old fiddle was looking a little dog-eared.*"

"*I really don't know what to say.*"

"*Just tell me you love me and be done with it.*"

He did that.

"*There's one condition.*"

"*What's that?*" *he asked as he raised the fiddle tentatively to his chin.*

"*Play for me later?*"

It was a beautiful day, if a little too windy.

The sky above was the deepest blue, as was the rippled surface of Loch Inchard. The white boat stood ready, swaying to and fro against the jetty. The mooring lines creaked and groaned as it moved, occasionally banging a fender against the wooden pilings.

Richard gave a small wave as the two figures walked down toward him, his hand finishing in his hair, holding it out of his eyes as the wind tugged at it.

"Are you sure you won't come now?" Peter Brennan asked once again.

Richard squinted and looked from his father to his wife, smiling slightly. "No, thanks. It's a little too breezy for me. You know how sick I get when it rocks too much. I'll just sit here and watch."

Peter shrugged. "Suit yourself. It's a great day for it. Still coming, Elisabeth?"

"Of course. Any excuse to get away from grumpy here," she said, reaching up on tiptoes to kiss Richard's nose.

He frowned. "Who's grumpy?"

"You are, my lovely. But I adore you still."

"Be careful," he said, kissing her back.

"Of course. Don't forget to wave."

"I won't. Don't forget your life jacket."

She rolled her eyes, then took Peter's hand as she stepped into the rolling boat. He cast off, raising the small sail proficiently. The lines hummed, feeding off the power of the wind, and the small craft edged away from the pier, rapidly picking up speed.

Richard sat watching for perhaps ten minutes until he stiffly got to his feet and made his way up to the small supply shop to see if he could scratch up some hot coffee. He was almost to the door when he saw someone come running out from within, shouting furiously and gesturing toward the loch. A weight plummeted through his stomach, ripping his insides as the sudden realization screeched through his mind. He turned slowly, following the man's hurried gestures.

Bobbing on the swells on the loch like some grotesque surfaced monster was the gleaming white hull of the small boat, the wide fin attached to the keelson moving in the wind like a distress call.

A s the last of the mourners passed him, Richard saw his father's tear-streaked face.

He reached forward with one hand, laying it slowly down on his sagging shoulder. The small mound of fresh-turned earth was painfully visible, a scar amid the perfect lawn of the cemetery.

"It's not your fault, Dad," he said, once more choking on the emotion. His father's jaw clenched, and his bottom lip moved as if he were chewing the words. With an anguished cry, Richard Brennan fell into his father's arms.

W ith tears coursing down my stubbled cheeks, and feeling wrung out and desperately alone, I rose and trudged back up the beach toward the empty bothy.

The afternoon had fled, and the sun was slowly being curtained by a thick cloud. Shadow gradually overtook me, leaching the color from the land.

11

Once again I postponed the inevitable by not staying there the night; instead I imposed upon the hospitality of the MacDermots in Kinlochbervie.

They were delighted to see me, and we spent the evening talking over small things.

In the morning, I returned to the cottage to make a full list of the things I would need to live there. I looked at the generator, and luckily enough, Dad had had enough foresight to post the instructions on the inside of the door. It was a modern, diesel-run motor that produced just enough power to light the house and run an odd implement or two. Next to the neatly stacked chopped wood and sods of peat were a half-dozen green jerry cans, all empty save one that sloshed when I shook it. I filled the tank, read the instructions, and gave it a trial run. It took me a couple of tries, but eventually the motor spluttered into life, settling down within a minute to a quiet hum. I wandered into the house and clicked on the switch. It was a cloud-cast early morning, and the bulb washed everything with harsh, unnatural light. I thought that I'd still probably use the candles and lamps, but it was a good thing to know I had electricity.

By midafternoon, I was on my way back from Dingwall, the boot of the car loaded down fit to bursting. There had been so much more that I needed, and although I felt I had found and bought most of it, there was bound to be something I had forgotten.

I returned to the croft exhausted, and after a short break in which I set a fire burning in the range, I began unpacking.

The first night was difficult. With my supper plate pushed away and a large wood and peat fire burning in the grate, I settled back, one hand toying with a glass of red wine. The cottage was alive with ghosts as the candles and lamps guttered fitfully. I wasn't running the generator. I didn't like the brilliance of the light, instead preferring the solace of the shadows and the flickering of the small flames. The room smelled of cooked food, wine, and smoke; it was all so familiar. It felt like I hadn't been away.

The breathing of the Atlantic was a sound I had sadly missed during my time abroad, and as I closed my eyes, resting my head in my hands, it lulled me almost as much as the absent Mozart I would have doubtless been playing had I the means.

Eventually, I adjourned to bed, and spent a restless night staring up at the rafters and starting at every noise. The silence was so complete, so full, and if anything, accented more by the gentle sound of the waves. A thin fingernail of moon was just visible through the cleaned glass of the window, and the wispy cloud before it was furred with its slight luminosity. Eventually I suppose I did sleep a little, but I awoke in the morning feeling tired and irritable, and

I spent the day moping around, trying to do a hundred small jobs, but each time having to forcibly focus myself. I hoped my moods would improve over time.

ii

A couple of weeks drifted past, the seasons began the slow turn to autumn, and finally the cottage once more looked like a home.

I had deliberately arranged the furniture differently; a voice in the back of my mind saying that I should try and start fresh. It took a number of trips into Dingwall, and one all the way to Inverness for a new bed, before I had everything that I needed. I purchased a small stereo, and often in the evenings I just sat listening to music, the front door open, or I would walk the short distance down to the sea and sit on the sand with my fiddle. I gradually began to feel better, more alive than I had in a long time. I felt like the wounds were finally healing.

I hadn't made any inquiries yet about work, but I had received one or two calls, doubtless routed via Jack, asking about me. It would not be long now. From Florence I heard nothing, but I wrote her a letter telling all that had happened and my ideas for the future. I also penned one to Bronwyn, but that still sat on the mantel, waiting for the time when I would have the courage to send it. I took up walking once more, and renewed all of my acquaintances with the local mountains and glens. I even started fishing in Sandwood Loch again.

Then something happened: a night passed that changed everything.

It mocked at my newly found complacency, and I still

do not know how much of it was dream, if any, nor if what I saw actually occurred. . . .

It was very late when I was suddenly awakened. I had fallen asleep at the table, my head resting on my arms. The fire had burned down to a bed of throbbing embers, and the surface of the table was puddled and spotted with melted wax from the dead stubs of candles.

I strained my ears, listening for the sound that had woken me. Without knowing it, I was holding my breath, only to exhale when the call came again: the bark of a seal.

I sat up, rubbing the sleep from my eyes and resting my elbows on the smooth wood. The aroma of burnt peat was strong, ingrained and heavy. The sound repeated, once, twice, then stopped.

I rose, scraping the chair back on the stone, and then, because of some unknown calling I didn't stop to question, I reached down for my fiddle. Pausing only to free it from its case, I pulled open the door and started out into the night.

Once off the soft machair, the loose sand of the beach shifted restlessly under my bare feet, and the wind tugged at my white shirt like a playful child. A bright, lemon moon hung like a pendant out over the ocean, lighting the water from the beach to the distance with a silver corridor of light; an image that was burned into my mind. The air was suffused with the crisp smell of the sea and of wildflowers, more memories that clung to me like brambles on a cliff-top path.

Mist gathered wraithlike in the hollows between the black shapes of the rocks and, knowing exactly where to place my hands and feet, I climbed up. I sat down, my back to a large boulder, facing the water, and after only the briefest hesitation, began to play, almost trancelike. It was an old Irish reel, one with probably a hundred names, but known to me as "The Lament of Limerick." I'd learned it from a dear friend of mine, the County Clare fiddler Martin Hayes, and as the title suggested, it was a hauntingly beautiful tune. It had been Bethy's favorite, and as my bow slowly stroked across the strings, I pictured her face.

The music released from within me was taken gently by the wind out over the moonlit waters. I imagined it like smoke, writhing and gradually dissipating, as if unwilling to release its corporeal form.

As the tune progressed slowly, I became aware of the small shapes bobbing in the moon channel, watching, listening. For each one that appeared, ripples would circle out across the still water. There were seven in all, and as I played, my eyes locked with the nearest, one I instinctively knew was female. The liquid pools, tinted with green—or was that a trick of the moonlight?—blinked knowingly, and for a moment, I knew she could see into my soul. She called out again, raising her face to the moon as she sculled out what sounded like a single word.

A name.

Richard . . .

The fiddle slipped from my numbed fingers, landing softly on the fine cushion of sand below. I stood quickly, my sleep-numbed muscles protesting at the sudden movement, and as I leaped from the rocks, stumbled, then ran to the water's edge, I cried, *"Elisabeth?"*

One by one, the small domes of the seals' heads dipped smoothly back under the water. The nearest lingered, just for an instant longer, then it too disappeared, and I was once again alone.

I fell heavily to my knees, ignorant of the sudden wetness. My fingers clawed at the heavy sand by my sides as my eyes searched the sea, as desperately as they had the loch, those six years past.

The moon slowly slipped behind a thin finger of cloud, and like a door gradually closing on the horizon, the corridor of light was extinguished.

I lowered my face into my cold hands and wept bitterly.

part two

COURTING THE GHOST

Music is the one thing that binds us together;
It doesn't matter which country you may be in,
If you know music, you can communicate.

—Ally Galloway, *English folklorist*

Superstition is the poetry of life.

—Goethe, *Spüche in Prosa III*

12

So did I dream it?

Like a madman in a claustrophobic padded cell, that question, and numerous variations on it, were all that tussled within my mind during the next day. The sensation was similar to if I had heard a catchy tune on the radio and could not stop humming the melody, and it was as annoying as it was disturbing.

I awoke again at first light, in bed and at once aware of what had happened. There was no delay while my waking mind fought to catch up with my alert body. For a moment, I just lay back on the cool pillows, my eyes closed but my mind open and working. The image that haunted me was not that of the seals nor of the night-dark liquid eyes that stared at me from across the mirrored water, but of the glimmer of the moonlight on the sea. Every time I squeezed my eyes closed, I saw a negative picture of the shining water—as if I had looked too long at the sun.

I eventually got up, slipped on a pair of loose black pants, and walked slowly out to the kitchen. I expected my movements to be somewhat awkward and stiff, but my legs felt normal. There were no slight tugs on the muscles, nor any stiffness, which I thought was odd because I could distinctly remember stumbling on the sand and feeling something pull.

Looking back with a day's hindsight enlightening me, I think that was the first sign (of many) that I might have dreamt the whole thing, from start to finish, though I doubt if I'll ever know for sure. It's so easy to rationalize things *after* the event.

I set the metal coffee pot on top of the freshly stoked range and sat down heavily enough in a chair that the wooden feet squeaked shrilly on the floor. I remained there for only a few seconds, absently itching at the side of my nose, then I got up and opened the front door. I was irritable and restless.

Outside, the land was washed in a frail, weak light that only seemed to illuminate the dull half-tones of the grass and sand. A thickening veil of gray was slowly coming in off the sea, and whatever it passed over, it leached the color from. Patches of dull, sullied blue were visible in the places where the cloud became more scrubby, and although I instinctively knew it would not rain for a while, it was going to be a damp, miserable day. Silently, I reflected that the weather had been altogether too good so far, and that usually boded for a harsh and biting winter. I was beginning to feel the cold more and more, and silently I considered whether or not I was prepared to brave a Scottish winter again.

The sea was as grim and flat as a chalkboard, and I walked down to the shore, and to the rock I vividly remembered. Everything was very silent, very still, though I thought I could hear the lone toll of a marker buoy far out to sea, its ringing strangely reminiscent of a church calling its worshipers to service. The wind was nothing more than a vague ebb of breath that barely managed to stroke my hair into life, but it carried on it a slight chill, a mocking reminder that summer was coming to an end and that the dark season would soon hold sway.

I reached the rock and rested for a minute, my hand against the cold roughness of the stone as I tried to rake my memories into some coherent order. I just could not remember how I had returned to the cottage. The last thing I could recall was kneeling on the beach, flooded with grief. I sighed, then unenthusiastically started back up toward the cottage, wondering what had happened to my wet clothes. The smell of fresh coffee drifted out of the open door, and with one last longing look at the sea, I went back inside.

With a mug of coffee held loosely in my hand, I wandered into the bedroom and found last night's clothes easily enough; they were tossed in a temporary pile on the floor at the end of the bed. Sorting through the small jumble, I lifted my jeans clear, and as I held them out before me, I looked at the knees.

Nothing. No sand, no wetness.

I knew there was no way they could have dried in the few short hours between last night and this morning, and as I threw them back on the floor and left the room, I felt myself becoming frustrated.

In a last, final attempt to confirm my rapidly disintegrating beliefs, I looked for my fiddle. It was in its case, cleaned and perfect, with no trace of any scratching dropping it onto sand would leave. The bow was in a similar condition.

So I must have dreamt it.

I sat down heavily at the table and angrily drank my hot coffee in several painful gulps, banging my mug down when I had finished. I don't know why I was so irate. I guess that I should've been relieved that it *was* all a dream, but the disappointment I was feeling was tremendous. I so desperately needed something to believe in at that point, something to tell me I'd made the right decision in coming home and that things weren't going to be worse here.

I spent most of the day wandering around in a state of abstract numbness. It was as if cold had crept out of the shadows early and was sucking hungrily at the warm marrow of my bones. I got absolutely nothing done and any jobs that I did attempt were either left half-finished or abandoned completely. My music too suffered, as I couldn't banish the feelings from my mind as I practiced, even through some of Pablo de Sarasate's more complex and intricate compositions.

Perhaps I was finally going mad.

ii

During the next few days, the feelings of helplessness and anger gradually subsided, slipping down within me to be cloaked, along with everything else, by modern-day rationality.

For a while, I didn't dream, or if I did, the dreams were not distinctive enough for me to remember clearly, and life turned from what in my mind had been the mysterious, back into some semblance of normalcy.

It was a Sunday morning, and although time really had no meaning for me, mentally, everything seemed quieter and more at peace. Over a slow breakfast of freshly baked soda bread and strong tea, I contemplated how I would spend this day of rest. It didn't take me too long to decide; I would go fishing.

Along with walking, angling had been one of my favorite pastimes, and it was one of the few hobbies I'd been able to actively continue in Australia, though under different conditions. I preferred the still tranquillity of the freshwater loch to the choppy sea, despite the chances being greater in the ocean. I'd found Dad's old rod, crammed into a corner of the shed, covered with a fleece of cobwebs and dust, but still usable. His tackle box I had discovered, for some unknown reason, under the sink in the bathroom, and it was in good condition despite some large resident spiders and spots of rust on the various hooks and disgorgers.

So, with my jacket zipped tightly closed, I stepped out from the warmth of the cottage into the dreary autumnal morning.

Gray rain drizzled inextricably down from a flat sky the color of damp slate, clouding the rumpled hills with a foggy luminescence and lending them a ghostly aspect. A breeze rich with the wet smell of the earth and the sharp poignancy of the heather rolled down the glen, gently shaking the water from the frail-looking trees and frothing the caps of the tiny waves that tumbled at the foot of the beach.

It was perfect fishing weather.

My glasses spotted over almost immediately, and I removed them, carefully stashing them away in the safety of an inside pocket. I wasn't exactly blind without them, but I still felt oddly vulnerable. I wished I'd had the foresight to buy a hat on my last visit into town.

I had a little trouble righting the curragh (which was heavier than it looked), and for a moment I thought I felt something pull in my wrist, but the pain went away, and dragging it across the sodden grass was easy enough; it was no more than sixty yards or so, and the rain made the surface slick, as if oiled. The stream that issued from the loch into the sea was swollen and fast-flowing with the rainwater, and looked more like a small river as it cut a twisting groove through the sand of the beach. Once I had returned for the oars, I deposited my gear under the seat and cast off.

It had been a long time since I had rowed, but like riding a bike, it is one of those skills that never really leaves you, and pretty soon, I was cutting the blades into the water, skimming the boat along effortlessly. I whistled a merry tune as I watched the pale shape of the bothy diminish in size.

When I reached what I judged to be a likely spot, I stowed the oars on either side of me and dropped the heavy mud anchor. The slippery nylon rope snaked into the water for quite some time as the lead weight fell, and for a moment I thought perhaps I had gone too deep, but then the rope went slack and I secured it off.

I sat back, my arms hanging loosely by my sides as I savored the sudden silence after the heavy breathing of my exertions. All I could hear was the distant monotony of the sea and the gentle gurgle of the loch water lapping against the sides of the boat. The rain mizzled around me, not really disturbing the surface of the loch, but rather turning it from a depthless mirror into an impenetrable sheet without reflection.

My actions as I put the rod together were unhurried, almost hushed, as if I were fearful to break the peace that was so complete around me. Baiting the hook with a square of bright yellow sweetcorn, I tentatively cast out, allowing the light line to be carried slightly by the whispering wind.

The weights plopped into the water, breaking the surface with a dozen tiny expanding circles, then sank, leaving only the bright tip of the float as any indication. I settled in to wait, burying my hands into my pockets, and although I wasn't really cold, hunching deeper into my coat.

The cleaned fish lay spitting in the pan.

I drizzled over a little more oil, then left it to cook a while longer. Moving around in the dim light of the room, I lit the half-dozen candles and stoked the open fire while I waited for my dinner to finish cooking. A bottle of dark ale sat opened and ready on the table, next to my plate, cutlery, and glass. Soft music, a quartet of flute, strings, and woodwind, seeped slowly from the speakers of the stereo, all but absorbing the barely perceptible hum of the generator outside and the mumbling of the sea. More than any other night so far, the atmosphere within the bothy was alive and welcoming, and I think that for the first time the place actually felt once more like my home.

Heavy rain pattered rhythmically against the windows, and the ocean breeze hissed against the tightly packed thatch of the roof. They were comforting sounds, almost blending perfectly with the music, and as I tipped the sizzling fish onto my plate, I reflected upon my happiness.

It felt as if I had purged my grief that night down by the ocean over a week ago.

Perhaps I had finally let Bethy go?

I'm not sure, as I felt somewhat traitorous following that line of thought. But imagined or not, since then my whole outlook had been lighter, less self-obsessed. My playing had taken on a different note too; when I picked up the fiddle, I once again felt the fire flowing from my fingers—something I had not fully experienced for years. I was growing edgy and excited about playing professionally once again. I felt I was ready, and if anything, I think I was better than ever.

True to its promise, the fish was delicious. My years of living alone had taught me two very valuable skills: how to cook, and how to clean up after myself. I was more than a little proud of the former. The latter had always seemed natural.

With the plate mopped clean and pushed away, I filled the glass with the last of the heavy beer and moved from the table into one of the soft chairs by the fire. I stretched out my feet toward the warmth of the grate and sighed contentedly. It wasn't too long before the crackling of the fire, the faded music, and the soft percussion of the weather had lulled me into a half-doze.

A sudden squall sent the rain drumming urgently at the glass and somewhere within the cottage, a window banged open. I lurched upright in the chair, the glass I had been cradling spilling the dregs of the ale into my lap. I cursed loudly, for a moment not knowing whether to clean up the cold, staining beer or find the offending window. I staggered clear of the chair, tipping the pool of ale from my lap onto the safety of the stone floor. Ignoring the discomfort for the time being, I stumbled, my mind still slightly numb, toward the bedroom. After the quietude of my sleep, the noise the window made sounded hideously intrusive and deafening, as if it were being physically rent from its hinges.

I reached the room and flicked on the light. It was the large window over the bed. Somehow, the loose catch had worked free, and once the wind's fingers had grabbed the frame, it had played with it mercilessly. Rain sheeted in victorious, already halfway to soaking the covers on the bed. With three sharp steps I was across the room and wrestling with the window. The wind seemed to sense what I was doing, and suddenly increased its tugging on the glass, as if reluctant to let go. My fingers were squeezed painfully between the frame and the sill, and I shouted another expletive as I slammed the window shut. With more force than was probably necessary, I put the latch across, then set about nursing my bruised fingers. I brushed back my damp hair and turned back toward the door.

Something caught my eye; through the fogged glass I thought I saw something move. I raised my hand and rubbed at the condensation, my skin squeaking on the cold smooth surface. I peered through, squinting as I gazed out into the turbulent night.

The pair of thinning trees, just visible through the gloom, swayed painfully as they fought the drenching rain, and in the distance, shrouded by the night, I fancied I could see the shimmer of the loch.

Something moved again, quite a distance away, a shadow within the darkness, fleeting and unidentifiable. My heart skipped, and the hairs along my spine rose as if caressed with the tiniest of electric wires. The low light from the bothy danced amid the cascading sheets of rain, making my eyes flick from place to place as they sought out the intruder. I had felt so secure tonight, so safe and at peace. A sudden surge of irrational anger rose within me, and I bolted for the front door.

I flung it open so hard that it crashed back against its hinges in a fit of protest, and I thundered out into the black. The sea was an even sheet of darkness before me, broken only by the continuing curve of the whitened waves. Within moments of leaving the warm confines of the bothy, my shirt was clinging coldly to my skin, but the discomfort was secondary. I made my way around the cottage, my hand shielding my eyes from the venom of the spitting sky. The cold wind slapped at my face, reddening my cheeks as if punishing me for my insolence, and as I cleared the generator shed, I stopped and searched the night. The rain was falling in staggered sheets, making it difficult to see more than a dozen yards. The blooms of light from the windows of the bothy were washed away almost immediately, and if anything, the slight glow was more a hindrance than a help. I could see nothing, but something within me shouted at caution, that whatever it was I had glimpsed through the glass was still here.

Watching.

For the brief moment, the wind died down to a wheezy sigh, and the driving rain lost most of its vehemence. I could see as far as the disturbed waters of Sandwood Loch.

Nothing.

I looked again, turning a slow full circle as I scanned the darkness.

Everything was as it should be, and other than the skeletal trees, there was neither bush nor rock to hide behind.

My voice striped with anger, I shouted, "Who's out there!" but the wind just took my words and smothered them as it rose back up to its former tempestuous fury, lashing the raindrops at me spitefully.

I dropped my arms as reality struck me. I hadn't seen anyone. It had probably been no more than a reflection in the glass. Part of me agreed readily to that thought but somewhere, deeper down, I balked away, as I knew I had seen something out here.

For a moment I even wondered if it had been the mysterious Sulika, returned to see why there were lights on in the bothy.

My hair was plastered over my scalp, cold, saturated, and uncomfortable; the wet fabric of my sodden trousers chaffed at my clammy skin; and my socks squeaked inside of my boots.

I returned to the bothy and changed into warm dry clothes. I eventually settled back into the chair, but every so often, I would get up and peer out into the darkness, rubbing the glass clean with my palm and looking at nothing more than my own distorted reflection.

It was a very restless night.

iii

My mind began to play sly tricks on me.

A number of times in the two weeks since the imagined figure out in the rain, I awoke in the middle of the night certain there was someone outside the cottage, stalking in the night-deepened shadows. Several times I ran out into the dark, clothed in nothing but my shorts, shouting blindly at some trespasser who simply wasn't there—or at least could hide very well. I found myself using the lock on the door for the first time. I think it was the only period in its history that the door of the bothy had been secured while someone was inside. It was a truly unnerving time, and once I even considered leaving for a while and taking up residence at the tavern in Kinlochbervie or once again testing the hospitality of the MacDermots, but I dismissed that idea as quickly as it arose.

I refused to be driven away a second time.

I was continually looking out of the window like an obsessed paranoid, desperately trying to convince myself that there was nothing out there but the night.

It always happened at night, though there was one afternoon when I felt it too. I had been taking a stroll over the nearby hills when I became totally convinced I was being followed. It was more than just a feeling through; as I walked I would occasionally hear the skitter of rocks behind me, betraying the presence of someone else.

I quickened my pace, thoughts tumbling through my mind like sycamore seeds. Eventually, I hid behind a large outcropping of granite, intent on confronting my shadow once and for all. After a length of time that I could clearly measure with the deafening beating of my heart, I heard movement and leaped out from my place of concealment, shouting dramatically, my face flushed with anger.

I don't know who was more surprised, me or the helpless sheep I had just terrorized.

But I still remained convinced.

iv

I finally decided to find out for myself.

The question of Dad's final few months here had been burning me since I had arrived, so one morning, I made a short call and within an hour, I was off into town to meet with Maggie Cunningham, Mother's old friend and apparent international informant.

I knew Maggie passingly well, and she was a nice enough woman, if a little too nosy for my liking. Unless things had changed in the past six years, I assumed she was still regarded as the town gossip. She and Mother had become

of her, but they'd only met her on one occasion, and could supply nothing more, other than to confirm that Dad had been more than content in his last few months.

But if he'd been that happy, why wasn't she mentioned in the will, and where was she now?

The fires of my curiosity had been fed, and I knew now that I would have to at least try and find her. I guess I felt a little jealous of her too, that this mysterious woman had been privy to such a happiness with him that I had missed out on.

I had other avenues to explore, and no shortage of time in which to do so.

V

The bothy was as cold as a tomb.

I couldn't tell what time it was, so replete was the darkness in the bedroom. Everything was still, silent, holding its breath. I could only just hear the sea as it whispered upon the sands, though it too was strangely muted.

Waiting.

I lay there, fear pressing against my chest like a cold clammy hand, my ears straining and my eyes wide, searching.

There was someone inside the bothy.

The air was damp, slimy, and it stirred restlessly against my sweat-sheened face. I don't know how I knew, but I could just *feel* the presence somewhere within my home. I sat up in bed, slowly, as if movement or noise might provoke attack from my unseen intruder. I swung my legs carefully out of bed and stood up on uncertain feet. Free of the duvet, I was freezing, though I was sweating, and my whole body was trembling, though through cold or fear, I wasn't sure.

I dry-swallowed and tried to will some life into my legs. The door to the bedroom stood open, but I could see little, as the room beyond was painted with darkness. Whoever it was, they were out there somewhere, hidden in the deep shadows.

I took a step forward, then stopped. The wafting air from the main room brought with it a terrible stench, wet and malodorous, not unlike the smell when the sea spits up something that once lived onto the shore to rot in the sun. For a moment I gagged, so strong was the stink, but with my hand clamped over my mouth, I shuffled toward the open door and whatever waited for me. I don't know what it was that stopped me from just cowering on the bed— perhaps the terror itself. I *had* to know what was out here.

As I neared the doorway, I could finally begin to see. A thin shaving of moonlight came in through the seaward window, just enough to paint a slash on the stones below and haze the room with a slick silver glow. Slowly, I eased my head around the jamb, convinced that who or whatever was waiting was just the other side, poised to strike.

Nothing.

The room was empty.

The smell was stronger here, and though I saw nothing I couldn't relax because I *knew* something was here.

I stepped out into the living room proper, past the table, and crossed on cold burning feet to the window. Outside, the land was calm, undisturbed, as it should be.

I let out the breath I had been holding, and unconsciously released my strung muscles, feeling the exhaustion as the fear finally began to fade. Despite the smell, I took a deep breath and tried to steady myself. It must've been another nightmare, but it was so different from the others that I had believed it true. But that still didn't explain the . . .

It felt like someone had taken a chilled knife to the flesh of my spine. The sound behind me shredded any relief I was feeling with a suddenness that nearly had me falling to the floor. I stood stock still, my eyes wide, staring out over the ocean, listening with all my being, *praying* my ears had been mistaken. But I heard it again all the same.

The creak of wood and the soft sigh of leather.

I turned like a marionette, slowly, woodenly, my expression not changing.

There was someone sitting in the chair before the long-dead fire.

I could see the outline of the back of the chair, and the small raised shape that could only be a head.

As if waiting for my acknowledgment, the figure rose, slowly. I could see that it was a man, or at least once had been.

As he stepped away from the chair, I saw his clothes were old and rotten, trailing creepers of seaweed that were still wet and glistening. Rough, homespun trousers ended at his calves, sodden and frayed, clinging to him, and his jacket was torn and holed as if it had been dashed repeatedly upon the rocks. He turned slowly and stood, facing me with an almost solemn air. Water pooled around him, running off the seaweed and dripping from his clothes.

But it was his face that truly terrified me, for I thought that I recognized him, or at least who he had been.

The skin of his features was blue-gray, like old soaked meat, his face bloated and waxy. The two eyes that stared impassively at me were filmed over with milky cataracts. His mouth was nothing more than a ragged slash, the lips long since eaten away, and the revealed teeth and raw gums were split and broken. Hair so like my own hung in long, withered ringlets around his skull, and its dark luster only served to accent the hideousness of his long-dead face.

The only two flashes of color in the whole room came from the two gold earrings that somehow still hung from what was left of his ears. The stench from his decomposing body was almost physical in its intensity, and it flooded over me like rancid bogwater.

For a long time, I just stood, face-to-face with my past, then, as he raised one skeletal hand and pointed at me, I crashed to my knees and vomited as the terror overwhelmed me. All I could see before me was that petrifying, *putrefying* face, those water-blind eyes boring into my soul as he spoke a single word, filled with more anguish, regret, and imploring than I could ever hope to comprehend.

"Please . . ."

vi

When I awoke in the morning, I was lying on the cold stone floor of the living room.

Curled up tight in a fetal position, the images of the nightmare rushed through my mind straightaway, and I scrambled to my feet, crying out in pain at the cramps that wracked my body from sleeping on the stone.

Breathing raggedly, I searched the room, but of course, I was alone. The room still stank, but it was the acid aroma of my vomit rather than that of the drowned man. Just thinking about his face made me rush to the toilet, where I spent a good few minutes retching into the bowl, bringing up nothing but chyme and bile.

I splashed cold water over my greasy face and washed

my mouth out thoroughly. My body was screaming at me, and it was all I could do to hobble out into the living room and sit down at the table.

For a long time, I just stayed there, near-naked and oblivious to the cold as I stared at the now-empty chair by the fire.

13

Unlike the others, that dream was harder to put behind me, and there were many nights when I woke up, my throat sore from screaming because I'd relived it in my sleep.

I just couldn't banish the horrific face from my thoughts, and if, during the day, I found my mind wandering, I would eventually discover myself back there, unwillingly staring into the sickly cataracts again.

I'd spent time trying to analyze it, to pick the images apart piece by piece, but even in the waking hours, with the sunlight on my face and the reassuring sands of the beach under my feet, the horror stayed with me, as strong as the first. It was almost as if it had been a totally different nightmare from my others, though it still had the basic underlying theme:

Drowning.

I also wondered if I had indeed been haunted in the true sense of the word, because for many years around Sandwood the legend has lingered about the ghost of a drowned fisherman with gold earrings, though I knew of no one who had actually seen him.

Until now.

And as for his single word to me, "please," I had no idea either.

It was a mystery I was eventually to solve, though its resolution would be devastating.

ii

With autumn fully upon me, and the wind bitter with the first dry smells of snow, I finally found proof for all my suspicions about being watched.

It was a bright night, sharp, clear, and biting, when I first heard it. I had been in bed perhaps an hour, and although I had not yet fallen completely asleep, I was in that half-place between consciousnesses that was alive with dreams. My eyes slowly opened, and for a minute, I didn't comprehend what I was hearing, then the last vestiges of sleep fled and I understood.

It was singing.

Like the gentle breath of a warm wind through summer flowers, the song floated slowly across the land. It was in complete harmony with the slow rhythm of the sea, achingly beautiful yet compellingly sad, like an old lament once heard, never forgotten. I sat up slowly in bed, fearful that sudden movement might break the spell, that perhaps in some way I was dreaming. The voice was just on the edge of my perception, and sometimes long moments would insinuate themselves into silences before I picked up the song once again.

Carefully, I slipped on my pants and a dark shirt, and crept from the room. I absently thought about putting shoes on my feet, but something in my mind demanded

careful haste, an unremitting urgency, as if I only had a few
minutes to find the source before it would be gone forever.
I threw a quick glance at the clock next to the bed; it was
almost exactly midnight.

The witching hour.

I eased open the door and stepped silently out into the
night. The moon was high, illuminating everything in a colorless light that was at once enchanting and incredibly
beautiful. Ghosts danced around me, wraiths and spirits of
the night brought to life by the light from the full-dark sky
and the warm blossom from the door of the bothy. The
glen looked like a place out of faerie; all colors were gone,
sucked away to be replaced by an impossible palette of
silver shadow. Quite suddenly, all of old MacKay's stories
seemed a whole lot more likely.

I cocked my head, listening over the soft rush of the
waves, then, sensing the right direction, I trod off toward
the high dunes that fringed the shore of Sandwood Loch.

My bare feet made no sound as they whispered over the
sand, and as I began to climb the low mounds of marram
grass, the singing became more distinguishable. It was a
woman's voice; the wondrous, dulcet tones of an angel,
cradled upon the thin air like the delicate scent of a rose.
It pulled at my heart and slipped its tendrils slowly into my
mind, and though I couldn't understand the words of what
she was singing, it tugged at my hidden memory, as if part
of me had heard it before. The melody that carried the
alluring song was alien to me also, though again, it seemed
I had somehow known it all my life.

As I neared the crest of the dune I slowed, dropping onto
my hands and knees to crawl the last few yards. The thick
blades of the rushes were deceptively sharp, like honed ra-
zors, but I was unmindful, so intent was I upon seeing what

it was I heard, I *felt*. The shallow puffs of my breath left my mouth in rapid succession, clouding quickly in the frigid air for a moment before being carried away and shredded by the fingers of the fitful, gusting wind. The sand beneath my hands and feet was numbingly cold, and as I clawed my way gradually toward the top, it felt as if my every movement were resisted and struggled against, as if I were wading through thick, icing water.

The singing continued, a lilting, almost hypnotic sound that pulled at the inner core of my being. Carefully, I lifted my head to look over the dune onto the gentle slope down to the water.

I saw her immediately.

I don't know if I can truly do justice to what it was I viewed, such was the magic in the very air. It fogged and impaired my mind like a shot of strong whisky, leaving me feeling euphoric and more than a little afraid. Down on the moon-tricked shores of Sandwood Loch, a figure was clearly visible in the brilliant burning luster reflecting off the still water.

It was a young woman.

She was naked, and she was dancing.

The moon rode high in the perfect, star-spotted black, full and replete, shining down like a winter sun. Pure silver light struck the dancer's skin with an argent phosphorescence, giving her the appearance of a porcelain statue come to life. Arms outstretched, she spun slowly, every movement as fluid as mercury, as sublime as a ballerina. Her head was thrown back, the features of her face swathed in shadow as the light played off her flawlessly. She was almost precisely placed between me and the moon, so only the edges of her body were fired by the witchlight, the rest enveloped in shadow as she danced alone on the sands.

Even from this distance, I could see that she was small of stature, though not in a childlike way, for there was no doubt it was a woman that whirled in the moonlight. Her hair, though not long, fanned outward gracefully, and looked to be shot though with a glittering pearlescence, as if some of it were reflecting the moonlight more than the rest. She gradually raised her arms up over her head, and I caught a flash of light upon her face. Her blue-kissed lips were parted, the song spilling forth like springwater from a well, but her eyes were closed. There was the faintest of scents riding bareback on the breeze, a tantalizing mixture of heady wild heather and something else, like the shiver of mist where the tide splinters against the rocks.

For a moment I wondered if this was finally the elusive Sulika, but her hair was the wrong color, and somehow I knew she was a different woman entirely.

I sat, utterly spellbound.

There was a compelling quality in the air, not just the song, but the ethereal presence of the dancing figure that struck me into stillness. It was as if there were some sort of a primal recognition somewhere within me, a stirring of my soul that was not altogether pleasant. I can't say that there wasn't a strong sexual attraction—there was, but it was due more to the perfection of the scene, the unquestionably erotic quality of the song, dance, and night rather than simply seeing a beautiful naked body.

I ached for my fiddle, that I might strike up a counter-melody to her wondrous, beguiling voice, but I knew that to move would be to betray my presence, and then the spell would most certainly be broken. A slight twinge of voyeuristic guilt flashed through my mind, watching as I was, but in a way it felt right; it was almost as if I were *meant* to watch her. She offered no indication that she knew I was there, and as the song finished, the last notes hanging impossibly on the air, she slowly collapsed to the sand, as if it had been an exhausting physical effort for her. Instinctively I moved, concerned that she might be hurt, or that the cold might have taken its toll, but at the first shift of my leg, her head suddenly flashed up like a startled animal. I don't know how, but as she crouched there, as if coiled to strike, I saw the glint of her eyes; they were wide and sparked with anger and I think . . . recognition?

Although I could see no indication, something in my mind knew that they were the color of polished emeralds, of the sea on a spring morning. Our gazes locked, and for a moment, something within me was opened; it was as if layers of my mind were pared slowly away by the power of her stare, and my whole person, conscious and unconscious, was laid open. My chest constricted and my breathing halted. Emotions tore though me, confused and entangled, from the very basest of human desires and needs to the higher, more hidden feelings and instincts that we all carry but never fully utilize. I was painfully erect, but throughout the unchecked river of desire, there was a rip of terrible, encompassing guilt and responsibility—for what, I didn't know. I saw myself stripped bare, clothed in nothing but my humility. My vision blurred and the pulse at my temple throbbed painfully. I ran my hand down my face, trying to summon back some semblance of sense.

All this happened in a split second, and when I lifted my gaze once more, she was gone.

Panic rose within me, and as I searched the shore of the loch, I caught a glimpse of her running away, her actions impossibly smooth and grace-filled. She was gone before I could rise from my knees.

I sat back down on the soft cushion of sand, my hands

and feet tingling with cold as I looked at the shallow incline she had run down. Without a doubt, I knew she had taken something from me.

I think she had stolen my soul.

14

I slept late the following day.

 I awoke to some sort of alarm, some part of my mind telling me to get up quickly. It took me a moment to realize what it was: my phone was ringing. I got out of bed in an explosion of sheets and limbs and ran out into the kitchen, where I stood still, concentrating intently. The faint chirping ring of my mobile came from somewhere within the main room, and for a moment, I remained motionless, the faint echoes of consternation building within me as I tried to remember where I'd left the damn thing. Dashing across to where my coat hung next to the door, I patted it roughly until I felt the slight telltale bulk in my pocket. I fumbled my phone out from within the folds, first nearly dropping it, then answering it clumsily with one hand while trying to extend the short aerial with the other. As I listened to the thin, heavily accented voice on the other end of the "line," I walked from room to room, trying to improve the reception. The clarity this far north was tenuous at best, and I would've gone outside had it not been for the rain.

 Thinking for a moment, and making a decision I hoped I was ready for, I agreed to the man's offer and strode across to the table and began writing down details on the small pad I kept there. I started to shiver slightly in the chill, and I absently wished I'd put some clothes or a robe on.

"So you start at eight, but you want me there by seven?" I asked, frowning slightly as I tried to listen to what he was telling me while frantically scribbling notes.

I waited a moment while he spoke, nodding sometimes as I underlined what I had written, then I asked, "I don't suppose you know how often the ferries run?" A squeal of static burst into my ear, probably something to do with the building storm outside, then I heard the man's reply.

We continued talking for a moment, then I thanked him and pressed the button to end the call. I sat the phone down on the table and looked at what I had jotted on the pad for a moment. I'd agreed to my first job: a private party on the Isle of Skye, playing with a couple of other people brought in especially for the night.

I looked at my watch and, seeing as it was just after midday, felt a slight stab of concern as I realized just how late I had overslept. Although I had nothing to speak of to do, I still managed to get up fairly early each morning, usually by about half past eight at the latest. For me to oversleep so soundly that I nearly missed the phone . . .

Then the events of the night before came clattering back down onto me. I sat down on the chair, my hand in my hair as I remembered it all in vivid detail.

The music, the night.

The woman.

After she'd run, I'd remained crouched for a time in the dunes, dumbstruck and hoping beyond reason that she might return. Then I'd walked slowly down to the shores of the loch and traced her footprints in the sand. I'd considered following her, but I'd no idea where she had gone to. The small impressions her feet had left in the golden sand were proof that she was real enough, but still . . . there was nothing north of Sandwood Loch, except for a ruined, decayed bothy and the lighthouse on the peninsula at Cape Wrath, and that was over five miles away over rock-strewn terrain.

As I set about making my "breakfast," my mind toyed with different ideas as to her origins, and they varied from the possible to the downright stupid. Rationally, I knew she must have come from some sort of a farmstead, one that perhaps isn't marked on the maps—an altogether not unlikely answer (though I do remember reading somewhere that the maps now are done by satellite, and I doubted that any new homesteads would have sprung up in the scant months since). The other possibility was that she was a hiker, a backpacker traveling the path around the northern rim of the country. A walker who happened to like dancing naked on starlit, blue-cold nights while singing.

I amused myself for a time thinking up different ideas, but they were all tinged with a streak of self-mocking irony that I couldn't shake.

But occupy my thoughts she did.

I just couldn't rid myself of that feeling of cognition that had struck me when our eyes had met. It nagged at me like an unseen splinter, and I must admit it scared me a little too. For the briefest, tiniest of instants, I considered if I had seen a spark of Bethy within her, but my foot came down on the ember of an idea, stamping it out before it had a chance to kindle.

The next time I looked at my watch, it was a quarter before three, and as I wondered where the afternoon had gone to, I set about getting my things ready. The deal for the job included a night's accommodation at the hotel on Skye, so I had to pack an overnight bag as well. From here, it was a good two-hour drive south down to Kyle of Lochalsh and the Skye ferry, and from there another twenty minutes north to Portree, so I was going to have to be ready to leave soon.

Part of me wondered whether or not I should have taken this job; maybe she might return again tonight, but with the wind and the rain drumming against the windows, I thought it unlikely. Besides, it might be good for me to get away from the solitude for a while.

I was ready to go a little under forty-five minutes later. I packed the Rover up with my things and, hunching into the wind, returned to lock the door to the generator hut and to the house. Rain tapped down from a seasick sky; not particularly hard, just steady and insistent. I silently added another half-hour on my driving estimate and wondered if I would have time after all for a bath when I arrived. The waters of the Minch were rolling, and the waves that shattered against the sands were large and ill-tempered. I stepped up into the cab of the four-wheel drive and shut the door, sealing myself away from the elements. The engine started on the first turn of the key. I reached into the glove box for Jack's book, and while I waited for the heater to warm up, I looked for the best route.

Turning the heater down a shade, I reversed, then drove carefully over onto the naked track. The wipers whirred rhythmically, flicking the water smoothly from the windscreen as I navigated my way alongside the three successive lakes. Several times the thick tires were forced to spin as they sought purchase on the boggy ground. Thin mist danced around the low mountains like a gossamer skirt, shielding the details from view and seeping across the track as it looked for patches of dryness it might've missed.

Turning onto the A838 at Rhiconich, I put on some speed as the road became wider and newer—black tarmac that glistened in the rain instead of unsealed gravel.

From Ullapool onward, the drive was easier. The rain still fell, but the fog had lifted, and I managed to make back the time I had lost. I stuck a CD of Enya's music into the player and frowned ruefully at the slight pang of nostalgia it gave me. Bronwyn always used to tease me about her, how the music was written purely for the delectation of advertising agents and their ilk.

When I arrived at Kyle of Lochalsh, I was stunned to discover that a bridge had been built over to the island. I was devastated; I'd always thought that one of the beauties about Skye was that it was an island accessible only by boat. No longer, apparently. The obscene concrete structure leered out over the bay like a gray laughing tongue, illuminated already by a plethora of spotlights. Of course there would be no more waiting, no lengthy ferry trip, no heavy seas, but then that was all part of visiting Skye.

The new bridge had put me in a surly mood, and as I wended my way up the A850 to Portree, I found it hard to shake my feeling of snappiness.

I'd spent most of the drive thinking about *her*.

And I was both self-conscious and embarrassed by my almost prepubescent moonings. But try as I might, I just could not shake the image of her graceful dancing from my mind. The odd thing was that no matter how hard I worked at remembering, I just couldn't recall the wondrous song. As a musician, I pride myself on my memory of music, but this . . . even with the car stereo silent, it slipped though my mind like a fine spray. Several times I would find myself humming it, but as soon as I'd realized what I was doing, I would lose it once more. It was familiar and ancient, compelling, but annoyingly elusive.

So intent was I about trying to remember everything about her that I *almost* managed to put the strangeness surrounding my father out of my mind.

I pulled into the restricted car park and sat for a moment looking up at the building. It was called the Storr Hotel, in deference, I suppose, to the great mountain of the same name a little further on up the road. To me, it looked to be Victorian in design, gables and arches aplenty, all washed a brilliant white and highlighted by strategically placed floods. Square windows revealed the warm glows from within, no doubt trying to entice more wealthy travelers in off the cold road.

The man who had phoned me, Angus, was a guitarist who, like myself, belonged to no particular band. Angus specialized in putting together ensembles for particular needs, hence he found it easier to gather the required musicians around him each time rather than have a set line-up. It begged for a little worry when it came to synchronizing of styles, but it made things interesting. I'd not worked with him before, but I knew of him. Tonight's bash was for a group of affluent Americans and Canadians, over here on the usual jet and luxury coach tour of Europe. They were staying at the Storr for two nights, and had expressed a desire to hear, as Angus had put it: "real damn folk moozic." We were to oblige them. The money was very good, but I had no idea how many people it would be split between. For all I knew, this Angus could've rung a dozen musicians.

I slung my soft bag over my shoulder and carried my fiddle case in toward reception. The carpet under my feet was rich and deep, the color of cranberries, and the walls

were painted white with tasteful gold fixtures. From a door
to my left came the sound of soft music, laughter, and chatter—obviously the bar. There were a pair of Chesterfield
sofas and a separating table against one of the walls, and
several paintings of local landscapes hung around me.

The woman behind the front desk efficiently attended to
another couple while I waited; then, with a cheerful smile,
she took my name and directed me up the stairs.

The room was small but functional; definitely not one of
the suites doubtless displayed in the brochure. After briefly
checking out the tiny bathroom and looking inside all of
the cupboards, I left, locked the door, and went down to
the bar to seek out Angus.

If ever there was a stereotypical Scotsman, it's Angus.
Although I'd never actually met him before, I knew him the
moment I stepped into the smoky room. He was at the bar,
leaning on it heavily with one hand while he gesticulated
with a pint of frothy beer in the other. A tremendous red
beard erupted from his ruddy face, tangling perfectly with
his long hair. As I crossed the floor, I could hear his booming laugh over all the other patrons' noise. He was talking
to two other people, a middle-aged woman and a furtive-
looking man who seemed vaguely familiar. I went up to
introduce myself, but before I could speak, he spied me
and, leaving the bar, stumped over.

"Richard Brennan!" he declared by way of a greeting.

"The very same. Angus MacCluskie, I presume?" He
nodded eagerly and shook my hand with a tiger's grip that
nearly made my eyes water.

"Careful," I warned him with a pained smile. "I might
need those fingers later."

His laugh once more filled the room, causing one or two
of the more sensitive patrons to mutter and tut. "Come

along," he said, "I'll introduce you to Keith and Carmen."

Keith was a short man with quick, nervous eyes that barely focused on one thing for more than an instant before finding something else more interesting. As it turned out, we had met before, though I could barely remember. He was an accomplished piano accordion player out of Glasgow, and according to him, we'd worked together once at Windmill Lane in Dublin, though, like I said, I couldn't really remember. It was probably one of those great sessions that had ended up at the nearby Dockers pub, marinated in whisky and that old dark devil, Guinness.

Carmen was quiet, intense, and softly spoken. She played the Scotch smallpipes, a softer-sounding cousin to the dread Highland bagpipes. She regarded me almost cautiously as she sipped at her tea, asking slight though detailed questions about my playing style and musical history. For about half an hour we swapped tales and drank while Angus efficiently filled us in on what was expected, the rough set list, keys, etc.

I managed to break away for ten minutes to get showered and changed, and by the time I came down, the bar had filled with loud American voices. Doubtless if I had looked in the car park I would have seen one of those huge white double-decker coaches waiting patiently for the next morning's excursions.

There were a few locals sprinkled within the crowd, identifiable mainly by the tolerably humorous, knowing smiles on their faces.

We kicked off the first set with a series of stomping jigs and reels, each of us waiting for Angus to call the changes, but we were all professionals, so everything went relatively smoothly. We stuck to the more well known of the folk tunes, and when the song called for it, Angus stepped up to the microphone and sang a few songs, sometimes in Gaelic, which seemed to please the tourists all the more.

Carmen sat just to my right, the pipes spread out across her arms as she fuzzed out the tunes, and she smiled slightly as I rolled my eyes at several Americans who looked to be line dancing. The waiters and waitresses kept the drinks coming, darting in and out of the throngs with a practiced ease, and the atmosphere in the room bubbled away nicely.

B y the middle of the fourth set I was beginning to tire. The long drive had taken it out of me, though I was still buzzing from being onstage again.

I tightened the frog on my bow and shook out my aching hands as I waited for the start of the next song, and was reasonably surprised when Angus turned to me with a mischievous glint in his eye and said, "You start. Solo. Improvise if you like. Just call out the key and nod your head when you want us to join in, and we'll see what we can all come up with."

I smiled and told him it would be a modal D piece, and as I started to play the three-part jig, a favorite of mine called "Banish Misfortune," I closed my eyes, tapping my foot to keep the rhythm.

I was about halfway through the tune when the extraordinary music from the night before abruptly came to me, and with a rush of clarity I switched my playing before it drifted away again. One tune melted into another like warm honey, and as I seized the full melody, I opened my eyes. Angus was looking at me oddly, as was Keith. Neither of them were joining in, and Carmen was only playing a droning chord accompaniment. I hadn't noticed it until then, but the room had gone quiet and graveyard-still, as most people just stood listening. Occasionally a white shirt would flash past as one of the barstaff went about their jobs, but most were motionless. The music progressed, drawn effortlessly from my subconscious. I had no real conception of what I was doing; my fingers just seemed to know where to be at the right time.

I blinked slowly, and as I took a deep breath to finish, I thought I could smell her; the jasmine, the spray of the sea. I saw a splash of movement at the back of the hall, a sudden snapshot of red-gold hair and white skin. As I drew the last note from my fiddle, my first reaction was to jump from the stage, but the music had a calming effect, and for some reason I held my ground. In the back of my mind I thought that perhaps my brash impulsiveness was constrained somehow to the area around the bothy. Besides, I knew it could not possibly be her. Not all the way out here (unless of course she *was* a backpacker and it was a grand coincidence).

My newfound peace wasn't to stop me scouring the crowd afterward though.

The audience was quiet for a moment longer, then erupted in a cacophony of applause—including Angus, Keith, and Carmen. I was to have numerous requests later on for an encore of the tune, but try as I might, I just could not recall it.

It didn't surprise me.

ii

I must have died.

When my eyes cracked open, I groaned aloud and screwed them shut against the brilliant, blowtorch shaft of sunlight that splashed white-hot over the bed. Diamond shards were stabbing themselves purposefully into my brain just behind my forehead, and something had *definitely* crawled inside my mouth to die. I opened my eyes again slowly. I was lying starfish on the bed, arms and legs spread, fully clothed. Fragments of the night before slipped in and out of memory, scenes of dancing, drinking, and drama, and also some fragment of recollection of singing an Elvis song in Gaelic, much to the delight of the encouraging Americans.

I groaned again, covering my eyes with the back of my hand. I would doubtless remember it all in vivid detail later on, or one of the others would take delight in reminding me. I hadn't gotten this drunk for a long, long time, and now I remembered why; I'd always had a fairly low tolerance for alcohol.

Motion brought a whole new set of experiences to the fore, and for a long time I just sat on the side of the bed, cradling my sore head gently in my hands and asking, "Why me?"

I staggered to the toilet and relieved myself of an impressive amount of fluid. I shrugged off my clothes, wrinkling my nose at the stench of stale cigarette smoke and alcohol, and positively fell into the shower. Oddly enough, I didn't feel all that nauseated. Overindulgence of drink never made me sick, which is probably a good thing. As the water stung against my stubbled face I began to feel a little better. The headache hammered on, but my eyes had become used to the light. I reached out for my toothbrush and began fastidiously scouring out my mouth, trying to remove all trace of the dead creature that had once used it for a lair.

Dressed in clean clothes and freshly combed and shaven

(my shaking hands had only let me down twice, but the cuts had stopped bleeding fairly quickly), I felt like I could finally face everyone else. The clock, which was a lot easier to decipher sober, read twenty to eleven, so I knew I was too late for breakfast. I didn't want food anyway. Just coffee, lots of it.

As if knowing I would awake in this condition, the morning had dawned bright and disgustingly sunny. Of the rain that had fallen consistently yesterday, there was no sign. I walked slowly down the stairs and through the double doors into the dining area. All the tables and chairs stood empty, but on the long food counter I spied a steaming jug of filter coffee and a bowl of fresh fruit. I crossed the deserted room and poured myself a cup. There was no milk in sight, so I had it black, suiting my mood.

I pulled out a chair and sat down slowly. The view out of the wide patio windows was beautiful, a panorama of the long island of Raasay just across the gleaming blue water, and on any other day I would have wandered over to gaze. I tried to remember the events of the previous night, but it was like trying to catch the steam coming out of the coffee cup. I *did* recall accepting several invitations to Texas and one to Canada, and I smiled slightly as I remembered the enthusiasm with which the patrons had greeted our music. My hands had been constantly filled with glasses of spirits and beer, and I seemed to recollect smoking a great big cigar, much to the delight of some man in what my mind remembered as a ten-gallon hat, though it was probably just a cap or something similar.

Halfway through my second cup, the young woman who had shown me to my room the night before came through the doors and, seeing me sitting at the table, she walked purposefully over.

"Good morning, Mr. Brennan," she said, with a warm smile that lit up her face. In her left hand she was holding an envelope. "I have a letter here for you, from Mr. MacCluskie. He had to leave early this morning, and he thought it best not to wake you, considering your . . . state."

I smiled wanly. "Probably a good idea." She handed me the envelope and made to leave. "You wouldn't happen to have a couple of paracetamol tablets I could possibly have, would you?" I asked thinly, rubbing at my temple with a rueful expression.

She said, "I'll see what I can do," and returned a little while later, cupping two small oval pills in her hand. As she gave them to me I said, "Thanks." She bobbed her head and before she left, I asked, "What time do I have to check out?"

"By two o'clock, if you could. The room's booked for tonight."

"That's fine. Thanks again."

"Don't mention it. Call if you need anything. The chef's just through there." She pointed to a set of swinging doors. "If you want to grab a bite to eat, ask her nicely and I'm sure she'll be able to knock something special up for you."

"I don't think I'll be eating anything just yet," I replied as she walked from the room chuckling to herself.

I put my coffee cup down and slowly opened the envelope. Inside was a wad of brand-new fifty-pound notes and a short handwritten letter from Angus. It read:

Dear Richard,

Hope you are feeling better—that was some party! Here's your money, plus a £100 tip that some old fool

wanted me to pass on. Not bad for three hours' music, eh!
Sorry I had to leave without saying good-bye, but I have
to be in Fort William by nine and the snores coming out
from under your door were more effective than the Do Not
Disturb sign. Really enjoyed the tunes, especially that one
of your own—I'll give you a call soon and we'll sort out
some more work.

Fair play to you,

It was signed with an elaborate squiggle that I suppose
passed for his name. I folded up the money and put it away
in my breast pocket, buttoning it down securely. I shook
my head slightly as I thought about how much the man
Angus had written about must have tipped in total. This
was in addition to the screwed-up bundles of notes I had
found stuffed in the pockets of my reeking jacket.

I finished my coffee and wondered what had happened
to Keith and Carmen. As I passed back through the hall,
the receptionist told me they had both checked out earlier
on in the morning. I was slightly irked by that—I always
made a point of saying good-bye to the people I had
worked with. Still, I suppose I should have got up at a
decent hour without the indecent hangover.

By the time I had packed my stinking clothes away, the
headache had dissolved down to a low throb that I could
just about live with. Despite the brightness of the day, I
found I wasn't really looking forward to the drive home. I
checked on my fiddle, briefly putting it under my chin as
I tried to remember the tune I had played so easily and
naturally the night before, but to no avail. I sighed as I
packed it away.

It might come to me in time.

...
iii

October

It was just over a fortnight before I saw her again.

Well, actually, that's incorrect. It was a fortnight before I *heard* her again.

That time, the first *definite* encounter since the night by the loch, I didn't skulk from the house like some thief. I opened the windows wide, admitting rushes of cold air, and just sat warming myself by the fire, barely breathing as I listened in mute rapture. I don't know how long she sang for—it felt like all night, but it could have been no longer than an hour. She was louder this time, more defined, and though I still couldn't pick out any words in the song, I came closer than ever to recognizing it.

I don't know how I knew, but somehow, as the evenings passed, I came to realize she was singing *for* me, that it wasn't just a personal thing. Several times I had sat in the house listening to her perfect voice filling the air with sweet melody, and I had been filled with the crushing desire to find her, to watch her as I had that first night. I would creep from the house, quiet as I could be, but no matter how stealthy I thought I was, she would always flee, before I got anywhere near her. Usually, she sang down by the shores of the bay, a diminutive silhouette (clothed now!) outlined against the sea, but a couple of times, I had thought her voice had drifted down from the cliffs to the north and once, when the moon had flooded the ocean with white light, I thought the singing came from atop the great gray stone pillar of Am Buachaille, but it was probably just the wind playing its tricks.

Sometimes, I became aware of her presence as I practiced late at night, and I tried to convey all of myself, my feelings and desires, within my music, but whether she understood what it was I was trying to do, I don't know.

I didn't become accustomed to her—never that—but I lost that sense of . . . mystical awe? that I had held her in. I was now fairly sure that she must come from another croft somewhere to the north. But still, I found nothing when I hiked out up there on numerous occasions. It was as if she only lived by night.

It was to be another two weeks before things changed again.

I got back to the bothy a little after eleven. I had been over in Durness, playing a wedding gig. It had been the usual affair, set-dancing and the regular sort of tunes, and as I stepped down from the car, I was silently thankful it was over. Still, it was all work, and it paid well.

I lowered my fiddle case carefully to the ground and reached inside the Rover for my coat. The night was clear and glassy cold, with a chilling wind blowing in off the dark, stirred depths of the Minch, seething through the trees and over the rocks like a phantom. The sky above me was ablaze with a thousand scintillating stars and an impossibly full moon that looked like a glowing globe hung low by an invisible thread. My breath clouded before me as I fumbled the key into the lock of the car, and once the mechanical whir of the central locking had ceased, I bent down to pick up my bag.

And the song began.

Whether it was the breath of the wind or the perfection of the night I do not know, but she sounded so close, so clear. I remained crouched by the car, my ears filling with the sound of her splendid voice, my soul drinking her down. I looked over to the sea, my sight skipping across the stippled water and back over the moon-washed sands. The metal of the car's engine pinged as it cooled down, and my heartbeat drummed in my ears, an awkward counterpoint to her melody.

Slowly, impossibly slowly, I unlatched my case, freeing my fiddle and bow, my eyes still searching for some trace of her. Shuffling on noiseless feet, I cleared the bulk of the car and squatted down next to a rough, ancient trunk of sea-bleached driftwood.

It was then that I saw her, down by the water, perched on one of the two large rocks that reared grandly from the sea.

She wasn't moving, but stood, arms outstretched, her outline clearly distinguishable before the silver corridor of moonlight that wedged out from the horizon.

For an instant my heart faltered and skipped, and hot and cold creatures chased tails along my spine. I thought that perhaps all of MacKay's stories were true, for I could not see her legs, only a single column of shadow that fanned outward where her feet should have been, looking for all the world like some sort of aquatic tail. All the legends I had ever heard or been told plummeted through my mind, each vying for prominence. I felt sick to the pit of my soul. It was a truly terrifying moment, to be confronted head-on by mystery and myth, and to wonder at my own history and sanity. The breath halted in my throat, refusing to go any further as I crouched there, stunned to the core of my being.

Then she moved a little, and a split of light caught on what I assume was a long skirt that barely moved in the vagrant breeze.

The feeling of relief that billowed through me was indescribable, but still I held on to my breath, so afraid was I that she would once again take flight.

Without even checking the tuning, I slipped the fiddle under my chin and readied my bow. For a long time I just hunkered by the log, my mouth counting the beats of her song until I could find a way in—or was I uttering a prayer?—then, with my eyes half-hooded, and expecting her to run, I played the gentlest notes ever heard.

They swelled slowly out from the steel, pony hair, and mahogany, seeping into the air, complementing her ethereal voice perfectly. I stayed simple, content just to play key notes underneath her flawless melody. She kept on singing, almost as if she were unaware of the sound of my fiddle, but as she turned her head, catching the silver, I knew she had heard the music and seen the man.

I grew more confident, weaving a subtle tune of my own in with hers. The music we made together was aching and beautiful, and such was the mood that I felt tears gathering in the corners of my eyes. I stood up slowly, my gaze never leaving her, and continued to play. Still she did not run. It almost sounded like there were other instruments with us—distant, throbbing pipes and a husky flute—but perhaps that was just the shallow breathing of the land around us and the ever-present heartbeat of the sea.

With the music emboldening me, I took several painfully slow steps toward her. From where I stood to the rocks on the beach was a fair way, and I knew there was no possibility of me gaining much ground before she ran, but still I walked on, compelled into action by the music.

The song took on a different note, a harder, more fervid tone that sent goose bumps rippling down my sweat-beaded back and raised the hairs along my arms like a static charge. I responded in like, almost challenging her with the passion in my strokes. The music became stunningly complex, chilling, and the variations in her voice pushed my talent to new limits. I closed my eyes, concentrating as hard as I could yet trying to stay free so that the harmony between us remained unbroken.

It's difficult to try and explain what was happening between us.

The music we were releasing was not technically brilliant or astoundingly fast, it was more than that. I knew that somehow I had to put my whole soul into what I was playing with her, that nothing else would possibly do.

It wasn't requested; it was demanded.

I realized our duet was drawing to a close. I don't know where the awareness came from; it was like knowing exactly where I was within a chord progression without counting the bars, and as I built up to the finale, I felt the pressure building within me, almost like the slow climb toward orgasm. Tears were flowing freely down my cheeks, and unrelinquished feelings broiled within me. I felt enriched, desolated, euphoric, and ruinous, a morass of conflicting emotion that bombarded through me like a tempestuous storm.

The final note was a blissfully powerful, almost discordant harmonic chime that echoed plaintively back off the mountains and soared down through the valleys like an eagle at wing.

When I finally lowered my fiddle and opened my eyes, I couldn't see her. I brushed away the tears and looked again, but the low rock she had danced on was vacant and lonely. I let out a slow breath and cast my view along the beach.

And there she was! Standing ankle-deep in the inky water, watching me. Her arms were hanging loosely by her sides, hands clutching at the thin fabric of her dress, perhaps holding it free of the clinging water.

She was looking directly at me.

Her head was slightly tilted to one side, as if in contemplation, and her raggedly cut hair fluttered fitfully in the sea breeze. I stayed perfectly still, trying to memorize every detail of her that I could see in the wan light. The tumescent moon was directly behind her, so the details of her face were still denied me, but what my eyes couldn't see my mind filled in. Her hair was definitely streaked with a lighter color, but—and I don't know how I came to this conclusion—it looked to be totally natural. I remembered the flash of color I had thought I'd seen on Skye, and mentally, I painted her auburn and gold. Like me, her breath ghosted on the night air before her, struck into luminosity by the moon before drifting noiselessly away. She was breathing rapidly, perhaps as spent as I by the music and magic. At least I knew she was a creature of flesh and not of spirit.

How long we stood there staring at each other I really couldn't say; maybe it was a lifetime? Then, with a sudden gesture that might've been an acknowledgment, she turned and ran lightly along the beach, her slim feet skipping up sprays of glittering water. I watched her run the length of the sands like a child at play, and before she disappeared from sight, I shouted, "What's your name? Tell me your name!"

If she answered at all I couldn't be sure, but I thought I heard a light, tinkering laugh floating on the wind just above the foam-flecked waves; then she was gone.

iv

I awoke in the morning, cold, damp, and naked, the sheets tangled around my legs.

I sat up shivering, last night's events like the raveled threads of a dream that I could not quite gather together.

With one hand pinching at the bridge of my nose, the other patted noisily across the bedside table, searching until it found my glasses. Putting them on, I raked my hands through my mop of hair, then wrinkled my nose as a peculiar aroma assaulted my nostrils. Brackish and pungent, the air was sharp with the smell of seaweed and the ocean, but not at all in the same way as when I'd dreamed about the sea-dead. This smell was almost pleasant, reassuring. Tugging on a pair of jeans, I padded toward the bedroom door, then stopped suddenly as I caught sight of a small puddle of water just on the threshold. My first reaction was to look up to the ceiling, and other than seeing no hole, I realized it had not been raining. I opened the door fully, letting it swing gently outward. What I saw sent a thrill of, well, fear and excitement I suppose, gliding down my back like ice.

Sunlight slatted through the thick, watery glass of the windows, spilling off the table and chairs and onto the cold floor. Dust motes danced merrily within the pillars of amber light, swirling like dervishes as I disturbed the still air. The fire was long dead, and both the oil lamps had burned down to the quick.

But it wasn't the postcard quality of the scene that so beguiled me, it was the dozen or so little pools that led from the bed to the outside door like small footprints. I crouched down by one, picking up a thin strand of black weed and rubbing it thoughtfully between my fingers. The smell was stronger in here, like rock pools in the sun, but there was something else, a wildflower-like undertone that spoke in whispers to my primal, and possibly masculine, self.

The exterior door was slightly ajar, and as I slowly opened it, I had to shield my eyes from the sudden brilliance of the sun that had at last been granted entrance. The small band of verdant *machair* that led from the cottage to the beach looked normal, and as I walked slowly down, I could see no more of the curious watermarks.

There was no sign of whoever had paid me a visit. With skin prickling from the frigid breeze (but I wasn't really cold), I went back inside. My curiosity was afire; I was a little afraid, but also almost childishly excited. Shutting the door, I paused to look out of the window at the calm blue of the ocean.

Something had happened, some barrier had been passed.

It would be night. Always night. I knew that much.

I also knew the time would ebb excruciatingly slowly till the next dawning of the moon.

15

Nothing happened the next night, nor the night following.

Steadily, as the week drew to a close, I began to worry, and doubt began to creep into my mind. The joy I had felt during our shared music quickly sublimed into something else that resembled frustration and almost despair. Had I pushed things too far with our duet? Perhaps if I had been content to just sit and listen instead of being so impulsive. . . .

A half-empty glass of red wine sat on the table before me, the dark liquid reflecting back the flutter of the candles like the lights on a carousel. Pinning the last of the meal with my fork, I slipped it into my mouth and chewed thoughtfully as I regarded the sudden change of season.

As the fingers of winter deliberately pressed their nails into the soft land around me, the pleasant, steady evenings I had enjoyed disappeared almost entirely. Now there was the thin, bleached light of the afternoon, then around four o'clock, the sun sank swiftly, and within fifteen minutes, it was dark.

With the perfect black beyond, the windows of the bothy

shone with the reflections from the inside of the room. I
pushed away my now-empty dinner plate and leaned back
in the chair, once more becoming anxious and edgy as I
wondered if she would appear tonight. I glanced to the
chubby hands of the clock I had fixed above the mantel,
and frowned as I saw it was still only early; just after seven.
My fingers formed a loose tent before me, bending at the
knuckles as I flexed them restlessly. With a heavy sigh I
reached over to where my notebook sat, and opening it up
at the last entry, picked up my pen and began to write. I'd
never kept a diary before, and living in solitude as I was, I
had thought it a good way to spend the evenings when I
wasn't playing—it was better than sitting here listening to
the fishing forecasts crackle over the radio.

But the journal had just turned into rambling reflections
on the strange woman who haunted me. There were pages
of speculation and observation, as well as a few sketches I
had penciled in (I could draw passably), and little else. For
a while I passed the time jotting down a few thoughts, then
that too became boring and I closed the book with a snap
and skidded it across the table.

I drummed the pads of my fingers against the heavy grain
of the wood, once more looking at the clock, then out of
the window. I got to my feet and walked across the floor,
cupping a hand to the glass that I might see better. I could
just make out the pale movement of the sea, and the indistinct shapes of the clouds, but nothing else. I lowered my
hand, a frown rippling across my forehead as I thought for
a moment, then I grabbed my heavy coat from the hook. I
draped it over the chair while I went into the bedroom and
dug out a thick, Fair Isle jumper. Slipping that over my
head, I pulled on the coat and buttoned it up, hoping that
it was going to be warm enough. I blew out one of my

paraffin lamps, leaving the other burning on a low wick against my return. The fire was well stoked and would burn for hours yet. Just to be safe I put the concertina grill across the grate to catch any sparks that might leap out—not that they could ignite anything on the stone, but still . . .

I flipped my hat on over my head, and on a sudden impulse, picked up my small Irish tin whistle in case I should chance upon her. Bracing myself against the chill, I stepped out into the night. After the intimate warmth of the cottage, the brittle wintry wind struck me like a gloved fist, and as I turned to pull shut the door, I could feel my cheeks burning already as my skin contracted alarmingly.

I stopped off at the generator shed to pick up one of the oil-fired storm lanterns that hung on the wall. It had heavy shutters to protect it from the wind, and although there was a fair bit of light from the moon, I thought it might come in handy.

I took a deep breath, savoring the feeling of the air burning through my nose and into my lungs. High above me, impossibly shaped clouds hung, gently shaded by the bloodless moonlight. Several pinpricks of white starlight were visible through the patches, though the moon itself was curtained for the time being. Looking once at the cottage, I set off slowly toward the curve of the shore. The sands of the bay were blanched with a gentle glow that was strangely calming and lent the beach a mysterious, otherworld feel.

With my heavy boots sinking slightly in the soft sand and the lantern tapping quietly against my coat, I walked to where the sea muttered against the mermaid rocks, the place I had seen her singing. Am Buachaille was an ill-defined, shadowy presence at the limit of my sight, only visible if a pale cloud were to pass behind it, and then only revealed as a monolithic finger pointing determinedly to the heavens.

I stuffed my warm hands into my deep pockets and stepped silently up onto the place where she had stood singing. For a time I just crouched there, gazing out to sea, letting my mind drift as easily as a boat out on the tide. The playful wind ruffled through my clothes and whispered secrets in my ears. Moonlight came and went like the headlamps of a car as the large pillows of cloud wandered steadily in from out to sea, and the shifting sands seemed to change; sometimes brilliantly lambent, other times near dark.

I hopped down from the stone and began to walk slowly up the beach. I picked up pebbles from close to the tide line, pitching them with lazy, overarm throws into the black water. Occasionally, carried by the wind, I would hear the hoot of a distant owl or the screech of some other night hunter prowling the glen or the skies above. I crossed the shallow stream easily enough and, with the low rocks rising to my right, continued on toward the fractured headland. The deep night was having a calming effect on me, and as I wandered, my feet scuffing the sand and my eyes scanning the lines of the cliffs for her, I found myself slightly embarrassed by my feelings. I don't know what it was about her that so beguiled me; I'd sat on many nights jotting down random feelings and ideas, but when I reread them, they failed to make sense or shed any light. It was as if something primal within me reacted to her on a level I failed to understand. It was like suddenly smelling a fragrance and having it conjure images long buried. I felt like I knew her, but I also understood that there was no way we had met before. Even sifting through my memories of my childhood here, I still could not recall her presence (despite the fact that she was obviously much younger than I was).

I'd spent time hiking around the valley, Strath Shinary, even once climbing the craggy heights of Creag Riabhach, but I had seen no trace of another used habitation. There were several old bothies, now nothing more than vacant shells that were the homes for sheep and rooks.

It was as if she just vanished. Yet I *knew* she was still here.

I put the lantern down, resisting the urge to light it as some sort of beacon, and sat down upon the southmost of the two mermaid rocks. Unconsciously, my body hunched against the bitter wind coasting in off the sea. There'd been no snow as yet, but I knew it was only a matter of time, and when it came, it might cut me off here for a time. I'd already stocked up with food, wood, and diesel for the generator, but my thoughts were still filled with a kind of childlike anticipation laced with no small amount of fear. What would happen then? When the land was mantled in thick white and all paths were impenetrable. Would she still come?

Time would tell, I hoped.

I dug out the old tin whistle and trilled a couple of hesitant notes, but the night was just too cold, and away from the sanctuary of my pockets, my fingers quickly became numb and stiff. So for a while I just sat there, looking out over the indifferent depths of the Minch, all the time wondering where she was.

Eventually, with the moon now completely covered by the thick drape of cloud, I started back down the beach toward home. I took my time, all the while looking back over my shoulder and trailing my sight along the dark broken line of the cliffs, but I didn't see her.

ii

I was just into my second cup of morning coffee when I saw it, sitting on the mantel next to my other precious memories.

For a moment I just sat there looking at it, not really registering that what I was looking at hadn't been there the night before.

It was a large, ivory-tinted seashell.

The feet of my chair squealed against the flagstones as I got up suddenly. My cup was still gripped tightly in my hand, and the hot drink within was burning my palm through the china. I crossed the room slowly, as in a daze, my mind trying to remember if somebody had just given it to me and I'd forgotten.

I put down my cup and reached out, lifting the shell from the shelf. It was heavier than it looked, and easily filled my hand. Outward from the central swirl rose delicate points of powder white, like horns, while the underside that led down inside was a scintillating pearlescent pink that gleamed and shimmered, changing hue as I turned it around in my hand. I ran a finger around the glass-smooth entrance, then, with a slightly foolish grin, I held it to my ear for a time, listening to the illusionary dull roar of the sea.

I knew it was from her; I could smell her on it, in it. What I didn't really know was why.

I thought that perhaps it was some sort of gift, a token. I was beguiled by the offer, confused but strongly pleased.

With the shell held tightly in my hand, I turned, my eyes tracing the route she would have taken to the door. There were no puddles of wet, in fact no indication that anyone had come inside at all. I kept the gray flagstones free from dust, so there were no telltale marks of feet—wet or dry. I reached the outer door and pulled it open. The gray light of the dawn reluctantly washed over me as I walked out into the frigid morning.

Nothing.

If she was waiting to see my reaction, I could not tell. Squinting into the harsh wind, I made a slow circuit of the cottage, my eyes and ears straining over the crash of the sea, the rush of the breeze.

I returned to the door and stood facing the choppy waters. Holding the gift to my breast, I shouted, "Thank you!" into the bay.

If I had been expecting some sort of reply, some acknowledgment, I would've been disappointed, but I wasn't, and with a silly smile on my face, I made my way back into the warmth of my home.

I placed the shell back on the mantel, between Bethy's stone cat and the tiny bone fiddle a friend had given me. I stood looking at it for a time, feeling the warmth of the gesture seeping into my soul.

For the rest of the day I stayed home, a slightly overblown feeling of anticipation ripe on my tongue.

Two mornings later, and a second gift awaited my awakening.

This time, I discovered it at the foot of my bed, a sudden splash of vivid color sitting atop the dark green cotton of my bedspread. Where, at the beginning of winter, she found such a flower, I do not know. It had an odd look to it: long-lobed, lop-sided petals brushed with a brilliant amber-yellow color danced around a center that was darkest damask and smelled fresh, almost citrusy. There was no stem, just a large flower head that filled my cupped palm. It reminded me a little of the summer orchids or the lilies that sometimes floated around the banks of the more sheltered locks and pools, but this flower was unlike any I could remember. But then, I was hardly a botanist, and I'd read somewhere there were pockets of land in Sutherland where almost subtropical flowers and plants bloomed—a little like the Burren in Ireland, I suppose. I lowered my face to the center of the petals and took a deep breath. The scent evoked images of the hills, and also, oddly enough, the aquamarine ocean floor.

I shivered with both the cold and a delicious sense of excitement knowing that last night she had stood here, as silent and noiseless as a ghost, and watched me sleep. I wondered why I felt no apprehension, no concern over the intrusion into my privacy. More than anything, I was hoping I would see her during the day, that perhaps she might make herself known at last on a more personal level. That day was coming, I was sure, and the expectation was almost gnawing at me.

I padded barefoot from the bedroom into the kitchen, wondering what I should do with the gift. Left as it was, the flower would surely be dead by the end of the day, and there was no way I could put it in a vase. Eventually, I filled a shallow bowl with cold water, sprinkled a little sugar into it, and just let the flower head float. I placed the bowl in the center of the table, marveling at the sudden splash of color the room quickly borrowed from it.

I returned to the bedroom and got dressed quickly, pulling on a pair of jeans and a thick sweater. Rebuilding the fire in the range, I set a pot to boil and crossed to the front door. Again, there was no trace of her passing, and as my fingers curled around the cold iron of the handle, I wondered if her hand had done the same only hours, or even minutes, before.

Opening the door, I was greeted with one of the most beautiful sights I had seen in a long, long while. The first true frost had fallen overnight, and the land from here to the sea was encased in a crystalline beauty that literally shimmered in the bright winter sun. I moved outside, a look of wonder on my face, my shoes crunching on the frozen grass as I stepped into the sun. I walked slowly around the bothy, looking up at the sloping turfed roof, now dusted with a gleaming, sprinkled coat of ice that bestowed upon the small cottage a storybook aspect.

Leaving deep footprints across the crisp grass, I slowly made my way round until I faced Sandwood Loch, and for a long while, I just stood there, looking at the wonderland before me. The pair of scraggy trees stood resplendent and almost proud in their new borrowed coats of shining crystal, the sluggish ebb of the stream was crusted with a thin veneer of clear ice, and even the rocks that lined the sides of Strath Shinary had been silvered by the frost. Sandwood Loch looked impossibly blue, and in the stunning sun its glory almost hurt my eyes. Small cotton twists of mist hung above its surface, gently folding on the breeze, and further off to the east, a gannet pulled in its wings and dived into the water, sparkling it briefly before suddenly reappearing and taking clumsy flight with a small fish. The morning air was as glassy as the ice, and it had an invigorating effect on me. I felt more alive than I had for a long time, and in a part of my mind now opened, I wish Bethy could have been here to share this. Her memory no longer brought the stab of pain into my chest, rather just a dull ache, a sense of penetrable loss that I knew would always be there, but one that I was finally beginning to accept and understand.

Further up the desolate valley, a single bird soared effortlessly on the gentle updrafts, spiraling higher and higher before turning and riding the wind down toward me. My heart gave a lurch as I realized it was a golden eagle: an exceptionally rare bird of prey, now all but gone from Scotland. With an elegance that was breathtaking, it wheeled on the wind, beating its broad wings slightly as it turned to the north. I watched it, my mouth open, until it finally dipped below the hill and vanished from sight. As I ambled back to the cottage, my heart full, I thought I could hear its aching cry echoing hauntingly around the bay.

As I neared the bothy, I broke into a run as I heard my phone ringing from somewhere inside.

A sudden feeling of irrational urgency broke over me, and as I flung open the door and made for the table, I was silently seething at the interruption.

I pulled up the aerial and jabbed a finger at the 'on' button. Raising it to my ear, I barely had a chance to say hello when: "For Christ's sake! It's a bloody *mobile* phone! You're supposed to take it with you, dickhead!"

"Morning, Jack," I replied in what I knew was an infuriatingly calm voice. My anger dissolved at the pleasure of talking to a friend.

"Where were you?" the loud voice asked. "Taking your morning dip?"

I smiled. "Something like that. How's things?"

"Same as always. So what's going on up at your end of the world?"

I filled him in on what I had been doing, where I'd been playing, things like that. I didn't mention the woman. I don't know why not. Perhaps I was worried she only existed within the boundaries of my own imagination.

"Well," he said cheerfully. "I've got an offer for you you're not going to believe—it'll get you away from all those poxy weddings and wakes you've been playing at. What are you doing for the next couple of months?"

"Nothing," I told him hesitantly. "Go on." A slight twist of worry was beginning to knot inside me.

"Remember that band you once played resident with, the Soapbox Preachers—you know, the *Cumbria* tour all those years back." His emphasis on 'Cumbria' was all that I needed to remember.

"Oh yes," I said with a grin, recalling all too well. They were a sort of folk band that blended traditional instruments with electric guitars and keyboards, and what they lacked in originality, they certainly made up for in enthusiasm—on and off the stage.

"Well, they're together again and they've got a tour coming up."

"And?"

"Michael asked for you specifically."

I frowned down the phone. "Michael Harris and I didn't exactly part on good terms."

"I *know* that," Jack told me. "But it's been ten years!"

"I suppose." I didn't sound too keen. "What's the deal?"

There was a brief pause, and I could hear Jack sucking on a cigarette. "England, Ireland, and Canada," he said after a moment.

"Canada!"

"The albums are huge over there, and some Vancouver folk society is sponsoring them out."

"How long?" I asked.

"Including overseas? Three months. It's the usual setup: travel, expenses, and the dosh up front per show. It's good money, Richard."

"Yeah, but three months . . . I've only just got settled, Jack."

His voice took on a slightly different note. I think he was surprised I hadn't jumped at the chance. "Christ, Richard, the tour'll get you away for most of the winter! And once it snows up there, you're not going to be able to work for a while anyway. Think about it! It's damn near as perfect an opportunity as anyone could wish for!"

I was quiet while I listened to him arguing out the points, then, hesitantly, I said, "I don't think so. The timing's not right. I'm sorry, Jack. I just need a little more space, time by myself, you know."

I was thinking of *her*.

I could feel the wave of disappointment coming from the receiver, then he said softly, "All right, you mad bugger, but if you change your mind, let me know. You've got about four days before I've got to offer it to someone else."

I nodded and replied, "Thanks, Jack, but I think I'm certain."

His mood lightened. "Ah well, your loss, you fool. I've got something else—if you could lower yourself to menial studio work amongst humble musicians."

Our conversation returned to the usual jokey manner, and by the end, I had accepted a booking for two days' work down at Park Lane in Glasgow, laying down fiddle tracks for a fairly popular band. I'd spend the nights at Jack's place—no, I'll rephrase that; I'd spend a fraction of the very early mornings at Jack's place, as he'd already told me his plans for our two nights on the town.

iii

NOVEMBER

I had decided to drive into Inverness.

There were some things that I thought I ought to buy before winter really set in, supplies and equipment that I could not get in Dingwall or Ullapool. I'd finally run out of blank manuscript paper, and the nearest musical shop was there also. Doubtless I could have found what I was looking for by driving from village to village, but in truth, I wanted to mix with "society" a little, and the bustle of Inverness would fulfill that desire perfectly.

I pulled the Rover up next to the shed and lowered the tailgate. Whistling a melody that had come into my mind of late (and of course I couldn't write it down—hence the trip), I loaded the large jerry cans into the back, two at a time, then threw an old blanket over them to stop any rattles. I would have to refill them at a service station at some point today—I had to get diesel, so it was going to be a long, smelly procedure, but I'd rather spend the money and time than be caught with no power.

By the middle of the afternoon I was almost finished. I'd very nearly forgotten to buy a set of snow chains for the Rover, and only the sight of a dealer's display had reminded me. The back of the vehicle was loaded up with odds and ends, maintenance things really: spare parts for the generator, oil for the lamps, candles, bulbs, a new, wide snow shovel, tinned and packet food, a few months' supply of decent coffee beans and the like. Just the essentials.

I was walking back along the high street, still humming the damn tune, when I stopped at the window of a clothes shop. For a minute, I just looked through, the seeds of an idea in my mind, then I ventured in, emerging a while later with a heavy woolen shawl. I remembered distinctly how little she wore when she came to see me, and although it occurred to me that it didn't seem to bother her all that much, I thought that perhaps it would make a good gift. The wool had been hand-dyed a deep rusty red, and I thought it might strike a fire with her amber-streaked hair.

Nearing the car park, my attention was diverted once again, this time by a small, quiet gift shop tucked away in a corner under a drooping black-beamed gable. I deposited the rest of my purchases in the Rover and returned for another look. From the outside, it appeared to be just another run-of-the-mill tourist trap, but as I pushed open the door and the tiny bell tinkled over my head, I found it to be much more. Deep shelves ran the entire length of the single cramped room, positively brimming with small curios. They were not the usual tacky tourist matter, but intricately made local crafts that were astonishing to behold. The top shelf, running three-quarters round the walls, supported a positive brigade of handmade teddy bears, from tiny, glass-bead-eyed mascots to large, near-life-size monsters that looked to cost an arm and a leg. Below sat a village of miniature painted cottages, a multitude of styles from Anne Hathaway's, complete with a garden positively exploding with flowers, to Windsor Castle and some that looked to be the product of a very fertile imagination. I picked one up, smiling as I wondered at the attention to detail. Underneath, it was signed by the sculptor and priced quite clearly. I put it back *very* carefully. I shuffled along between the stands and shelves, sometimes examining things, mostly just admiring.

An old, well-dressed woman appeared from behind a curtain at the back of the shop, a mug of what I assume was tea in her hand and a friendly smile on her face. "Can I help you with anything?" she asked politely.

I shook my head. "No thanks, I'm just browsing." I paused for a minute while I looked at a watercolor painting of a beach scene that was hanging in a gap between crammed cupboards. The attention to detail was utterly phenomenal; the landscape was similar to Sandwood, but the beach was rougher, harder, and less romantic. In the background, heather-dusted hills rippled down to a sand-streaked bay peppered with sea-smeared rocks. The clouds depicted above were full and sodden, and the feeling one got from the picture was a sudden burst of warmth, fore-boding rain. "You have some incredible things here," I said softly, marveling at the artist's genius use of half-light and shadows to set the mournfully beautiful and desolate mood.

"Thank you," she said, coming to stand next to me. "That's one of Natasha Newlyn's. She's an artist who lives over in Connemara. She's only young," the woman re-marked, sipping her tea. "But she draws like a veteran."

"It's so beautiful," I breathed, almost awestruck. It was easily the most evocative piece of art I had laid eyes on.

The woman smiled knowingly. "I know. I can't get hold of enough of her work—she turns them out slowly, and I sell them pretty much as soon as they arrive. You should see her pencil-only drawings—they're extraordinary. I've been in this business forty-six years, and I don't think I've seen her like."

I drank in the intricate, meticulous detail. Just when I thought I had seen all of the painting, I would pick out more: a person walking along the beach in the distance, a gull tumbling on the breeze, a subtle shape in the clouds. "She has an incredible eye," I said, shaking my head.

"It's a bay in Connemara," the woman told me. "Near Letterfract, I believe." She stepped back a little, to give me some room. "It's called *View of Inishboffin*."

I nodded. I wasn't a hundred percent sure, but I thought I knew the beach, but I'd never seen it like this before.

"I give her ten years, just to mature her style, before she's at least the equal of Waterhouse."

I raised my eyebrows, but this lady seemed to know her stuff, and judging from the picture, in front of me, I was inclined to believe.

"How much is it?" I asked, touching the polished oak of the frame slightly.

"Twenty-five hundred pounds," she said without preamble. "And that's a steal. It'll be worth at least twice that in a year or so."

I didn't even need to think. "I'll take it."

If she was surprised, it didn't register. She merely blinked and nodded. "I thought you might," she said, putting her mug down and taking the painting carefully off the wall. "That tends to be the way with Newlyn's work—someone'll come in, stare at the picture, and buy it just like that."

I smiled. I don't know why I'd bought it—I knew nothing about art and actually had never purchased an original in my life, but there was something about the painting that touched me, and I knew that I would never grow tired of gazing at it. Flicking through my wallet, I pulled out my credit card and handed it to her. I stood there, waiting for the transaction to clear while the woman carefully slipped the picture into a thin but sturdy box. I glanced around, and something by the cash register caught my eye. It was a small parian figurine of a Renaissance-style mermaid on a low rock. She was reclined, wringing out her long hair with a slight knowing smile on her face. I picked it up, looking at it a moment thinking what a perfect present it would make.

"Could you possibly write down your name and address for me?" the owner asked, breaking my reverie. "It's just Ms. Newlyn always likes to know where her work goes, and she gives all the owners first choice on any specials or limited editions."

"Sure," I replied, taking the offered pen and pad. "By the way," I asked, writing my name down, "how much is this?" I indicated the little statuette with the pen.

"Five pounds, but I'll include for free," she said with a slight wink.

I shook my head, a cheeky grin on my features. "I should think so."

She smiled back and began wrapping it in soft paper.

When she was done, I asked, "Could I leave them here and pick them up later? I don't really want to lug a painting around town and I'd rather not leave it in the boot of the car either."

"Of course. How long do you think you'll be?"

"Oh, hopefully no more than an hour," I told her.

I walked the short distance to the Inverness Town Hall and eventually found myself at the door to the Births, Deaths, and Marriages section.

I entered the room and found myself facing a dark wooden counter fronted by a middle-aged man with a sour expression. Taking a breath as if bracing myself, I stepped up to him.

I didn't really know why I was here. I just felt like I needed to see Dad's death certificate. I knew he drowned, but I wondered if there was anything more to it than that, and though I knew the certificate wouldn't really tell me anything, I wanted to be sure all the same.

"Afternoon," I said as cheerfully as I could, "I'd like to see the death certificate for Peter David Brennan of Kinlochbervie." I was surprised at how easily I'd been able to say that.

"I'll need to see some identification and the, ah, date of death," the man told me. I dutifully produced my driver's license and told him what he needed to know. After only the most cursory inspection, he asked me to repeat the information, which he wrote down on a pad before disappearing off amid the corridors of files.

I had been all ready to quote the 1994 Data Protection Act to him if he'd refused, but in fact, he was the picture of cordiality.

He returned a few minutes later with a thin manila folder. "That was quick," I said.

He smiled and laid the folder down before me. "There aren't too many Brennans in Sutherland. This is all there is. Your whole family in front of you. I'll leave you to it. There are seats and booths over there." He pointed behind me. "If you need anything, just tap the bell."

I thanked him and crossed the room to the nearest booth. Sitting down, I opened the folder. Straightaway I saw Dad's death certificate—obviously the most recent addition. I slipped it out and read through the neatly typed lines but found nothing. Just behind it was the coroner's report. I wasn't expecting to find this, but I suppose if the circumstances were anything but "normal," there would've had to have been an inquiry.

This was a little more informative. The official coroner's verdict was Death by Misadventure.

I suppose drowning is classed as misadventure.

I read on, and was surprised when I recognized the signature at the bottom. It was of Doctor Williamson, our local GP.

I made a few notes, then, with my curiosity getting the better of me, I leafed through the rest of the folder. It was all there, right the way back to a faded tatter of paper that was Padraig's death certificate. It was well beyond reading though, nothing more than a scrap of skin-thin parchment.

I felt a stab of pain as I saw a copy of my own marriage certificate to Bethy, and for a long moment, I just sat there looking at it.

I found Dad's birth and marriage documents, then sat back with a puzzled frown as I saw another with a name I didn't recognize.

It was a birth certificate for someone called Liam Brennan.

I racked my brain, but could remember no relations by that name. We weren't exactly a large family either. The date of birth was thirteen years earlier than my own father, and although Liam Brennan's father, John Brennan, had been my grandfather, I didn't recognize his mother, Mairéad.

There was no surname.

It took a moment to sink in, but then I realized Dad had a brother—well, a half brother.

Just for confirmation, I checked his own birth certificate, but his parents were definitely who I regarded as my grandparents: John and Maggie Brennan.

So who was Mairéad? And more importantly, who was Liam Brennan?

I spilled the contents of the entire file out onto the table, but could not find a death certificate for him. I did a quick mental calculation and put his age at eighty-one. So it was possible he could still be alive. Though he might have moved away and died elsewhere, in which case it was unlikely I'd ever find him.

I leafed through again, and as I had thought, there was no marriage certificate for John Brennan and Mairéad.

So Liam was born out of wedlock?

I wonder if my father even knew? And if he did, why did he keep it a secret?

Mairéad had given birth to the child in Sutherland, that much was clear, but where she had died (I was assuming she was dead, or else well into her late nineties, maybe more) was a mystery, as without a surname, I could not trace her.

I sat back in the uncomfortable wooden chair and ran my fingers through my hair. The musty room had become quite uncomfortable, and I wanted to leave as soon as possible.

In a shaky hand, I scribbled down as much as I thought appropriate, then returned the folder to the front desk. I could have got some photocopies, but I didn't really see the need. The gentleman asked if I had found what I had been looking for, and I could only nod.

Despite what I had discovered earlier, that evening I wandered the bothy like a child on the night before Christmas.

I'd left the shawl, wrapped in paper, on the small rock

about a dozen paces from the front door. I thought that if I'd left it inside, she might not have realized it was a gift. There was very little wind and the skies were clear tonight, so I knew it would not get wet or blow away.

I managed to sit down and practice steadily for several hours, and I replied to a couple of work-related calls, but despite my good mood, my heart wasn't really in anything I did.

I went to bed early, which was probably not a very good idea, as I lay there tossing until finally, only an hour or so after I had retired, I got up, flung on some clothes, and went out into the main room, crossing automatically to the window and looking out. The little package was still where I had left it, and the pale wrapping paper shone softly in the faint light from the window. I picked up my book and flumped down in one of the chairs by the fire and tried to read. Occasionally, I looked up from the pages to stare at the new painting. At first, I had wanted to fix it above the mantel, in the most prominent position, but I had thought that it might not have been a good idea over the heat of the fire, so I had put it on the wall opposite the door. When the light hit it just right, it looked like a third window, with a view out over the sea. It was an utterly beautiful piece of work, and I knew I'd never grow tired of looking at it.

Sighing, I leafed open the book to where I had marked the page and began to read halfheartedly.

My head snapped back, and my eyes opened.
    For a moment, the disorientation was so great that I didn't know where I was. The book I had been so disjointedly reading lay across my lap, the pages spread like

the wings of a gull. The fire was low, casting a subdued but still warming glow across me. I looked at the clock and was surprised when I saw it read twenty to three. It felt like I had been dozing for only a few moments.

I locked my fingers together and stretched my arms up over my head, groaning loudly as the stiffness reluctantly left my body. I carefully picked up the book, marked my place, and put it over on the table. I got up slowly and walked to the window, still flexing my arms, a big yawn distorting my face. Blinking like an owl, I looked out into the night, the corners of my mouth curling into a smile at what I saw.

The shawl was gone.

iv

The following day and night passed by without incident, but the morning after, I found a beautiful quartz crystal on the table next to my bed.

It caught the sunlight from the window and shattered it, sending the different-colored shards all over the room. As I lay there looking at the display, I once again marveled at her silence, her ability to come in here and stand this close without me waking. I'd always thought of myself as a light sleeper, starting at any sound, but I guess not that light.

I spent the morning tidying the bothy up a little, then I got ready for work. I had a small gig this evening in a pub near Wick, on the east coast. The drive there and back was probably going to take longer than the actual performance, but I didn't mind. I was also going to use the opportunity to check out a Brennan that was listed in that area's phone book. I'd tried ringing, but the man who had answered my call had been reluctant to talk to a complete stranger over the phone. There was very little chance that he was related, but it was something.

I took my time.

The roads were getting slippery, and there were occasional patches of black ice that slewed the wheels momentarily. I drove distractedly; I was a little disappointed that my lead had turned out to be nothing—the man in question was the son of an Irishman who had only crossed the sea a dozen years back, and was therefore no relation. I would be a liar to say that I hadn't been getting my hopes up.

But what occupied me more on the trip home was the inklings of a tune beating around in my head, and when I eventually returned home late that night, I left the figurine out on the rock and sat at the table writing. It was the first music I actually *finished* composing for a long time. The melody seemed perfect, a beautiful counterpoint to the landscape around me and the feeling in my heart. I found myself frequently gazing at the painting for inspiration as I searched for a note or phrase.

Eventually it was to be my one truly personal gift to her.

The items continued to be exchanged.

Not every night, but with fair frequency during the following week. I think out of all the presents she gave to me, my favorite was a flat piece of driftwood that she left propped up against the side of my bed one morning. It must've been a beach find, and though I'd heard stories of people who'd found things similar, I'd never seen anything like it myself. Roughly two feet long and about eight inches wide, the wood was made up of two shattered planks still joined together. The wood was completely saturated but still firm to the touch, as if it had only recently been submerged. The waters of the sea had colored the timbers nearly black, but the numbers and scraps of flowing script were still quite visible.

sti 1669

I had no idea what the name of the ship had been (I'd tried to look up wrecks known around that date or later, but there were so many different possibilities on the name, and as the old librarian had told me, the vessel may never have even been listed as lost). The letters of the name had obviously continued on from another piece of the wreck, and though my curiosity was piqued, I knew it would remain forever an enigma. I often wondered if it was connected to the heavy gold doubloon that she had once left near the range. Of course there were rumors of a Spanish galleon that ran aground near here centuries ago, but then you find those rumors wherever you find fishermen.

I placed the gift up on one of the beams, carefully securing it with thin nails. It seemed very appropriate there.

V

It began to rain.

Starting as a fine drizzle late in the afternoon, the vast shapes that hung in the sky out to sea seemed to assemble, then decide to move inextricably toward land, the heavy rain trailing below them like a thick black gauze. It washed over me vehemently as I stepped down from the Land

Rover, lashing at the grass and sheathing the trees and rocks with a heavy coat of water. With the weather so inclement I knew there was little chance of her visiting to-night.

The surface of the gray sea was stippled and untrue, and the white-capped waves that broke against the shore were tall, strong, and resentful. I walked slowly, deliberately, through the wall of water that the sky spat hatefully down onto me. Reaching the solace of the cottage, I thundered inside, banging the door shut moodily. The water dribbled off my waxed jacket, seeking the joins in the stone floor at my feet.

With the sun long gone and a small fire flickering before me, I sat in a chair next to the window, looking out longingly.

A single finger tapped a dull tattoo against the old, thick glass, a counterpoint to the churning murmur of the tide that continued on regardless of my moods. The rain had not eased, and far away, occasionally visible to me, sudden streaks of white lightning would stagger down from the sky. The crofter's cottage smelled strongly of earth, stone, and smoldering wood, and the base aromas were somehow comforting and welcoming in their complexity, bringing me slowly out from the darkness. I was no longer as angry as I had been, but rather just disappointed and morose. I thought about playing some music, but my hands were still stiff and cold, and I knew there would be no hiding behind a tune. I'd settled into a deliciously melancholy mood, neither truly sad nor completely at ease, but one worthy of a musician or a writer all the same.

Sighing, I once more rubbed the glass free of condensation and looked back through the square of window. Outside, the storm raged on, lightning illuminating the scene from the shore to the horizon like a photo flash. Thunder rumbled down the glen, building slowly, then finishing in a climatic shatter that rattled the windows. The wind chased down the chimney, howling gleefully around the fire while the flames fought on, clinging to the wood tenaciously with fragile amber fingers.

I crossed to the grate and laid a couple more of the split logs over the flaring embers, sending a shiver of sparks cascading upward. I poured myself another glass of red wine and resumed my vigil by the window. I didn't really expect to see anything, but I had always liked watching storms, and I had nothing else to do. For a time I considered venturing out into the wet and starting up the generator, so that I might listen to some music, but that idea passed as quickly as it came; I knew the rain would soak me to the skin as soon as I passed over the threshold and besides, it was more atmospheric just sitting here with the flickering fire and the bobbing flames of the candles.

I held the glass loosely as I sipped slowly, feeling each mouthful warm me inside. The sky was split by another bolt of electricity and . . .

I saw something, down on the beach!

Sitting up suddenly, I furiously wiped at the pane while I blindly fumbled the goblet down onto the table. The thunder shook the house, and my ill-balanced glass crashed to the floor, smashing into a thousand glittering splinters and spraying wine everywhere. I barely registered the noise, so intent was I on the beach.

I waited, almost holding my breath for the next flash. When it came, it was so bright it hurt my eyes and made me start with its sudden vehemence, but I saw the figure down there, standing still.

Waiting for me.

The image stayed with me, burned onto the backs of my retinas like a negative. Without bothering to put on a coat, I dashed out into the storm.

My mind became a blur; the only thought I could seriously keep focused was of her. Within seconds I was drenched. The teeming sheets of rain saturated my jumper, seeping through to stick to my skin. My jeans took a little longer, but I can honestly say that by the time I jumped off the belt of grass onto the sand, I was as wet as if I had dived into a pool.

I drew to a halt, digging my feet into the sand. I tore off my useless glasses, stuffing them into my pocket as I waited for the next flash. When it came, I saw that she had moved from the rock, and was standing on the breakwater, only two dozen yards or so from where I was. My vision blurred from the rain and lack of aid, I looked at her steadily. Although I could barely make out the detail, I knew, I *felt* her regarding me.

For the briefest of moments, the storm died around us; the wind dropped to a shallow murmur, the rain eased, and the thunder abated. My head was spinning a little, whether from the wine or the situation, I did not know. I brushed the water from my eyes and scraped back my sodden hair, not knowing if I should approach. For a long moment we stood like that, facing each other across the sand. I could tell that she was again wearing only the long dress—how could she not be cold?—and somehow I could tell her feet were bare. I thought that I could smell her, the bite of the sea and the aroma of jasmine.

I took a tentative step toward her, my hands held forward at waist height as I asked, "Who *are* you?"

The wind picked up, almost as if it were carrying my words to her. She said nothing, then—with a wondrous sound that will always live in my memory—she laughed.

And ran.

Without hesitation, I followed.

She was like a wild animal, elegant, swift, and impossibly graceful, and as I lumbered after her, I called out for her to stop, knowing full well that she wouldn't.

The chase had begun.

The storm, fed up with being just a spectator, renewed its fury almost as soon as I took my first step. The rain belted down, painfully lashing against my skin like a lead-tipped whip. It flicked into my eyes like a hundred angry fingers while the wind tugged at my hair and snarled in my ears. The waves pummeled the shore mercilessly, sending sheets of spray into the air to fall as mist. The waters of the Minch rode up the sands swiftly, engulfing my ankles as I ran, seemingly reluctant to let go, as if it wanted to pull me into its inky world. The sand clung to my boots, weighting my steps so that speed became impossible. I shouted to her again as she left the beach, jumping effortlessly onto the rocks, then leaping over to the grass on the other side.

I pulled myself up as best I could. My lungs were burning with the exertion of sprinting, and my body, fueled by the chase, had burned away the chill. Heaving, I scrambled onto the highest of the boulders and stopped for a moment, fearful that she had lost me.

But no, there she was, standing waiting a little way ahead. I took a step forward and slipped, falling heavily onto my knee. I heard the fabric of my trousers rip and felt a sudden hot iron of pain as the rock tore my skin, then I was up and jumping onto the grass. I fell again, my boots skidding on the waterlogged slope, and as I scrambled to my feet, she started away again. It was as if she were teasing me; letting me get close only to dash my hopes like the sea against the cliff. I heard her laughing, and the merry sound fired me to greater efforts. I ran as if I were possessed. Time ceased to have any meaning as I hurtled first up the hill, then down the valley. I had no idea where I was, or where we were heading, and I didn't care.

Only she existed for me now, the woman and the storm that bellowed around us almost encouragingly.

I was caked with heavy mud, from the sticky mass of my hair down to the insides of my boots, but still I ran on. The sky split wide, spewing forth a great serrated bolt of lightning that shattered somewhere off to my left while the clouds laughed thunder down on me. In some small, rational part of my mind I realized the delay between the sound and the vision was growing as the storm passed over us and headed inland. The torrent of rain had eased off too, falling down steady and insistent, rather than a deluge.

I couldn't stop myself as I reached the bottom of the steep glen, such was my momentum, and with arms wheeling like windmills, I fell headlong into a small brook. The water hit me, a shard-filled slap in the face, and as I reflexively breathed in, I sucked down an improbable amount. I coughed violently, retching hard as the exertions of the last . . . hours? caught up with me. I clutched at the sudden cramps in my stomach and vomited peaty water.

I fell back onto the slick and saturated banks of the small stream, the back of my hand across my eyes, utterly exhausted, spent.

When I removed my arm, I saw her, standing on the other side of the brook, her arms by her sides, watching me.

For a moment, I either didn't grasp it, or I didn't care, so ruined was I by the pursuit. When I had once again rubbed the mud and water from my eyes, she was still there, as motionless as an effigy, and as enigmatic. I pushed myself up onto my elbows, and gradually got to my feet. I reached into my pocket for my glasses, hoping they had not been damaged, and with an inward sigh of relief I rubbed them as clean as I could and slipped them on. I needed to see her, not just a vague outline or a shape against the water as she had been before.

I could finally make out her face, her eyes. She was all I had imagined, all I had drawn, in my mind, my journal, and my heart.

She seemed smaller than I thought; diminutive but not tiny, but there was an air of strength about her, a feeling not unlike that of the land or the sea. Her face was pale, almost alabasterine in the frail light, and fine-featured, a delicate nose, cheeks, and chin surrounding lips that looked almost violet. Her hair, cut short and feathered to about the level of her neck, *was* shot through with gold, and it contrasted dramatically with the deep titian shade of the rest. How I could see so much I don't know, for the moon was only just beginning to warily peek out from behind a break in the clouds far to the west, but I did. To me, she was as vivid as if I viewed her on a summer's day. Her smell was strong, almost primal, as if she lived wild. It was both uncomfortable and intoxicating at the same time.

But it was her eyes that held me.

In one total moment of clarity, our gazes knitted together. Large and unblinking, she looked down on me with eyes the color of the waves breaking on the shore, of the sun on wet grass. There was power there, behind her stare, fathomless beauty and an unremitting strength that threatened to break me, to dash me helpless against the stone.

But despite the hardness, there was recognition. Like playing our ethereal duet, or when she had caught me watching her dance, I saw something else in her eyes. Doorways opened, doorways into the past and into the future, of lives gone and those to come. I surrendered wordlessly to her, all thoughts of my personality gone in an instant as she reached out and took my heart and humanity.

She blinked, slowly and deliberately, and the cord between us was momentarily severed. Pain flashed in my skull, like the splinter of a headache; it drummed in time with my pulse, the punishment for running so hard. I squeezed my eyes shut briefly, trying to banish the discomfort.

When I looked up again she hadn't moved. The rain hissed around us, between us, everywhere, gradually dying. To my right, which I suppose was east, forks of lightning still stabbed at the land. My breathing sounded irregular, laborious, and impossibly loud in my ears, while she seemed barely out of breath.

I cleared my throat, and in a voice little more than a whisper, I asked, "What's your name?"

For a long moment she stood, just contemplating me, and I thought that she would once again flee—and this time I was in no state to follow.

I nearly jumped when she spoke. Her voice was as musical and clear as her singing. For the slightest of instants, I didn't understand her, then something in my brain registered.

She was speaking Gaelic!

It had been a long time since I had used the language of

the Western Isles, and though I knew it, I wondered at my
fluency. Taking a breath, I rephrased the question and
asked her again.

Her eyes blinked—almost with surprise, it seemed, and
taking on a seemingly mischievous air, she replied, "There
is a magic in the giving . . ."

"Slower, *please,* it's been a . . . long time."

She fixed me with another stare, and started again, at a
gentler pace this time.

"Why should I trust you enough to give you my name?"
Her voice sounded so rich and vibrant to me. It felt so right
that she should speak Gaelic.

I swallowed, not really expecting the question. Phrasing
my answer carefully, I replied clumsily, "I thought the trust
was already there . . . you"—I struggled for a moment—
"left me gifts . . . the flower, the shell. . . ."

She shrugged (at least she could understand me).

"Please," I almost pleaded, "won't you just tell me your
name? I'm Richard, Richard Brennan. But I guess you already know that."

She just looked at me, boring into my head with those
eyes, then, like the breath of the wind across the water, she
said, "I am Ailish."

The silence between us was palpable, uncomfortable; as
thick as the rain had been only moments before. I wanted
so desperately to break through it, but I didn't know what
to say. Instead I drank her down, savoring every detail,
from the slight eddying of her wet hair to the simple brown
spun dress that rippled gently about her slim frame like a
loose robe. Eventually, with my courage returning, I asked,
"Who *are* you?"

She smiled, a just perceptible turning up at the corners
of her mouth, and took a couple of steps backward. I

knew she was going to leave, but I made no effort to stop her.

I didn't expect her to reply, but halfway up the slope of the glen she stopped and said, "I am who you would want me to be."

There was nothing at all subservient in the way she spoke those words, but instead there was an undercurrent of mocking running deep in her voice.

Then, with another humor-filled, tinkering laugh, she lifted the dark, rain-stained hem of her dress clear of the grass and walked purposefully from view.

I kept her in sight as long as I could, and though I was tempted, something stopped me from once again following.

16

With the western sky pinking, the sun set slowly, brushing the last of the fleeing rain clouds with a rosy lambency, as if there were soft bulbs inside the swells of each.

The sky above me was a depthless violet, the wondrous halfway tint between night and day. Almost breathless with anticipation, I paced the beach, kicking at stones and driftwood while I waited.

When I could delay no longer, I went back inside to fetch my fiddle. It sat on the table, where I had left it earlier, surrounded by scattered sheets of music manuscript, all scrawled over with my spidery writing. Notes and rests danced across the parchment-colored paper, to the untrained eye in a seeming random fashion; but to me, to lift one of the pages to my eyes was to hear music in my soul.

I left the papers where they lay—their job was done now, and, taking up my instrument, I hurried back outside. Tuning it briefly, I crossed the soft sand down to where I had sat before, amid the dark outlines of the rocks. At first, I had thought to play the piece in the open, sitting in the very middle of the beach, but then I recalled her predilection for shadows, so I moved down to the dark amid the mermaid rocks.

I took a deep breath and prepared myself, hoping I could remember all of the tune. As I looked out over the indigo blue of the late evening sea, I tightened the frog on my bow and wondered what might happen. I was filled with a kind of tingling expectation as the magic gathered in my hands and mind. Above me, a sky only slightly lighter than the waters of the Minch shone with the beginnings of a star-scattered night, and a heavy, sodden moon was gradually lifting into the sky. The wind was frigid and keen, and as it hushed past my ears I sensed that it too was waiting as it lingered around the bay.

The night was so alive with sounds and shadows. Apart from the usual lulling rhythm of the sea, there was a whispered, almost hypnotic anticipation abounding across the land. For a short time I just sat there, back against the rock while my long legs stretched out before me, drinking in the life, the heartbeat of the bay. The tide was completely out, and the tiny shingle it had uncovered was a stark, vivid contrast to the gently glowing sand of the rest of the beach. The small stones shone a deep black in the ethereal light, adding yet more atmosphere to the already fey scene.

Sighing slightly, I once more checked the tuning on my fiddle. The sky was completely dark now, like an infinitely pinpricked wafer sheet of jet paper before a light. The sea lapped at the last of the shore, content to sit back and watch for a time.

I itched my cheek, having a quick look around me before I began proper. I could see nothing but the ghost-lit hills, the faint glow from the windows of the bothy, and the gentle sparkle from the thin ribbon of stream coming from the out-of-sight lake.

Resting my bow against the first string, I closed my eyes and gently drew back my arm, issuing out a pure and unbroken note, a call. The fingers of my left hand began to walk slowly over the fingerboard, sometimes pausing to spin out some vibrato or slide into a note. The air was filled with the perfect sound, a melody as pure and unbroken as the mirror that glided away in front of me.

How long I played for I couldn't really say. The piece I had written lasted just over ten minutes, but as I played it in its entirety, it went on much longer as I discovered variations within the music. It was an odd work, neither traditional folk nor classical, but rather a mysterious blend of the two.

With my eyes closed, my other four senses were enhanced greatly. The metal of the strings tried to bite into the calluses on the pads of my fingers, but to no avail, while the wood of the bow was content just to be held lightly. I could feel my hair flicking over my face, and the oddly comforting tingle of the wind on my cheeks. My nose and mouth were afire, not only with the brumal air but with the myriad fragrances and tastes that danced on the breeze as if to the music while the wind murmured its reassurances to me.

I played on, opening my eyes while a smile crept over my face; Ailish was there, somewhere, watching, listening.

I couldn't say how I knew; I had neither heard her approach nor smelled her fragrance, but I knew just the same. My playing renewed its vigor as I tried to squeeze all of the emotion from the instrument and from myself. The melody flowed well, and I thought it had captured the essence of her spirit as I perceived it.

I finished, drawing out the last note for as long as I could, then I lowered the fiddle to my lap and let out a

long breath, as if wearied. The moon was high now, suspended in the black like a silver medallion, and the shaft
of phosphorent light that reached out across the water was
brilliant and almost dazzling.

"Good evening, Ailish," I said softly, carefully phrasing
the Gaelic.

For a moment, I heard no reply, then, gently, like the
stirring shingle, "Hello, Richard." Her voice was halting,
but not nervous, unlike mine.

She was somewhere behind me, perhaps on the rocks.
Her use of my name sent a slow shiver down my spine,
and though I longed to turn and look at her, I resisted the
desire.

Swallowing dryly, I hesitated a moment, then asked,
"Did you like the tune? I wrote it for you."

Again, the unendurable quiet. "Very beautiful. It reminded me of home," she said after a moment.

"And where is home?" I inquired, trying to keep my
voice calm and unfaltered but not believing I was actually
having a conversation with her.

"Close by," she said, noncommittally. "Why do you not
look for me tonight?"

I think I could sense amusement in her tone, and, smiling, I replied toward the sea, "Because I fear you may run
away again."

When the laugh came, it was from a different place, further away to my right. "You are wise," she teased.

I finally lost control, turned my head, and saw her standing on the beach. To my delight, she had the shawl
wrapped around her narrow shoulders.

"Won't you stay?" I called after her, getting to my feet
slowly but making no movement toward her.

"Not tonight," was her reply. Did I detect a trace of disappointment in her voice?

"Do you like your shawl?" I asked, desperately trying to find a spark of conversation so that she would remain a while longer.

She gripped the corners of the wrap, absently pulling it tighter around her. "Thank you," she said shortly. "It is very warm."

Then I did something foolish.

I was feeling heady, euphoric almost, and I began to walk toward her. Immediately she took two steps backward, then turned and ran a short way. I stopped, angry at myself but reassured when she too halted and spun round to look at me again. I knifed a few notes of the fiddle, and my heart soared when she raised her hand in good-bye. I lifted my bow in a salute, smiling broadly as she continued along the beach at a slow walk. Part of me wanted to follow her, but I also knew that to do so would be to jeopardize what had been accomplished.

I watched her disappear into the darkness at the end of the beach, then with another long sigh, I made my way back to the welcome warmth of the bothy. "I guess I'm not that wise," I said to myself as I closed the door on the darkness.

17

Slowly, and with a steadfast resolution that rivaled the sea wearing away at the cliffs, I came to know the intense, delphic Ailish.

At first, she would only appear to me down near the beach, near the sea, and only at night; never when I expected it. Whenever she was close, the hairs on the back of my neck would rise, stiffen, as if she gave off a slight charge.

At the beginning, we conversed little, and I was content just to sit outside, wrapped in my heavy coat against the chill, and play music for her. Sometimes, I would hear her singing and once, very early in the morning, I had seen her dancing a second time, and although the image was filled with magic and wonder, it lacked that unexplainable element that had been there at first. No, that's not right, the power was still there, I think it was just that I knew I was the intended audience this time, not an uninvited peeping Tom. But then, looking back, perhaps the first dance had been intentional too.

I know we communicated far more deeply with our multitude of tiny gestures, looks, and feelings than most would with plain speech. I still gabbled away, my mouth often running away from me as I fought to contain my emotions by covering them up with idle banter. It's odd, but before I had met Ailish, I was always thought of as a close-mouthed person—I really didn't like filling up the spaces in conversation with random talk, but now. . . . Still, my verbosity didn't seem to concern Ailish at all. If anything, she encouraged me to talk all the more, and would sit listening to me with her face painted with patient interest and curiosity.

I could tell she was becoming more accustomed to me, not so wary and certainly a lot less skittish. But Ailish was still very much an enigma, and though we did talk, I never managed to glean as much from her as she seemed to coax from me. She was continually eclipsed by shadows; both her physical form and her speech, so much so that I really had to rely on my mind to sketch in the finer details of her character.

An arcane reek clung about her, a tantalizing mystery that I came no closer to solving during the very beginnings of our . . . friendship. There were many meetings that I could go into detail about, as each was uniquely precious to me. They are like a scattering of bright diamonds against the black backdrop of my past, like softly blinking stars in a summer sky. They're all constantly replaying in my head, particularly as I lie in bed at that foggy juncture between sleep and wake. At those times, fantasy takes over, and I would imagine myself closing the gap between us, touching her cool skin, kissing her lips . . .

I think it was the twenty-sixth of November, it was certainly a Sunday, and as I shrugged the heavy blankets and duvet off myself, I hurriedly got dressed, my bare feet burning on the cold flagstones.

Absently, as I gingerly walked into the bathroom, I berated myself for not buying more throw rugs. Still, I supposed there would be a little more time to go to town before I was cut off completely. The water I hastily splashed over my face was as cold as the floor, and by the time I had briskly rubbed myself dry on the towel, I was fully awake. Entering the kitchen, I found I was looking forward to being isolated with a mixture of excitement and dread. Would Ailish still come to see me in the heavy winter months? Logic suggested that there would be no way for her to get through the snows, but my heart seemed to think somehow she would.

I cursed under my breath as I saw that the range had gone out over the night. The heavy iron door was cold to the touch, but inside, the ashes were still warm, though by no means hot enough to relight. Sighing, I fetched the brush and pail and cleaned out the interior, sweeping the flakes of burnt wood and detritus into the bucket before arranging the fresh splints and faggots around the smelly white square of fire lighter. The small block caught on the first match, and fairly rapidly the flames ate through the twigs and began hungrily licking at the larger pieces of wood. I shut the door, peering for a moment through the thick glass porthole to make sure the flames took. When I was satisfied, I stood up, brushing my hands down my jeans. Crossing the room, I found the fire in the grate still throbbing dimly, and it took me next to no time to get it going again. When I had finished, I finally set a pot of water to boil and glanced around.

The winter sunlight that streamed through the windows was brilliant, almost dazzling, and I padded over to the front door, intent on letting some in despite the brumal air. Pressing my thumb down on the latch, I stepped back as the door swung in toward me. For a moment, I didn't realize who it was I was looking at; then, like the clown in a comedy film, understanding dawned with a sudden jolt. I blinked like an awoken owl in the bright sunlight, totally surprised. A shard of cold glided up my spine that had nothing to do with the outside temperature.

"Good morning, Richard," Ailish said softly.

I stayed where I was, too surprised to even think about moving toward her. "Good morning," I replied haltingly, leaning against the doorjamb. She was sitting on the small boulder where I had left her gifts. Facing me, she was casually leaning forward, her legs slightly apart and her elbows resting lightly on top of her knees. Her hands hung down loose between, playing slightly (nervously?) with a slight hole in her dress. She looked up at me, the long curve of her neck accented by the position.

Ailish looked to be at ease, but I knew how mercurial she could be, so I made no move. This was the first time I had seen her during the day. That fact struck me like a blow, and in the instant before I spoke again, my memory took a snapshot of her, a picture that I knew I would carry with me forever. Comparing her in sunlight to how I knew her during the night, there was only one difference that I could pick out. Her lips were no longer violet, they were a deep crimson red, and they were struck to color against her skin like blood drops on snow.

Her face was set in a neutral expression, though as always, I thought I could detect a slight trace of sardonic humor about the corners of her mouth. Her hair fluttered around her face, framing the pale oval with an ever-changing shift of red and gold that was mesmerizing. The almost unnatural tints of her hair were made even more vibrant by the flat gray of the sea behind her. Her skin was still translucent, almost as white as the sunlight on a stream, but her eyes shone green, like bottomless pools. Ailish was still wearing the (what I assume was the same) plain, rust-colored dress, and it feathered about her ankles, sometimes lifting slightly to reveal a slender calf lightly dusted with fine, downy hair. My shawl hugged her shoulders loosely, not fully wrapped but hanging like a rough cloak. As she sat, leaning forward, I couldn't help but notice how the dress fell away under her neck, revealing the beginnings to her small breasts. A thrill ran through me, both of excitement and shame, and I quickly pulled my eyes away. I knew she was fully aware of my scrutiny, but it didn't seem to bother her in the slightest. If anything, I think it amused her.

For a moment, I struggled for what to say. It had completely fazed me, seeing her here like this, and I was at a loss.

"Would you like to come in?" I asked, my voice sounding frail and weak in my ears. I gestured inside as she looked at me steadily, before shaking her head slightly.

"Thank you, no. Not yet."

"But you came in before," I said, frowning. "Why not now?"

She shrugged her slight shoulders, an odd movement as the look she gave me was anything but vacillating. "That was . . . different," she told me finally.

The look of bewilderment was evident on my face. She would creep in during the night while I was asleep, but refused a proper invitation? "Would you like some tea? Some coffee? . . ." As if on cue, the kettle I had left on the stove top began to whistle shrilly. I began to feel the panic building in me. The rising conflict of whether to stay here with her or stop the bansheelike wail and risk her disappearance was terrible. I held out a hand toward her, one finger pointing up in a slight gesture of pleading. "Please, don't go. I'll just stop the . . . stay there, okay? I won't be a . . ." I almost danced on the threshold with indecision, and as I nipped back inside, I thought I saw a slight smile on her face.

As quickly as I could, I grabbed another mug from the shelf and tossed a tea bag in. The tea I fixed us was hurried and weak, and as I made my way back to the door, it sloshed over the rims of the cups, burning my fingers.

She was still there, sitting on the rock with one leg drawn up under her now, arms wrapped tightly around it as if she were feeling the chill. I stopped at the door, not knowing if I should try and approach.

"Are you cold?" I asked, looking at her pose.

Ailish shook her head. "No," she replied quickly. "I like this weather."

I shrugged slightly, thinking of how much I normally wore when I was just puttering around the cottage. The conflict of whether or not to walk over and hand her the mug was almost painful. Ailish regarded me quizzically, and, taking a deep breath, I strode toward her.

"Here, I made you a cup of tea. Well, it's more of a mug really and I doubt if it'll be any good but . . ." I reined in my mouth as I was beginning to ramble. I had also forgotten to speak Gaelic.

The distance closed between us until we were near enough to touch. Her scent was nearly overpowering, a complex mix of night flowers and her own musk. There was a silent, almost static moment as I stood over her offering the mug, my fingers aflame from holding it around the rim, then her slim hand slowly rose to grip the handle. I released it and lingered a moment, lost in the emerald of her eyes.

I stepped back, returning to the safety of the doorway.

I watched her tentatively lift the mug to her lips. It was almost as if she had not drunk tea before. Perhaps she was just as nervous as I. She took a sip and winced, making a slight noise and looking at me with a rueful expression.

"It is hot," she said, rubbing her lips with her fingers.

Instantly, I made an apologetic face and replied, "It's powdered milk, I'm afraid. I don't have a fridge and it's a long way to the farm."

She frowned, looking at the light brown liquid almost suspiciously before taking another taste—carefully this time. She smiled as she lowered the mug. "It is good."

I frowned with mock consternation. "Not that good," I replied. "You should try one of my Irish coffees."

"Coffee?"

My eyebrows shot up. "You've not had coffee before?" Ailish shook her head, once more taking a cautious sip. I suppose her not having tasted coffee wasn't all that un- likely—we were living in one of the remotest places in the British Isles. I'd known people here who had quite seriously never seen a television—not that that's any great loss. The steam from our mugs misted in the air, mingling with our breath. I squinted in the sunlight. "You're in for a treat. Next time . . ." I left the sentence hanging, not wishing to seem too presumptuous.

"Next time," she agreed quietly.

ii

That night I saw the drowned man again.

I don't know whether I dreamed of him because it had been such a remarkable day, or if it was just a coincidence. Actually, for that matter, I'm not entirely sure I was even asleep.

I had been lying in bed, my mind skittering over a thousand details of the day, from the color of Ailish's eyes down to every word we'd spoken, when I saw him, standing in the deep dark at the foot of my bed.

It was one of those terrible visions one is haunted by from childhood, the monster in the bedroom, and my ghoul was as real to me then as any.

I saw the outline of his head, his shoulders first as I lay there gazing at the ceiling, but when I actually took up the courage to move my eyes and look at him, I could no longer make him out. I stared, opening my eyes as wide as I dared in the inky night, but he was gone; yet as soon as I moved my head, I could see him, skirting the very fringes of my consciousness. I began to tremble, a cold, slimy sweat breaking out over my brow and body. I blinked, looking directly at him again, but . . .

Gone.

The stink was there too, but less demanding than the first time, more like the sickly tang of passing a fishmonger's.

I began to wonder if I was just imagining it.

I have, in my younger years, had occasions where I have woken in my bed in the small hours, sure that whoever had been visiting me for dinner or the like was still there in the house and that I had rudely fallen asleep. The feeling usually only lasted a few moments, before reality gradually caught up with me; so perhaps, in a couple more heart-beats, I would suddenly realize that I was looking at the outline of my dressing gown or a peculiar shadow from the window.

As I turned away I distinctly caught the glimmer of the weak moonlight on something metallic.

A gold earring.

I swallowed and turned on my side, squeezing my eyes closed and trying not to imagine him crossing the floor to stand over me while I was sleeping. Childishly, I pulled the covers up over my chin, and turned my thoughts to Ailish, as if her memory could drive the demon from my room.

Somehow, it worked, and I slept.

18

Four days later, and I saw her sitting on a rock just the other side of where the stream cuts through the sands to the sea.

It didn't take me long to discover she was there, waiting. I came out of the front door with the pail full of warm ashes and almost immediately I felt the hairs on the back on my neck chill. I put down my load and turned with a boyish smile on my face. When I saw her I waved, then gestured for her to wait. Dashing inside, I fixed us two cups of tea from the pot that was still hot under the cozy, and crossed the sands to where she waited patiently. For a time I wondered if I was indeed supposed to approach her, but she made no move to leave, and after the . . . friendliness of the other day, well, I was buoyant.

"I brought you another tea," I said in Gaelic, offering her the cup handle-first. She took it, sniffed a few times, then took a sip, carefully again.

Neither of us spoke, then, "Would you like to walk?" Ailish asked.

Surprised beyond words, I could only nod. She gracefully slipped off the rock, still holding her tea, and began strolling toward the steep escarpment at the north end of the beach. Still not believing what was happening, I followed anxiously, not even having the sense to shut the door.

We walked north for about an hour, talking about many different topics. I found her surprisingly forthcoming, yet still withdrawn about certain things like exactly where she lived. I didn't push her. I was fearful that the thin thread of our friendship would snap if I tried to gather it too close. I felt like she gave me enough anyway, more in fact, than I really needed. I only wanted to know *her*. As we walked, she was careful not to stray too close to me, but there was almost a sense of her *wanting* to. I knew it would only be a matter of time; from the glances she would occasionally throw my way and by the slight flames of warmth in her voice. Her voice. Its tone sent cascading ripples of delight through my body like some illicit drug. As I followed her, my eyes stroked across her back like a caress, savoring every movement of her body like a miser storing gold.

With the empty mug hanging loosely from her hand, Ailish stopped, waiting a moment for me to catch up, then pointed. "Do you know the Bay of Keisgaig?" she asked, looking down the small ravine at the rock-strewn beach, barely more than a break in the cliffs. I nodded, lowering my hands onto my knees as I puffed.

"The Bay of Seals," she said quietly, her words being taken by the gusting wind.

"Is that the translation?" I asked, my breath still catching.

Ailish shook her head. "No. It is just what it's called by some." She turned to me and smiled, an expression that was as pure as the sheet of blue sky above us. "Come 'long," she told me, starting off toward the gully that ran steeply down to the bay. I groaned and pushed myself upright, my attempt at sufferance going unnoticed. Tired, but feeling better than I had for years, I left my long-empty cup at the top and followed after.

I marveled at Ailish's agility. Not once did she dislodge a rock as we made our way toward the sea. I clattered down the stony defile like an avalanche, my footing unsure and clumsy as I tried to imitate her pace. In the end, I realized that she wasn't going to run away, and there was no real need for my haste, so I slowed, picking my way carefully amid the small pebbles. The thought of being stranded here with a broken ankle was quite prominent in my mind.

The bay itself was a deep, desolate crescent guarded on either side by rearing faces of angry, broken cliffs that looked nothing short of intimidating. There was no beach as such, only a patch of ground where the stones became smaller where the sea broke upon them. The noise of the waves against the rocks was booming, almost frightening, as the sound reverberated around the sheltered bay.

I caught up with Ailish, who had stopped about fifty feet from the sea. She was standing still, looking down to the water with an unreadable expression on her face. I stood next to her, acutely aware of the closeness of our bodies, and asked, "What is it?"

Slowly, she pointed. I followed her direction, looking at the mass of rounded stones down near the breaking waves. I was about to ask her again what it was we were looking at, when one of the stones moved.

They were dozens of seals.

Even though I'd spent a great deal of my life here, I'd never seen them this close before. Usually, they were just bobbing heads out to sea, or distant basking cows seen through binoculars, but this . . .

The images from my dreams passed fleetingly through my mind, but danced away suddenly as Ailish began to walk toward the seals. I raised my hand to stop her—I didn't want to disturb them, not when they were this close, but she merely turned, halting my action with an expression akin to reassurance. Boldly, she walked down to where they lay, warming their bodies in the brief winter sun. As she stepped up onto the slight ledge that ran out into the water, heads raised, muzzles sniffing the air warily but without apparent distress. I was holding my breath; could they really be that tame?

She knelt down by the nearest, reached out, and laid a hand on its head. Her skin stood out in stark contrast to the mottled brown flesh of the mammal. The seal's eyes blinked slowly, and it raised its head a little like a dog might.

"If you walk slow, he may let you approach," Ailish told me, her voice subdued and soft, but still carrying over the shattering waves. I swallowed down my apprehension and willed my legs to move. The herd (was that the right term?) must've numbered about twenty-five or thirty, and as my clumsy feet crunched over the loose shingle, they raised their heads as one to regard me with those depthless, impossibly intelligent eyes. For some reason I was afraid. I felt as if I were trespassing, that this bay was not meant for humans. I could feel the distrust emanating from the animals, and as I neared Ailish, I asked anxiously, "Are you sure it's all right?"

She nodded, still patting the massive bull. They were much bigger than I had imagined, almost the size of cattle, and as I neared the place where Ailish crouched, I felt the stare of the ancient seal boring into me—so similar to the way Ailish's did!

"Come here," Ailish said, nodding to the place beside her. "Now, reach out your hand slowly."

With a face filled with wonder, I did as I was asked. The bull murmured slightly as I put my hand down onto him, and Ailish kept whispering unintelligible words in his ear. The seal's skin was tough and leathery, but surprisingly warm and oddly comforting. Despite the layers of protective fat, I could feel the power in him. The others watched dispassionately, sometimes snorting. The stink of fish was almost overpowering, but I did my best to ignore it, so enthralled was I by being this close to a wild creature. I continued to stroke the seal, my hand circling up toward the small apertures that were its ears. My fingers brushed over Ailish's hand. The contact was tentative at best, but we both looked up, and I wasn't sure who was the most alarmed. For a long moment, we just looked at each other. The touch had been unconscious, but I was fully aware of the softness of her skin, and the slight tingle that had run through my veins at the first contact. I opened my mouth to speak, to perhaps apologize . . .

There was a sudden bark, and as one, the herd started. The great bodies heaved into the water, falling off the ledge like tumbling rocks. The bull shuffled away from us, its body rippling as it made for the safety of the ocean. I snatched my hand back, suddenly fearful, my heart beating in my ears as the tension was broken. Within moments they were gone, and not even the low dome of a head appeared out in the water.

Ailish laughed, a light, amused sound that banished the alarm from me instantly. I found myself grinning like a fool. We crouched there for a while longer, listening to the dull roar of the ocean, each terribly aware of the other, then, like the seals, we stood as one and without a word, began the slow climb back up to the cliff top.

ii

The last time I had seen him, Doctor Iain Williamson had been a small, balding man of advancing years.

He had one of those "doctorly" faces that instantly put him out from the crowd as someone to trust. He'd been our family GP since before I was born—in fact his late wife, Miriam, had been the district midwife and had delivered both me and Florence. So as I sat in his waiting room, I felt an odd sense of déjà vu.

His surgery was just off the main street of Kinlochbervie, situated in a wonderful old building that still somehow managed to smell like a house rather than a place for the sick. Sea scenes dominated the walls of the waiting room, and there was a small coffee table that was positively toppling under the weight of old magazines. There was one other person in the room with me, a young woman whom I neither knew nor recognized. As was typical of waiting rooms, we studiously ignored one another while secretly trying to guess what was wrong with each other.

I didn't have to wait long. Although the woman had been here when I arrived, the nurse-cum-receptionist came out through the door and called my name. I was about to tell her I would be willing to wait a while longer when she handed the other woman a prescription and she left.

The nurse ushered me through into a room that looked not to have changed since my childhood. About the size of an average living room, the surgery was dominated by a huge oak desk that had probably sat there since the construction of the house. The walls were lined with book-shelves and several glass-fronted cabinets that contained a variety of weird and wonderful medical instruments. I always remember being fascinated by their contents as a child, and by the macabre stories Doctor Williamson used to tell about their uses.

"Remembering the lip clamps for naughty boys, eh, Richard?"

God, he even *sounded* the same. Iain Williamson rose from behind his desk and walked across the carpet to shake my hand. He looked little older, a few more lines here and there and his hair was almost gone, but his eyes still shone with that light that so mesmerized me as a child. I towered over him, and almost felt like I should stoop down to talk to him.

"Doctor Williamson, it's been a long time."

He smiled. "I think you're old enough to call me Iain, Richard, and yes, I do believe it's been what, thirteen, fourteen years?" His voice still contained a shard of that clean, clipped English cadence, the only giveaway as to his origins. I remember him telling me how he had moved up to Scotland from Sussex after the end of World War II, when doctors were in dreadfully short supply. As with most, he and his wife only came for a few months, just to help out, but had ended up staying. And for Kinlochbervie, I have to say they were godsends. It took them a while to be accepted, but the townsfolk soon realized they had a wonderful pair on their hands, and some even joked that they made themselves ill and got pregnant just to make Iain and Miriam stay.

"You're looking well," he remarked.

"As are you!" I told him. "Why haven't you retired?"

He gestured toward the padded chair opposite the desk

and I sat. "The day I retire will be the day old Hugh MacGraw comes in here with one of his coffins."

I smiled as I made myself comfortable. For a few minutes, we talked about the past, and I told him what I had been doing with myself in Australia.

Once we were both relatively up to date, he asked me, "So what it is I can do for you today—you don't exactly look sick, now."

"I'm not," I said. "Truth is, I wanted to talk to you about Dad."

Doctor Williamson nodded as if he had been expecting that. "I see. Well, you're my last patient for the day, so I have the time. Just what is it you'd like to know, Richard?"

I shrugged. "Anything you can tell me, I suppose."

"Ah, so you're not exactly here for grief counseling then." For a moment, I thought he was going to say that he couldn't, or wouldn't, but then he spoke. "Donnie Campbell, the postmaster, found him. Apparently your father's mail had been gathering at the post office for a few days, and seeing as how he was going out to Balchrick anyhow, Donnie decided to drop it in personally late one afternoon. From what he told me, he arrived and found the bothy empty.

"At first he thought your father had just gone for a walk, because the makings for supper were still on the table, even though the range was out." Williamson stopped and picked up a pen, which he began absently playing with. "Donnie found your father down on the beach," he continued, looking at me with sympathy in his eyes. "There was nothing he could do—the poor man had been dead two days."

"And he . . ."

"Drowned, yes. That was my official statement as cause of death. It was assumed he was out walking and slipped on the rocks, knocked himself out, and drowned."

"And your unofficial opinion?"

He looked at me hard; then, seeming to make a decision in his mind, he said, "I didn't quite mean it like that. There is absolutely no doubt that Peter Brennan drowned. But saying that, I don't think he knocked himself out, or else I would have seen evidence of stress on his skull, but that still doesn't discount the possibility that he slipped."

"Is there anything suspicious about it at all?" I asked bluntly.

"If you're asking if Sulika had anything to do with it, which I assume you are, then no. And don't go listening to that awful Cunningham woman. She's got nothing better to do than sit around and stuff her nose into other peoples' goings-on." He paused and collected himself. "There were no signs of a struggle, or of trauma to any part of his body." He raised his hands and let them drop onto the table. "I'm no detective. He just drowned. I'm sorry, Richard. Peter was a good friend. I never met Sulika, but I know they were in love. Peter told me so himself." He laughed softly to himself. "Funny, the last few months of his life, he was like a little boy again. Amazing what the love of a woman can do."

He put down the pen and sat back in the leather chair. "I don't know what happened to her either," he sighed. "I imagine she packed up and went back to wherever she came from."

I opened my mouth to ask another question about her, but then stopped. I was reading conspiracies in where there were none, and seeing ghosts where I should only be seeing shadows.

The silence in the room was broken only by the low methodical tocking of the large clock next to the window.

The light outside was falling, and I knew I'd soon have to leave. Before I left, though, there was one last question I wanted to ask:

"Who is Liam?"

Doctor Williamson went very still, and for a moment it was impossible for me to read his mood. I couldn't tell if he was about to explode in anger or shrug and ask me the question back.

He surprised me.

"Do you know how long I've been waiting for one of you to come in here and ask me that?" He shook his head and leaned forward so he was resting his elbows on the thick protective glass that covered the surface of the desk. "How on earth did you find out about Liam?" he asked me in a peculiar tone.

"I saw his birth certificate," I replied.

"Ah yes, of course. Isn't it odd how the most hidden of secrets can be so easily undone?"

"So you know him?"

He raised his eyebrows. "Personally? Oh no, but I know *about* him."

I sat forward too, eager to hear about my father's mysterious half brother.

"I don't know if I should really be telling you this in this age of lawsuits, personal privacy, and liability, but I'm an old man and I think you've a right to know. Hell, it's not as if they can lock me up for long, is it."

"I suppose not," I answered, impatient for him to start.

"And you are family. Now, if you've seen the birth certificate, I take it you know who his mother was?"

"Mairéad."

"Yes. Now, I got this from the previous doctor that inhabited this surgery, a cantankerous buffoon called Mac-

Donald who still kept a bone saw and a jar of leeches on the table. The only reason he knew about the baby at all was because it was a difficult birth and your grandfather John ran all the way into town to fetch him."

"Difficult how?" I asked.

Williamson shrugged. "Like I said, I don't know the finer details. But I know the baby was born deformed." He saw my look and headed it off with a raised hand. "Again, Richard, I don't know how. I only became acquainted with Doctor MacDonald a short time before he died, and he barely told me anything—what with me being a despicable invading English bastard." He grinned, then turned serious. "MacDonald was a nasty man, given over to a kind of meanness I can't abide. He only told me the story as an example of what he called 'far north inbreeding.' " Williamson suddenly seemed to realize what he had said and apologized profusely.

I waved away his embarrassment.

He grew reflective for a moment, sinking back into the chair, and when he spoke again, his voice was low, as if in reflection of the gloaming evening that was enveloping the street outside. "Mairéad had the child late in the summer of . . . 1914, I believe, and by the first snows of winter, she and the babe were gone."

"Gone? Gone where?"

Again, Williamson shrugged. "If MacDonald knew, he never told me, so he took the secret to his grave. No one saw the child except for him. Hell, for all intents and purposes the baby might never have existed! I don't think your father—or your grandmother Maggie, for that matter—even knew of his existence. Then of course when your grandfather died, shortly after your father was born, there was no one left who knew but me.

"It's funny that you're here now, asking this," he said, "because I've often wondered what became of the boy—and Mairéad, for that matter. For all we know he could have lived his life out right here."

"He might even still be alive," I whispered.

"I suppose there's a chance. It would all depend on the deformity."

We were both silent. On the other side of the door, I could hear his assistant puttering about.

"Let it go, Richard," Williamson said softly. "It does no good to go raking over the coals of the past. Liam has obviously wanted to remain apart, or else he would have made an appearance."

"Unless he too has no idea who he is," I suggested.

"There's that."

I nodded, feeling slightly peculiar and detached from the story I had just heard. It was as if everything was just that, a story, and not something that had happened to my immediate family. Still, it was over. I had no more avenues to explore, and short of turning up some new amazing piece of evidence, I would have to be content with what I had learned.

"Is there anything else you would like to know?" he asked.

I shook my head and stood up. "No, thank you. I've already taken up too much of your time."

"Nonsense. I'm glad I've finally had the chance to pass all this on."

I paused by the door and offered my hand. "If you remember anything else . . ."

"I'll let you know."

"Thank you, Iain."

He nodded and opened the door. "Oh, and Richard . . ."

I turned.

"Welcome back."

iii

DECEMBER

Days turned into weeks, and soon enough, the final month of the year was upon us.

November's last dying hours had bequeathed the first snows upon the land, nothing more than a light sprinkling that sifted down from the flat gray sky late one evening. The fine flakes quickly powdered the hills, blowing in spiraling eddies around the cottage and out onto the beach. The air was dust dry, almost hard, and as the gently undulating white blanket deepened around my home, the land took on the hushed and patient quality that was wondrous, as if the very earth were holding its breath.

That first evening, I sat on the doorstep of the bothy, watching with an almost childlike delight as the snow fell silently around me. I wandered outside onto the grass, wrapped in a heavy jumper, arms outstretched, feeling the pinpricks of cold on my hands, and looked up into the dull gray sky, staring up into a seeming infinity of tumbling white specks. I'd not seen snow for seven or so years, and it lingered in my memory as a fantasy, rather than the bitterly cold and uncomfortable reality. I knew that would come soon enough, but for the time being I was content just to enjoy it.

I became worried when Ailish failed to appear that night, and more so the following morning. By the early afternoon, the worry had faded down into a concern that was laced with bitter disappointment. Perhaps the snow was deeper where she lived, and she had no way of getting here? A dozen possible questions, scenarios, and answers flitted through my mind, but none of them sounded convincing. Little did I know then that my tenuous friendship with the abstruse woman was about to change dramatically.

I'd set about passing the time by making myself dinner. I had prepared a rough casserole of vegetables, wine, and herbs, and had decided that some fish would top it off nicely. So, with rod in one hand and tool bag in the other, I had set out toward the loch. The snowfall had decreased to just a few large flakes that seemed to take an improbable amount of time to drift to the ground, and as my boots squeaked through the thin coating of white, I hunched deeper into my coat as the cold wind bit at me. A heavy woolen scarf was wrapped around my throat, mouth, and nose, but still the gelid air scorched my lungs. My breath seeped through the scarf, instantly misting, and when I reached halfway, I had to pull the wool clear of my mouth, as it had become damp and cold with the moisture. Underneath all my clothes, I was as warm as toast, but my hands, feet, and face were stinging.

Reaching the edge of the water, I tentatively knelt down on the soft cushion of snow and tested the layer of white-dusted ice. With as much strength as I could muster, I brought the hammer down, wincing at the numbing shock that coursed up my arm and made my wrist throb. The ice was barely marked, except for the ring of cracks that circled around the slight dent I had made. I tried again in several other places before I judged the ice safe.

Warily, I stepped out onto the slippery surface, treading my way slowly out until I thought the water might be deep enough. Digging out my drill, I screwed in the largest bit I had found and began carefully boring into the ice. I broke through after a couple of minutes, and was surprised to find the crust looked to be several inches thick. I put the drill back in the leather tool bag and produced a lethal-looking, thin-bladed saw that was designed especially to eat through ice.

By the time I had cut a ragged square (ever tried cutting a *circle* in ice?) I was perspiring heavily, and my ragged breath sounded like it was echoing through the glen. I lowered my prepared line though the wound in the ice and settled back to wait.

Within an hour, I had caught three reasonable-sized fish, and thought that they would do. Packing up the rod, I brushed the light collection of snow from my shoulders and stood up, trying to coax some warmth into bones that had been sucked clean. Even through my thick boots, my feet had no sensation whatsoever.

I decided to leave the hole clear in case I chose to return at another time. Getting to my feet, I looked around me for a moment, savoring the hushed, anticipative silence of the glen. Then, with one last deep breath, I pulled my scarf back over my mouth and started toward the shore.

It was a pathetically obvious accident waiting to happen, and even with the benefit of hindsight, I suppose I should have taken more care, but . . .

My foot came down on an uneven bump of ice and I slipped.

My arms windmilled automatically, and my tool bag and rod went flying. The sensation of falling was intense; one moment I was looking at the shore, the next the whole world tilted. I remember shouting a profanity, but the sound was muffled by my scarf. It felt like it happened in slow motion. I struck the ice almost flat, and the pain spread instantly through my body. The sound when my head hit was terrible, as was the jagged bolt of pain, but nowhere near as dreadful as the noise the ice made as it gave way beneath me. The splitting crack was like a thunderfit, and the air that left my lungs in a forced rush was a low roar. For the briefest of moments, I imagined there was quiet, then the water claimed me.

The sudden cold was like nothing I had ever experienced before. It rushed into me, ignoring my clothes, and bit into my very bones. I felt nothing but the cold.

The pain was incredible, like being immersed in a vat of lava. Reflexively, I must've opened my mouth to scream, or to reclaim the breath that had been brutally forced from me, because I have the frightening memory of being entered by the lake, like a violation as it raped my warmth and tried to steal away my life. Then, with my eyes, my nose, all my senses alight and overloaded, I blacked out.

I regained consciousness briefly seconds later and a montage of images was recorded somehow by my brain.

The sky, gray and flat, blocked suddenly by Ailish's perfect face, looking down on me as if from a great height. I could see the concern in her eyes, the way the bitter breeze was content just to toy with her hair.

Flashes from my dreams—nightmares—came to me, of dark things swimming in black waters, of teeth, razored and tearing, and of the terror of drowning.

My clothes, suddenly tight as I am dragged forcibly from the darkness.

Pressure on my back, the impossible amounts of water fountaining from my mouth and nose.

I felt warm.

The wondrous sensation of her holding me, cradling my head and speaking things I couldn't understand, her voice distant, as though she were trying to communicate from far away.

My face smarting suddenly, my eyes tearing as consciousness and perception grudgingly returned.

Her voice: "Can you stand? *Richard!* Can you get up?"

I looked up at her, and for one moment, everything was quiet and perfect, then I began to cough, great racking heaves that ripped at my insides like talons. Roughly, Ailish shifted me into a sitting position until the spasms passed. I voided yet more loch water, a thick stream mixed with bile that hung from my chin afterward in a tendril. Without apparent concern or disgust, Ailish wiped it away and looked at me, the worry evident in her impossibly green eyes. I tried to smile at her, to give her some sort of reassurance, but I was seized by another coughing fit.

My memory of our walk, or should I say, our stumble, back to the cottage is hazy and very indistinct at best, and only two tenuous images lingered afterward. The first was of the brightness of the sky, of the sheer power of the light despite the heavy blanket of colorless cloud, and the second was that Ailish didn't hesitate when it came to entering the bothy. I sat before the fire, entombed in a dozen blankets and the duvet but still shivering.

I don't think I was cold anymore—I certainly didn't feel it—but my body was still reacting as if I were. I'd been submerged in a hot bath for what seemed like hours (thank God I'd decided to buy a small immersion heater a few weeks ago). Beads of sweat chased lines down my face, yet my teeth rattled within my mouth. My head drummed as if it were being bashed by a mallet.

The grate had been well stocked, and I don't think such a large fire had been kindled within it for some time. Some old childhood-remembered warning about setting fire to the chimney had flashed through my mind, but feeling the warmth, both physical and mental, radiating out, I had said nothing.

I turned slightly in the chair to study Ailish as she moved swiftly around the kitchen. She'd dumped me here (after I had managed to convince her that I was well enough to change my own clothes), wrapped me up despite my pathetic protestations, then got to work. Silently, as she had put the pot of prepared stew within the oven and set about readying the fish, I watched her, beguiled in spite of my disposition. She possessed an economy of movement that was just so graceful and elegant to behold. Her feet (still bare) whispered over the cold flagstones almost without touching them as she pulled pots and plates from cupboards without any hesitation.

I watched her a while longer, snuggling deeper into my protective cotton cocoon. Every so often, she would look over at me, and I would return her glance with a pained smile that was only half to do with how I was feeling physically. She looked so small, especially when she stood next to the black enormity of the range, but I knew she contained the strength and steadfastness of the sea. The change in her was almost astonishing: from the edgy, warisome woman I knew only from a distance to this confident, almost assured person who moved about my cottage as if it were her own. An air of timorousness still squalled about her, but her demeanor had shifted, sidestepped, as if what had come before had been but a display. I wondered if she was just naturally cautious, or whether it had all been for my benefit, and if so, why?

I snapped out a chain of sneezes that made my eyes water, and Ailish stopped what she was doing and glanced over at me again. My eyes teared, and I wormed a hand out from under the blankets to wipe them with a crumpled tissue and to nudge my glasses back on properly. I blinked and looked up to see Ailish standing over me, a tumbler of what appeared to be red wine in her hand.

"Here," she said, handing it to me. I was surprised to find the glass almost too hot to hold. "Sip it slowly," she told me. I raised it to my nose and sniffed, my eyes watering once more as the pungent aroma of cloves and cinnamon assaulted my senses.

"Mulled wine?" I asked, sipping carefully.

She shrugged. "Sort of" was the elusive reply. Her expression was teasing, puckish, and she whispered, "Perhaps more."

"As long as you don't turn me into a toad," I told her.

Her face took on an intrigued look. "Why would I do that?"

The wine was incredibly spicy, and burned my throat like whisky. I thought I could taste hot pepper and ground nutmeg—along with something else . . . something bitter, almost herblike. The liquid left a trail of fire within me as it trickled down my throat to my stomach, then the warmth spread out like heated, searching fingers throughout my damp, chilled body.

She smiled again, and this time there was something else there too; I had a definite perception of an emotion akin to compassion, or perhaps empathy. It was almost like the look a doctor might give to a sick child, but tinted with just that little bit more. . . .

Promise?

She lowered her face so that it was level with mine, and in a voice soft and almost husky, Ailish asked, "Better?" The inflections her voice gave the Gaelic sent a delicious tremble down my spine.

Her eyes flicked over my flushed features, an almost sensual caress. I nodded, my lips and mouth almost numb from the drink as I swallowed. She held my gaze easily, dominantly, her face unreadable. We were so close I could make out three minute spots of brown in her eyes; tiny islands of darkness within emerald oceans. I saw her looking at my nose, my lips, and for a moment I honestly thought she was going to close the gap between us and kiss me.

The moment hung in the air, almost palpable.

Ridiculously, I imagined the tiny sparks arcing between us, closing the fractional void with tiny stuttered leaps and the tiny odor of ozone. I could have been the one, leaned forward and brushed her lips with mine, but in all honesty I was terrified. She even *smelled* powerful, daunting; that heady mix of wild heather and the other, more hidden aromas that still produced profound, subconscious reactions within me. My head was spinning like a carousel. I'd been through a lot today, I was chilled and sick, and now this . . . I wondered if had I not fallen through the ice if she would still have this effect on me. Without thinking too hard I knew she would. How I was responding to her had nothing to do with any cold or fever I might have.

The contact broke abruptly, and she pulled away, but did I feel a sense of disappointment—or was that just my hopeful imagination? Ailish stood, looking down on me silently for a moment, then returned to the kitchen.

"You can eat now," she said, opening the range oven door and hefting the large pot out.

I could only nod.

We ate in near silence, listening to the steady accompaniment of the sea, both sitting at the table, with me still wrapped in my blankets, at Ailish's insistence.

While I wolfed down the thick stew, Ailish only dabbed at hers with a piece of bread, or occasionally picked out small chunks of meat with her fingers. I didn't care about the manner with which she ate, so intent was I upon my meal. It felt like I hadn't had food in weeks, and the heavy mixture of fish and vegetables warmed me considerably. Despite the thick blankets, I had never felt so cold in my life. The brief respite from the chill I had felt earlier had been just that.

We exchanged few pleasantries, I asked what had happened, though in my mind it was simple enough. Ailish had responded to my question with one of her own: why didn't I just fish from the edge? The embarrassed smile that spread across my face almost covered up the blush that ran from my neck to the roots of my hair.

After the meal we sat for a time, almost awkwardly regarding one another, then Ailish stood and stretched like a cat. "You ought to get some sleep," she suggested.

I nodded, a yawn already coming unbidden to my mouth.

I got up slowly, wincing slightly at the pain that thrummed across my back, circling up to my head in a sudden flash of anger. For a sudden moment I thought I was going to faint. I teetered by the table, the blankets puddling around my legs as I reached out to steady myself. Instead of the table, I found Ailish at my side, a surprisingly strong arm going around my waist as she guided me toward the bedroom.

Once inside, she lowered me slowly to the bed, then returned to the other room for the covers. By the time she came back, I was lying on my side, my legs pulled up trying to reclaim some of the heat I knew I had once possessed but which had since been stolen. The thick duvet was thrown over me, fully clothed, and two blankets spread over the top. The weight was reassuring and welcome, but I still felt like I was in a freezer.

"Are you warm enough?" Ailish asked when she was done.

I nodded, my still-chattering teeth not exactly adding weight to the blatant lie. She fixed me with another one of those contemplative looks, then left the room in a swirl of cloth. Over the noise of my shivering, I could hear her blowing out the candles and lamps, then banking up the fire. Soon, the light in the bothy was extinguished to all but nothing, and I lay there, waiting for the click of the front door as she left me.

But there was nothing but the silence of the dark, then:

The slight scuff of feet on stone;

A gentle sigh of breath;

The rustle as the blankets and duvet were pulled back.

My surprise when Ailish slipped under the covers with me was very nearly overwhelming. For a moment, as she shuffled up next to me and her body molded against mine like the second piece of a two-part puzzle, I thought I would burst. Even through the layers of clothes I had on and her woolen dress, I could feel her, the gentle protrusion of her breasts, the firmness of her legs as they pressed against the backs of mine. Her offered heat seeped into me, more healing than any balm or elixir. If she was aware of my state of . . . discomfort, she gave no sign, and after the initial shock of feeling her pressed up against me had dulled, I relaxed slightly. There was nothing sexual in what she was doing, though I knew it was only my current state of disability that stopped me from embarrassing myself, and her.

After endless minutes of near silence, with me practically holding my breath, Ailish said, "Better?"

It was the second time she had asked me that tonight, and for the second time, I could only nod.

An arm slowly reached over my shoulder, hanging down before my chest, almost a gesture of possession, I thought. Very tentatively, as if I rested on eggshells, I shifted position and reached up with my hand, brushing her pale fingers with a feather stroke. When she didn't withdraw, I lengthened my caress to the whole of her hand. I could feel her breath against the back of my neck, warm and steady. I traced the lengths of her fingers with mine, riding up over her emphasized knuckles to draw invisible patterns along the back of her hand and wrist before dipping back down once more. My movements were slow, measured, almost painful—so aware was I of the feel of her.

Finally, I took her slim hand in mine, holding it close to me as if I were fearful she would suddenly leave if I broke contact.

I don't know what time it was when I woke, only that it was still very much night.

A faint, snow-fed glow trickled in through the glass of the closed window, dappling across the rumpled blankets and projecting half a square on the cold floor.

It took me a moment to recover my wits, then I turned over suddenly.

The bed was empty. I was alone.

For a moment, I wondered if I had dreamed the whole thing, but as I pulled back the covers I saw the slight depression made by another person. I reached out a hand slowly, cautiously, almost as if I were fearful. The vague light that filtered through the glass bleached my hand into black and white, darkening the grooves and pores while striking my knuckles and hairs into prominence. Gently touching the shallow indent in the sheets, I could still feel the warmth from her body. Brushing my fingers across my mouth and nose, I could still smell her.

I whispered her name questioningly into the shadows, my voice dry and little more than a hiss, but there was no reply. Pulling the other pillow closer, I inhaled deeply, my eyes closing as I savored the wondrous, almost erotic scent that lingered there.

I huddled down under the duvet and blankets, a broad smile on my sleep-filled face.

19

I stayed in bed for most of the next day, only venturing forth to use the bathroom or get myself a drink and fix a quick snack.

I didn't actually feel that unwell; in fact, the only thing I could detect that was out of place was the deep cough and the dull pain along my back. Still, a day in bed couldn't hurt.

Ailish turned up early in the afternoon, letting herself in as silently as always. I must have been dozing in a half-sleep filled with dreams when she arrived, for when I opened my eyes, she was standing at the foot of the bed watching me. I edged myself up on the pillows, a welcoming smile on my face as I slid on my glasses.

"Bad dreams?" she asked after a moment.

I frowned, trying to recall the faint images that still lingered fleetingly in my mind. "I'm not sure," I replied hesitantly. "I think so, yes. Still, they're not as bad as they were."

Ailish was looking at me oddly, her head slightly cocked as if she were considering another question.

"How do you feel?" she inquired after a moment. For

some reason I knew that hadn't been her original train of thought.

I smiled, and with a slightly impudent turn of phrase, answered, "Better."

She caught the slight attempt at a joke, and a shy smile crept across her lovely features. As always, she was wearing the long russet dress, and I thought I could see a light coating of snow over her narrow shoulders. As if reading my mind, she absently brushed the flakes from her shoulder and removed the shawl, hanging it across the end of the bed. The subtle action wasn't lost on me, and as our eyes met again, I could once again see the nuances there.

"You should get out of bed," she told me in no uncertain terms. "You are not sick."

"Yes, doctor," I replied, in a somewhat surly tone of voice. I was a little put out because the only reason I had stayed in bed so long in the first place was for fear that she might appear and be angry with me for getting up.

I swept back the covers and lowered my bare legs to the floor, muttering slightly as my warm feet touched the blue-cold stone. At some point in the morning I had removed most of my clothes, for I had become intolerably hot.

With an almost mocking smile that I somehow knew was directed at my physique, Ailish turned and went into the kitchen.

I got dressed as quickly as I could, but my bruised back was still a little painful, and before I made my appearance, I paused in the bathroom to swallow down a couple of paracetamol tablets. I think some of the water went down the wrong way, and I spent several painful moments coughing heavily, my hand gripping the smooth side of the enamel sink while my body heaved. I blew my nose and tossed the tissue into the toilet.

I entered the living room to discover a bright, cheery fire burning in the grate and a kettle of boiling water rattling away merrily on the stove in the kitchen. The light through the windows was washed and moody, and I could hear the laughter of the wind around the cottage as it sought entrance. Ailish was seated just back from the table, her hands in her lap, watching me silently as I slowly prepared us a pot of coffee. I heaped a few spoonfuls of whitener into her cup, and added a teaspoon of sugar in reply to her nonchalant shrug. I managed to make it without spilling a drop, despite the fact that I had overfilled the cups as usual and my step was a little infirm. I set the mug of steaming coffee down before her and carefully pulled out a chair for myself.

"It's hot," I warned her, with a smile. Her look told me to stop being so condescending, but I nearly chuckled when she confidently lifted the cup to her lips and promptly burned herself again. Her face was filled with chagrin as she took another sip—carefully this time. "I think I prefer the other," she said, placing the cup down on the dark wood of the table.

"What, you mean the tea?" I asked.

Ailish nodded and was silent, as if considering the taste. "Though it might be nicer if it was sweeter."

"Easily remedied," I said, reaching for the sugar.

I finished up my cup and made my way back over to make another, all the while feeling Ailish's eyes upon me. I was afloat with self-consciousness, and though the potent emotions I had felt the night before were still with me, once again I sensed her hesitancy, and although it was nowhere near as great as it used to be, it was there all the same.

I returned to the chair and shifted it around closer to the fire, closer to her. I looked at the clock and discovered it was a quarter before four. Glancing out of the window, I saw that the light was already beginning to fail. It didn't look to be snowing, but the wind that chased down the chimney was bitterly cold, even after passing through the thick forest of flames. There seemed to be more drafts than normal, though that might've just been my heightened susceptibility to the cold.

Smothering the first ticklings of a cough, I gulped down a mouthful of coffee and silently wondered if she would stay tonight.

I was in a mind for some music and, excusing myself momentarily, I put on my coat and went outside to start the genny. The twilit sky was a dark magenta, deepening almost visibly as the unseen sun dipped below the horizon. A blanket of featureless cloud hung silently out to sea, making its way slowly and surely toward the land, and I knew it would snow again sometime toward dawn, and probably quite heavily. I reached the shed as quickly as my sore body would let me and once inside, I hurried about my business, not wanting to spend any more time outside than was necessary. The shed was ripe with the sharp smell of diesel and treated wood, a musty combination that was not altogether unpleasant. I topped up the large fuel tank and, priming the plugs, pulled out the starter. The motor caught on the second tug of the cord, and after a few fitful moments of gurgles and splutters, it mumbled down to its usual low hum. Briefly checking the voltage gauge to make sure all was well, I shut the door, secured it firmly with the latch, and hurried back to the bothy. As I walked over the frozen crust of snow, my boots crunching as if I trod on old leaves, I could see Ailish through the window of the kitchen, her slight frame outlined by the low light of a paraffin lamp she must have lit while I was gone. The glow from the window was ghostly, and she looked like a specter as she drifted out of sight.

Opening the door, I entered quickly in a cloud of frosted breath and frigid air. I almost slammed it in my haste to be back in the warmth, and as I took off my voluminous coat, I turned to Ailish. "It's cold!" I told her emphatically.

She smiled in agreement and I noticed that she had poured herself another coffee and was spooning in an improbable amount of sugar.

Hunching my shoulders and rubbing my hands briskly together, I crossed to the fire and leaned against the mantel, sighing as the warmth bled into my body. When I felt I had heated up sufficiently, I crossed to the small stereo and crouched down in front of my collection of compact discs.

"What shall we listen to?" I asked her, casting my eyes along the thin columns of spines.

Ailish was quiet, then replied, "You decide."

I shrugged. "How about some Solas . . . oh, no, I know what would be perfect." I pulled out a case, opened it, and carefully laid the gleaming disc in the tray. I pressed play, turning the volume right down so we could still talk. After a short pause, the first rippling chords of Luka Bloom's wonderful album, *Turf,* shimmered from the speakers. I stood, listening a moment, then stepped back and sat down in the soft chair by the fire. Ailish remained at the table, just off to my right, and I watched her for a moment as she listened to the gentle, lilting voice that drifted around the room like smoke.

"He sings like you play," she remarked after the first song had finished.

I sat up a little, and turned to face her. "What do you mean?" I asked, intrigued.

"It comes from the heart," she replied simply.

"What about *your* singing?"

"That just comes from here." She gestured to her grin-split mouth with a finger.

"It sounds like it comes from all around," I told her.

Ailish shrugged. "I just sing. It's there."

"I've never heard anyone sing the way you do." I think she blushed a little at the compliment. "Would you sing for me later?" I asked hopefully.

"Perhaps."

We were both quiet again while we listened. I hadn't really meant for the music to be this distracting, but that was one of the qualities of Bloom's music; it could silence the rowdiest of rooms.

"Who taught you the music?" Ailish asked, shifting in her chair a little and leaning toward me slightly. The fire played with the highlights in her hair, kindling life into them, and struck her skin with a rich glow.

"An old man called Billy Stewart," I told her. "He lived on his own in Kinlochbervie. It kind of happened by accident." I stopped to reflect. "Or maybe it didn't. Anyway, I was just starting the long trek home from the post office when Florence—my sister—and I decided to play a trick on him. He was a bit of a hermit, a crotchety old man that I don't think anyone really liked—at least that's what my father told me." I looked over at Ailish briefly. She had made a tent of her hands and was resting her chin lightly on it, watching me intently. I noticed how rarely she seemed to blink. Pushing aside the extraneous thought, I smiled and continued. "Flo's idea was to knock on his door and run away—a silly prank really, but I was only seven or so, and at that age, it was a feat of great daring.

"We both stood by the door, and Flo raised her hand to

knock. It was then that I heard the fiddle music coming from within. It bewitched me completely. Like I said, I was only young, but the melody seized me so totally that I didn't even realize Flo had run until the door was opened and I was yanked inside by the collar of my shirt.

" 'You're that Brennan boy, ain't you!' he roared at me with a voice like thunder. To this day I still remember the sheer terror I felt seeing that balding, old face leaning over me, shouting just inches from my own." I grimaced. "The smell of his breath nearly made me gag—Billy didn't believe in brushing his teeth," I remarked.

" 'What's the matter?' he bellowed. 'Didn't have the sense to run like yer sister?' I couldn't even reply, I was that scared. I remember stuttering something about hearing the music, and his face softened slightly—not much, mind you, but a little. He took me into a room, sat me down, and began to play the most chilling, aching music my young ears had ever heard."

My eyes lifted to hers again, and for a moment I paused, the memories thick. I sat back in the chair and the air escaped through the worn leather like a sigh.

"I think he had meant to scare me with the music, or at least warn me away, but it had the opposite effect. I went to see Billy every day for six months before I convinced him to teach me, and even after he agreed—reluctantly, I'll add, and probably more to stop me begging him—I had to perform chores around his filthy home as payment—I once swept out his cellar while surrounded by gigantic rats I was convinced were going to eat me alive.

"I pestered my poor father relentlessly to buy me a fiddle, and finally, he abated—again, probably to stop my whining. It was a half-size—tiny and toylike compared to Billy's, but I cherished it.

"God, he was an angry old man, furious with the world and the sea for everything and anything, but by Christ could he play!" I shook my head slowly. "For eleven years—right up until I left for Edinburgh—I went to him at least three times a week, almost without fail. He had no children of his own, no wife and no family, and I knew he was trying to cram a lifetime of tunes into my head in those short years he had left."

I sighed and ran my hand down my face. "He died eight months after I left for university. I think he was finally happy—he'd passed on his legacy. I only hope one day I can do the same."

My face clouded over, and I looked at the feathered flames of the fire as they danced along the charring logs. The heat brushed at me in welcome waves, and the amber light filled the room with deep dancing shadows. I heard soft footsteps, and Ailish sat down quietly on the rug before the chair, folding her legs up under her. She stared at me for a time, her fathomless eyes blinking knowingly, then she said gently, "Tell me more?"

I regarded her a moment, then replied, "As long as you do one thing for me."

She appeared a little shaken, as if she didn't quite know what to expect. "What?" she asked cautiously.

"Make some more of that incredible mulled wine?"

The smile that split her face warmed me more than the fire, and she got lightly to her feet and pattered into the kitchen.

W e talked late into the night.
Well, *I* talked; Ailish was content to sit on the rug, one leg drawn up close to her body while she listened to

the stories of my childhood. The hot strong wine made me a little heady, and I think I rambled a little more than was necessary, but Ailish didn't seem to mind. She probed me with slight though meaningful questions that made me open up whole new doors on my past. I told her of my growing years here, of Florence and my parents. Ailish added in her own little comments here and there, but for the most seemed content just to sit and listen to me going on.

I didn't get as far as telling her about Bethy; that part of me I held back. I thought it might seem crass of me to go into details about her, though I think I secretly wanted to. I realized now I needed someone to share my grief with—what little there was left. I think Ailish was that someone, but I had to be sure.

She was exceptionally skillful at diverting my questions about herself, a fact I didn't really appreciate until later on, when I had a chance to reflect on what we had spoken about. When I asked her where she had come from, she gestured loosely westward.

"Ireland?" I said hopefully.

She shrugged. "Sometimes."

And that's how it went.

But despite the reticence on her part, I did learn things about her, little items of trivia that thrilled me, though left me wanting more. Her age was still a mystery; sometimes she seemed barely nineteen, other times, older than me. Physically, I suppose she was in her mid-twenties, but again, it was hard to really tell with any degree of accuracy. Like I said earlier, I never really minded her secrecy. Something sacred and wondrous had entered my life, and I knew one of the conditions was that I couldn't question too deeply. I was content just to let things happen. If she chose to tell me every detail of her life, fine, if not, so be it. I would have been more than happy to take her just as she was. Besides, there's something highly arousing about secrets, and though I doubt that was everything, it certainly played a part.

The clock read just after three.

The fire guttered fitfully, and the amber-crested shadows that crouched in the corners were visibly deeper. Through the thick glass I could see the large flakes of snow that were falling steadily outside. They spiraled down through the bitter air like tiny ghosts, each taking its own circuitous route toward the hard earth. Already a good quarter-inch bar of powdery white had gathered on the sill.

Ailish moved slightly, shifting her legs up under so she was almost kneeling. I knew she was about to leave. I had spent the evening desperately hoping, wondering, if she would sleep with me again tonight, but apparently not.

She rocked forward onto her arms and looked at me. I sat up in the chair, rapidly trying to think of something to say that would make her remain here with me.

"Please," I asked, almost pleading. "Won't you stay? It's cold and snowing. I . . . I can sleep out here if you'd prefer or . . . " She reached forward and placed her fingers against my lips, silencing me. They were impossibly smooth and firm, and it took everything in my power to stop myself from kissing them.

She was regarding me almost sadly, a look of genuine regret painted on her beautiful, firelit face, and I caught the almost imperceptible shake of her head. Then she did something that, although I think I had been expecting, still shook me to the core. Slowly, without her eyes ever leaving mine, Ailish lowered her hand and leaned forward and brushed her lips against mine.

The kiss was slight, dovelike, but her cold lips seemed to almost burn mine, and the intentions were barely veiled. Reflexively, my arms began to reach for her, but she stood fluidly, in one movement, and looked down on me with an almost compassionate expression.

The disappointment and delight must have been evident on my face, for she raised her hand, taking mine in a brief gesture of farewell before stepping back. Our contact was broken reluctantly, fingers interlocking momentarily, then trailing before we separated.

She whispered, "Good night, Richard."

Then, before I could even respond, she was gone.

ii

The nightmare was *almost* the same as the others.

The vivid silver disk of the moon hung before me, lighting my way as I ran down toward the sands. I opened my mouth, shouting until my lungs were deflated, but no sound issued forth.

Nothing.

No hiss of the small waves or sibilant whisper of the mocking wind.

My bare feet churned the cold sand, kicking up storms of dust as I sprinted to the water. The beach seemed impossibly long, stretching away from me like the view in a distorted mirror. I could see the ocean, black and deep, like a sheet of molten jet reaching out as far as my eyes could register. Nothing marred its surface but the ever-expanding circle of ripples I knew I had to reach. My legs pumped, and arms ending in fists as I threw myself over the sands.

Massive-bodied seabirds perched all over the rocks to either side of me, an attentive audience that made no comment. The stones beneath them were white-smeared, limed with their stinking excretions and scattered with the tiny bones of fish.

Still there was no sound.

I reached the water, and though I knew somehow what would happen, panic demanded no less. I dived in without a thought, my body straightening as I knifed through the ebony mirror.

The pain was intense, almost bordering on the exquisite, like something filling with liquid within my head, then bursting like a swollen blood blister. I dived further this time than before; I felt like I was almost at the barrier, the membrane that separated me from her, but like before, the agony became too much.

I surfaced with an explosion of dark water and a sucked-down instinctive breath that began in the very center of my being. I dived under again, trying to find her, to save her, but it was no good. Everything was too dark and the pain was insufferable. Breaking through again, I raised my head and my hands to the moon and screamed.

The ragged cry split the silence like a knife to a balloon, raising the birds to sudden flight. Their calls were raucous and mocking as they tumbled around me on unfelt currents.

With my hands stiffened into claws of pain and unquestionable loss, I watched the water, shining now with both gold and silver light, trickling between my fingers.

So reminiscent of the life I had just lost.

iii

"You're what?"

"Pregnant, Richard. It happens sometimes."

"Oh my God!"

"What's the matter?"

I was at a loss for words. "You're my sister!" I told her.

I could hear the light laughter in her voice. "What's that got to do with it . . . oh, I get it; this is one of those *brotherly* things, isn't it! I've got news for you, Rick, I've been having sex for quite some time, you know."

I felt my face coloring, and I realized I had been talking nonsense. "I'm sorry, Florence," I said humorously. "Congratulations are in order. It's about time, really."

"Why, thank you for your approval, *Uncle* Richard."

"Sorry I won't be there."

"I don't think I *want* you there!"

"I didn't mean that. Pat Dan on the back for me, will you?"

"Of course. So how are things up there?"

A broad grin came onto my face as I saw Ailish through the window, trudging through the thin snow toward the bothy from the direction of the beach. "Good," I replied, opening the door. "Really good."

"Snow?"

"Yeah, but not as much as I thought yet. Still, it's only December."

Florence sighed. "I miss the snow."

"Believe me, once you get over the novelty, it's more a pain." I tossed a wave to Ailish, who raised a hand in reply. My heart was beating so loud I wondered if my sister could hear it over the phone.

"So what's going on in your life?" she asked. "Quickly now, this call's costing me a fortune, what with your number being a mobile and all."

I filled her in rapidly on what I had done, mainly little details about the bothy, my work, and Scotland in general. I paused, then ploughed ahead and told her about Ailish.

When I had finished, she asked plainly, "Are you in love with her?"

I looked up to see her coming through the door, the shy smile on her face. "I think so," I replied quietly, blushing again despite the fact Ailish couldn't have known what we were talking about.

"That's great, Rick," Florence said, her soft voice serious. "Just remember to try and be nicer this time, more open."

I nodded my head and smiled, glancing at Ailish. "Take care of yourself, sis," I told her finally.

"You too. And don't forget to send that damn letter you've been promising for months! I'm getting tired of reminding you. You are just so hopeless at that kind of thing, Richard. *Don't* forget!"

I grinned. "I won't. Scout's honor. Oh, Florence . . . "

"Yes?"

"Well done. Bye now."

iv

We talked again that evening.

I made us a rough meal while Ailish sat at the table, once more listening to my talk of the past. And as before, she was incredibly attentive. I uncorked another bottle of wine (I only had a half-dozen bottles left now). Setting a glass down before her and holding mine loosely in my hand, I returned to the kitchen.

I arranged the last sheet of dried pasta over my rough mixture of sauces and sprinkled over a copious quantity of grated cheese that I had bought fresh. With a hand wrapped in a tea towel, I opened the oven door and slipped the lasagne inside. I washed my sticky fingers and crossed the room to sit next to her, still drying my hands.

After we had eaten, Ailish rose and explored the bothy more thoroughly while I tackled the dishes. I got the impression that she hadn't really investigated before, that she had been waiting for some sort of approval. I had certainly given it. Every so often, I would glance up from the sink and watch her for a time as she wandered around, picking up and examining different items. She pulled out several books from my small shelf, leafing through the pages almost negligently before putting them back carefully. I think she took as much delight from Natasha Newlyn's breathtaking painting as I did, for she spent a long time standing silently staring at it.

Finally, Ailish said, "She has much magic too," and trailing a finger down the glass almost longingly, she looked over to me for a moment. She continued on, wandering almost wistfully between the chairs, her dress shifting around her as she stood before the mantel. I put down the towel and crossed the stone floor, pausing to light a few more candles on my way. Wordlessly, I stood behind her, my face close to her hair, breathing deep of her spirituous redolence.

"This is beautiful," she said, gently holding the stone cat Bethy had made.

I swallowed, my throat suddenly dry, and said in a hushed tone, "It belonged to someone very special." I hesitated, then continued in a voice little more than a whisper, "My wife."

Ailish seemed neither shocked nor particularly concerned. "Where is she now?" she asked, carefully putting the figure back.

"She died. Six years ago. In an . . . accident. A boat she was in capsized out on Loch Inchard." I was surprised at how easily I could say it. I sat down slowly in the chair behind me.

I looked up to see Ailish's eyes reading my face, an odd expression on her delicate features, not so much sympathy as understanding, and it warmed me more than any fire. Slowly, almost deliberately, she knelt down before me, close enough to touch.

"You loved her very much."

I inclined my head slightly.

I don't know why, but I began telling her everything, from the first time I had met Bethy up to the day of her death. I left out nothing, raking through the ashes of memory until I had exposed even the faintest glow of the embers that still burned. Memories that even *I* had thought forgotten. I knew that I had never laid myself so bare before another person in my life—perhaps not even to Bethy herself. There was something about Ailish, some enchanting, marvelous thing that made me want to share myself utterly, without any restraints or conditions. She listened without comment, but sometimes, when my words became thick with emotion, she would reach a hand to touch me, or the expression on her face would coax me gently into continuing. It was she who helped dig out and remove the tiny but painful shards that still lingered deep in my mind.

"You blame yourself, don't you," she said after I was through. It wasn't really a question.

I stared at her, moisture gathering in the corners of my eyes, and nodded.

"Why?" she asked.

I removed my glasses and brushed the tears from my face. "I don't know, I guess because I knew it was too windy for sailing, but I didn't stop them, and I saw Bethy didn't have her life jacket on."

With a deceptive simplicity that would've been condescending from anyone else, Ailish said, "It wasn't your fault."

I took a deep breath, the pain easing a little. "I know," I whispered. I think I had always realized that, but the admission that there was nothing I could have done had been almost impossible for me.

I continued talking awhile longer, running through all the different, ridiculous reasons why I stood myself accused.

Time passed, and I finished in little more than a whisper, the tears running down my face unashamedly. I felt free of the anguish I had carried with me for six years. It was as if the last fragment of a festering splinter had finally been removed. Deep down, I knew it hadn't been my fault, that it had been an accident, but I'd had to deal with the tiny part of me that had almost enjoyed the melancholy, and the much larger piece that had refused to let Bethy go. It was an incredible sensation, finally letting go, and though I wasn't so sure about life after death, I knew Bethy would have been pleased, wherever she was.

The small room was rich with shadows, and the white walls were painted with a brassy blush that melted down onto the stone squares of the floor. The air was wonderfully warm and infused with the weighty aromas of peat, wine, and woodsmoke. In the background, the andante from Mozart's Bassoon Concerto in B-flat Major hung like mist, mixing in with the natural atmosphere as if it had been originally written here.

I realized I had been dozing slightly, content and happy in the warmth. Blinking, I took in a deep breath and yawned.

I looked down and saw that Ailish was leaning back against my legs, facing the fire, and that my hand was gently sifting through her satin red-gold locks. I remained silent, drained but feeling cleansed, fearful that I might be taking a liberty, but she made no move away, and if anything, she leaned closer to me, curling her hand around my leg. I extended my stroking, caressing with feathered fingers down through her fine hair until I touched the soft skin of her neck. My desire for her was building, like a slowly approaching summer storm. Fragments of imagery flashed through my mind: Ailish dancing, her music filling the night, the chase, our first words. How I had reacted then was but a shadow of the emotions that were thundering through me now.

I continued my movements, lightly brushing her face with my fingers for what seemed to me to be an age, until the fire popped loudly and rumpled the mantle of peace that had descended over us.

Ailish shifted position, turning round so that she knelt before me. She laid her hands down on my legs just above my knees, a gesture that sent a ripple of longing through me. She looked at me, and I saw her eyes were shiny, perhaps with tears.

"What's the matter?" I asked, sitting up a little.

She said nothing, but there was a look in her eyes, almost like a kind of pleading. She shook her head slightly, no more than the tiniest of movements that barely stirred her hair.

Once more the moment hung between us. The bothy was silent but for the ethereal music and the muted crackle of the fire. I moved toward her, my head tilting slightly and my eyes closing.

But she stopped me, once more with a finger against my lips.

The confusion must have been as evident on my face as the desire, but before I could speak, Ailish asked, "Is this what you want?"

I swallowed thickly, knowing what I wanted to say but somehow not knowing if I should.

"Yes," I said finally. "With all of my soul."

Again, there was that look of almost . . . regret? on her face, then she leaned forward to meet me halfway.

The kiss was soft at first, gentle and unhurried. I felt Ailish's slim arms reaching around my head, and I slipped mine about her waist, drawing her closer so our bodies pressed together. We separated for a moment, eyes searching each other's faces.

There was a tangible sense of surrender in the air, but did it come from me or from her?

We joined again. Need flared, and my hands slid slowly up along her back and around her neck to cup her face. My mouth opened, and Ailish's tongue danced within, skipping across my teeth and tracing the circle of my lips. I ran my fingers gently down the length of her back, feeling her taut muscles beneath the fabric of her dress. My hands began a slow, circling ascent of her body, stopping just below her shoulders. I could sense the softness of her breasts against the insides of my wrists and inextricably, I moved my hands around. A low sigh eased out from her, and I felt her deft fingers undoing my loose shirt.

Still joined, she peeled it from me, my hands leaving her body for only the most fleeting of instants. I loosened the row of buttons that ran down from her neckline, and with the minimum of pressure from my hands, I pulled the dress up over her shoulders. She was naked underneath, and the warm firelight played across her pale skin, flawless like porcelain, casting shifting patterns upon the cool surface. Her breasts were small, like those of a young girl, and the nipples were dark and stiffly erect. Her stomach was flat, and as I slowly ran my fingers down, goose pimples sprang up in their wake. Her sex was a downy, orange-red bar that disappeared into the deep, fire-fed shadow between her legs. I leaned down and tenderly put my mouth at the juncture of her neck and shoulders, steadily working kisses and the gentlest of bites down her body until I took a single nipple within my mouth. She tasted tangy, a vague mix of her own scent and salt that was strangely erotic. As my tongue swirled around her, one of her hands tangled itself in my hair while the other worked at my belt. I stroked my hands down her sides and out along her firm legs. I stood slightly, and Ailish tugged my finally loosened jeans and shorts down, halting slightly as she eased them over my fully erect penis.

Free of our clothes, we fell together on the floor, one of my legs between hers. I could feel the soft deep pile of the rug crushing under my knees, then the deliciously cool sensation as our bodies rubbed together. Our mouths sought each other out again, and as our tongues dueled, a distant part of me thought that perhaps I had never been so aroused. Her fingers, stretched into soft claws, raked inextricably down my back to clench at my buttocks. I bucked reflexively. My penis was pressed up against her leg, swollen and hot. I could feel her wetness kissing my thigh, and in a sudden move, I lifted my other leg inside of hers. She shifted position, raising herself slightly. For a moment we broke, and my head hung above hers, the gray-dusted curls of my hair tickling her face. Ailish's eyes reflected back the wavering light, her emerald-encircled pupils wide, her mouth open. I moved my hips forward slightly, lowering myself. There was little resistance as I slid smoothly into her, and as her eyes closed, I heard her breathe out a small sigh that eased into a soft calling of my name. I stayed perfectly still, my senses delirious as I felt her about me. She murmured something unintelligible in my ear, and pulled me closer, tighter.

The sudden realization that I was inside her flooded my mind, cutting off all other thought. For a moment, I honestly think I almost lost consciousness, so intense and all-encompassing were my feelings for her. I could perceive the fire flaring within me; starting as a tiny flickering spark in my mind's eye, it traveled through my body, circling, building up pace steadily, until the slightest movement of myself within her triggered its furious release. It burst from me with an emotive violence that would forever suture me to this woman in my mind.

Ailish's thighs slipped up along mine to my hips, and she gripped me passionately, possessively as I emptied myself into her completely. She was looking up at me, *into* me, her breath coming in short gasps. She was the rock that my tide broke against. My orgasm was impossibly long, drawn out, almost agonizing, and I cried out almost piteously. I held on to her so tightly, crushing her sweat-sheened body to mine as I was wrung dry. It lasted forever, and as I lay in her arms, trembling and spent, I felt embarrassed, ashamed even, that I had come so soon without regard for her.

I remained within her, still aroused and erect, despite the ejaculation that had burst from me. Ailish held me, her legs tightly wrapped around my waist, keeping me inside. I looked at her, and for a moment, something passed between us, and she raised her head and kissed me wildly, her teeth clinging to my lower lip. There was a sudden thorn of pain, and I tasted blood with my tongue and could see the butterfly spot of red on her lips. Her eyes were wide, and a slow smile spread across her beautiful flushed face.

"You belong to me now," she breathed softly, the words sending a thrill of ice down my back. She drew me down, pressing my lips to hers as she began moving languidly beneath me. All thought of what she had said and done fled as I began stirring within her once more.

At some point during the night, when the fire had burned down to nothing more than glowing ash and the lamps had long since burned dry, we moved into the bedroom, walking naked, our bodies constantly touching, stopping to embrace every few steps. I had to bend down almost comically to reach her.

We made love through most of the dark hours, sometimes vigorously, mostly with slow, wild sensual abandon. She swallowed my soul that night, completely, totally, and as the late light of the moon filtered softly through the thick glass, I knew I would never be the same again.

20

The dazzling morning sunlight streamed through the window and down onto the bed.

It splashed over the walls, not painting them with warmth, but rather with the intense light of an early winter morning. For a time, I watched the brilliant spray from the small crystal flecking the rough plaster of the ceiling with a hundred colors, but not for long. My eyes were continually drawn back down to her, and had she not been lying in the bed beside me, I would not have truly believed what had happened.

Ailish slept on, her small face serene and peaceful as she nestled within the large pillow, the duvet spread loosely over her body. My heart filled with longing as I silently lay there watching her, and the warm feeling spread through me not unlike intoxication. She was lying on her side, facing me, her eyes fluttering almost imperceptibly as she dreamed. I resisted the urge to reach forward and brush the strand of red hair away from her face for fear that I might wake her. So I just lay there, hair disheveled, eyes bleary, propped up uncomfortably on one arm. My gaze wandered

over her features like a silk-soft caress, following the con-
tours of her face, the lines of her defined jaw. Like this, she
lacked the sense of mystery that so surrounded her when
she was awake; the power of her eyes temporarily contained within closed lids.

I took in a deep breath and carefully ran a hand through
my hair, sweeping it back out of my eyes. I didn't have any
idea what time it was, only that the day outside was glo-
rious. Sitting up as I was, I should have been cold in the
chill morning air, but the fires of our lovemaking still
burned bright inside of me. With a lopsided grin, I thought
back over the last night. I had responded to her with the
energy and enthusiasm of an eighteen-year-old boy, not of
a man fast approaching forty. Even now, the tiredness
failed to claim me. I could feel the life flowing through my
veins, almost burning in its intensity. The desire for her was
as vehement now as it had been half a night ago, and I
found myself both longing to wake her, yet anxious not to.

I have to admit that she did frighten me.

It wasn't so much a feeling of being scared of her, but
more like being wary at what was happening between us.
I'd always loosely believed in love at first sight—to a degree. But when I'd seen Ailish, it was as if I had thrown
my common sense out of the nearest window. I'd been
struck by a thunderbolt, and the sky was still storming. But
I felt no regret whatsoever, no apprehension. What was
occurring between us felt so *right,* so proper, that I couldn't
find fault. And I couldn't take heed of the voice of reason
and concern that whispered at me from the smallest corner
of my mind. Who was I to try and justify love?

But was it love?

Or was it just infatuation, obsession, foolishness?

After all, I had met her when I had most needed someone, when my emotional state had been at its most vulnerable.

A memory came sharply to mind, of a time many years ago in Brisbane. I'd not long been in Australia, and my grief was probably at its apex. I was by no means an alcoholic or a chronic depressive, but I was what might be called socially catatonic. Flo had introduced me to one of her friends—Juliet was her name—in the hope that she might have helped me to get over things. At first, it looked like everything might work out. Juliet was a good listener, and unconsciously, I began off-loading my sorrow and self-loathing onto her. What had started as a possible friendship had shattered within three weeks as my emotional deluge swamped her.

Was I doing the same to Ailish?

I didn't think so. It *was* different this time; she wanted everything, and when I wasn't forthcoming she would gently, subtly coax me out. No, it *was* another time and place entirely. I'd had nearly seven years to deal with my past, and although the present situation had brought it strongly to mind, I knew deep down that Bethy was put to rest.

The sunlight brushed against my face, warming it slightly despite the absence of heat in the small room. I settled back down, my face resting scant inches from hers. I could feel the soft ebb of her breath against my cheek. A pulse throbbed in her neck, its beat slow and steady—in complete contrast to the hammering that was going on in my chest. Mostly hidden by the shelter of the heavy covers, I could feel her naked body against mine, impossibly smooth and oddly cool, yet reassuring. Tentatively, I reached out with my right hand. My eyes left her face and trailed down, following my fingers over the white skin of her shoulder and down along to her thin-boned hand. The gentle swell of her breast was partially concealed beneath her upper arm, and the restricted view only served to heighten the intimacy. I watched the minuscule, almost colorless hairs that furred her arms spring up, catching the morning light like silver thread. I played the tips of my fingers back up along her forearm, smiling slightly as she sighed, still asleep. I wandered up the curve of her neck, tracing around her ear, then over her mouth. I leaned down slowly and stroked my moist lips across hers. Ailish's eyes flickered open, and for a moment, just the slightest instant, there was a look of . . . anguish? on her face; her brow wrinkled, her mouth opened slightly, and her emerald irises contracted in the bright light. For that split second, it was as if she didn't know who I was, but then sleep must've fled, and a wide smile reached across her features, warming me more than any sun. Two thin creases bracketed either side of her delighted grin, and with the green fire blooming in her eyes, she drew me down.

ii

Two weeks passed as swiftly as the weather changed, and each day our love deepened.

Just when I thought nothing could surprise me about Ailish anymore, she would do or say something, and a heart that I already thought was full would swell even further. I loved her more intensely and all-encompassingly than I would ever had imagined possible. She quite literally became my life. All other things were secondary, even the music, although that too took on another dimension for me.

Ailish seemed to take an incredible delight in even the simplest things I did. She was everywhere I was, her fingers touching, eyes searching as she observed me living. Most mornings, she would sit on the end of the old enamel bath, watching fascinated while I shaved. I must admit that it wasn't so perfect for both of us, as I became aware of her scrutiny—often painfully so—and as likely as not, my nervous hands shook. But Ailish was always there to "kiss away the hurt," as she put it, and sometimes I wondered if, unconsciously, I cut myself shaving on purpose.

She loved music, both when I played for her, and the prerecorded discs on my shelf. Several mornings I awoke to the sounds of the radio, blasting out tunes at a twilight hour (I had shown Ailish how to start the generator, and although she seemed repulsed by the smell of it, she had grasped the idea immediately). During the evenings, we sat by the heavy fire, talking, playing games—I taught her to play chess, and she beat me every time—but usually just filling ourselves with music.

The first time she sang with me, I had nearly been overwhelmed. Her voice was stunning, as crystalline as the streams that threaded the hills yet as eternal as the mountains. It possessed a strength and a purity that I don't think I had ever heard before—and I made my living playing fiddle to some of the greatest singers of our time. I would be playing a tune, usually something slow, and quite without announcement, Ailish would begin singing, making up the words as she went along. I always watched her with awe, trying desperately to keep my mind on what I was playing while being conscious of every hair on my neck rising up as if to listen. Her voice literally sent goose bumps rippling over my body as if I had slipped into a cold bath. Our music sessions nearly always ended in lovemaking. It was as if the melodies and tunes awoke a similar need in both of us. The spring would begin coiling within almost as soon as the first notes bled from my strings, and it would continue tightening until one of us—and it was not only me—could stand it no longer.

How could life possibly be better? I had asked myself one evening as we lay entwined together before the hearth, our sweat-shining bodies glistening in the enthusiastic firelight. Ailish seemed as happy as I, but sometimes I would find her wandering the cottage, humming a melancholy tune—a mood that would always be dispelled as soon as she saw me, but still. I never could linger on my doubts for long—her infectious nature made sure of that.

No more snow had fallen, and with most of the month over, I silently wondered if we had seen all of it for this year. The days and nights were still bitterly cold, and in the mornings, it took all of my willpower to leave the fervent heat of the bed for the near-arctic conditions of the bathroom. The thin white blanket that coated the Highlands had frozen into a treacherous, crispy layer that glittered in the brilliant sunlight like the frozen surface of the loch.

At night, under the gaze of the moon, Strath Shinary would take on the mantle of a magic place, with a thousand eyes hiding in the deep shadows further up the valley. Night creatures would call out; foxes on the hunt, capercaillie, and occasionally the silhouette of a stag would be seen, silver-lit against the black of the sky, running majestically along a ridge as if fleeing the hunt. The silent shapes of owls and other nocturnal birds would drift overhead like ghosts, not even the soft beat of their wings breaking the silence. The river, Lón Mòr, meandered its way swiftly down from the higher ground, spilling gracefully into Sandwood Loch before resuming the short journey across the sand to the waiting arms of the sea.

More than ever, Sandwood engraved itself into my mind during those first few weeks of our relationship. I saw beauty where I had overlooked it, and found a grace that I had always known was there but had never truly seen. I knew it was all due to Ailish, and I felt like all that had gone before had just been in preparation to the existence I now enjoyed.

A re you sure?" I asked, the disappointment probably obvious on my face.

Ailish nodded and smiled in that way that made it impossible for me to argue with her.

"All right then. See you soon."

I opened the door, stepping back slightly as the cold air gusted inward. I felt Ailish's hand on my arm, and I turned just in time to receive a passionate kiss on the lips. Her touch was lingering and filled with the usual promise, and for a very real moment I considered not going.

"Hurry back," she said, resting a hand on the side of the door and holding it open for me. With another quick kiss, I stepped out into the freezing gray afternoon.

I was on my way to Kinlochbervie; a short trip just to pick up some food (I hadn't counted on there being two of us) and anything else I might find. I'd tried to persuade Ailish to come along, but she had politely refused, preferring instead to stay within the warmth of the bothy. An odd choice for someone who had no regard for the temperature.

My boots crunched through the hard layer of ice that

had once been soft snow, and as I walked over to the Land Rover I was careful not to slip. Down to my left, the waves chased each other lazily up the beach, curiously sedated considering the evil wind that howled down from the north.

The lock in the car door was thankfully ice-free, and I all but jumped in. The engine turned a few times before grumbling reluctantly to life. I flicked all the heater controls to defrost and popped the boot open, then I shut the door and wandered round the back, raising the large hatch. As I did, I looked back at the bothy. Ailish stood in the doorway, silently watching me. Even though it was only just after midday, the sky was grim enough that she was outlined by the faint glow from the fire. I raised my hand, grinning when she did the same.

Fishing around in the clutter of junk, I pulled out the ice scraper and the plastic bottle of antifreeze and proceeded to clean the crystal-hard shell from the windows and mirrors. Frost chips flew about me like snow, spotting on my face for a moment before melting into drops of water that the wind quickly tried to refreeze. The smell of the antifreeze spray was sharp and bitter, reminiscent of some of the more exotic liqueurs I had drunk in my youth, but it did the job well.

By the time I was done, I was sweating within my coat. I banged the scraper clean on one of the large tires and chucked it back inside with the bottle, slamming the boot down. I got inside the now-warm interior and revved the engine a few times, then stuck the smaller of the gear levers into four-wheel drive, high ratio. I pulled the other down into D, then drove up past the bothy to the shed to load the few empty jerry cans before crawling on toward the beginning of the crude track. With a final vigorous wave to Ailish, I began carefully picking my way toward the road.

I had a few hairy moments. The section of the path that ran between Loch á Mhuilian and Lochain nan Sac was deadly with ice, great peat-dark sheets that stretched across the two furrows like frozen rivers, and at one point, I was forced to leave the track, my wheels biting fiercely at the diamond-hard earth as I steadily edged the Rover forward.

Thankfully, the road from Sheigra to Kinlochbervie was in a better state. It was not important enough for the snow-plows, but the movement of traffic had all but cleared it of snow.

Kinlochbervie was quiet as always, but down at the harbor it looked to be life as normal. The biting cold was no excuse not to work here, and the trawlers and boats that were docked were crawling with fishermen off-loading catches and preparing for the next trip out onto the sea.

I pulled into a space next to the small grocery shop and switched off the engine. Deprived of the heater, I was surprised how quickly the air in the cabin cooled. Picking up my jacket and wallet, I opened the door and stepped down onto the street. In a sudden flurry of limbs and frosting breath, I hurriedly put on my coat. With the zipper done tightly up to where my scarf lay coiled around my neck, I shoved my hands deep into my pockets and set off at a brisk pace. It was nearly Christmas, and Kinlochbervie had a festive atmosphere about it. Decorations and fir trees decked out with tinsel stood in windows, lighting the dull afternoon with flashes of cheerful Technicolor brilliance, and the door to the Compass was adorned with a massive holly and ivy wreath. The smell of burning wood was in the air, as the wind tugged at the ribbons of smoke issuing from most of the chimneys. I walked on past the Compass, and my nose was assaulted by the wonderful odor of roasting chestnuts, something I had not smelled for years. It conjured many images in my mind of Christmases past, and as I walked to the first of the shops on my list, I was whistling a merry carol.

About an hour later I was just about finished. All I had left to do was fill the jerry cans and top up the tank with petrol. Brushing back my sleeve, I looked at my watch; just after three. I was contemplating driving into Ullapool. It had occurred to me that Ailish didn't have any clothes other than that russet dress (she had taken to parading around in some of my older things, a look I found delightfully ridiculous), and I thought that I ought to buy her some other items to wear. I'd actually asked her if she wanted to return to her home to fetch anything, but she had dismissed me with an answer something along the lines of "I live here now."

I paused, the key half in the lock, and looked at the sky. The clouds were moody, but it didn't look like it would storm or snow. With my mind made up, I opened the door. I knew I only had an hour of daylight left at best, and it was a sixty-odd-mile round trip, but now the idea had taken seed. Driving away swiftly, I pulled an illegal U-turn and headed south on the A894, the music of Atlantic 152 issuing from the speakers.

Despite the tang of the sea and the crisp bite of the night air, I could still smell the aroma of burning bread.

I wrinkled my nose and looked over at the bothy as I slammed the car door.

Light bloomed out suddenly over the white-coated grass

and Ailish rushed out into the night, barefoot and ignorant of the cold. Before I had a chance to put down the great burden of bags, she was in my arms, her head in my shoulder. What had at first been amusement quickly turned to concern as I realized she was quite upset.

"Here now," I said, dropping the remainder of the shopping to the floor to hold her close. "What's the matter?"

She mumbled something into my coat and looked up at me. Her normally bright and mischievous eyes were dull and glistening with tears. I reached up a hand and stroked her cheek, smiling as reassuringly as I could. "Did you have an accident?" I asked gently.

She shook her head.

When it became clear I wasn't going to get an answer from her immediately, I said, "Let's get inside where it's warmer, then you can tell me what's wrong."

Ailish nodded, sniffing slightly. I kissed her once, then bent down to pick up the bags strewn at my feet. Ailish did too, but I said hurriedly, "Not that one!" and she looked up at me in surprise. My manner softened, and I looked a little coy. "That's a surprise."

She smiled and I felt some of the worry drain away.

Walking into the bothy, I noticed the thin layer of smoke that hung on the air, and, dropping the bags, I went to the oven and opened the door. Inside, rather burned but probably just about edible, was a large loaf of bread. Wrapping a towel about my hand, I pulled it out and set it down on the sink.

Ailish came in, closed the door, and sat down in one of the chairs.

"Did you forget about this?" I asked, gesturing to the charred loaf. She nodded glumly. "It doesn't matter," I told her, with a flash of a grin. "I like them well done."

She smiled wanly at my poor attempt at humor. I pulled off my coat and scarf, hanging them on the peg as I crossed to kneel before her.

"What's up?" I asked, laying my hands on her legs. Her dress was cold, chilled by the wind, but I could feel the life beneath.

For a moment, she was silent and just sat there looking at me with those liquid eyes, then she said, "I was worried." Her voice was little more than a hushed whisper.

The relief broke through me like a wave, and I almost laughed as I hugged her tight. "Oh, you silly thing," I said lovingly, cupping her chin with my hand. "What on earth were you worried about?"

She looked down briefly, swallowed, then replied, "I didn't think you were coming back . . . that you had left me."

I rocked back on my heels, a hand holding the arm of the chair for support.

I was stunned.

A tiny fraction of me—the self-centered, churlish part— was reassuringly pleased by her answer, for it meant that she must feel roughly the same way about me that I did about her. Wincing, I instantly regretted the thought.

"Hey," I said, pulling her forward into my arms. "Come here."

I don't think she'd been crying, but I knew she was still morose. I was a little alarmed that she had reacted this way, but then I suppose, being out here all on her own . . . once again, I pushed that train of thought from my mind as I held her tightly to me. I burrowed my nose into her hair, marveling at its scent. Ailish still smelled distinctly wild and untamed, and there was the slight nip of salt there too, and possibly damp, and absently I wondered if she had washed her hair.

With my face still over her shoulder, and my hand running up and down her back, I said, "I went down to Ullapool. I'm sorry—it was a spur-of-the-moment thing." I gently pushed away from her, my eyes seeking hers. "I won't go away again," I told her. "I promise." I silently wondered what would happen when I gigged—a problem we'd work out together when it arose.

She smiled and nodded, and everything seemed all right again.

"Here," I said, rustling one of the bags up between us. "I bought you a few things. I know it's not Christmas yet but . . ."

She rummaged through the white plastic carrier, her hands coming out with a dark green dress. Without any hesitation, she jumped up from the chair and shrugged off the one she was wearing. I blinked at the sight of her before me, the sudden nakedness, and felt a slight twinge of disappointment as the heavy emerald-colored cotton glided down over her. I'd got the color just right (the vividness of her eyes never left my mind), and as she stood in front of the fire, her hands gripping at the fabric, I asked, "What do you think? Do you like it? I had to guess the sizes, but I reckon I got them just about right. . . .," I think I was almost as eager as she was.

For a moment, Ailish was silent, then she dropped to her knees and kissed me with rough abandon, her hands gripping my head tightly. "I'll take that as a yes," I murmured when she released me. "There's more . . .," I began, turning to another bag, but she was quicker, her deft hands pulling out the other items before I had a chance. Skirts, a pair of dark jeans, shirts, a jumper, shoes, and underwear were all consecutively tried on while I sat there, my back to the chair, slightly bewildered by Ailish's almost childlike reactions to what I barely gave a second thought to. She looked different in the new clothes, more . . . civilized, I suppose, but no less special. Ailish's enigmatic quality was inbuilt. She thrilled me no matter what she wore.

"I thought it best to stick to browns and greens—considering your hair and eyes," I told her. Ailish just shrugged.

By the end, the only items not to really meet with her overwhelming approval were the pair of shoes and the underwear, which were both deemed uncomfortable. Who was I to argue?

Dressed finally in the jeans and heavy autumn-colored sweater, Ailish flumped on top of me suddenly, knocking me sideways. Her small body straddled me, and her hands, surprisingly strong, pinned my arms up by my head. For a time she just looked down at me, with nothing but my slightly winded breathing breaking the crackling monotony of the fire. Then slowly, with a rather serious expression that sent my stomach rolling, she lowered her face until it was scant inches from mine. I felt my body responding; already aroused by the sight of her trying on the clothes, it took little to tilt my feelings from appreciation over to desire. Strands of her hair tickled my nose, and I resisted the urge to blow them clear, so rapt was I by her countenance. In the half-light of the room, her pupils were impossibly wide, so much so that her eyes looked almost black.

Bottomless pools I knew I was to drown in.

Lips the color of holly berries parted slightly, and down amid my waist, where our bodies met, I thought I could feel the drumming of her pulse, or was it mine?

The quiet was replete, perfect, then:

"I love you, Richard."

She spoke the words in English!

Her accent was thick, lilting, perfect, and the shudder that ran through my body was devastating. My mouth opened, trying to form words, a reply, anything, but it was stuffed with cotton wool and nothing would emerge. It had been so unexpected, so startling, but God how I had *needed* to know.

My arms now free, I reached up and drew her down onto me, one hand brushing the hair back from her face, drawing comfort from her weight on my chest. I held her so tight I thought she might break, my head again in her hair so that she wouldn't see the tears that coursed down my face.

iii

Christmas came and went as quickly as it always did.

We didn't really celebrate it properly, like most adults, I guess. Since losing my childhood I wasn't all that enamored of the whole concept (I've always jokingly said I'm more a pagan than a Christian), and Ailish seemed to have an interest, but no overwhelming enthusiasm. For her, it was the New Year's Eve that was there to be enjoyed, so we agreed to do something that night. But still, one of the other articles I had bought in Ullapool had been a reasonable-sized goose (I positively *hate* turkey), and we spent most of Christmas morning preparing and cooking it, a true joint effort, along with potatoes and as many different sorts of "greens" as I could find this time of year in the local shops.

Ailish added a few articles that, although at the time I

looked on with an expression close to distaste, later proved to be delicious. The two that will stick in my mind were the seaweed (boiled and surprisingly tasty) and something else I was not privy to the name of, a green, cylindrical vegetable of some sort that tasted somewhat like a turnip. I knew she'd got them from the rock pools down near Am Buachaille. A peculiar inclusion on the traditional festive menu, but then, that was Ailish.

But it was a good meal, even if the meat was a little greasy, and afterward we even exchanged a few small presents.

What to buy her (other than clothes) had been a slight dilemma to me as I had plodded the streets of Ullapool. She wore no jewelry or ornaments, and I disliked buying things like that anyway. No, what to get for her was a definite problem; there was a distinct lack of the materialistic about her.

Eventually, I had found something in an old shop down one of the side lanes. Its dark, almost dilapidated-looking front was undecorated and not the style to inspire instant buying potential, but I entered all the same, unsure if it was even open. Inside I had been greeted by a surly-faced man and a Pandora's box.

"Here," I said, handing her the small rectangle of bright paper. As usual, we sat before the fire, our faces ruddy from the glow. The room was shrouded in shadow, no other lamps were lit, and the effect from the flames was wonderful and eerie. A round disk of iron sat to one side on the fire, resting on a specially cleared bed of glowing embers. A handful of sweet chestnuts lay scattered over its surface, roasting slowly, and their wonderful woody aroma filled the air.

Ailish took the present apprehensively, turning it over in her hands while looking at me curiously.

"Open it up," I urged her, the anticipation almost bursting from me. Carefully, she undid the parcel, intricately peeling back each piece of sticky tape. I had to credit her patience—I would've ripped it apart.

The thin, leather-bound book slipped into her hand, and she looked at it, eyes wide, fingers stroking the cover worn smooth from years of hands doing the exact same thing. She opened the first page and traced the flowing script, then looked up at me again. "What does it say?" she asked quietly.

For a moment, I was utterly astounded. Could she really not read? Were there really communities up here that still relied on oral tradition? Surely not! Then it hit me, and I slapped the flat of my hand against my forehead.

The book was in *English!* What an idiot! With frustration screwing up my face, I apologized profusely.

"I'm so, so sorry. I didn't think. When I saw it in the shop, I thought it would be so perfect. It's a first edition—1952, but . . ." I clicked my teeth together to shut off the tirade. Ailish was looking at me with that laughter smile of hers, and in a slower manner, I told her, "It's called *The Old Man and the Sea*. Ernest Hemingway?" I raised my eyebrows, but she shook her head. Undaunted, I carried on. "It's about an old man . . ."

"Really?"

I scowled with mock consternation and the interruption and tried to continue, finding it difficult under Ailish's humorous expression. "Who . . . catches a really big fish," I finished somewhat lamely.

"I knew a man that caught a big fish once," she said in a light tone.

"What happened?" I asked, getting sucked in as always. "It swallowed him."

For a moment I just sat there and looked at her. Being serious was going to be impossible, I knew. Ailish was in one of her puckish moods, but then just as I thought she was going to continue her line of impishness, her eyes became serious and she said, "Thank you." There was a gap of silence, then she asked, "Would you read it to me?"

I nodded. "Of course. I'd love to. Tonight, if you like."

"I would like that very much," she replied, leaning forward to kiss me. When we separated, I could see her eyes glinting with mischievousness once more, and she swiftly got to her feet.

"I have something for you also," she told me, hopping nimbly over my legs and disappearing into the dark of the bedroom. I heard the soft shuffling of clothes, then she reappeared, her arms behind her back and a fractious grin lighting her pixie face.

"Close your eyes!" she ordered. I did so, trying not to peek through the chinks as I heard her sit down next to me. I could feel her warm thigh against mine, and the ill-suppressed mirth on her sweet breath.

Something cold, hard, and glassy was pressed into my opened hands, and as I closed my fingers, I knew it was a bottle. "Can I open my eyes now?" I asked.

"Yes," Ailish replied, and I felt her sit back slightly.

I was right (what else could be that shape?); it was a deeply amber bottle. I held it up before me and pushed my glasses back on my nose slightly. There was no label and the cork was covered in the remnants of what must've once been a wax seal. The liquid inside looked to be clear, but with the darkness of the glass it was difficult to tell. There was a feeling of oldness about it, and my curiosity was piqued.

"What is it?" I asked, holding it up to the light.

Ailish replied, "Whisky. I think."

My eyes flicked to her face, and I looked at her over the rim of my glasses. "You don't know?"

"Well, it *should* be whisky," she went on, "but it might have spoiled."

"Why?"

Her frown wrinkled but her face remained lit. "It's a long story."

"Wait a minute," I said suddenly. "It's off that wreck, isn't it?"

Ailish nodded, delighted, and clapped her hands.

"My God. Where did you get it?"

She made an obscure gesture, and I looked back at the bottle in awe, shaking my head slightly. During the Second World War, a cargo ship had sunk off the west coast, down near Skye, I think, though I couldn't remember exactly where. One of the ship's cargoes had been hundreds of bottles of whisky, bound for America. Since then, lucky fishermen, beachcombers, and divers had found bottles of the wonderful drink all along the western beaches—most of it unharmed, preserved by the years at the bottom of the sea. I seemed to recall a recovered crate of the stuff selling for thousands at Sotheby's. I'd thought the wreck just about played out after all this time, but apparently not.

"Can I open it?" I asked. Ailish nodded vigorously.

I stood and went to the kitchen, clattering though the cutlery until I found the corkscrew. I picked up two glasses and sat back down next to her. I chipped off the rest of the wax seal and tossed it into the fire. Thankfully, it looked to have covered most of the cork. Rather than risk pulling out the cork by hand, I decided to use an opener. There was a fair bit of resistance as I twisted it in, a good sign that the cork was still sound. With the bright metal fully inside, I stopped for a moment. "You know it might just be old vinegar?" I warned her, but Ailish dismissed my worry with a wave of her hand. I put the bottle between my legs and pulled. The effort needed was considerable. I suppose time must have swelled the cork considerably. For a moment, I feared it might break off inside, but then, with my face beet-red, there was a sudden loud squeak, and my arm flew back, almost catching Ailish in the face. I apologized again.

Tentatively, I lifted the opening to my nose and sniffed. The sharp bite of whisky almost made my eyes water, and with a broad grin plastered over my face, I poured out two small measures. Raising the glass to my lips, I took a tiny sip. The liquid burned over my tongue and trickled like molten metal down my throat. It was wondrously smoky, rich flavored, and strong. I nodded encouragingly and took another. It was a good quality single malt, and though I knew whisky didn't really improve once in the bottle, it was the thought of drinking something so old, so precious, that made it wonderful. Ailish had already drunk hers, finishing it up with a cough and a slightly startled expression of delight. Up until that point, the best whiskies I had tasted had been Jack's twenty-year-old things that he only dragged out occasionally. This eclipsed them all, but then, the present company probably also played a part.

I put down my glass and gathered Ailish up into a great hug. "Thank you," I said into her ear. "Merry Christmas."

iv

In the pure, unbroken darkness of midnight, I sat upright in bed, one hand reaching back onto the pillows for support while the palm of the other covered my mouth.

My eyes were wide, desperately searching the impenetrable black for some splinter of reality to cling to, but there was nothing, only the night. A cold sweat beaded over my body, and bitter shudders still trembled through my limbs like the aftereffects of some disease.

The nightmare had been truly terrifying—all the more so for my inhibited recollection now I was awake, and the ripples of fear that had electrified my nerves while I was asleep were now only just fading. Sickening sensations washed over me, and the saliva gathered in the back of my throat. For a moment, I hung terribly close to vomiting, but somehow I managed to step back.

Beside me, I felt Ailish stir, her voice soft and sleep-numbed as she asked what was wrong. I shook my head, my hand still over my mouth, not realizing the gesture would be unseen. A small hand slipped up over my slick shoulder and squeezed, indicating I should lie back down.

The silence was intense, as bloated as the pitch-dark night without our home. For all I knew I sat at the bottom of the abyss, so complete was the sensory deprivation.

I swung my legs out of bed and walked shakily from the bedroom.

Entering the living room, I pulled out a chair, positioning it in front of the remains of the fire, and sat down heavily, as if exhausted.

I leaned down and rested my elbows on my knees and hung my head, my eyes looking numbly at the fire. With one hand across my sweat-damp face, I wept.

For what, I didn't yet know.

21

Cape Wrath is well named.

I stood at the top of the adjoining hill, looking out over the ragged bar of rocks to the sea. From this height, the cliffs were little more than a vague discoloration below me, with only the tops visible where the grass suddenly stopped, and certainly no indication of their height. I knew that there were places where the sheer granite visage dropped over eight hundred feet into the pounding sea below. The highest in Britain. Tonight, as if aware and somehow responding to our presence, the sound of the sea was muted, blending in almost perfectly with the rush of the ferocious wind that grabbed at my coat and scarf. I stood, my ears and eyes open and receptive to the night. The solitude and isolation up here were palpable, even more so than Sandwood. It felt like the top of the world, with no one other than Ailish here with me. Directly overhead, the sky was close enough to touch, and the thousands of stars provided a delicate light. The thin sickle of moon was hidden behind a deepening wall of ghostly cloud that was rumbling in majestically off the sea, and though the easternmost edges of the mass were feathered with silver most of it was only a shade lighter than the water. Across the surface of the Atlantic, tiny facets glittered like coins at the bottom of a well. Rhythmically, the sky was lit by a pulse of light, a beacon as the lighthouse up on the cape flashed out its warning.

Ailish's voice drifted up to me from the side of the next hill, carried on the obliging wind. "Come on, Richard!"

I stuffed the errant end of my scarf back under my collar and started after her, careful of my footing on the back-breakingly hard ground. I kept my hands out of my pockets, primarily in case I slipped on a rock and fell, but also because my wrists were aching like fury. As I trumped along behind her, I tried to remember if I had picked up anything heavy in the past few days or banged my hands, but nothing came to mind.

I was a little worried—what musician wouldn't be? My hands were quite literally my livelihood, and any injury was a potential disaster.

Still, I couldn't feel anything wrong, and I could move them both reasonably well, so I hadn't strained them or done anything serious. The throbbing was deep, as if I had somehow bruised the bones.

I glanced up from where I had been watching the ground and looked at Ailish's back. With the pain all but forgotten, I hurried after her.

Our walk up here from the bothy had been invigorating, tiring, and dangerous, but worth it. The distance to the headland was only about five miles, but we had allowed three hours, and both of us knew we would spend most of that time descending into deep gullies, scrambling out of coves, and generally avoiding the frozen marshes. Then of course there was the darkness to take into account.

It was New Year's Eve, and God only knows why we'd

decided to walk up here, when most rational people were in by the fire. But Ailish and I weren't exactly the most rational people, and it had seemed like a good idea.

I stepped over the tall frozen stems of the tussocks, drawing level with her once more. With my panting breath vanishing behind me, I looked over and smiled. As always, Ailish seemed barely winded. She looked slightly comical wrapped up in one of my oversized coats.

"Not far now, eh?" I whispered, not knowing why I kept my voice so low. She grinned, her teeth almost as startling white as the beam from the lighthouse that scythed through the night. I mirrored her expression, then felt her cold hand worming its way into my pocket. Giving it a reassuring squeeze, I lowered my head, watching my footing as we walked on.

We reached the cape about ten minutes later, knowing we were close when the lime-washed lighthouse building appeared on the horizon. The waves were noticeably louder here, as if the exposure of the headland somehow amplified their never-ending war upon the land.

We walked past the building, giving it only the briefest of inspections. Up until only recently it was staffed, but now, with economic cutbacks and downsizing, it had been turned into one of those automated affairs, locked and bolted, probably completely controlled from a dry, warm room in Glasgow. We reached the edge of the cliff and stopped. Access to the pinnacle was denied by the rather severe drop down onto the thin bridge of rock that joined it to the land, so we were content to sit down on the grass, as close as we dared. I slipped the light bag off of my shoulder and dug out the flask of whisky (just Glenfiddich this time) we had brought with us, pouring out two small drams and passing one to Ailish. Once more the light arced overhead, lighting our faces briefly before sweeping on. The alcohol seeped into my blood, strong and potent. I put down my cup and looked at my watch. We'd timed it almost perfectly, as there were only five minutes to go before midnight.

We didn't need to speak, we were just content in each other's company. Without a doubt, this headland, standing as it does at the most northerly point of Sutherland, is the wildest, most primitive place in all of Britain. The feelings that coursed though me as I rested there were almost primal in their intensity. This was not the place for humans. There was just too much power in the air, the sea, and the land. I looked over to the west and felt a slight jab of alarm as I saw how much closer the bank of clouds had come toward us. There was no sight of even the small fleck of silver light on the water, and from the heavy, leaden feel to the wind that ran at its fore, I knew it was going to rain.

I didn't care.

The night was so perfect, just being here with her. I clenched her hand tighter within mine, and Ailish leaned over to kiss me. We huddled together, not really for the warmth, but more for the feeling of closeness, and I slipped an arm around her. With under a minute to go, we both stood and embraced, waiting patiently, just drinking in the sight of one another.

"Happy New Year," I said to her, first in English, then Gaelic.

She spoke something in a language I wasn't familiar with, though the words tugged achingly at my subconscious, then, barely audible over the smashing of the waves, she whispered, "Together. Always."

My heart thumped at what she had said, the way her face had looked, so solemn and sincere, yet filled with love.

I was feeling peculiar, almost drunk, and when the wet wind fervently caressed my head, I turned round suddenly.

Even though it was night, I could still see the wall of rain that swept in, smothering the cliffs and hissing on the grass of the headland. Like a heavy trailing cloak, it enveloped the lighthouse building, but even in its fury, the rainstorm could not contain the stabbing light of the beacon fully. It hit me like a fist, instantly drenching my hair and rattling like hundreds of nails off my coat. I heard Ailish's sudden cry, then delighted laugh.

It was a marvelous sensation. The water entered my eyes, ears, nose, everywhere. It was cold, stinging, and intrusive, but I didn't care. It may have been the alcohol, but my core was burning with wildfire, and I turned round, picking Ailish up and spinning her around as the storm lashed passionately around us. We turned one way, and the beam of light overhead, thick and visible now, a horizontal column of brilliance, followed. I put her down, laughing madly like a fool as I roughly kissed her cold, wet lips. Her eyes were sparkling like emeralds, and with her hair plastered around her head and the rain running in rivers from her chin, I thought she had never looked as beautiful.

"I love you!" I shouted in Gaelic, the wind doing its best to steal the words from my mouth but failing. The look on her face was incredible, stupefying, and I repeated the words, laughing them down joyously onto her. She jumped into my arms rapturously, her slight weight nothing against the strength of the emotions that were exploding within me. I heard her reply, the words choked and muffled, but as clear to me as my own. We disengaged a little, and I raised my hands to the raging sky like a prophet calling down a blessing.

"I love you!" I roared again, face to the storm, my voice

breaking as I battled the sheer rage of the elements. An almost ecstatic grin split my face as the rain drummed its icy fingers over my skin, as if demanding entry. I closed my unseeing, water-blinded eyes, once more feeling Ailish's strong arms going around me. She held me tight, possessively, almost squeezing the final cry from me like the wind from a bellows.

Then, still together, we fell, slipping on the perilous grass and tumbling into a single heap, the love and laughter spilling from us like the rain from the sky.

22

I knew I was going to have to go back to see Doctor Williamson.

This time though, I would not be going to seek out more information, I'd be going as a patient.

The pain in my wrists had been getting steadily worse, to the stage where I could barely play fiddle. It was an odd kind of pain, as if I had somehow knocked them both against something and perhaps bruised the tendon. There was no specific point of pain though, like a bruise or a blemish, though they did hurt if I pressed into the joints.

At times, the pain was bad enough that I had trouble doing menial tasks like washing up or even holding something. Mostly, it was a low, pulsing ache that caused me to walk around the house rubbing my wrists constantly. The cold did nothing to help me either.

I was scared.

I imagine that the thought of arthritis or some other form of debilitating disease of the joints is a very real fear for most musicians, if not everyone. To have my only means of living and my one true personal passion stripped away would do nothing short of destroy me.

Although I kept my fears of disease to myself, Ailish knew I was in pain and did what she could, which meant everything to me. The evening I finally decided to go to the doctor's, she sat opposite me before the fire, her cool hands gently massaging my sore and swollen wrists while she sang to me. It was probably just my imagination, but it did seem to help. Perhaps it was just that her voice and presence took me away for a time. She was utterly wonderful, and her tenderness touched me more than I can say.

I was pretty sure that what I had was nothing more than some sort of infection, or at worse, tendonitis, in which case I would just have to cut back on my playing for a time. Although hard, that wouldn't be impossible, especially since it was winter and gigs were few and far between at the moment.

I supposed I'd find out in the morning.

There was a low mist hanging out over Sandwood Loch. The valley was utterly still and silent, as if it were holding its breath. Occasionally, my eye would be drawn away from the tranquillity of the water by the flicker of movement as a dipper or some other waterbird that fed on the shores suddenly took flight. The sky above me was shatteringly blue, and I could just make out the faint disk of the moon, even though it was just after midday.

I rubbed a hand down my face and looked back over the water.

Never before in my life had I felt such a sense of utter despair. It's as if we go through life with no real control over anything that happens to us. Sure, we *think* we make decisions about our careers, the path we take, how we lead our lives, but really, we're at the mercy of random chance. I've never been a particularly religious person, but I was beginning to think that if there was a God, he or she was up there at the moment having a right royal laugh at us.

But then I suppose, like Doctor Williamson said, nothing is certain.

A h, Richard, back so soon?"

"This time it's purely professional," I told him as I crossed the room and sat in the familiar leather chair.

"What can I do for you this fine morning?"

Taking a deep breath, I told him in as much detail as I could about the problem. I've never been all that comfortable around doctors, but Iain Williamson soon had me telling him a hundred little details through a series of pointed questions.

When I had finished, he capped the pen he had been taking notes with and came around the desk. Sitting on the edge, he took my hands in his and began manipulating the joints. His skin was cool and waxy, but his touch was firm.

"You've a fair bit of swelling in them both," he remarked.

"It's actually not quite so bad this morning," I told him, hoping it was a good sign.

He moved my hands around for a few moments, then asked, "Can you pop off your jacket and roll up your sleeves, please."

I did so, and he spent a few minutes feeling around my elbows, concentrating on my right one. He seemed to have found something, and when he returned to sit behind his desk, I had a quick feel and felt a small lump I'd not known was there before.

Williamson made a few more notes, then sat back looking at me. I could tell by the expression on his face that it wasn't going to be good news.

"Now, none of this is certain," he began, "but I'm pretty sure you've got some sort of arthritis."

I shook my head and sat forward. "What do you mean 'some sort'? Isn't arthritis just that?"

"No, 'arthritis' is just a general medical term. There are over a hundred different types varying from negligible to crippling."

My voice was still remarkably steady. "So what kind have I got?"

"That's what I'm going to find out. I'd like to send you for a few X rays and take some blood for tests. But I have to tell you, your symptoms point toward rheumatoid."

Now I did feel a cold weight plummet through me.

Rheumatoid arthritis.

I remember seeing pictures of deformed feet and wrists and hearing stories from a friend whose mother was all but disabled from it. "But aren't I a little young?" I asked incredulously.

Williamson shook his head. "It can happen at any age—even to children. In fact, judging from your history, you're almost a prime candidate, what with your music, and that your father suffered with it too. The only thing you have in your favor is you're male. The other thing that makes me think it's rheumatoid is the nodule behind your right elbow. They're symptomatic with RA. Look, Richard, it's far more common than most people think. Some doctors suggest that up to one in six people get it."

"How do I find out for certain?"

"I'll take some blood and it'll be tested for rheumatoid factor, which is an abnormal substance that is found in the blood of about eighty percent of RA sufferers. Even then nothing is absolutely certain."

"And if it is rheumatoid arthritis, how do we cure it?" I asked.

"There is no cure, I'm afraid. But there are a number of very good treatments."

"Treatments? What, you mean drugs?" I was beginning to feel sick.

"Not exclusively, but yes. There are anti-inflammatories, and if things get worse, disease-modifying antirheumatic drugs. Many people have a great deal of success and lead normal lives."

"But then most people don't play fiddle for a living either," I replied somewhat aggressively. I think it was only just beginning to sink in.

"No, but you don't have to stop that altogether. Look, until we get the results back, all this is conjecture."

"But you're pretty sure . . ."

He hesitated a moment, then nodded. "It looks that way, but let's wait until we're really sure before we start planning for the future. For the time being, I can prescribe you a course of anti-inflamatories that should take down the swelling, and I'll give you some painkillers to use if you need them. You're going to have to lay off any lifting for a while, and be careful—if it is RA that you have, then you'll experience good and bad days. Don't go hurting yourself because everything feels all right."

"What about my playing?"

"Same thing. Just use your own judgment and try and be careful. If in doubt, don't."

"That's easy for you to say," I told him.

He looked slightly taken aback, but quickly smoothed it over. "It's all a matter of adaptation," he said. "If it is RA—and even if it isn't—there's no telling just how it will affect you. It could be that you'll go through the rest of your life with nothing more than the occasional sore wrist. Or . . ."

"Or?" I prompted.

Williamson made a gesture with his hand. "It could get worse." He paused, then began talking about different kinds of treatments and therapies. I could tell by his voice that he, at least, was convinced.

I sat back, the old leather of the chair sighing under me. I was trying to take in what he was telling me, but my mind was still reeling.

All I could keep thinking was *why me?*

I removed my hands from my face and immediately felt my skin contracting with the cold.

I don't know how long I had been sitting there, my mind adrift, but I was beginning to get cold, despite my thick coat and scarf. The wind picked up slightly, ruffling the smooth waters of the loch into tiny flecking peaks and bending the straggle of leafless shrubs off to my left. In the distance, I could hear the breath of the sea as it exhaled upon the shore, and the occasional plaintive cry of a gull.

I took in a deep draft of air, holding it for a long time before blowing it out as a cloud of steam.

Why me?

Because my life now was just so perfect? Did I somehow deserve this because I had grown lax and content? I did wonder.

I didn't hear her approaching footsteps, but I knew Ailish stood behind me. When it got tired of gusting down toward the sea, the wind would occasionally turn and bring to me the most delicate traces of her, carried like a child's handful of delicate wildflowers. Even though we had been living together intimately, I was still not in any way used to her.

Nor do I think I ever really will be.

As it had been from that very first night, I was bewitched by every facet of her nature, from her stunning beauty to her mannerisms, even her smell. Just knowing she was near calmed me.

For a long time, neither of us spoke.

It was Ailish who finally broke the silence, and although I had somehow known she was there, she startled me with just how close she was.

"It is bad." It wasn't phrased as either a question or a statement, but rather just a simple definition of what I was thinking.

I nodded and turned around. She was only a foot or so away from me, standing perfectly still on the edge of the grass that courted the small sandy inland beach. She looked incongruous in a pair of jeans and a chocolate sweater, slightly different somehow, as if by dressing her in the mundane I was burring off the edges of her wildness. Her feet were, as always, bare, and the fresh breeze played with her hair and reddened her cheeks.

For a moment we just looked at one another, then I held out my arms. She smiled sadly and took two steps forward, closing the distance between us. In one fluid movement, she turned and sat down between my legs, leaning back into me. I wrapped my arms around her waist and pulled her tighter still, resting my chin on her shoulder as we both gazed out over the loch. As she had been doing a lot recently, Ailish absently took my hands and began rubbing them. Her touch was angelic and infinitely soothing.

Could I do it? Could I really give up my music? I wasn't sure that I was really being asked to go that far, but judging from the gravity in Williamson's voice, I knew it was a very real possibility. *Would* I even be able to give up something that was as integral a part of my life?

I lowered my face so it was resting against the back of Ailish's head. She smelled so perfect, so wild yet so comforting.

I closed my eyes and wondered.

It was perhaps half an hour later when she spoke again. I had been content sitting there holding her, and I thought that perhaps she had fallen asleep, but her voice was clear.

"No matter what happens, we will always have each other."

I replied, "That's the only thing that matters to me."

And even after what I had been through today, I knew in my soul that I meant it.

23

Do you believe in ghosts?"
I put the book down onto the duvet that covered my
lap and looked at her curiously. Ailish had been oddly quiet
for most of the evening. Usually, while I read to her from
Hemingway's book, she was alive with queries and comments, but not tonight. She still responded to the story, but
there was something on her mind. She lay deep under the
covers of the bed, with only her oval face visible.

I gave her question a little thought, itching at the side of
my jaw with a thumbnail for a moment before answering.

"I don't know," I replied honestly. "I think that maybe
sometimes things happen that can leave an . . . imprint, on
the land, something that might be called a haunting, I suppose. But it would need to be something pretty horrific, like
a plane crash or a murder . . . or a drowning," I added,
thinking of the ghost I thought I'd seen right here in the
bothy, though I had to confess that was one particular nightmare that did go away.

"What about spirits?"

"Same thing, I would imagine." I sighed and looked at
the play of moonlight across the room for a moment. "Every
religion has to have its own afterlife, otherwise, what is there

to work for? I think we all have an intrinsic need to think that it doesn't just . . . *end* when our hearts give out or the cancer claims us. This is getting heavy," I added.

"Do you believe in myths?" she asked softly, phrasing the question carefully.

"You mean like fairies, magic, and mystery?"

She nodded, eyes uncannily bright. For a moment, I felt like joking, but there was something in her manner that quelled all thoughts of humor. "I guess so," I said as truthfully as I could. "I think myth and legend are part and parcel of being a folk musician. You can't play this sort of music all your life *without* questioning the source. Obviously, if that sort of thing did exist, I doubt if it's anything like the way it's portrayed in all those books." I stopped and smiled; then, as if the realization had suddenly come to me, I said, "Yes, I think I do believe. Sometimes when I'm playing, I can almost *feel* the magic in the air. And when I first saw you, I felt it then too."

The enigmatic smile slipped across her face. I reached over for the bookmark and slipped it between the old, cream-colored pages before putting the book on the table next to me. I turned a little and propped myself up on my elbow as I regarded her face, then shifted position again as I felt a twinge in my left wrist. The light from an almost full moon glittered through the window, and through the open door, I could see the dancing glow from the still-burning fire.

"Actually, I've always been meaning to ask; did you know I was watching you that night?"

Her laugh was infectious. "Of course!"

"Then why did you run?"

"To see if you'd follow."

I stared at her openmouthed. "I thought you were afraid!"

A mock frown creased her forehead. "Afraid of you?" she asked incredulously. "Why would I be afraid of you?"

"You mean to say . . ."

"It took you a long time to pluck up courage to follow me," she said with a chuckle.

In a sudden tangle of sheets, I rolled on top of her, trying to pin her arms but failing miserably. I settled instead with peppering her face with kisses. She shrieked, trying to evade me but failing.

"What if I'd have caught you?" I asked when the laughter had died down.

"What indeed," she replied huskily, and I felt her legs twining around my waist.

"Hey, that's not fair! I'm supposed to be mad at you!" I cried as I felt myself responding to her caresses.

Ailish shrugged. "You can still be mad if you want." And with that, she reached up and kissed me.

I dozed in the warm afterglow of our sex, lazily content and almost numbingly happy.

Surprisingly, my wrists had been giving me little trouble. Doctor Williamson had called me into his surgery a few days ago to confirm that it was "almost definite" that I had rheumatoid arthritis. I had greeted the news with a resigned kind of lassitude that I think bothered him.

The truth was, I was so happy with Ailish that I refused to fully deal with the implications of the disease that might well rewrite my whole way of thinking.

In the end, Williamson had prescribed a series of non-steroidal drugs to begin with and given me a wealth of literature that told me how to live my life. It still sat on the table. Unread.

I could feel myself drifting off to sleep when I heard my name spoken, the voice sounding miles away.

"Richard?"

I ignored it, thinking it the beginnings of a dream, but

when it came again, I roused myself, and my eyes flickered open.

"Richard?"

"What's the matter?" I asked, a sleepy smile appearing as I saw Ailish's face inches from my own.

"Promise me something?" she said, and all sleep fled as I heard the seriousness in her tone.

"Anything."

She brushed the lengthening hair from her eyes. She was silent, and for a moment, I thought I would have to agree again, but then she said softly, "Promise me we'll always be together?" Her voice was odd, almost meek, and coming from her it sounded somehow wrong.

"Of course we will."

She didn't look convinced. I sat up and took her face gently in my hands, kissing her with all the seriousness I could muster. "I promise, Ailish," I told her between kisses. "I've only just found you. I'm not about to let anything happen."

She looked a little more reassured. "We're joined," I continued, forcing a lighter tone into my voice as I lay back down. "Nothing could separate us now anyway."

"Not even death?"

"*Especially* death—with all its nasty pointy fangs," I remarked, with a stupid grin, and though I was rewarded with a smile, I think the Monty Python was lost on her.

"There *is* a bond between us," she agreed. "And it is stronger than anything."

Strangely enough, *I* felt better when she said that.

Her voice changed, taking on a humorous note. "Would you come for me if I was at the top of the highest mountain?"

"Right away."

"Biggest desert?"

"Without second thought."

"Longest valley?"

"Absolutely."

"Deepest sea?"

I hesitated, sensing the sudden difference in her tone. I looked into her eyes. "I promise," I said seriously, then smiled as the tension broke. "What about you?" I said, turning it around.

"Go on, then," she said.

"Darkest dungeon?"

"Yes."

"Widest plain?"

"I suppose so."

"Dirtiest city?"

She frowned. "Maybe."

"Maybe!" I said indignantly. My hands found sensitive spots under the covers and pinched. Ailish suddenly jumped. "Maybe?" I repeated, lower this time.

I tweaked again with my fingers and she squeaked loudly. "Richard! . . . no, *please*, I . . ." She thrashed on the bed, weeping with laughter and trying to beat me off. One of the earliest things I had discovered about Ailish was how exceptionally ticklish she was. I pressed my advantage until she confessed she would swim through lava, dive off cliffs—all the usual lover things.

ii

MARCH

Most of the snows had gone except for one or two smears that lingered on the lee slopes of the mountains.

The winds that came in off the sea were still bitterly cold, but they carried with them an air of rejuvenation, as if they knew spring was just around the corner. The ground was still frozen solid, and each morning, we would awake to a countryside encased in a heavy frost that was just breathtaking. As the days grew gradually longer, Ailish and I took to walking the hills along Strath Shinary, sometimes starting out while it was still dark so that we could watch the magnificent sunrises. On a clear morning, the blazing orb of the sun would gradually climb above the rugged indigo line of the distant mountains, the golden warming rays of its light chasing out before it, gilding the frosted land. It was a truly stunning sight, one made all the more meaningful and intimate when shared with the beautiful woman next to me.

I found that my feelings for Ailish were still increasing. It was almost as if we transcended all barriers for lovers, and just kept on growing together. We shared everything, there were no secrets between us. Our lovemaking wasn't just great, it was stupendous—surpassing my every fantasy, real and imagined. She was the warmest, most physical person I had ever known, constantly kissing or touching me, as if she needed to reassure herself of my existence. And for my part, I was just about the same, if not worse.

The first couple of weeks of the month passed slowly, lazily, with the only real point of reference being the arrival of the much delayed tea chests from Australia. For Ailish and me, it was almost like Christmas all over again. Although I knew what was inside each of them, there was still some sort of delight about pulling them apart. Ailish found it all intriguing, especially my much exaggerated story of what had happened to them during their voyage around the globe.

24

It would only be for an hour or so," I told her, looking over from the table.

My fiddle sat before me, once again shining after I had rubbed it clean of rosin deposits with some rosemary oil.

"I don't know, Richard . . ."

"Come on, Ailish," I said lightly. "It'll be good to get out. It's only Kinlochbervie, after all. A little music, some chat . . ."

She smiled, her shoulders sagging as if weary. At last, she replied, "Can we come home if I want to?"

"Of course," I told her without hesitation. "Whenever you want."

She perked up a little. "All right then."

Ailish crossed the room, kissed me for no reason, then asked brightly, "What shall I wear?"

"Anything you like," I replied, putting the fiddle in its case with something that was almost a sigh of relief. I knew that if she had wanted it, I wouldn't have gone without a second word. "It's only the Compass, after all." She was quiet a moment, as if thinking. "Your green dress is washed," I said.

"Yes. Will you play some music?" she inquired, leaving me and padding into the bedroom.

"Maybe," I shouted to her. "It depends on who's there. Why? Thinking of singing?"

She returned, clothed in the emerald dress, hair covering her face as she looked down to do up her buttons. "Perhaps," she said, with a hidden smile.

When she was dressed, Ailish came over to me and laid a hand on my shoulder. I reached up and took it in one of mine. "Are you sure *you* feel like it?" she asked, twining her fingers around mine.

I knew straightaway she was referring to the arthritis. There was no point lying to her—not that I could have anyway—but if the truth be told, for the past month the pain had been little more than a discomfort. The swellings had gone right down, and although I remembered Williamson's warnings about remission and the dangers of pushing things too far, it was something I wanted to, no, *needed* to do.

"I'm fine, Ailish," I reassured her. "And if they start to hurt at all, I'll stop right away."

"Promise?"

"You have my word."

She looked at me hard for a moment, and I quite honestly thought she was going to argue the point, but she surprised me.

"I'll have more than your word."

It was another half hour before we were ready to leave.

Ailish had never been in the Rover before, and she was quite nervous.

Actually, I found out later on that it was the first time she had been in *any* sort of car, so I drove especially carefully. Her initial apprehension soon melted into joy, and by the time we reached the outskirts of Kinlochbervie, I think she wanted us to drive to the moon. I stepped down from the cab, hurrying round to open Ailish's door. Her bare feet whispered onto the black tarmac, and once again I found myself hoping she would be allowed inside. Still, the long dress swished around her feet, covering them most of the time, so perhaps no one would notice.

With my fiddle case under one arm, and the other around Ailish's slim waist, we walked the short distance to the pub. Ailish was constantly looking around, her mouth opening with silent exclamations as she saw the houses and buildings of the town. She questioned everything, sometimes pointing like a child in a museum at something I would have given no second thought to, like a lamppost or a street sign. I took delight from her wonder, explaining as much as I could in the short time. I suppose to someone from the wilds Kinlochbervie *would* look . . . different.

I pushed open the door and we stepped into the sheltered porch, where we halted for a moment. "Remember," I said, "we can leave whenever you want to." Ailish nodded, and as I turned to open the other door, she gripped my arm. I turned and she caught me with a kiss. I stepped into her embrace just as the inner door opened and an elderly couple stepped out. We moved out of their way, me apologizing profusely while Ailish laughed into her hand. The old fella found it funny, and made some remark about youth and love, but the woman just tutted. I felt myself blushing as I opened the outer door for them.

Shaking my head and frowning at Ailish with mock anger, I stepped into the other bar. It was a Friday night, and the small bar was full. I had an uneasy sense of déjà vu as we walked across the floor—the last time I had seen it this busy was the evening of the wake. I reached the bar, silently wondering if MacKay was here somewhere. I turned, slowly scanning the crowd, but could not see him. I did see some of the men—young and old—giving Ailish appraising glances though, and I flushed with pride to be with her. Surprisingly, she seemed to be taking it all in her stride, replying to the comments with a polite incline of her head or a few words. Nearly everyone around these parts spoke Gaelic fluently, so her language was not a problem. Indeed, some of the older men's faces lit up with delight to see a young woman speaking the old tongue.

I waited my turn at the bar, then ordered a pint of local bitter for myself and a whisky for Ailish (she'd taken a shine to it during Christmas). The barman hurried about his business, ignoring the plaintive heckles from other patrons. I turned around and Ailish stepped back into my arms, somehow managing to avoid the fiddle case at my feet. In the quieter corner, I could see a few people holding instruments, sitting patiently listening to a woman who was standing and telling a story. Although we couldn't make out the words from here, it was obviously funny, judging by the sudden bursts of laughter. Just to the right of them, I spied the MacDermots, and as they saw me, they gestured for us to come over and join them at their table. I raised a hand in acknowledgment and indicated I was waiting for our drinks.

"That's John and Aggie MacDermot," I said into Ailish's ear. "Friends of Florence, mainly, but I know them quite well."

She nodded and turned around, a big smile on her face. "This is fun," she said merrily. I was relieved she was enjoying the bustle. Nothing had been said about her lack of footwear, and I hoped no one would tread on her toes. Picking up my drink and handing Ailish hers, I pointed and we made our way slowly through the crowd toward John and Aggie.

"Hello, Richard, good t' see yeh, at last!" declared John in his usual brusque, good-natured manner. I reached forward with my hand and shook his callused one. "And who is this?"

"John, Aggie, this is Ailish . . ."

Before I had a chance to explain, John leaned forward and took her hand. "May I say yeh are quite the most lovely person I have e' seen."

Ailish smiled slightly and looked to me. With a quick chuckle, I translated for her. She laughed and shook his hand.

"Please pardon my ignorant husband," Aggie said in perfect Gaelic, leaning forward also. "He neglected his studies at school, instead choosing to chase a ball around a muddy field all day."

"What was that?" John asked, looking from Aggie to me.

"Eh, Aggie said you don't speak Gaelic," I replied somewhat concisely.

"My loss, it would seem," he said, looking once again at Ailish as she sat down next to me.

While Aggie engaged Ailish in somewhat tentative conversation, John leaned over to me and whispered, "So where'd you meet her?"

I shrugged. "Hereabouts."

"When?"

I sipped the head off my bitter. "Oh, Octoberish," I answered with faked nonchalance.

"And this is the first time we've been introduced? What have you been doing up there through those dark winter months?"

"Oh, this and that," I replied, with an enigmatic smile that Ailish would have been proud of. John looked between us, a slight blush coloring his already ruddy cheeks. As if she had understood, Ailish nudged closer to me, and I felt her hand slide up my leg. I think she was enjoying herself after all.

A voice cut through the noise of the bar like an ax.

"Is that Richard Brennan I see over there wi' a fiddle at his feet? In a case an' all!" She made it sound like a crime, and I turned, feeling dozens of eyes on me.

"Hello, Margaret," I said feebly.

"Hello, yourself. Yeh going t' get tha' thing out, or is it just a fancy footstool?"

People around us chuckled, and with a sigh of mock resignation, I produced my fiddle, tuning it briefly before holding it under my chin. Ailish looked on, expectation in her eyes.

"Well, it's about time!" Margaret declared, picking up her guitar and strumming a few chords. "See if you can follow," she said, finger-picking an intricate rhythm in an open tuning. Without any preamble, the man next to her raised a flute to his lips and began to play. I waited until the end of the measure, then joined in. The tune was simple; a dark Shetland reel called "The Gravel Walk," and I had no trouble keeping up. At the end, I changed the pace, slipping into a jig and flashing the challenge to Margaret with my eyes. The flutist stopped, but a bodhran player began, her action heavy and deep.

There was a light smattering of applause when we finished, with Ailish's ringing out loudest. Leaning over, I
asked her, "You all right to stay awhile?" She nodded en-
thusiastically.

About half an hour later, I lowered the fiddle back into
its case and took a tired gulp of the fresh pint that had
been placed down before me. For a time, I just sat there,
talking to Ailish as quietly as the chatter would allow. It
felt good to be away from the bothy for a change—not
that there was anything wrong with the isolation. It was
also great to play with a crowd. My wrists were surprisingly pain-free. A little tired, true, but I think that was due
more to the lack of practice.

I put my mouth next to Ailish's ear and asked, "Would
you like to sing, if I play?"

For a moment, she made no reply, then she nodded. I
kissed her ear, pleased. She turned around to face me.
"What shall I sing?" she asked.

I shrugged. Most of her songs were on-the-spot improv-
izations, all sung in that oddly familiar-sounding language.
"How about I just play a tune and you see what happens?"

Looking over at Margaret, who was the unofficial tune-
caller, I indicated that Ailish and I would like to perform
a duet. She spread her hands, indicating the floor was ours.
I took up my fiddle, absently tightening the frog on the bow
as I wondered what to play. I placed the pony hair lightly
against the strings, then, making up my mind, began to
play.

The notes seeped from my fiddle, slow and aching, and
as was usual when I played, I closed my eyes and opened
my heart.

After the first few bars, Ailish joined in, her voice light
and impossibly clear, slicing through the gabble like a di-

amond blade. I continued, taking my cues from her.

The tune we performed sounded like the old Scots piece "Ailein Duinn," but the words were different and the melody far more subtle.

Then something remarkable happened.

The noise in the pub dulled, then ceased completely, something I had only ever heard happen once before, at a tiny festival tent in Galway when Máire Brennan (no relation) from the band Clannad had stood up and performed an impromptu solo.

But this was better.

Ailish's voice soared over the crowd, circling the room like a bird. It touched everyone, stilling them into silence, then filling them with profound awe. My playing became secondary. I barely concentrated on what I was doing, so rapt was I by the expression on her wondrous face.

When we finished, and the last note left her throat to die softly in the room, the sudden quiet was amazing, then the roar of applause filled the pub. I reached forward, pulling her to me and swallowing her in a great hug. I felt my heart would burst with pride for her. Hands appeared, patting us both on the shoulder while people called for more. Ailish blushed and tried to shrink into my arms, completely overwhelmed by the attention. I was weak with delight, shivering with the remnants of the song, and too bewildered to do anything other than thank people for the response.

One ancient-looking lady came over to us, her face filled with joy, and in heavy Gaelic said to Ailish, "I didnae think there was anyone left alive tha' could speak Cornish—ley alone sing in it."

Ailish thanked her while I sat there, stunned. I'd thought Cornish to have died out about eighty years ago. Apparently not, for not only had Ailish been singing in it, but the old woman had recognized it.

Eventually, when they realized there was to be no more, the crowd stilled, and eventually the regulars struck up again (though with a little less vigor!).

I think most of the occupants of the Compass dropped past us at some time afterward with a quick word of encouragement and thanks. The atmosphere in the pub and the attitude of the people were wonderfully accepting, warming.

I kept congratulating Ailish, telling her how fantasticshe was until her smile was nearly as big as mine.

It was then that I saw him.

He was standing in the shadow to one side of the fire, watching, his form almost totally encased in half-light.

MacKay knew that I had seen him, and for a moment, our eyes locked. Despite the darkness under his cap I could see the odd look that lived in those dark places. My heart skipped a beat as he leaned forward and walked toward us determinedly.

He stopped at the edge of the table and stared down, still with that peculiar expression on his face, like sympathy and knowing. Then, resting a gloved hand on the edge, he bent down, leaning past me to speak to Ailish. His odor filled my nose; noisome and wretched, he stank of sweat, whisky, and something else, like the docks on a hot day. I opened my mouth to speak, but he cut me off without looking, greeting Ailish with a word that sounded something like *Granuina*.

I frowned, trying to work out what he had said, when he continued, speaking to her in a language I didn't recognize. It teased at me, reminiscent of some type of old Gaelic, perhaps a far-north dialect, and there were words that I came tantalizingly close to recognizing, but it all went over my head. It certainly wasn't the beautiful language Ailish had sung in earlier.

She didn't reply, but I saw her eyes flick to me once, the alarm evident. My stomach rolled, and my pulse beat in my head. I'd had enough. Whatever he was saying to her, it didn't sound pleasant, and I raised my hand to draw him back.

But he'd finished.

With a final, long, contemplative look at me, he pulled his cap back on over his wisps of white hair and stepped back into the crowd, leaving behind only the reek of his body and the fear in my heart.

"What was that all about?" John asked, frowning.

I shook my head, looking first at him, then at Ailish. Her eyes were wide and pleading, and without speaking, I knew she wanted to leave.

"I think we'd best be going," I said to them in English, zipping up my fiddle case. "It is getting on, after all."

We went through the usual round of invitations back to their house and polite refusals, and I suppose it was about five minutes later that we finally stepped out into the clear cold of the night.

"What happened in there? Was MacKay rude to you?" I asked her as we drove up the lit high street and then out down the black lane. Ailish sat with her knees drawn up to her chin, her head against the window as she hummed a sad tune. I could see the reflection of her face as she stared out into the dark.

"Ailish?"

She turned, her eyes cloudy and tired-looking. "Umm?"

"What did MacKay say to you?"

"Nothing."

I frowned. "Come on, it was more than nothing. I could see that much from your face."

"I'll tell you later, Richard," she said quietly. "I don't want to talk about it just yet."

I abated, but still the worry for her nagged at me.

Surprisingly, we made love that night. I'd not even thought about it, and had gone to bed quietly, without asking her any more questions. I knew she'd tell me in time. I'd lain there, staring at the ceiling, when I'd felt her reaching for me. Our sex had seemed endless, wildly tender and strangely disquieting in its uncurbed passion, and afterward, she held on to me tightly, murmuring unintelligible things in my ear until I had fallen slowly into a dream-filled sleep.

I awoke in an empty bed, and for a moment, I had remained there, anticipating her return.

The room was distinctly cold, and a fresh wind was stirring the loose section of the sheet that hung over the bed. I waited.

Sitting up, I slipped on my glasses. "Ailish?" I called inquisitively, receiving no reply. With the first twists of worry building within me, I pulled on my thick bathrobe and stepped into the living room. I found the source of the draft easily enough; the front door was wide open. Pulling the knot on the belt tight, I looked out into the colorless morning, breathing an audible sigh of relief when I saw Ailish down on the beach.

For the moment unmindful of the cold on my body, I walked across the grass, then the sands, toward her, my bare feet feeling as if they were on fire from the cold. I noticed the waves were tall and white flecked, crashing upon one another as if driven forcibly up toward us. The wind whistled around me in warning, and I felt the first spots of sleety rain on my cheeks.

I neared her, speaking her name once more, but she didn't turn. I noticed she was wearing her old russet dress and thought it odd; she'd not worn it since before Christmas. I could see her fingers curled around her elbows as she hugged herself, as if cold. Her hair, just over her shoulders now, snapped in the breeze like a flag, and even the feeble light on the sky couldn't dull its vivid sheen.

I reached out, laying a hand on her shoulder and feeling her start suddenly.

"Hey, hey, it's only me," I said reassuringly.

She turned around, and immediately, I could see she had been crying. "What's the matter?" I asked gently, the hand on her shoulder reaching up to brush away a tear.

Ailish swallowed, the normally vibrant eyes subdued and still, unlike the rolling sea just beyond, and said, "Do you love me?"

"You *know* I do," I replied, the disbelief in my voice.

"I have to go away for a while," she said after a moment, her eyes flicking past me and scanning the land as if looking for more. The slight bur of worry I had been feeling suddenly wrenched at my guts like a tightening fist, and for a moment, as what she said sunk in completely, I felt physically sick.

"Why?" I whispered painfully. Her eyes were back on my face, pleading with me to understand, and I knew she wasn't going to answer me properly.

"It has something to do with what MacKay said, doesn't it?"

Ailish shook her head. "No. Not really. It's . . . it's something I have to do. I won't . . . be long, then we'll be together always—I *promise!*" The last word almost ripped from her, and I could see the tremble in her body.

The anguish in her voice triggered something within me, and I felt the first tear roll down my cheek.

"How long will you be gone?" I asked, my voice breaking.

"Not long."

"Can't I come with you?"

"Not this time," she replied, and for the tiniest instant my mind wondered what she had meant, then the sadness drowned me.

"I love you," I said simply.

Her hands were on my face, tracing my features, her eyes in my soul.

"I'll come back," she told me. "I swear it."

"I'll wait," I replied, not knowing what else I could say. Then we embraced, and I tried to convey all of my love for her in that one kiss. The fog in my mind lifted slightly, and quite clearly, I knew she *would* return.

"Don't be too long," I said, forcing the joviality into my strained voice, "or I'll find someone else!"

"Impossible," she said, turning and taking a slow step toward the north. "You belong to me."

Our arms stretched between us, our hands still joined, then our fingers slipped apart.

I watched her walk up the beach. I remained there for a long time after she had slipped out of sight, before returning to the cold, empty bothy.

part three

SWIM THE MOON

The Western tide crept up along the sand,
And o'er and o'er the sand,
And round and round the sand,
As far as the eye could see.
The rolling mist came down and hid the land,
And never home came she.

—Charles Kingsley, "The Sands of Dee"

We are as near to heaven
by sea as by land.

—Humphrey Gilbert, an English navigator
1539–1583 (from *A Book of Anecdotes*)

25

After what happened on the beach, I had expected to be nearly inconsolable; the pain as I had stood helpless while Ailish walked away was very nearly too much for me.

As I had done before, I buried the sorrow away to be confronted later, at a time when I thought I could handle it better.

But that other time hadn't arrived.

That initial day had been terrible. I felt her absence keenly, and for the first time since I had moved there, I was truly alone. My joints ached like fury, and I was forced to take a couple of the painkillers Williamson had given me.

The daylight hours had dragged their heels, though for that I was glad. I dreaded the night, and the images that I felt sure would haunt me.

If I did dream, I didn't remember anything when I awoke, and the sense of peace that pervaded me was almost as wondrous as her presence. It sounds cloying, but I knew she was here in spirit, and most importantly, I knew she was coming back.

This day had passed as quickly as the others. I puttered around the cottage, completing a few jobs I had neglected of late, and I even found time to go into town. As I walked slowly between the shops, people recognized me, waved, and inquired about Ailish. It appeared she had gained some reputation after her singing the other night. I answered their polite inquiries cheerfully, careful not to let her absence show on my face. Most seemed happy that I was settling in well and had found myself a "nice girl."

I didn't see either John or Aggie, of which I was glad, and by the time I left the road by Blairmore, it was raining quite hard. The windscreen wipers clicked to and fro, doing their best to sweep the water from the glass. Outside, the glen was washed by sheets of hard gray rain. The stubbed, roughly conical shape of the marker cairn appeared to my right, appearing out of the haze like a misshapen ghost and disappearing just as quickly. The wheels fought for traction, and I could almost feel the mud gumming hungrily at the tires.

I made it through easily enough and, not really wanting to get wet, I parked the Rover right up by the side of the bothy. Gathering the few things I had bought under the safety of my coat, I hesitated only a moment, then flung open the door and made a run for the cottage. The grass was slippery as if greased, but my boots bit into the soft soil. The boiling sky spat down the rain onto me, as if angry that I had avoided most of its wrath. With a loud clatter of hands on wood and a spray of water, I was inside, shutting the vengeful fury out.

I put the last of the dirty bowls in the sink, then put the pot on top of the stove to cook.

Rubbing my hands briskly on a tea towel, I picked up my drink and walked to the chair by the fire. With a slight stab in my heart, I reached down and picked up Ailish's book, running my hands over it and tracing the name engraved on the spine. The lettering had once been rendered in elaborate script, but was now no more than flecks of gold leaf against the worn red vellum.

"The Old Man and the Sea," I said to myself softly. Then, with a slight shake of my head, I placed it safely on the table.

I sat down, feeling incredibly weary. I rubbed one hand over the back of my neck, trying to alleviate some of the stiffness of muscles that felt like old leather stretched over a board. I jumped slightly as the windows were suddenly lit up by a dry-sounding crackle of lightning; then, only moments later, the low reverberation of thunder echoed around the glen. Rain still drummed against the heavy glass, and I could hear it running in thick rivulets down from the gutterless roof to splash on the earth below. I closed my eyes, sipping at the whisky slowly as I let my mind wander. For some reason I thought of my father, and wished he could have met Ailish. They'd have got on famously. Both Ailish and my father shared an almost identical sense of humor, and practically the same outlook on life and the land. Still, it sounded like he'd found his own Ailish in Sulika. I sighed, letting the alcohol-tainted breath out slowly.

I jumped again, startled out of my reverie as another hammer of noise boomed through the house. My mind was still elsewhere, then it suddenly dawned on me that there'd been no lightning. The sound came again, and with a slight tendril of apprehension slithering down my spine, I realized it was someone knocking hard on the door.

I leaped out of the chair, barely managing to put the

drink down before almost running across the flagstones, my heart in my mouth as I realized she had come back.

I flung open the door, mindless of the rain, a delighted expression painted on my face, and my mouth opened to welcome her home . . .

Somehow, despite the façade I was putting on for my own benefit, I had *known* it wasn't her. Ailish had never felt the need to request entrance, for one thing, and the knocks were too heavy, too lead-fisted to have come from her fine-boned hands.

The darkness outside the bothy was almost complete. The sea was hidden by the seething, shifting curtain of rain; the gray grass disappeared into the black after only a few yards. The figure standing just outside the low gable was lit tenuously by the guarded glow of the cottage. Features half-consumed by shadow stood set, regarding. Eyes under heavy brows, almost deeper than the night around.

There was no mistaking him, hidden or not.

It was MacKay.

He stood there, still making no attempt to shelter under the slight porch. Rainwater ran off the peak of his sodden hat, streaming past his steady face and soaking into his tweed jacket. In one gloved hand he carried an old walking stick, a single, twisted piece of wood that looked like blackthorn. The other hand hung by his side, bare and red with the cold.

We stood there, just looking at one another, both equally regardless of the inclement weather, then MacKay said, "I need t' speak with yeh."

I stepped back without thinking, and he doffed his cap and in a quick motion crossed over the threshold into the bothy. I closed the door, standing by it while he remained still. The water trickled from his saturated jacket onto the floor to form a shining ring around him. The sound was a contrast to the low hiss and crackle of the fire.

"You can put your coat there," I said evenly, pointing to the peg on the door. He nodded once and shrugged off the heavy item, reaching slowly past me. Loosely draped, the water now ran down the splits and cracks in the woodwork. Underneath, he wore a grimy shirt half-covered by a woolen waistcoat. These too were soaked through.

"If you'd no mind, I'll use yeh fire," he said, his voice deep and gravelly, and without waiting for my reply, he shuffled to the mantel, leaning against it heavily.

There was a moment's quiet, a sudden stilling while his eyes searched the flames, then I asked, "What do you want, MacKay?"

I saw the thin line of his lips tighten, as if in a smile. "What do I want?" he repeated to the fire.

I felt angry. "You've surely not walked all the way from Kinlochbervie just to warm yourself."

He looked my way, and I saw that it was a smile that patterned his worn face. "Indeed no," he said, turning slowly and sitting down in the chair.

"Well?" I asked.

He glanced at the whisky, then back to me. "I'm here t' save yeh life. And stop somethin' that's been goin' on too long."

I shook my head, my face screwing up with disbelief. "What?"

"I've got t' tell yeh a few things." He rubbed his mitten roughly over his face, as if the whole of it itched suddenly. "There's no way I can alter the past, but p'haps the future . . ."

I was suddenly afraid. I didn't want him here; this place was sacred, scared to me, and to Ailish. He was invading it with his stink and words. I wanted him out, gone, but I knew I had to hear what he was to say.

"Why don't yeh sit down, Richard," he said. "What I have t' tell will take a fair time."

Despite my unease and apprehension, I did so. I even went as far as to pour him a glass of whisky. MacKay made a satisfied sound and put down the tumbler.

"Ah, it warms better than any fire, and that's the truth."

I was about to ask him to hurry up, to say what he had to and then go, but he looked over the table at me.

"Before I begin, I want your word that yeh won't interrupt me until I'm finished—nae matter what yeh may think or believe. Yeh *must* hear me out first."

I raised my eyebrows incredulously, the anger replaced by something that was almost—not quite—humor, but the look in his eyes extinguished that spark of mocking within me, and I couldn't get the words of scorn past my lips. Silently, I found myself nodding.

MacKay seemed to find my agreement convincing enough.

"It started with Padraig," he said finally. "You of all people should be aware o' your family's history, although still, yeh don't know as much as some.

" 'Tis true he came here from Ireland in a fishing boat, and that it was an accident. Most of the story that is told in the pubs round these parts from time to time is true. 'Tis just the finer details that are hidden."

He took another, gentler sip and continued. "Padraig— God rest his poor soul—stayed no through any respect for the land, nor through love for a local lass—though I suppose yeh could say it played a part." Once again his stare fixed mine, and I felt the rawness there.

Without any preamble, MacKay told me: "Padraig captured a selkie."

A rational man would have laughed, and indeed, I did smile slightly, but it was a bitter, ironic expression that marred my face. I suppose he was waiting for me to comment, or to jump to my feet shouting, but when I neither moved nor spoke, MacKay continued on. "Her land name was Sheelagh. They were together long before Padraig mey and married your great-grandmother—Mary-Jane, I believe?" I dipped my head once in affirmation and reached for my whisky. He smacked his lips, shook his head slightly, then went on. "Now, according t' tradition, which is t' say Law, Sheelagh stayed with him, and I suppose in their own way they were happy, but unlike most other selkies, Sheelagh never found her skin.

"She died on land, lonely and a long way from her kin." He paused again to empty his tumbler, and without a word, I found myself refilling our glasses. The clink of the green bottle against the crystal and the slosh of the whisky was strangely comforting.

" 'Tis a terrible thing," he said, speaking softly and looking back at the fire, "to die alone. Oh, Padraig was there, but even at the end, when she was no more than a shriveled bag of withered muscle and brittle bones, he would nae relent and tell her where her sea skin was hidden.

"You see, they are *water* creatures, and though they can abide on land for a while, it eventually destroys them. To be sure, it may take years and the process is gradual, but steady nevertheless.

"Sheelagh were the daughter of Eithne herself, and her grief we' as much as any mother tha' loses a child. Retribution was demanded, and it was deemed that from tha' time, the male line of the Brennan family must pay the sacrifice."

Now I did laugh. I knew where it was leading, and I refused be baited there. MacKay watched me steadily while the laughter bled from me. I should have realized then that he was affecting me, for my amusement was just too great, and by the time I had finished, there were tears in my eyes, but not from the mirth.

"I suppose you're going to tell me that Ailish is also a selkie and that she's here to lure me to a watery grave?" My sarcasm was lost on him though, for throughout my small tirade he just sat still, looking at me with an immense feeling of pity in his eyes. That made me all the more angry. "I've not heard such crap in all my life!" I shouted, feeling the heat rise in my face. "Are you trying to say that Padraig, my grandfather, my *father,* were drowned by *selkies!* They were accidents, for Christ's sake! Not actors in some children's fairy tale!"

His voice was deceptively calm. "Do yeh know how they died, Richard?" he asked.

I pushed my glasses back up my nose. "You know damn well they all drowned!"

"They all died alone," he said clearly, emphasizing each word. "At night. Here." His finger thudded onto the table. "They walked out into the sea."

My voice was weary but still sharp. "What's your point? I'm not about to go jumping in the Atlantic."

"Aren't yeh now?" he commented quietly. His calmness only served to make me all the more infuriated, but before I could continue: "I got to know your father quite well before he drowned," MacKay said in an oddly conversational tone. "Peter was a good man. I'd thought him spared—since he'd moved away t' Glasgow and all that, but no—and *it's the same with you*. He found himself drawn back here, and within two years, he was dead. Drowned. Although I know for a fact he went willingly."

Again he stopped, but I remained silent. "As yeh know, her name was Sulika, and by t' gods she was a beauty— long hair the color o' night, and a face so perfect. . . . The selkie that took your grandfather was called Mairéad. Yours is Ailish."

A blunt finger rose to point at me. *"It's the same with you,"* he repeated, his voice rising a little, but still remaining deep. "Until the last of the male Brennans born here is gone. Dead."

"I am the last," I said softly to myself, eyes flickering over the heavy swirling grain of the table. A sudden thunderfit boomed outside, rattling the windows and shaking the door. The wind cried down the chimney, a single, low howl that sent the hairs on the back of my neck up.

"If it's any consolation to yeh," he added in a whisper, "they all went willingly. There was no pain, no regret . . . charms and magic. That's what it is. But still, a nasty business indeed. . . ." MacKay shook his head and drained his glass once more. I could smell the whisky on him now, a piquant, acidic bite that gnawed through the wood smoke easily. He fixed me again, and in a tone I will always remember for its sobriety, warned, "She will destroy you."

There was a silence, an absence of words while we both listened to the raging storm without. My feelings mirrored the rain; my insides were awash with turmoil. I felt like laughing at him, yet . . .

I didn't believe, *couldn't*—who would? But there seemed to be something there that struck against the truth like the ring of a hammer against an anvil. Words, sentences, sprung to mind, and as they bobbed with the other flotsam

on the surface of my memory, I tried to seize them, to twist
and bend them into making sense.

"... *You belong to me now* ..."

"... *Nothing could separate us* ... *not even death.*"

"... Especially *not death* ..."

"... *I love you* ..."

I screwed my eyes closed, my hand tightly gripping the
cool glass. God, how I missed her.

The sum of my loss came bubbling to the surface in a
sudden disharmonious cacophony of random phrases and
half-remembered images and actions. I saw her dancing
down by the loch, moonlit and perfect; solitary and singing,
capturing my heart and more; sitting on the rock, waiting
for me in the early morning sun; her fire-shadowed face as
we made love for the first time; the anguish as MacKay
faced her in the Compass.

My anger was suddenly vented, and it broke through the
sentiment viciously, sweeping it aside like a pile of autumn
leaves tossed by the wind. Who was this man to try and
ruin the peace I—we—had found at last?

"Get out," I said, my voice sounding alien to me.

MacKay didn't move. His eyes were still on me, boring
into my skull relentlessly as he looked on with that pathetic, self-knowing expression.

"Despite of what yeh might think," he growled, unblinking, "I'm here to try and help yeh. ..."

"Try and *help* me?" I shouted, my voice dripping with
bitter derision. "You come here, spinning some old fisherman's yarn about sea creatures killing my family, then go
on to tell me I'm in *love* with one, and you're only trying
to help!"

"Richard, list ..."

"No, *you* listen, you cantankerous old bastard! Listen to

yourself! Why? That's what I want to know. Why tell me all this? I just don't understand. Do you truly despise me so much that you're willing to go to these lengths? Did I do something as a child? Or was it . . ."

"What more do yeh want?" he barked suddenly, cutting me off.

I got to my feet quickly, knocking the chair over with a loud clatter of wood against stone. "Want! How about some *proof!* That's where you fall apart; there's no proof whatsoever! Dad's dead, Ailish has gone—God only knows where, after you said whatever you did to her the other night. There's nothing, *nothing* but your word, and there's little you can say that will sound convincing." I spat the last, my breath spent. The air rumbled again, and a flash of lightning lit up the window, but I barely noticed. My skin prickled with the outrage that flowed through me, squeezing itself out of every pore, and I dropped my hands down onto the surface of the table, leaning as I looked up at him with hate in my eyes.

MacKay rose from his chair slowly. All the more ominous for the lack of speed or anger evident.

"Proof," he said quietly, almost to himself. "Yeh want proof."

I said simply, "Yes."

The rain drummed on the windows. His eyes shone dangerously, revealing some inner strength that seeped across the distance between us and once more splintered fear into my heart.

"Proof!" he roared, startling me with his sudden fury. "Look around yeh, *fool!* What more proof do yeh need? Can yeh not see it? She appears from nowhere and yeh fall in love. Surely you're no *that* naive t' think that it was natural!"

I opened my mouth to voice an objection, but he cut me off. "Where's she from? What did she do before yeh met? Have yeh asked her *anything?* Do yeh *know* anything about her? My bet's no. Yeh were too wrapped up in living out your own little fantasy that yeh refused t' even question—or if yeh did, I suppose yeh blocked it away or came up wi' some convenient answer." He took a step forward and stabbed a finger at me to emphasize the words. "She's nae human. Plain and simple. What? Did yeh think it was *talent* that reduced the people in the pub to near tears? Are yeh *really* that blind? That's the magic."

"What would you know!" I shouted blindly at him. The fire that ran through me was consuming in its intensity. "You're nothing but the town drunk! The abusive bully that everyone laughs at!"

Two sudden paces forward and his meaty hands grabbed my shirt. The room tilted and rolled as he spun me round roughly, and I felt my back slam into the mantel. The ornaments by the side of my head rocked but didn't fall. His stink overwhelmed me, and his breath burned my cheeks as he lowered his face to within inches of mine.

"What would I know!" he bellowed savagely, *"I'll show you what I know!"*

The terror that ripped through me was dreadful. I felt my innards coiling, from my mouth right the way through to my bowels. A flare of lightning struck us, like the flash from a camera, and I think I saw his face in more detail than anyone ever before. Lines and creases etched his features, deep and abysmal like trenches. His eyes, oh God his eyes, were nothing more than black, glassy pits surrounded by blood-streaked whites. His hair was perfectly colorless, indeed all of his face was forced into monochrome by the sudden snap of brilliance.

He released my shirt, and his gloved hand appeared between our faces, old, filthy, and reeking. With those shark eyes never leaving mine, he reached over with his other, bare, hand and ripped off the woolen mitten. For a moment, I held his gaze, then, as if drawn by a magnet, I looked down.

The hand was identical to the other except for one detail: His fingers were webbed.

A sharp breath, cloyed with the smell of him, rushed into my lungs. The skin joining each digit was pale, almost transparent except for the network of veins that spidered through each. Thin flesh ran the length of each finger, right up to the pad, then rolled down slightly to join the next. I could see at once that this was no deformity—the uniform nature of the membranes was just too perfect, too symmetrical.

The cold that rushed into my bones numbed me, and the anger drained away to be replaced by a knife of dread that slowly pared away the skin of my rationality.

An image came to me, a sudden thing as instant as the lightning, of Ailish standing on the rock singing, her legs joined as if one. I remembered the all too real fear that had billowed through me. I faced it again now.

"But your other hand . . . ," I stuttered, my gaze still locked on what was before me.

He held it up slowly and turned into the light. The webs weren't there, but I could see now what he had done. The length of each of his fingers was striped with a ragged, puckered red scar. Small slithers of dried old flesh, like peelings from an apple, still hung, inflamed and sore. I tried to imagine the pain it must've caused—still caused—but I couldn't.

"Why?" I asked chokingly, looking once more to his stolid face.

MacKay shrugged and lowered his hand. Quiet now. "I thought that perhaps I could change myself. Deny my past, my history. But when I took the blade to my hand it was like cutting at my soul."

Realization struck me. It all fitted together suddenly, and I wondered why I hadn't seen or thought of it before.

"You're Liam, aren't you."

MacKay stepped back, his face still except for the blinking lids across his deep dead eyes. For a moment I thought he wasn't going to answer me, but when he finally did speak, he surprised me yet again.

"Nae lad, I'm no Liam, though I know o' him and may ha' met him once or twice."

"Who was he?" I asked, still stunned by all that had happened.

"An accident," MacKay replied simply. "Mairéad fell pregnant t' yeh grandfather, and we' forced to leave wi' the child lest the truth be revealed before the appointed time."

"The truth?"

"Of her origins—and of the child's. She returned t' John years later, long after your grandmother had passed. By then, time had dulled the betrayal so much that she we' able t' finish her task." He paused to itch at his sore hand. "It only took Mairéad six weeks to beguile your grandfather into following her to his death. Of Liam I know nothing more."

"Who *are* you?" I said, ignoring the predictability of the question.

He sighed and lowered his hand slightly, moving his head as if contemplating my words. "I am a half-born," he said after a moment. "My *father* were a selkie—a merrow, t' be exact."

I think he saw the look of confusion on my face, because he explained further, despite the fact it obviously caused him distress. "Children born o' a selkie mother can return to the sea if they so wish, but those sired by the coupling o' a merrow and a mortal woman are . . . incomplete." He held up the webbed hand and sighed. "All that remains o' my father's legacy. This, and a slight knack when it comes to things o' the water. In other times, I'd have been drowned at birth as a divil or the like."

"But that story you told . . . of the selkie that fathered children, then took them away . . ."

"Were just that; a story. Fact and fiction mixed together t' form a suitable tale for a dark night. Though I suppose I we' thinking a little of Mairéad and wee Liam, if truth be told."

For a moment, my anger was displaced by overwhelming sympathy for this man. He'd lived a long life having to hide his history from everyone underneath the mask of a rotting mitten and a harsh face. I tried to imagine the pain he must have felt mentally as well as physically to want to try and remove the membranous webs.

As if he'd read my mind, MacKay said, "I don't want your pity. I've lived with *my* choices. The only thing I regret is what has happened to your family. That's why I'm here. I canna change the past, but I can do something about the present. Padraig may have deserved it for his cruelty to Sheelagh, but yesself? I think not."

He stepped back to the table. There was another thunderous detonation outside and the flames of the fire faltered as the wind screeched over the roof.

"She *will* destroy you," he told me quietly, intensely.

The sympathy vanished, eradicated once more by the burning rage.

"I don't—*can't*—believe it," I replied through gritted teeth. "I love her too much, and I *know* she feels the same about me."

"Yeh must leave, Richard, if yeh value your life."

"My life is nothing without her, don't you see?"

He shook his head. For a moment, I felt the tension building between us again, like static, but he crossed to the door and put on his sodden jacket. MacKay thumbed the latch of the door, letting in a sudden squall of rain, wind, and wet leaves. He slipped his cap on over his hair and put the mitten back on his hand, but before he stepped out into the night, he turned to me once more.

"Then yeh are already dead."

With the rain lashing around him like a hissing veil, he walked through the door.

The night took hold of him, and within two heartbeats, he was gone.

26

I sat staring at the door for a long time after MacKay had left, my eyes absently following the staggered paths of the grain.

The fire had died down to a low bed of embers that still throbbed out heat to warm at the right side of my face, and the rain continued to pelt against the windows relentlessly.

Nothing outside had changed.

I was numb to everything else. I remained still, my mind turned in on itself as I constantly thought over what he had said. It had all been nonsense, of course. That's what I kept telling myself over and over, but somehow the seed of doubt had been sown and was growing rapidly.

Each time I looked back on a memory with Ailish, I found myself seeing things in a different light. Not only that time when I had glimpsed her on the rock and thought her something else, but other, smaller pieces of trivia that now began to fit into a bigger pattern.

That long night, I think I reevaluated every half-phrase uttered, every gesture made that I could possibly recall, but still I could not make up my mind. The normal, rational part of me laughed inwardly while the other, deeper segment of my consciousness warned.

Inextricably, I found myself wondering about Bethy's death. If for some reason what MacKay had revealed was true—and wasn't his hand proof enough?—then had they been responsible for that too? The more I thought on it the less I wanted to believe, but the more I did. Resentment was stirred up, in turn for Ailish, myself, MacKay, even my father. No one escaped my sudden bouts of blame.

I tried to stand back from myself and look at my relationship with Ailish, but even with forced aloofness, I knew I loved her wholly, totally.

I was forced into conceding that even if it were all true, and she had been the cause of the deaths in my family, I could no more stop loving her than I could bring back those lost to me. She was inside me completely, and though I wondered at MacKay's warnings of magic, I thought that perhaps she loved me the same way.

Either that or she was the greatest of pretenders—or I the greatest of fools.

There would be a confrontation, of that I was certain, and I also knew that I would be willing to reach any compromise to stay with her.

Morning passed into midday, midday on into afternoon.

I ate nothing, I felt too sick to even contemplate food, and I spent most of the day sitting at the table, my head resting on my sore hands, staring into space, staring within. In spite of my supposed forced acceptance of what was to come, I still found myself slipping into black angers where I would stamp around the house, shouting at unseen phantoms. Eventually, the rage would be replaced by deep melancholy, and though I didn't actually shed any tears, I could feel the buildup of grief, like the waters pressing against a weakness in a dam.

I would remain at the table for a few minutes, then rise and move to look out of the window over the sea, desperately searching the beach and surrounding lands for her. I never once left the bothy. It felt like I was restrained to remaining within the confines of the cottage, as if to venture outside would be to forfeit.

Later on in the afternoon, I took out my fiddle and placed a chair at the door. I played for over two hours without stopping, regardless of the pain it caused me, as if somehow I thought the music might summon her back. The tunes bled from me, taking what was left of my composure with them as they floated out over the now-still water.

By early evening I had slipped into a mode of near complacency that, like the sorrow, was besplit by a dangerous charge of fury that felt like it was just waiting to erupt. I'd been trying to find myself some menial tasks to occupy my hands, such as banking the wood onto the fire. Mechanically, like a robot on a production line, I placed the quarter-logs on the still-burning collection of embers, until one of them had stuck me with a long, jagged splinter. Not moving, I stared at the rivulet of bright blood that trickled down the crack in my palm, watching as it pooled just under my ring finger. The fragment of wood was like a tiny dagger embedded into me, sticking out as if the job had only been half done. The sight was almost mesmerizing; the pale, sun-starved flesh of my hand, the brilliant silver of my ring, and the deeply crimson blood. Then I'd felt my face begin to burn, and my hands to shake. The wrath that was unearthed in me was intense and a little frightening.

Still I did not move; then, like a tsunami shattering against an island, I had hurled the rest of the wood at the fire, spitting curses and not caring that I had filled the grate to a ridiculous level.

By the time night had fallen proper, the blaze in the hearth was ferocious, lighting the house with a dazzling picture show of cavorting, dancing shapes that somehow managed to mock me all the more. The loss of the sunlight seemed to stabilize my mercurial moods somewhat, and I managed to calm down a little.

But despite my hopes, she didn't appear that day.

She returned at night.

ii

I don't know what it was that made me start up from the chair, perhaps some sound that I had heard unconsciously or maybe just the feeling that she was near.

My arms had been crossed upon the table, supporting the weight of my head as I had lightly dozed in the scorching heat from the fire. My fiddle and bow were before me, resting now after yet more furious playing half an hour earlier. The smell of the fire was strong, and the high flames filled the bothy with a sound like ice continually being broken. The vivid tongues of heat licked at the bottom of the wooden mantel, but I didn't care.

I leaned back suddenly, my hands automatically finding my glasses and slipping them on. I pushed back the chair, my fingers lingering for a moment against the wood before I moved. For some reason, I picked up the fiddle. It was an unconscious action, and one I didn't realize I had done until a little later.

Despite the urgency in my mind, I walked slowly across the cold floor to the open door, resting slightly against the frame while I looked out into the night.

The shore, the grass and sand that gently wandered down to the lapping water, was bathed in the silver of the full moon that hung heavy on the horizon. From the beach out to as far as I could see, the Minch was wedged with a sparkling corridor of moonlight that undulated and rolled as if it rested on a breathing, living creature. A single thin twist of gossamer cloud rode in the dark sky, fired into an indistinct, hazy lambency by the large glowing ball of white. The hills and cliffs to the right and left of me were nothing more than massive ghostly shapes looming just out of sight, hiding in the shadows as if waiting to strike. Their rugged visages were highlighted, and as they plummeted into the sea, the outlines looked like stark snapshots of lightning.

There was a feeling of ominousness about the air, a blanket of unnatural black smothering the dark gray of the night. I could hear night birds calling to one another, far away up Strath Shinary, their sudden shrieks echoing like the last cries of the dying. The gentle aroma of wildflowers was lifted along by the cool breeze, perhaps the first sign of the early fingers of spring that would soon explode from within the cold ground. The sea was there, as always, in sight, sound, and smell, and tonight it was oddly subdued, little more than a shiny, rumpled cloth pinpricked by tiny triangles of light that flicked on and off erratically.

I began to play slowly, standing still, a single figure outlined by the moon. The tune that came to me was slow and difficult, but I played on, listening as the pain-filled notes rang back from the hills. The hairs along my arms rose alarmingly, as if chilled by the melody or the night.

I opened my eyes.

And saw her immediately.

Down on the beach, about three-quarters of the distance between the bothy and the water. She was walking toward me slowly. Her hands hung loose by her sides, swinging gently. The dress danced around her softly, tugged and taken by the unseen breeze. Her hair followed the same pattern, eddying about her shoulders freely. Even from this distance, I could see the light that shone in her eyes.

I lowered the fiddle to my side.

I don't know what I'd expected. Perhaps that was why I'd jumped as I had; maybe I'd hoped to catch her in the act of changing. But there she was, walking calmly up the shore as she had always done. No magical explosion of light, no strange sounds or whatever was suppose to occur when these things happened.

For what must've been the hundredth time, I found myself seriously doubting the words of MacKay. Seeing her now, coming toward me, I discarded all the warnings to the wind. I saw her hand rise, a gesture of greeting, and my stoicism broke and melted away like snow.

I ran to her.

My feet thudded over the grass, then dug into the sand. As I neared, I saw the smile on her face, but I slowed as I realized something had changed. There was a sense of . . . of what? determination? resignation, perhaps? about her that halted me at once.

We closed to within a few feet, and for a long time, maybe even half of the night, we just stood looking at each other. It felt like it had been years since I'd seen her. I swallowed her beauty like a starved man, savoring each detail of her face again, feeding my memories, my soul.

Something passed between us, a momentary understanding, then we fell into each other.

Ailish nearly crushed the life out of me, and I think I did the same to her. I dropped the fiddle and bow onto the sand at either side of us, not caring about anything other than the woman in my arms. I think I murmured things into her ear—I don't remember, but I know she spoke to me too.

We broke away, though still held on to each other's hands tightly. I could see moisture shining in her eyes, and I knew mine looked the same. My breath was short; not from the run but from the terrible feeling of passion and fear that was burning within me.

It was Ailish who finally broached the silence, and when she did, her words tore through me.

"I cannot come here anymore," she told me simply.

For a heartbeat, I suffered the most incredible sensation of dread. I went instantly numb to the bone, while my face flushed hot crimson. I felt intensely sick, my mouth watered and my stomach tightened as if I really were going to vomit.

I managed to swallow, then utter, "Why?"

"I must go home," she replied. Ailish shook her head, and despite the rampaging grief, I could see she was in as much pain as I.

"Can't you stay?" I asked her, squeezing her hands. It still had not occurred to me what was happening.

Another shake of her head. No.

The thought of losing her was replaced for a moment by a cold slash of realization that cut away the last vestiges of rationality I still had left.

"It's all true, isn't it," I said, phrasing it more as a statement.

I'd thought the anger would burst from me, or that I would just simply not believe her. I knew then that I had never really given any credence to what MacKay had told me, despite the hours of reasoning and argument.

Ailish simply answered, "Yes." Not even having to ask what it was I spoke about.

A cry broke from me, a wretched, dismal sound, and I felt myself falling. My knees sunk into the yielding sand, and through the fabric of my trousers I could feel the beach's cold grip. Ailish crouched down with me, her arms coming about my shoulders. I tried to shrug her off. All I could see in my mind's eye was Bethy and my father . . . and Padraig, whose ghost still haunts the bothy.

Dead, drowned.

I remembered the sight of the boat, overturned on Loch Inchard. Gross and unnatural as it wallowed in the water, the harsh reality of my father's coffin as it was slowly lowered into the earth.

So much loss, too much grief.

Ailish was talking to me again, but through my weeping, I could only hear the end.

". . . were not responsible. Elisabeth's death was an accident, nothing more."

I looked up at her through tear-smeared eyes. "What? What did you say?"

"My kin had nothing to do with the loss of your wife. It was an accident."

"How can I possibly believe anything you say!"

Ailish shook her head, her hair fanning slightly. I could see that she too was crying.

"Is it *all* true?" I asked. "Was everything to do with vengeance?"

She looked at me steadily, and sat down opposite, unmindful of the cold sand. "I don't know what MacKay told you," she started, voice hushed. "I was to be your downfall, following the example of all the others before me. It was my . . . task, to make you love me, to foster an obsession that would border on madness, so that when the time came, you would follow me blindly."

"You did well," I said, my voice overflowing with disbelief and sorrow. I looked into her eyes. "I'd've done anything for you."

Ailish didn't reply. I sniffed and brushed the wet from my eyes. "So what went wrong?" I asked after a time. When she didn't answer for the second time, I glanced at her again. Tears were running freely down her face, and I felt my heart breaking steadily.

"I fell in love with you," she confessed, the words sounding thick.

My eyes held hers. With my whole body trembling with emotion, I reached out my hand and cupped her face. She moved her head, leaning into my caress. "I . . . I couldn't help it," she sobbed softly. "There was something about you . . . the way you opened up to me completely . . . your trust. I knew it was happening, from that first time when you spoke to me—during the storm. I could feel it, I couldn't stop . . . it just happened."

She paused, wiping at her eyes with the sleeve of her dress.

"I wanted to stay with you, to forget my history and continue living as we had, but I could only deny the past for so long, and eventually, I knew I would have to return."

"Was it what MacKay said to you?" I asked.

"No. He only asked me to spare you. That there had

been enough loss already." She swallowed, then continued, "It was his words that sent me back. I wanted to see if it could be stopped."

A flush of shame ran through me as I considered the way in which I had treated a man who had really only wanted to put things right.

"So where's . . . where's your skin?" I asked after a moment, trying desperately to force a lighter tone.

She gestured vaguely to the rocks. "Hidden, down by the water."

I nodded, wiping my running nose. "The mermaid rocks."

Ailish just smiled thinly.

"So what happens now?" I asked quietly.

"I have to go."

"Despite what you've just told me?" I asked incredulously.

"*Especially* because of that." She looked downward. "I don't blame you for hating me," she said. "But I want you to know there was no duplicity in my love for you, not then, or now."

I felt the tears coursing down my cheeks once more, but I found myself smiling. "I don't hate you," I told her gently. "I love you more than anything, more than my life. Can't you stay? Who's to know?"

"They are," she replied, gesturing over her shoulder. I looked past her, out over the water, and saw perhaps half a dozen small domes bobbing gently in the silver passage. Although they faced the land, their eyes still sparkled with the moonlight.

Seals.

"I am only young, Richard. In the minds of my people I am but a child who has failed. I cannot stay. I would die here, even if I chose to remain of my own free will, I would die."

I shook my head angrily. "You can't just leave me. There must be something we can do? Goddamnit, Ailish, you can't just leave." I broke down again as the full reality struck. I knelt sobbing on the sand, then reached forward for her. Our embrace was fierce and filled with pain. We both shook, rocked by emotions we were powerless to control. I knew there was no way we could be together—our worlds were within touching distance, yet a life apart.

Again, how long we held each other I do not know, but when we finally separated, we were both nearly inconsolable. Ailish stood, a hand still gripped within mine, and looked down on me. The bright moonlight lit her hair startlingly, highlighted the fine line of her chin, and gilded the length of her bare arm. Our eyes held for a moment longer, and I could see everything there, all I was and more; perhaps all I was meant to be. Fingers slipped apart gradually, then her arm swung back and she turned away.

I was bent double with grief, my palms pressed over my eyes as I refused to watch her go. My nose was blocked and my throat felt like it was swollen. Sadness flowed from me like a stream, running down my arms and vanishing into the unconcerned sand like a rainstorm in the desert. My mind felt as if it were collapsing like a card house.

I was nothing without her.

Nothing.

My whole existence revolved about this woman who had come into my life so suddenly, and was now leaving just the same.

I lowered my damp hands, pushing myself up suddenly. My eyes scanned the beach, but I could no longer see her. I ran, not stopping when I reached the water, but wading out as far as I could. The water was bitterly cold, and it swirled about me in silver-black currents as I battled my way out. I swept my hands up out of the sea, her name ripping from my throat.

"*Ailish!*"

There was a sudden crackling sound, like footsteps on dried wood, and I turned my body just as the roof of the bothy erupted upward in a rapturous flare of amber flame. The fires reached into the sky, chasing after the pillows of gray, moon-kissed smoke that boiled upward. My mouth opened, drawing in ragged, chilled air as I watched my home being consumed.

I turned back, facing once more out to sea. The molten-cast water trickled slowly from my twisted hands, and all too suddenly, it struck me.

The dreams.

They had not been flashes of the past, but rather premonitions of the future, of losing her. I threw back my head and cried out again, but there was no answer.

I searched the wedge of light, now looking through the sparkle of silver and gold and, seeing the small heads, I shouted, "Bring her back! For Christ's sake, *please!* Don't do this to me—to *us!*"

One by one, they dipped below the smooth water, leaving behind only shallow ripples that gradually dissipated on the tide.

Until only one remained.

I fancied I could make out the detail of the face; the emerald eyes, the delicate mouth. Somehow I knew it was Ailish, and as I tried to make my way out to her, I could feel the waves resisting me. The water lapped at my waist. I could hear it breaking against the shore, barely audible over the deep, victorious roar of the fire.

The moon was high now, suspended in the black like a heavy silver coin, and the shaft of luminous light it cast upon the water was brilliant and almost dazzling. Two shadows spilled away from me, one toward the land, and another, stronger one, toward the black.

The single seal lifted her face and called out, the same desolate plea as before, as in the dreams, and as I heard my name carried to me by the errant wind, I stood still and listened, my heart filling.

Come . . . Swim the moon . . . Swim the moon with me, my love . . .

I began peeling off my clothes, shedding my land skin with a single-minded resolution. It was all so clear to me. I'd never felt so lucid before. She could not stay, but *I* could go to *her*.

My white shirt floated away from me, folding in on itself as the tide gently tugged it toward land. My trousers followed, rising to the surface briefly before sinking again from view. Finally, I cast off my glasses, dropping them at my side. The sea swallowed them instantly.

Naked now, I dived smoothly under the black polished mirror of the sea. The sudden, incredible cold lanced into my mind, urgent and demanding, trying to find my sanity, but my desire and determination swallowed it, pushing it aside like a troublesome insect.

I broke the surface, and with a last, deep breath, I clung to my humanity, savoring it, cherishing it one final time, then I inverted myself, my arms wheeling, legs kicking as I swam down to the deeper places.

I pushed through the black, eyes stinging from the cold and the salt, then, with a fierce burning and a shuddering flash of pain, all cleared, and I knifed though clear, lagoonal waters, my strokes broad and effortless. There were shapes below me, amid the shoals of fleeting fish, floating with an almost ethereal grace, all recognizable, all beckoning, welcoming. I saw my father, my grandfather, all of them.

Ailish was there, her red-shot hair impossibly long and wafting around her like a silk pennant on a summer's day. Her perfect grass-green eyes were filled with joy, and her arms opened as she smiled.

My heart was bursting with love, happiness, and the incredible feeling of rightness that was pervading my soul.

Returning the smile, I swam to her.